NOTHING IS FOREVER

An absorbing historical family saga with a huge twist

GRACE THOMPSON

Revised edition 2022
Joffe Books, London
www.joffebooks.com

First published by Robert Hale Ltd.
in Great Britain in 2012

This paperback edition was first published
in Great Britain in 2022

© Grace Thompson 2012, 2022

This book is a work of fiction. Names, characters, businesses, organizations, places and events are either the product of the author's imagination or are used fictitiously. Any resemblance to actual persons, living or dead, events or locales is entirely coincidental. The spelling used is British English except where fidelity to the author's rendering of accent or dialect supersedes this. The right of Grace Thompson to be identified as author of this work has been asserted in accordance with the Copyright, Designs and Patents Act 1988.

Cover art by Jarmila Takač

ISBN: 978-1-80405-475-8

CHAPTER ONE

Ruth Thomas and Henry were walking through the fields on a cold, crisp day in March. The frost hadn't cleared from places sheltered from the weak sun and they were well wrapped up for their winter walk, but they were beginning to think of cafés and cups of tea. Walking in the countryside near where they lived was something they both enjoyed and at this time of the year with the trees bare and visibility at its best, Henry carried field-glasses and Ruth carried a camera. But Ruth was aware that today, Henry seemed unaware of the beauty of the place and walked silently beside her as though there was something on his mind.

'I'm tired of waiting,' he said, when she asked the reason for his sober mood. 'I want us to marry.'

'Of course we'll marry, Henry, but not yet.'

'I think we should name a day for later this year.'

Ruth laughed. 'Oh, you are funny sometimes. How can we with Tommy, and Bryn and his wife still living at home? How could I manage to look after them and live with you, unless you've changed your mind about coming to live at Ty Gwyn?'

'You've looked after your four brothers for ten years. Don't you think it's time to put yourself first? I want us to have children, Ruth, and time is passing.'

They returned to the car and Henry stopped outside a café where they regularly went on their days together. When he tried again to discuss plans for a wedding, she glanced at her watch and begin to hurriedly finish the cake she was eating. 'Come on, love, I have to get back, we can talk about this some other time. Brenda and Bryn will be back and Tommy too. They'll be expecting their tea to be on the table.'

'What about us?'

'The boys will need me for a while yet.'

'When Tommy marries, your work will be done, they'll all go off and make lives for themselves and you will have to do the same, don't you see that? You'll have to make a life of your own once you're no longer needed to run the family home. Think about it and make plans of your own, plans for you and me.'

'I can't leave Ty Gwyn. It's been the family home for two generations before us. Besides, even if Tommy marries he'll stay at home. Bryn and Tommy, being twins have been close all their lives and one won't go far without the other.'

Henry dropped her off at the house and drove off. She waved as he turned the corner then, smiling, she went into the house. She was happy. She'd had a lovely morning with Henry but this was where she was needed. Her life was full of the ordinary things that meant she was valued and that was what kept her content. Gardening, mending, struggling to find meals out of the restrictive rationing. Spring 1954 and the rumour was that the rationing would finally be lifted this year, almost nine years after the war had ended. She was looking forward to that and had promised the family a huge celebratory dinner. Her brother Geraint would come down from London with Hazel and stay a few days. Emrys and Susan would come over from Bridgend. She was still smiling, aware of her contentment. One day she'd marry Henry and that would be wonderful too, but not while the boys needed her; she knew that he understood despite his occasional complaints.

There was a note on the message board telling her that Tommy was bringing someone home later. No name, so she presumed it was one of his friends from the darts team as usual. They practised in the shed when the weather allowed but today, it being so cold and the heater insufficient to heat the place they would meet in the kitchen and reminisce over previous matches and plan how to win the next game. She was smiling as she set the table, bringing out the very small cake that the rationing allowed. She loved the kitchen. It was where they all met to tell each other what their day had held, good news and bad, this kitchen had heard it all.

Bryn and Brenda came in first. 'Our Tommy's bringing a girl to meet you, Ruth,' Brenda told her.

'Oh that's nice, I hope she isn't too hungry, I've only made food for the three of you.'

'I don't think hunger's on their mind.'

'Someone special? It can't be serious or I'd have met her before. Always brings his new girlfriends home, Tommy does.'

Voices outside, then the door burst open and Tommy came in shivering with cold, holding open the door to a young woman, whom he introduced as Toni, to enter. She looked, not exactly nervous, more on guard, Ruth told Henry later, as though expecting us not to like her.

'Toni, this is Ruth, my wonderful sister who has looked after us since our parents died. How long is it now, Bryn?'

'Ten years, and you still look as simple as you did then aged ten.'

'Here they go,' Ruth said with a laugh. 'They never stop tormenting each other.'

'I've noticed,' Toni said, but she didn't smile.

'Isn't Aunty Blod here yet?' Tommy asked.

'Don't tell me you've invited her as well. How many are there coming and expecting tea?'

A rattle at the door and an elderly lady came in. 'What's this all about, then, our Tommy? Royal command it was,

"Come to Ty Gwyn without fail." Won the football pools have you?'

'Better than that, Aunty Blod. This is Toni and we're getting married.'

It was a shock to them but it was Aunty Blodwen who recovered first.

'This is a surprise. Sudden, isn't it? You haven't announced an engagement yet, boy,' Blodwen said, sizing up the newcomer with a suspicious frown.

'It can't be very soon, plenty of time to get to know each other. It takes a long time to plan a wedding. I'll have to get one of the bigger front bedrooms ready for a start and—'

Tommy interrupted Ruth with a shock announcement. 'No need to fuss, our Ruth. We've found a place to live and the wedding will be in the register office and—' It was Tommy's turn to be interrupted.

'A place to live?' Ruth stared at the silent girl who had moved to take Tommy's arm possessively. 'Where? I thought Tommy would stay here like Bryn and Brenda, to save up for a while and maybe buy a house of your own. You haven't known Tommy long, or you'd know that he and Bryn are inseparable. Tommy won't go unless Bryn goes and I can't see him and Brenda leaving, can you, Tommy?' She looked at her brother, a frown on her face, waiting for an explanation.

'Don't be so upset, this is good news, Ruth,' he said. 'It's time we looked after ourselves and let you get on with the life you deserve. Marry Henry, Sis. Be happy. Wonderful you've been and we'll never forget it.'

'Thanks for sorting out my life for me,' Ruth said, then briskly, 'Come on, you'd better get this food eaten, or it'll go for next door's chickens!'

* * *

'So,' Henry said, when Ruth phoned from the kiosk on the corner of the road, 'the good news is, we can marry at last.'

'They'll still need me there for a long time yet. I don't suppose Toni will be able to cope straight away with running a home and working. I have to be there to help. And there's still Bryn and Brenda. They'll still come home from work expecting food, and the washing done and ironed.'

'So, our wedding?' His voice revealed a slight irritation. 'When d'you think you can fit that in?'

'While I'm needed I have to be here.'

'I'm off tomorrow to North Wales looking for furniture that I can sell at auction and hopefully a few smaller items for the shop. Don't forget lunch with Mam tomorrow. I'll see you when I get back, in about a week, and please, while I'm away think about us and let's talk about a firm date when I get back, all right?'

'I promise I'll think about it, Henry. Oh, and I'll pop in to make sure everything is secure at the shop.'

'My mother would like you to go there for lunch tomorrow; I'll leave from there. One o'clock?' Henry ran an antiques business from two small shops in the town and buying and selling at auctions. A third, smaller shop was managed by his mother. Ruth had never taken a great interest in what he did, but while he was away she would clean the place as a surprise for when he got back.

* * *

The plans were changed when Bryn and Brenda came in the following morning followed by Tommy and Toni.

A rather grim-faced Toni handed Ruth a piece of paper.

'What's this?' Ruth asked, before looking at it. 'You all look too serious for it to be good news.'

'Toni and me, we're getting married in three days' time,' Tommy said, putting an arm around Ruth's shoulders. 'That's good news, eh? Me and Toni are getting married and Bryn'll be best man and Brenda the matron of honour, I don't know whether they have bridesmaids in the register office, see,' he added.

'But you can't. How am I going to arrange a wedding in a couple of days? This is silly. You'll have to reconsider it. Later in the summer perhaps, or an autumn wedding would be lovely. But in three days' time? Don't be ridiculous, Tommy.'

'There's this flat,' Toni explained briskly. 'We heard of it yesterday and we've decided to take it.' She looked at Bryn and Brenda who stood white faced and anxious.

'The flat next door to it is for rent too,' Tommy explained nervously. 'Bryn and Brenda know they have put on you for too long so they're taking that one. Marvellous luck. Living next door to each other; it's too good an opportunity to miss, see. And Ruth, love, we'll be out of your hair. You'll be free of us.'

Ruth felt sick, her stomach churning with the shock, and angry too at the casualness of the announcement. How could they make plans without involving her in the discussions? She glanced at the cold expression on Toni's face and feared for a future without her brothers to care for. Toni was already making it clear that she was not going to fit into the pattern of Ruth's idea of family life.

Geraint and Hazel in London, Emrys and Susan in Bridgend, and now both the twins moving out without allowing her time to get used to the changes. She was afraid to ask the address of the flats. Surely they won't be moving far from Ty Gwyn?

Henry was travelling and Ruth had no one to talk to. She had made very few friends during the years she had cared for her brothers. Aunty Blod wouldn't understand; she had agreed with Bryn and Tommy that this was a good thing. Ruth knew that although they had known each other for such a brief time, she and Toni would never be as close as she and Brenda had always been. She was a stranger who had upset her life the moment she arrived.

What a shock this had been. She had wild dreams of being alone in this large house, waking to imagined sounds. She went to the kitchen and made herself a cup of tea and wondered if she'd be brave enough to go upstairs and get into bed knowing there was no one else there, and thought that maybe she'd sleep on the old couch beside the fire. She completely forgot the invitation to have lunch with Henry's mother, Rachael. So Henry had left without saying goodbye.

She left a message at one of the hotels in which he regularly stayed, but didn't make a real effort to find him. In a strange way she was angry with him, he should be here when she needed him, but even that emotion passed. She was so busy she had little time to think about anything other than the wedding and the fear of being alone in the house that had always been filled with people.

On the day of the wedding she kept herself busy, pushing aside her fears of the emptiness of the large house once the twins and their wives had gone. Outside the register office a young man watched the family gathered for a few photographs, wondering whether there was a family for him, just waiting to be found. He followed them back to Ty Gwyn where the party was joined by others, laughing, pushing themselves into the house, from where the sounds of laughter continued until he eventually moved away. The name of the house touched a chord and he wondered whether the family justified a few enquiries.

* * *

It had been a double shock, Tommy marrying Toni whom they had not met before this week, and with Bryn and Brenda leaving too, the four of them moving into a place of their own. All in a matter of days, the arrangements being made without her being told until everything was in place. That must have been due to this Toni. Neither Brenda nor the twins would have behaved so unkindly.

In the large old fashioned kitchen of Ty Gwyn, Ruth looked around her at the familiar room that would soon lose its familiarity. Today was her brother Tommy's wedding day and with Tommy and his twin brother Bryn and their wives all moving out there would be only the lonely echoes of the years of their childhood. The chairs would be empty, there would no longer be huge meals to prepare. The room would have lost its heart.

Tommy's wedding would be the last the house would see. Bryn and Brenda, who had stayed on after their wedding were about to leave, Tommy's new wife sweeping the changes before her without a thought. This sad, hastily planned wedding would be the last the house would know. She kept telling herself that she would cope on her own. She was frightened but determined to hide from the rest of the family.

Noises from the living room across the hall increased as jokes were told and teasing became more ribald. She had lost count of the friends and relatives for whom she was catering. Many more than had been invited for sure. She placed the sandwiches she had made on plates ready to take in to the guests. There had been so little time to prepare and with rationing still in force, she was disappointed at the simple spread she had been able to make.

She heard footsteps approaching and looked up, the smile ready for whoever appeared. She wouldn't show for a moment how she feared the loneliness to come. She hoped it was Henry but that was unlikely; she hadn't had a response from her letter telling him about Tommy's wedding. It had all been such a rush. She knew she should have made more of an effort to tell him about the unexpectedly sudden marriage of Tommy and Toni but things had happened so fast. She regretted not talking to his mother, she would have known how to get in touch. Too late now. Henry would understand.

The back door opened and three people she didn't know came in, waved vaguely and went to join the others. More friends of the happy couple, she presumed. She looked at the loaves and the last tin of corned beef, meat paste and the sad winter salads, plus a few treats from a farmer, of butter, cheese and a cooked chicken, hoping the food would last. The living room door opened and the sound of the party increased, Tommy and Bryn were singing, making up the words when memory failed. Someone had produced a mouth organ and was struggling to keep in time.

Aunty Blodwen came into the kitchen and flopped onto the old couch, looking incongruous in a frilly dress with a long skirt, most unsuitable for March, and furry slippers. The room was not what many would call a kitchen, with its scrubbed pine table and ill-matching cupboards, an armchair and couch, their faded covers hidden by cushions Ruth had made, and with a fire burning in the hearth winter and summer. In Ty Gwyn, the house that had been her parents' and grandparents' home, the rooms hadn't been furnished, they had 'just happened'.

'They're going to take up the rugs and dance when they've finished eating,' Blodwen reported. 'I don't think you'll have a very early night.'

'Tommy and Toni will be leaving soon, they're booked at an hotel for the night. The rest will leave soon after.'

'Well that's that, then,' Aunty Blodwen said. 'You've been a wonderful sister to them all, darlin', but our Tommy's the last. The next wedding, will it be yours? You and Henry's? Have you come to a decision at last or are you going to settle into middle age on your own?'

Ruth turned away to hide her frown, thinking of Henry and the proposals she had refused. 'Let's get this one over first, Aunty Blod.'

The wedding of her brother Tommy to Toni Gretorex had been a miserably small affair. Far less of an event than those of her other three brothers, Tommy and Toni deciding on a register office rather than a carefully planned wedding was as upsetting as the suddenness of it. Tommy and Bryn were twins and practically inseparable, and she was sure the reason for Tommy and Toni's sudden wedding had been because a flat next to the one about to be rented by Bryn and Brenda had become available. Tommy had quickly taken on the tenancy and arranged the civil ceremony with hardly time to let everyone know. Toni had dealt with it efficiently and without telling Ruth, and the four had made their plans together. Ruth was still feeling the shock of their announcement and the hurt of not being involved in the decision and the plans.

Tommy and Bryn worked together, enjoying a variety of gardening jobs and travelling around the local farms doing seasonal work. Several farmers for whom they worked on occasions were here sharing the celebrations and had also added to the food on offer. The money wasn't great, but Toni worked in a wool shop which would help. Brenda worked with Tommy and Bryn by keeping a note of their arrangements, and also worked at the farms doing housework during spring cleaning and at other busy times. She helped on a regular basis at the school, cleaning the kitchens after meals had been cooked. 'Bits and bobs', was how she described her occupation.

Despite the noise from the living room, and the constant comings and goings as friends came in for more plates of food, she could already feel the house changing from a busy, noisy one, to a hollow shell. A too large house in which she would rattle. Henry hardly entered her thoughts. She wasn't prepared for the sudden end to her busy life. With no one needing her, what would she do with the empty hours?

Since their parents had died of a flu epidemic when Ruth was only seventeen, she had looked after them all; four brothers and now, four sisters-in-law had all treated this as their home and the house had been filled every day with their friends, and now after ten years it was over, in less than a week.

Ruth had willingly given up the prospect of a career in hotel management to stay at home and keep the family together. After all, it was her duty, but it was also a joy. It was the family home and had been for three generations. She gave a sigh, and tried to put thoughts of the empty house aside. There was a lot of noise coming from the living room, shouted conversations above the music that was now playing. Ty Gwyn was filled with family and friends, mostly friends, people who had treated this place as a second home. To go from this to silence; how would she cope with that?

The bride and groom came through the door to the kitchen where she was putting the final touches to the plates of food still being collected and taken into the living room, and she smiled.

That smile had been fixed to her face all day and her jaw ached with the effort. She was trying not to think of tonight, when all the guests were gone and she faced staying in the huge house on her own for the first time ever. Night time was a long way off and there was so much to do she told herself, that she would sleep as soon as she crawled in between the sheets.

Aunty Blodwen heaved herself out of the couch where she had been dozing and gave her a hug. 'Can I ask a big, huge favour, darlin' girl?' she asked, her large brown eyes looking sorrowful.

'Of course. Anything, Aunty Blod.'

'Can I stay a few days next week? The workmen are coming to do some repairs and some decorating. Terrible hard it'll be to stay there with them all buzzing about like flies.'

Trying not to show her relief, Ruth agreed. For those few days the house wouldn't be completely empty. Looking forward to that would help in the days until then. But even so, the absence of her twin brothers and their wives would make her feel abandoned.

Guessing her thoughts, Blodwen said, 'Don't worry, Ruth love. They'll be in and out so much you won't realize they've gone.'

'It went well considering I had so little time to arrange it, didn't it?' Ruth said. 'It's a pity they couldn't have waited till food rationing had ended, mind. We could have had a big-huge spread then. It can't be more than a few more months. Imagine that, Aunty Blod, going into a shop and asking for a whole pound of butter after managing on two ounces a week for so long.'

Aunty Blodwen looked thoughtful. '1954, almost nine years after the end of the war and we're still rationed. I'm dreaming of buying a big-huge steak and eating the lot. But I doubt if I will, our stomachs must have shrunk after all these years.'

'I suppose they couldn't have waited,' Ruth mused. 'Tommy and Bryn are never happy apart, and a delay before the wedding might have lost them that flat. I wish they could have given me a bit more notice though.'

'Sudden it was, and no mistake, and you were amazing, Ruth, darlin', producing this spread. Strange it was such a rush job, mind,' she added thoughtfully.

'It was the flat. Once Tommy saw that place, right next to the one taken by Bryn and Brenda, there was nothing else to consider. You know what they're like for being together, living together, working together and never a cross word.'

'Just the flat? Yes,' Blodwen said thoughtfully. 'That's why there was the rush, sure to be. But it had been empty for a while, mind. Perhaps there's something we don't know about.'

'What d'you mean? We don't have secrets.'

Blodwen's face wrinkled in a comical frown. 'I think it's what Churchill said about Russia, "A riddle, wrapped up in a mystery inside a — whatsit.'

'An enigma.' Ruth finished for her. 'What do you mean, Aunty? Where's the mystery? They hate being separated, always have done since they were born.'

'Yes, it was just the flat, you're probably right.'

'All the brothers married now and I feel abandoned,' Ruth sighed, stacking the returned plates ready for washing. She smiled at the word, hoping it sounded like a joke. She was hardly abandoned, but that was how it would feel. After all the years of having the large family bounding through its rooms and narrow corridors the silence would be almost threatening. She pushed away the over-dramatic words and concentrated on filling more plates that were still being taken into the living room.

Tommy stopped before picking up the plateful of sandwiches she had just prepared and gave her a hug.

'Thanks, Sis. You've been wonderful and made this a very happy day.'

'The first of many I hope,' she replied, forcing the smile back on her face.

She wasn't the only one facing changes. Tommy and Bryn and their wives were starting a new kind of life as different for them as her own would be and she guessed they, too, were apprehensive, especially Tommy's Toni and Bryn's wife, Brenda. The changes were greater for women: living here with her running the home, coming in from work to a tidy house with a meal waiting, the laundry done; then suddenly having to face it all themselves.

Men didn't feel it as much as women. The men would come home from work and everything would be the same apart from their wives dealing with things instead of their mother, or, she reminded herself, in this case, their sister. The newly wed wives hadn't managed housekeeping budgets before, or had to plan meals on a small ration for two. Beds didn't make themselves and washing had to be dried and ironed and put away. No, the changes for Toni and Brenda would be harder than those she faced. But that reminder didn't make anticipation of the silent, empty house and the lonely days ahead any easier to bear. She shivered as she reminded herself of the few friends she had. Apart from Henry the people she knew were friends of Tommy and Bryn.

It had been such a shock to learn that the arrangements were all made. Toni hadn't said a word until everything was in place. She'd have expected to deal with it as she had with Geraint and Emrys and Bryn. It hadn't given her time to become accustomed to the idea of them leaving. Tommy marrying and moving out at the same time as Bryn and Brenda was the biggest shock. She thought that Tommy, like the others would have stayed at home for a while until they could afford to move out.

She kept telling herself that when they returned from honeymoon in Aberaeron, Tommy and Toni wouldn't be coming back, they wouldn't expect her to be waiting with their rooms ready and a meal prepared, but she still didn't believe it, the thought was too distressing. At least Tommy and Bryn wouldn't be separated, and she ought to be thankful for that. Besides, this being first time away from the family home and into their own places, she'd be needed, specially as all four were working.

'Hi, Sis,' Bryn said, as he helped himself to a piece of the fatless sponge cake she was about to take into the living room. 'Thanks for everything you've done. Toni and our Tommy are very grateful.'

The word 'grateful' was hurtful. It was too formal, the sort of thing he'd say to a stranger who had done some kind deed. But she forced a smile. 'It's been a pleasure, Bryn, you know that. I've only done for Tommy and Toni what I did for the rest of you.'

'You will be all right, won't you?' Brenda asked, walking in behind him. 'I know you'll find it strange, the four of us going, we've been such a noisy houseful.'

'Of course. I'll be fine.'

Tommy came in then and sat at the large pine table where so many meals had been eaten, the family filling the place with chatter, and arguments and laughter — she particularly remembered the laughter.

'Anyway,' she went on, 'Aunty Blodwen is staying for a few days next week, and until then I'll be so busy clearing everything away after you lot, I won't miss you at all. And you'll be back at the end of the week. And Bryn and Brenda will be popping in until then.'

The brothers glanced at each other. 'No, they won't,' Tommy said. 'They're coming with us.'

'On your honeymoon?' She laughed then. 'I can't believe you are all going to Aberaeron together. It's your honeymoon,' she said with emphasis. 'How were you persuaded to invite two more along?'

'Easy; it's a walking holiday and Bryn's better at map-reading.'

'I give up on you two,' Ruth said, with her first genuine laugh for days.

* * *

The party was getting louder with extra guests still arriving, some invited and others with the excuse of bringing a gift or a card. Music was played on the gramophone for dancing in the large living room. Ruth left them and went upstairs to start sorting out the chaos caused by the preparations for the wedding. Tommy's room was a mess. It had been used by Tommy and Toni to change out of their wedding clothes into casual attire ready to leave on their honeymoon. Besides clothes strewn across the bed and in heaps on the floor, there were torn and crumpled pieces of wrapping paper and string, cards opened and abandoned. Spilled make-up made crazy patterns on the window sill. She sighed with a mixture of despair and almost humorous acceptance. Her family certainly kept her busy: at least, it had until today, when everything would suddenly and frighteningly change.

Her other two brothers, Geraint and Emrys had stayed the previous night with their wives Hazel and Susan. In Emrys's and Susan's room, again clothes were thrown carelessly over the bed and an assortment of make-up was spread over the dressing-table. Shoe boxes and handbags were piled on the bed as though Susan couldn't decide which to use until the last moment.

Geraint's and Hazel's room was neat and the bed was stripped, the sheets piled ready for washing. Apart from the used bedding, nothing was out of place; it was as though the room hadn't been used. Ruth found this sadder than the chaos of the other rooms. Geraint's wife was so organized it made her feel utterly redundant when she was around. While she knew that was how it should be, and knew she was being stupid, it still hurt. She loved being the organized one; loved being needed.

Toni's parents, and Geraint and Hazel and a few friends left at seven o'clock, having to drive back to London. Others, mainly people Ruth didn't know, stayed on. The intention was for the party to go on until ten o'clock and then the happy couple would go to an hotel for the night ready to leave for their honeymoon the following morning. Unbelievably, Bryn and Brenda were staying at the hotel too. But with Bryn and Tommy, plans had a habit of changing.

At one o'clock, when the party had become more subdued but showed little sign of ending, dancing had ceased and party games were in progress. An hour later, Tommy and Toni had locked themselves in Tommy's bedroom and Bryn and Brenda were sleeping in what was still their bedroom. Two friends she hadn't met before slept on the settee in the living room and another in an armchair. Two local young farmers for whom the twins regularly worked, had announced it wasn't worth going home to bed, having to rise so early, were wrapped in blankets on the floor.

Someone else she didn't know came and told her that Aunty Blod was a bit merry. She had sung a few songs, attempted a dance and was now fast asleep. 'Merry', the euphemism for drunk, didn't alarm her. It was a wedding after all and Aunty Blod knew how to celebrate. Gently she lifted her up from behind the open door of the hall cupboard into which she had gradually slid, half hidden by coats.

'Come on, wake up, Aunty, we'll get you onto the couch till we can find a taxi.'

'Don't tell me I haven't got a bed?' Aunty Blodwen wailed. 'You can't turn me out in the middle of the night. March it is and freezing out there. I'll catch my death, girl!'

Ruth smiled and with a young man, whom she didn't know, helping her, she guided her aunt up the stairs and into her own bedroom. 'You'd best sleep here tonight. I'll sort out a bed for myself when that lot downstairs finally leave.' She pointed down behind her with a thumb.

The young man looked doubtful. 'Leaving? Settled for the night most of them,' he said.

Aunty Blod undressed with Ruth's help and was soon producing gentle snores. Ruth sighed and wondered how many more hours it would be until she could do the same.

In fact she didn't go to bed at all. Too tired to find a blanket and find an unoccupied place to sleep, she sat in the kitchen on the old couch they had been meaning to throw away for months, and dozed, in between people coming in and out for drinks and a bite to eat until three o'clock, when it finally went quiet. She stayed there until seven o'clock in the morning.

Her first thought on waking and remembering the reason for her unusual position was guilt for not making sure Henry had been told about the wedding. She must try and reach him today. He deserves an explanation even though it wouldn't sound very convincing.

The morning was more chaotic than the day before. Tommy and Toni, Bryn and Brenda were difficult to rouse.

'Give us another hour, Ruth, it isn't a long journey' Tommy muttered, when she banged on the bedroom door at eight o'clock.

'No panic, Sis,' Bryn said sleepily when she tried to call him. 'It isn't all that far.'

'Emrys and Susan are up and on their way back to Bridgend,' she called to them.

'Good on 'em,' both brothers muttered in unison.

The friends sleeping in the living room asked very politely if they could have a cup of tea and maybe some toast. A sleepy figure uncurled from behind the couch, someone she hadn't noticed before, and asked sleepily if he could please have the same, before falling back out of sight. Glad to be busy, Ruth obliged but warned them it would be toast with Marmite or jam without butter or margarine. The ration wasn't large enough to share and she'd borrowed on next week's to provide food for the wedding.

'Come on, get a move on,' Ruth called to the four an hour later.

'No rush, Sis.'

'Not for you maybe, but I have work to do. There's all this mess to sort out after I've fed you,' Ruth protested mildly.

'Manage fine you will. A marvel you are, our Ruth.'

There was a knock at the back door and she ran down to open it. 'Henry! I'm so glad to see you. Sorry you couldn't make it in time for Tommy's wedding; it was all such a rush. They didn't give me any time to plan it properly — you know what those two are like.' He didn't respond at once and she stood, wondering how to make her explanation sound genuine. 'I rang one of the hotels where you usually stay, but I'm so sorry, I didn't think to ask your mother to pass on the message. I'm so sorry, but it was such a rush,' she repeated lamely.

'Can I come in?' He smiled and she thought it seemed as artificial as hers had been all through the day before. 'I've just driven through the night from Porthmadog. Sorry I didn't make the wedding. I only heard yesterday, from my assistant. Why didn't you write to one of the places I was staying, I'd given you the addresses and dates?'

'No time for writing and anyway, I lost the list you gave me, in all the muddle of getting things done.'

'I see.' He stared at her and she knew he had been hurt by her negligence. 'And about forgetting lunch with my mother?'

'I'm so sorry, I'll write to her and explain.'

'I did try to get here, I would have liked to have been there to see Tommy and Toni married, join the celebration. I would have cancelled my appointments if I'd been told. It went well, did it?'

'Meagre food, but everything else was fine.'

'I'd have come, you know that, Ruth. Why didn't you tell me?'

She was saved a reply.

'I'm sinking for a cuppa. Any chance of some breakfast, our Ruth?' Tommy called, as he walked down the stairs. 'Oh, hello, Henry. Where were you? You missed a good party.'

Henry looked at Ruth and shrugged.

'I'm waiting for Toni, Bryn and Brenda to get up,' she said. 'If you can wait, you can eat with us.'

'I thought Tommy and Toni had booked an hotel. Nothing went wrong, did it?'

'Only too much alcohol and not enough sense! They all stayed here last night. And they're all going to Aberaeron together!'

Henry gave his loud, infectious laugh. 'Sharing a honeymoon with your brother, Tommy? And no special first night at the hotel? There's something wrong with you, man.' Tommy nodded in happy agreement and went back upstairs. Henry moved towards Ruth, put his arms around her and kissed her lightly. 'We'll arrange things differently when you marry me. If only you'd stop pushing me away and say yes.'

'I can't think about it yet.'

'First the boys were too young; then they couldn't be expected to give up their home, and you couldn't expect them to share it with me, then you had to wait until they were all married and away from home. What is it now, Ruth?'

'Give me time to get over all this, please, Henry. My head's all over the place. I've been so busy organizing Tommy's wedding, and now have to find my way of coping without them all.'

Henry looked at her a half smile on his face. 'Then, the cat's only twelve, she might live for a couple more years,' he said, with gentle sarcasm. 'Then there'll be nieces and nephews. When are you going to find time for yourself? For us?'

'Henry, I'm sorry but—' She was again saved from replying by a bump from above them. 'Sounds like someone has fallen out of bed, I hope it isn't Aunty Blod!' She hurried to the stairs and ran up calling to ask if anyone was hurt. Reassured, she turned back to Henry, but he was gone. He had driven off to one of his favourite places in which to sit and think.

* * *

Henry owned three shops selling antiques. One was run by his mother, Rachel, one sold only ordinary second-hand items, mostly furniture and was run by part-time staff. The other, selling more expensive quality items was where he lived and he left it in the care of Tabitha Bishop when he was away buying stock. He had known Ruth since they were children and had always assumed they would marry, but with her insistence that she had to look after her brothers they were still without any firm plans. He wanted marriage and children and there was no one else for him but Ruth and he doubted whether there ever would be.

* * *

The four honeymooners finally left at midday. Aunty Blod helped by tidying up the kitchen and dealing with the leftover food, then they sat with a cup of tea wondering where to start on the rest. Ruth was about to ask Blod what time she was leaving when that lady asked, 'Ruth, love, you wouldn't mind if I stay all next week, would you? The decorators are starting tomorrow and it won't be very pleasant having them push me here and there as they do the repairs. Then there'll be the painting and a new window's going in where Emrys chopped some firewood and sent a piece flying through the pane. Everything is packed away ready for them and the landlord will be supervising.'

'Good,' Ruth said jumping up and reaching for the vacuum cleaner. 'That's the incentive I need to get me going. Come on, Aunty, we'll start by getting a room ready for you.'

Aunty Blodwen was ready to leave at five o'clock, when she asked, 'What's happening about this house now the brothers are all gone? It belongs to all five of you. So will you sell it and share the money?'

'No. The boys discussed this ages ago and they all agreed that I can stay here until I choose to leave. If I decide to stay, then after my time it'll be sold and the money shared between the brothers and any children.'

'Things have changed. They'll be glad of the money now they're married, won't they?'

'They're grateful for the way I stayed and kept home for them. None of them wants me to have to leave. Besides, Ty

Gwyn is still their base, it's the family home and has been since our grandparents' time; I don't think they want to see it go to strangers.'

'Now they're setting up their own homes, though . . . Can you sit here on their inheritance, knowing they need it?'

'We had a couple of valuations a few years ago and to be honest, they didn't think the amount was worth tipping me out for. There won't be much more than one hundred pounds each after bills are settled, so they're happy to let me stay.'

'Unless you marry Henry.'

'The way I feel now, I'd be marrying for the wrong reasons. I can't marry Henry because I don't like living alone, or because the boys want to sell the house, can I?'

The bus took her aunt away at last and Ruth took a deep breath as she went back into the empty house. She couldn't shut the door. If she did she would be shutting herself away from the world and now the boys were gone, the world wouldn't be coming in. She propped the door open with a couple of bricks painted and left there for the purpose and went into the kitchen. Even that had lost its comforting feel. Being here alone wasn't going to be easy.

* * *

Henry came that evening and, as usual, Ruth couldn't decide whether she was relieved to see him or not. They had been seeing each other regularly for years, but had never reached the stage when marriage was a certainty. Henry popped the question from time to time but she had always used the excuse of looking after her brothers. She wondered whether the wait had been too long and the pot had gone off the boil.

She told herself she wasn't sure of his love, but that wasn't true. The true reason, which she tried to deny, was not being here when her brothers needed her. That commitment to their welfare would always be there.

The second reason was her doubts about her feelings toward Henry. Did she really love Henry, or was it just a habit, a convenient way of planning for a future in which she didn't have to cope alone? She wasn't even sure what love really meant. Her parents had argued all the time, sometimes violently, and they had frightened her as a small child with their fights. Yet they had stayed together and between their frequent disagreements, they seemed content. There had been occasions when their happiness and laughter had filled the house, but those moments were rare and the strongest memories were the bad times.

More recently she had seen her four brothers fall in love and marry and those relationships had overridden memories of the fights between her parents to a certain extent. Any marriage was taking a chance, she was convinced of that. Even with the obvious happiness of her four brothers and their wives she knew it wasn't the same for her and Henry. Perhaps they had waited too long.

She cleaned and tidied the house and washed the bedding, and threw out the oddments of leftover food into a bin for next door's chickens. The day ended, darkness came and, with it, the dread of the night alone in the large house for the first time in her life. It was with reluctance that she closed the door.

She didn't want to waste electricity by burning the light all night but couldn't face the utter darkness. She lit a candle and set it in a dish beside her bed. It's flickering light didn't really help. A movement of the flame set her wondering whether there was a draught from an open door to account for it.

Restless and a little afraid, she rose three times and went down the stairs carrying the candle as well as switching on the landing light. Each time, she checked every door and window but nothing had changed. At four she made a cup of cocoa and at five she gave up trying to sleep and made tea and toast, sitting on the old couch to eat it, an electric fire glowing in front of yesterday's ashes.

* * *

Jack had been in the area for a couple of months. He had escaped from his previous address just ahead of a police inquiry and with just enough cash to survive for a month. He had eked out his money by scrounging from other men sleeping rough and stealing when an opportunity arose. It was mostly food he took, but once he had found a purse temptingly easy to pick up and on two occasions an open window had enabled him to reach inside and take an ornament which he then sold when he was far enough away from where it had been taken. It was so easy. He laughed when he thought about it and his confidence grew.

In 1954 people still left keys hanging down behind their letterboxes and on that day in March, he risked entering a house after seeing a woman and three children leaving it and getting on a bus. Entering a house was something he swore never to do again, but he had nowhere to sleep and he was very hungry. He watched the bus stop and the family of mother and three children get in and find seats. He waited for a few minutes then pulled the key on its chain through the letter box and let himself him.

He went silently up the stairs and looked in drawers, carefully opening them and more carefully closing them again. With luck he wouldn't leave evidence of his presence and anything missing would be presumed to be carelessness. A bank book was under some clothes and inside was a pound note and five shillings in coins. Pocketing the money he continued the search. Downstairs he went into what was obviously the best room with its table and three-piece suite and sideboard. It smelled of polish with a slight tinge of dampness. In the sideboard were three books; insurance, rent book and one marked coal and gas. Another three pounds. Without intending to go in — it was time to leave — he looked around the door of the living room and to his horror saw an old man sitting near the fire.

'That you, Dolly? What did you forget this time?'

Jack ran and didn't stop until there were three streets between him and the old man. He travelled a long way that day, even using some of his money to go a few miles by bus, then, as darkness was falling, he found a barn and slept cosily and without any qualms of conscience. He was used to getting up with the dawn and as soon as a pale light appeared in the sky he was on his way before the farmer was aware of his presence.

In a café, he took out the notebook he carried and marked off another town on his list. No luck so far, but he felt sure he was in the right area. Today might be the day, he told himself, as he did every morning as, relaxed after a good night's sleep and with a full belly, his confidence was at its height.

He was searching for a family, but he didn't know where they lived, just that it was in South Wales and not far from the sea. He had spent time in several small towns, investigating families with the name he sought, but hadn't found the people who owed him money.

He made his way by thumbing lifts and walking, back to where his fiancée Abigail, and her mother Gloria lived. He had given up his job and with Abi's blessing was touring the towns of South Wales searching for the family whom he believed owed him an inheritance.

Abigail was not quite twenty but already a successful hat saleswoman. With a car, she travelled around towns of Wales and western England selling to hat shops. She and Gloria lived in a beautiful flat which they rented; she had the smartest clothes so she looked successful and every customer who bought her hats hoped to look as glamorous as she did.

She earned a lot of money for someone so young and knowing how badly Jack wanted to find his family and the money he felt he was due, she agreed that he should spend a few months searching for them.

Abi's mother was not happy about the arrangement and tried to persuade her daughter not to trust him. 'You're young and foolish,' she told her, when Jack had once more left to continue his investigations. 'You have a wonderful job and you earn a great deal of money, so why is he trying to find a family that might exist only in his imagination?'

'Jack has to get it out of his system, Mum. If he doesn't he'll regret it later and perhaps blame me. Now is the time, before we marry and have children.'

'Where is he now?'

'I don't exactly know,' Abi admitted, 'but I know he'll come back to me.'

* * *

It was three more nights before Aunty Blod came back and by that time sleep had begun to come more easily to Ruth. She wondered whether she would have to start getting used to the emptiness again, after having Blod's company for the week.

They spent their days sorting through drawers and cupboards trying to decide what to keep and what to throw away, Ruth's intention being to reduce the clutter in the house and make the place easier to run. Henry came for a meal twice while her aunt was there. He explained that he was off to trawl the second-hand shops in the west of England. Listening to their conversations, to Ruth the house seemed almost back to normal and it was a painful moment when Henry left.

Her aunt telephoned from the telephone box on the corner each day to learn of the progress on her house and Ruth crossed her fingers and hoped she would stay another day. It was only a few small repairs and some decoration and it hadn't been expected to last more than a week.

Aunty Blod, eventually and regretfully, left. Ruth went with her to the bus stop and walked back to the house as though to her execution. She opened the windows, even though it was a chilling late-March morning, and the front door stayed open. Foolishly she convinced herself that it offered the promise of someone calling, stopped her feeling so cut off and alone, even though no one was likely to come. Henry was in the west of England buying antiques. The twins and their wives were still away. It was a pity Toni had refused her offer to clean and tidy the flats ready for their return, and Brenda, less enthusiastically, echoed her brisk insistence that they would manage just fine. Ruth would have been glad to show them how much they would still need her.

Emrys and Susan lived in Bridgend and they called a few times at first. Geraint and Hazel lived in London running a business selling items by post. There were a couple of brief notes but no suggestion of a visit. She was beginning to feel invisible!

After her aunt's help the house was as clean as she could wish and she knew that before she gave in to her situation and succumbed to becoming less and less valued and no longer needed, she had to start looking for work, or something to fill her time, but the thought of a job appealed less and less. She was afraid. With a surge of guilt, she wondered if she should forget trying to build a career and marry Henry. She was ashamed of the way she thought about him, not as the love of her life but as an escape from everything she feared. She needed to do some serious thinking about where her life should be leading. It was changing in every way and she should face the future with confidence and hope, not use Henry in case nothing better turned up, like a shipwrecked sailor clinging to flotsam. But life without him would be unimaginable. At least the house was returning to its friendly atmosphere and at eleven o'clock she relaxed easily and comfortably into sleep.

She was woken by a sound from downstairs, like something breaking. She reached for a torch and leapt out of bed and switched on the light. Putting on lights as she went, she headed for the kitchen from where the sound had come. It was empty, but the back door stood wide open and on the table was a broken dish that had apparently fallen from the shelf. Holding the torch like a weapon, she locked the door then searched every room. Each room was empty and apart from the open door and the broken plate she might have convinced herself she had dreamed it. Someone had been in there, but who? No one except her brothers had a key and she picked hers up and gripped it tightly in her hand.

She decided not to tell anyone. She must have forgotten to lock the door, it was time she stopped delaying closing it. It had to be her forgetfulness, there wasn't any other explanation and a plate, propped against the dresser shelf could easily have slipped.

Outside, hidden in the shadows, Jack stared up at the house. Ty Gwyn? There was definitely something familiar about the name, but the book he had found in a drawer stated the name of the occupier was Thomas. Not the name of the family he was looking for. He wished he had listened with more care when the old man had talked about his childhood.

* * *

On the day Tommy and Toni, Bryn and Brenda were due home, Ruth had a casserole simmering in the oven, and fresh bread waiting on the board ready to slice. They'd be starving when they got back and she had left a note pinned to each of their doors promising them a meal would be waiting for them, in case they had forgotten her invitation. She had no idea when they would be back but everything was ready at nine o'clock.

At 10.30, she turned off the oven and sat with the wireless on low, listening for the sound of the gate. An hour later they came, laughing and apologizing for being so late.

'We stopped to have a meal on the way back, Sis. I hope you didn't wait for us.'

'It doesn't matter, Tommy. You can—' She had been about to say they could eat it tomorrow, but stopped in time. There were no tomorrows so far as her brothers were concerned. 'You can have a hot drink if you like?' she amended.

'We won't stay,' Bryn said, 'But we'll come and see you soon. Tomorrow?' he suggested.

'Not much chance of that,' Toni added quickly. 'We haven't finished unpacking yet and heaven alone knows where the saucepans are.'

'Would you like me to come and help?' Ruth offered. But all four shook their heads.

'Time we looked after ourselves, our Ruth. You've done enough.'

'Now it's time for you to find a life for yourself.' Toni spoke kindly, although there was a firm gleam in her eyes that startled Ruth. Then Toni stared at Brenda, who stared back, then nodded confirmation. Again, Ruth forced her smile. 'Yes, now it's time for me,' she agreed.

Ever since the wedding she had opened the back and front doors as soon as she got up and they stayed open until darkness came. That was the time she hated most, closing the doors and knowing there would be no one there until the following day — if then. She slept fitfully and often woke and sometimes read for a while in the hope of tiring herself. It was always still dark each morning when she went down to make tea and open the doors. Even after her fright of the night before she still found it impossible to close the door until dusk.

* * *

The following morning, Tommy stared at his wife and frowned. 'Where am I? And who are you?' he joked.

'My name's Dolores De-lightful. What's yours?'

'Bob Hopeless. Come here.' He pulled her close and she struggled playfully.

'Come on, we have to get up.'

'We don't! Isn't it wonderful? Our own place and we can do what we like.'

'No we can't. We have to get up and try to work out how to use the cooker for a start. Tomorrow it's back to work.'

'Ruined my mood you have, Mrs Tommy Thomas.' He kissed her and asked anxiously, 'Happy?'

'Utterly.'

'I love you, Mrs Tommy Thomas. Thank goodness the wedding's over. Now all we have to do is convince everyone that you can produce a six and a half month baby!'

* * *

Jack wandered through the villages and eventually found himself in a small seaside town, where the small shops suggested it was a popular place for holidaymakers. As he travelled he was looking for information, something that would help him find some member of the family — if there were any left after all this time, which he doubted. From the little he had learned, the family wasn't large and names could have changed and, after forty years, who would care even if they did remember?

He stopped at a newsagent's shop but he didn't go in. He didn't want to make the search official, not until he was certain how he would be greeted. He suspected that most would be only too glad to send him on his way. If only he could go from town to town working each one as a paperboy. That would be a way of finding out people's names. He had to talk to people and depend on luck. Meanwhile, he would take another look at the house called Ty Gwyn. He had little to go on, but the name rang that persistent bell somewhere in his memory.

* * *

One morning Ruth had just thrown away a cake she had made, wondering when she would learn to cook for one and stop wasting precious rations on food no one wanted. Would she ever stop making cakes in case someone called? Or learn to prepare small meals instead of continuing to throw excess food in the bin for the chickens? The postman touched the gate and shocked her out of her reverie.

Opening a letter from her aunt, she gave a huge sigh of relief. Aunty Blodwen was having trouble after the repairers had caused a leak in the kitchen. It would take a few days to fix.

'They can't do anything until next week, so I was wondering—' the letter said. Ruth wrote straight back and invited her to stay for as long as it took.

'All right, I'm a coward,' she said aloud to her reflection in the hall mirror. 'I will cope with this, I really will, but not yet.'

The house had five bedrooms, two of them small and overlooking the back and there were two larger rooms at the front. Ruth had stayed in the smallest room overlooking the back garden, which, being next to the bathroom was also the noisiest.

'Why don't you move into one of the bigger bedrooms, our Ruth?' Aunty Blod asked when she was unpacking her things. 'Seems daft squeezing yourself into the tiddly room at the back while the best rooms are empty.' She looked at her niece and added softly, 'They won't be back, you've got the whole house, so spoil yourself. Remember, no one praises a martyr.'

'Is that what I am?'

'No, but it's what you might become if you hang around waiting for your brothers to need you.' She hugged Ruth. 'Sorry, love, but you've got to stop being the big sister looking after them all. This is time for you.'

'That's what Tommy's Toni says.'

'And she's right. So what would you like to do now you're free?'

Ruth shrugged. 'All I know is looking after people, keeping the house looking nice, and making food.'

'You worked in an hotel once, what about that?'

'It won't be the same, Aunty Blod. Caring for your own is something special.'

'And lucky you are to have had the experience, but it's over now, love. You're free.'

'I love this house, and wish it could always be filled with people being happy. It's a beautiful place, isn't it?'

'Beautiful, and so are you. Too beautiful to incarcerate yourself here, waiting for someone to call. Tommy and Toni, Bryn and Brenda love this place too but soon they'll love their own places, chosen by them, filled with the start of their own lives. Like Geraint and Hazel, and Emrys and Susan. It's where they start making their own memories. As you will one day.'

* * *

The house was sparsely furnished as Ruth had offered furniture to both Bryn and Tommy to start building their homes. They had taken beds and a couple of armchairs, small tables and even a wardrobe which Ruth knew she would never need. They had also taken much of the cutlery and china of which there had been plenty. Ornaments too had been passed on to help make the flats feel like homes. One day the shops would be filled with everything a home needed, but until then they were glad to make use of what they were given.

When Henry called soon after Aunty Blodwen returned, he looked around the living room in surprise before settling in the old-fashioned kitchen. 'This is the most comfortable room in the house. And even this is short of several chairs. What happened?' he asked.

'Oh, Tommy and Bryn needed a few things, and I can't see me needing a houseful of stuff anymore.'

'Do you plan to move out now they've all gone?' he asked. 'Sell this place?'

'No need, they've all agreed to let me stay.'

'They've agreed? What about you? What d' you want?'

'It's too early for me to decide,' she said.

'I see, and it's not my business?'

'Come to dinner on Sunday,' Blodwen said. 'Ruth's invited the twins and their other halves. Emrys and Susan too. Make it a bit of a celebration, shall we?'

'Yes, but won't you tell me what we're celebrating?'

'We can talk about everything after they've gone,' Ruth said, avoiding looking at him.

A few days later, Henry turned up with one of his vans. Opening the back Ruth saw an assortment of furniture plus vases and even a silver tea-set with its tray. He invited Ruth to choose any replacements she might need.

Neither of them noticed the rather shabbily dressed man watching from behind the hedge of the next-door house.

'I know none of this will be your first choice,' he said. 'But you'll need a few extra chairs for Sunday if you're going to invite the family. You can choose exactly what you like, furnish the house in any way you please when you move in with me,' he said, looking at her with a serious expression on his face.

'Henry, I've been unfair to you, keeping you waiting with half promises. I do love you, I always have, but you deserve more than I can give you. The truth is, I can't leave this house and move into yours, not now, not ever. I'm sorry.'

'You can face a life alone, rattling around this house? Why?'

'It's my home and it's home for Emrys, Geraint, Bryn and Tommy too. I have to stay, keep it for them and their children.'

'That's nonsense and you know it. All right, if you don't love me, then say it! Stop pretending you're refusing me because of your brothers, who all have lives of their own and no longer need you!'

'They do need me! They're married, but they still need to know their home is here. Why else do they want me to stay here? It's their childhood, reminders of all the years they were growing up, and the only memories they have of our parents. I can't take it away from them.'

'And, just in case the thought has ever flickered through your mind, I can't live here, being constantly reminded that I don't belong in your special charmed circle!'

He threw down the kitchen chairs he had brought, put the silver tea-set on the table and, after calling goodnight to Aunty Blod, drove off without another word.

That evening, despite heavy rain and a cold dark sky, it would be very late before she closed the door.

* * *

Jack stood watching the house, standing in the darkest area between the street lamp and the light from the window. He seemed unaware of the rain although his clothes were sodden and smelling unpleasantly of damp, and rain ran down his neck and soaked his shirt back and front. He moved closer and could hear the radio and occasional laughter from the old lady he'd seen earlier. They had referred to her as Aunty Blod, but he couldn't remember if the old man had ever used the name.

Silently he walked through the open door and stood in the hall, darting into the hall cupboard when he heard Ruth mention making a cup of cocoa. He held his breath as she passed him to go into the kitchen and listened as she made hot drinks. She passed again to wash the cups before climbing the stairs with the old lady in front of her and helping her into bed. She came back down and locked the door and he waited in the darkness.

Was this the house he'd been searching for since he was fourteen? He waited until silence had fallen then opened drawers and cupboards, looking for something, anything, bearing the name he wanted. He'd tried so many places and felt no hope, but there was something about this house that made him feel more confident of having found the right one at last. He needed to search it thoroughly and he didn't know how he was going to achieve that. But he knew a way would be found. Money belonging to him was here, he could smell it, and it would be found, however long it took. He eased the bolt, unlocked the door and, picking up the silver tea-set, he left.

CHAPTER TWO

Ruth woke and at once felt a draught. A moment later she heard the tapping sound and guessed that was what had woken her. She grabbed her dressing gown and in the weird light of early dawn went downstairs. She picked up the torch but didn't light it. The grey glow slipping through the curtains was enough for her to see her way and slowly, quietly, again gripping the torch as a weapon, she descended the stairs. The house was silent, it was too early for traffic to be passing and the silence was oppressive, the place didn't feel like her home.

Slowly, her heart beating painfully, she looked in each room. The tapping sound she heard was repeated as she entered the kitchen and she saw that the back door stood ajar, a breeze moving it gently.

This time she was sure she had locked and bolted it, clearly remembered doing so. So how could it be open? The kitchen was where she sat for her late-night hot drink; on the armchair facing the door, so how could she have forgotten?

She ran across, locked it, withdrew the key and threw the bolt, then panic set in even stronger. If someone was in the house she had locked herself in with him.

She put on all the lights then looked in all the downstairs rooms before slowly, fearfully, beginning to climb the stairs.

She looked first into Aunty Blod's room without disturbing her, then the rest of the house. Nothing seemed disturbed until she opened the final door. What she found in the room that had once been Tommy's made her cry out in fright. The contents of the dressing-table had been emptied onto the floor, the drawers left on top of the bed.

No one could have got in. Not though a door bolted on the inside! It must be me, she thought. I must be doing this. There is no one else here. Sleep-walking maybe. She remembered her mother telling she had done so for a while when she was young.

Dawn was breaking and the increasing light gave her confidence. It must be her. She looked at her feet wondering if they showed signs of walking around outside. There was no other way she could find out about night-time wanderings; her dreams and presumably sleepwalking too, were rarely remembered. The soles of her feet showed no sign of tramping around. Yet it must be the explanation. There was no other.

Without stopping even for a cup of tea, she found a torch and went to the shed and from the tool box that had been her father's, took out a rusty old bolt and some screws. Tonight she would make sure no one could get in then, if anything was moved, she would know that she was sleep walking as she had when she was a child.

It took a long time, and the screws resisted her puny strength so she hit them in with a hammer to start them off and eventually there was a second bolt on the back door. She determined not to leave it open again, not even when she went to the clothes line, or to put rubbish in the ash bin.

She was too wide awake to consider going back to bed so she made tea, and it was then that she noticed that the silver tea-set had gone. She tried to remember when she had last noticed it and decided sadly that Henry must have taken it away again. She hadn't been very gracious when he had offered it.

* * *

Tommy and Bryn were setting off for work and, as they drove past their old home noticed that lights were on. 'Ruth is up early, Bryn. Should we call and see that she's all right?' Tommy slowed but Bryn shook his head and he drove on.

'I don't think she's happy living there on her own. Perhaps she'll move on and sell the house,' Bryn said.

'Handy if she would, we'd be glad of the extra cash.'

They were heading to a local farm where they were to clear out an old barn and repair the wooden walls. They passed Henry's shop and then saw Mali running down the road, pulling on her coat as she went.

Mali and her sister Megan shared the work in a café and when they were on the early shift, they were always in a rush to get there by 7.30. Megan had a little boy, called Mickie and the sisters shared the happy task of taking care of him, sharing the job in the café, alternating between the café and looking after Mickie.

'Hi, Mali,' Tommy called. 'Why didn't you and Megan come to our wedding party?'

'Mam went out instead of looking after Mickie as she promised in a weak moment and which she immediately regretted.'

'Should have brought him. Loved it he would.'

'Tell Mam. Never does a thing to help us with Dylan. Always complaining about him, poor little love.'

'She's the loser. Lovely kid he is.'

Mali ran on. She and her sister Megan knew they had to do something to get them away from their difficult mother. She was unhelpful and always complaining, making their lives miserable and two-year-old Mickie deserved better and so did she and Megan. If only they could afford to rent a house, it didn't have to be something grand, they'd all be happier in a hovel rather than the place they no longer considered their home.

'What we need,' Megan said, when they talked about their situation later, 'what we desperately want is a third to share. Then we could afford to rent a place.'

'What we need,' Mali said, looking at the sleeping Mickie, 'what we desperately need, is an angelic third, someone who can cope with our Mickie, bless him.'

* * *

Jack had found a place to sleep that he used for a couple of nights, sharing with another man, an ex-soldier who was unable to return to the life he had led before joining the army and serving in France. On the first night, each wrapped in a sour-smelling blanket on opposite corners of the leaky shed, they didn't speak. Jack slept fitfully, opening an eye whenever the other man moved, afraid of losing the valuable items in his bundle.

After a second night, the two men met in a field through which a small stream meandered. Jack was washing himself in the breathtakingly cold water and, seeing the man approach leapt up and stood warningly over his bundle.

'Got soap, have you?' the man asked hopefully and Jack offered the slim remains of a bar.

'Is there any place where I can get some shoes?' Jack asked. 'I'm right through the bottom of these, no mistake.'

'You English? You sound English.'

'Sure am.'

'Ex-army?'

'Shoes?' Jack asked irritably. 'Where can I find some shoes?'

'There's a church and in the basement they sometimes have stuff. You have to show them what you've got and if they think you need a better pair and they've got some that fit you might be lucky. Want me to show you where it is? I'll treat you to a cuppa if you like?'

'I'll treat you to a cup of tea.' Then Jack looked at the man and shook his head. 'But they won't let you into a café smelling like you do. Use that soap and I'll be waiting in the lane.'

'Bossy bloke, aren't you?'

'Don't be too long.'

The church was closed but a notice explained when there would be someone there and they settled to wait. In the porch of the church there was a carrier bag filled with woollen items that someone had left. The two men searched through and helped themselves to shirts and a jumper each. Not a good fit but clean and in reasonable condition. They hid what they'd found and waited patiently in the hope of some shoes.

After answering a series of questions, followed by advice on finding work and somewhere to stay, they were invited to join in a prayer, then each was given a warm coat and shoes and sent on their way.

'Can I trust you?' Jack asked, as the man was about to leave. 'If I can, I know how you can earn a few shillings.'

'What d'you want me to do? Nothing illegal, mind.'

'I have something valuable which I want to sell.'

'Stolen?'

'They belonged to my grandmother,' Jack replied.

'Then why don't you sell them?'

'I don't want my uncle to see me. Family heirlooms, mate; he'd be angry if he saw me selling them.'

'I thought you were from England?'

'Look, if you don't want a few shillings clear off!'

'All right, what is it?'

The silver was taken into Henry's shop and only Tabitha, his assistant, was there. She was tall, very thin and was dressed in old-fashioned, ill-fitting clothes. Her voice was low and nervous but she asked politely what the man had to offer in the bag he placed on the counter. The man looked at her and asked boldly if he could talk to the boss as he had something to sell. He didn't imagine for a moment that this person was in charge of buying and he needed to get rid of this, and fast. Whatever his partner said, there was something iffy about all this. 'Hurry up,' he said irritably.

'I'm afraid you'll have to deal with me,' she said, trying to sound firm. She was suspicious of the nervous man who offered the items for sale but he told a good story and she took a chance. Henry allowed her to buy occasionally, aware of her wide knowledge of silver, china and glass and she made a low offer which was swiftly accepted.

'Will you put your name and address on this form, please?' she said and, still unsure, she phoned the police station and spoke to Sergeant Miller who checked but found no report of the silver being stolen. Nervously the man wrote down an imaginary address in Cardiff and hurried out grasping the money tightly.

Jack gave him a generous percentage and the men parted company.

Tabitha didn't bother telling Henry about her purchase when he rang later; he had been in a hurry and she knew she had got it for a good price.

* * *

A few days later, Henry was driving along the road on Gower that would take him to Rhossili. He had left Penarth, where he had stayed the night with his mother, and now, instead of going back to the shop and the flat above, he had turned the van away from the town.

It was very early and he didn't expect to see anyone, apart from maybe a few dog-walkers. Today he wanted to avoid people, he needed a peaceful place to sit and think. His mother rarely interfered in his life, but she had been hinting for a while that it was time he gave up on any hope of marrying Ruth Thomas. 'Now, with the boys all gone she's still finding reasons to delay, and,' she had added firmly, 'I want you to face facts and let her go, find someone who will love you, who won't find excuses, who'll provide me with grandchildren one day soon.'

He walked along the wide cliff path where sheep grazed and gulls wailed their mournful cries, accompanied by the cackling laughter of the herring gulls, out to the point where he faced The Worm, an island at high tide but which could be reached once the tide went out. Today the tide was high and the Worm's Head was a safe haven for the birds.

He sat on the grass, his eyes following the path that led downward to where the tide played among the rocks. It was cold, with a wind rising and flapping his coat, but he seemed unaware of its chilly embrace. His thoughts were chilled too, thoughts of being alone, if he walked away from Ruth. He couldn't imagine sharing his life with anyone else. Could he accept friendship with no hope of anything more?

Passion was rarely aroused between them these days. Their meetings were usually when they were surrounded by her brothers and their friends. He felt that he was included in that group in Ruth's mind, with no value that separated him from them.

Even when he invited her out, to the pictures or for a meal to celebrate a birthday or something, she arranged for some of the others to join them. He frowned. Had he been a fool? Had she been trying to tell him how it was and he had been too stupid to see the signs? She had made vague promises that they would marry as soon as she was free from caring for her brothers, but they were gone and she still had no intention of giving up her home, or her hope that Tommy, Bryn, Emrys, Geraint and the rest, would still need her. The problem was, he needed her and he didn't know how to persuade her of that.

A woman walked towards him, a spaniel quartering the ground, his nose searching for interesting smells, his tail wagging furiously. He turned and waved, then quickly turned away, hoping she wouldn't want to talk. To discourage her he took a notebook out of his pocket and perused it diligently until she had turned and walked back towards the village. He glanced at his watch. Seven o'clock. Time he was moving too.

With no decision made, he walked back to the road then set off to drive slowly back through a village that was just waking, windows lit, garages opening, the sound of engines disturbing the quiet, a few people walking towards the bus stop, a boy delivering morning papers, a bike thrown against a hedge waiting for its owner to return. His mind was drifting lazily, but a dog suddenly ran out of a gateway startling him and making his brakes squeal. The dog began barking at his car and he stopped completely, afraid of hitting it.

'I'm sorry,' a voice called, and a woman appeared, grabbed the dog, cuffed it and began dragging it towards the gate. 'I'm sorry,' she repeated. 'It's my daughter's dog and so badly behaved.'

'No harm done.' Henry smiled and drove on. He wondered whether a dog would be good company for Ruth; he knew that sleeping in the house alone was not something she enjoyed. But no, it would probably become another reason for her not to marry me, he decided with a sigh. What they needed was time together to really talk.

He turned away from home again and instead, called to see Ruth. She was hanging sheets out on the line and he stepped across to help her with the awkward task, with the wind threatening to steal them from her hands.

'What about going out for the day on Sunday?' he said. 'Just you and me. We're sure to find a café somewhere for a light lunch and there's a good restaurant near Carmarthen where we can get an excellent evening meal. Let's make a day of it.'

'Oh, I don't know, Henry. I sort of expect Tommy and Toni, Bryn and Brenda on Sunday.'

'"Sort of"? That doesn't sound very definite. Can't it be changed? I'll put a note in their door, shall I? So they know we'll be out for the afternoon and evening.'

'No, I — I haven't exactly invited them yet. It's whether I can get enough meat to make a meal.'

'I see. Nothing definite, but you are definite that you don't want to spend a day with me. Right. I understand.'

He hurried around the corner of the house and, ignoring her calls, drove the short distance to the flats where Tommy and Bryn lived. He knocked, hoping for a reply. A note wasn't a good idea. A note could be easily removed. Ruth had a key to both flats, he thought with a grim smile.

Fortunately Toni was home and he explained his plan for Sunday, before returning to Ruth.

'Why was Toni home?' she asked.

'How would I know? That's her business,' he added pointedly. 'Now, how are you? You look tired.'

'I'm all right, but I don't sleep very well these days.'

'These days meaning since you have lived here alone?' He looked at her; there was something odd about her mood. She was edgy, but perhaps that was because she was trying to find an excuse not to go out on Sunday.

She was thinking guiltily about her casual attitude to the silver tea-set, which he had taken back because of her lack of interest. She had been so off-hand at his generosity offering replenishments to her home, especially the beautiful silver. He knew she would love it, so why had she managed to be so indifferent to the beautiful gift? Putting aside the thought of how she had hurt him, she asked, 'Henry, will you change the locks for me? I know it sounds silly but I have the feeling sometimes that someone has been here while I'm out and one morning when I got up I found the back door open. It must have been open all night. Yet I'm so careful about locking it.'

'Are you sure you lock it every night? You do leave it open until dark.'

'After one fright, and now another, and I also found the contents of the dressing-table drawers spilt on the bedroom floor in Tommy's room; yes, I am sure.'

'You mean someone came in and emptied the dressing-table?' He frowned. 'That must have been Tommy, surely? He must have some stuff left here, he can't have taken everything at once.'

'No, I asked him and he hadn't been near. Henry, I keep hearing noises and I panic, convinced someone is in the house. But there isn't a sign of a break-in. When I check everything is the same as when I last looked.'

'Nothing missing?'

'No, Henry, that's what so strange. There is nothing stolen, yet I'm sure someone has been here.'

He turned then as a sob escaped and which she covered up with a handkerchief and a cough. He looked at her anxious face and felt ashamed of his lack of concern. He wondered just how many times she was waking and coming down to reassure herself all was well. It was no wonder she looked tired. Without asking anything more, he went to look at the door then he frowned. The back door was locked and bolted from the inside; no one could have opened it from without. It was unlikely there had been an intruder but he said nothing of his thoughts to Ruth. If she was telling the truth there was no believable explanation. If someone had come in it would have to be through the front door and for that they'd need a key. The four brothers each had one, and they were used to leaving a mess for Ruth to tidy up. But he said nothing.

'I'll change the lock on the front door,' he promised, 'and from now on, make sure the back door is kept locked. Check and then double check the doors and windows. And a third time if you have any doubts. You'll sleep all right when you're absolutely certain everything is safe and secure.'

She nodded agreement but wondered if she would ever feel secure again.

'What about the drawers? Are you sure you didn't tip them out while you looked for something? With Tommy and Bryn leaving you've been in a bit of a muddle, looking for birth certificates and insurances and all that.'

She stared at him. 'I'd have remembered. Unless — Henry, could I have been sleep-walking? I do have some strange dreams these days.'

'It's possible, but don't worry, love, it will pass; you're finding it strange living in a silent house that has always been so full of noisy people.' He held her for a moment. 'Just make absolutely certain that everything is locked then you'll know that no one can get in and you'll sleep peacefully.'

When Sunday came she didn't want to go for a drive and dinner with Henry. But how could she explain that being out in the evening and having to face coming back to an empty house was something she was finding impossible? Guessing the reason for her refusal, Henry put an arm around her shoulder. This time he didn't ask, but told her he would come in with her and stay the night.

'No arguments, Ruth. I'll stay. When we get back I'll settle into the big, soft old couch and stay till morning.'

She began to disagree but he silenced her protest with a kiss. 'No creeping up the stairs, I promise. You'll just know you aren't alone. Right?'

'Henry, why are you so good to me?'

'I still believe I'll persuade you to say yes, one day. Hopefully, before it's too late for us to have children,' he added in a whisper.

* * *

The drive through Pembrokeshire was delightful. The day was clear with the sun shining and every bend in the road revealing another picturesque scene of green fields, some with crops already spearing through the earth, others dotted with sheep. Neat farms, whitewashed houses, well-tended hedges. Home baking at the café where they stopped for lunch adding to the pleasure.

'Henry? Ruth?' a voice called. To their surprise, Tabitha, the young woman who worked part-time for Henry in his antiques shop was there with her father, George Bishop, and George's fiancée Martha Howard. They had just ordered and George invited them to join them. Tabitha was embarrassed, and her face began to redden. She was dressed in the same dress she used for work, and it was well laundered which had leached the colour from what had been a dull green to begin with. By contrast, Martha wore a red dress and lots of jewellery. She glowed with confidence and put Tabitha even more in the shade than was normal. Martha and George talked over her when she made an attempt to join in the conversation and looked bored when the shy young woman managed a few words. Martha wasn't used to being ignored, and certainly not to being upstaged by the pathetic Tabitha.

Tabitha stuttered and hesitated when spoken to, didn't know what to say when Henry tried to include her in the conversation. Eventually he spoke of her rather than to her, telling George how knowledgeable she was and how fortunate he was to have her as his assistant. This embarrassed her even more and she spilt food on the tablecloth and stood up looking as though she were about to run away. Ruth went with her into the ladies room and helped wipe the food stains from her dress. She wondered how the woman managed to deal with customers in the shop.

'She used to spend hours with my mother,' George was saying when they got back. 'With a small car my mother used to go around the area knocking on doors and asking if there was anything she could buy. Talked to Tabitha for hours she would. Then she'd take her to auctions and talk about everything being sold.' He smiled at his daughter. 'Best education that was, eh? My old mum — and her mum, they taught you all you know.'

Looking down at her plate with its minimal amount of food, Tabs nodded.

Taking the attention from her to ease her misery, Henry talked about the early morning walk he'd taken a few days previously and about the beauty of Gower. As the meal progressed and conversation widened, Ruth learned to her surprise that Martha had known her parents. She, and occasionally George, filled gaps in her knowledge of them with amusing stories about when they were young. There were tales about her grandparents too, grandparents she hardly remembered.

'I've got some old photographs at home,' Martha said. 'Some of your mother and her sister, Blodwen, and even some of poor Ralph, the son who was sent away in disgrace. Lucky my mother saved them, your grandfather burned all he had. Poor Ralph.'

'You remember Uncle Ralph? I never knew him and whenever I asked about him the subject was quickly dropped. What did he do?'

'Nothing, if you ask me. There were suspicions and accusations and your grandfather wouldn't help him and he was sent away. Fifteen he was, and treated worse than a dog.'

'Do you know where he is? Is he still alive?'

'Never a word from him. He couldn't come home, not with your grandfather there. Knew he'd only be sent away again.'

As they were leaving, Martha said, 'I'll look for some photos, shall I? And, d'you know, I think I've still got a painting poor little Ralph did when he was at infant school. Throwing it out they were, when your mam and dad died, so I kept it. Not very good, mind, but he was only five when he did it.'

'See you on Monday, Tabs,' Henry called, as they were leaving.

In her breathless, nervous way, Tabitha said, 'I bought something on Friday. A silver tea-set. I was a bit doubtful so I rang Sergeant Miller and he hadn't heard of a theft, so I paid the three pounds the man wanted.'

'Well done, Tabs. I know someone who might be interested.'

On the way back Henry parked and asked Ruth what she knew about her Uncle Ralph.

'I don't even know what he looked like,' Ruth said. 'It will be wonderful to see some photographs.'

'What could he have done that turned his parents against him at the tender age of fifteen?'

'I was never told the full story, but he was believed to be a thief and was suspected of setting fire to a house belonging to a retired school teacher. They thought it was revenge for a caning he'd been given years before. It was all circumstantial and very unlikely from what Mam told me. But I don't remember much about him it's so long ago; Mam died ten years ago remember.'

'What about Aunty Blod, doesn't she know what happened?'

'She was eight years old and doesn't remember him at all.'

It was quite late when he drove her home and although the evening had been an interesting one, meeting Martha and George and Tabs, he didn't think he had made much progress in his plan to persuade her to marry him.

With Henry downstairs Ruth didn't sleep. Her mind was too busy after the conversation and also she was too aware of his presence. When she thought of him giving up on her she was more frightened than she had been at finding the door open.

Being alone was far worse now Tommy and Bryn no longer needed her. Was it love? She wasn't sure. More her foolish need to be needed.

* * *

At 7 Oak Terrace, not far from the shop above which Henry lived, Megan and Mali, the sisters, aged eighteen and seventeen, lived with their mother and Megan's small son. As he alighted from the car a few days later, Henry heard them quarrelling, their mother's shrill voice complaining, and the calmer voices of the two girls. As he walked towards his door he heard the little boy begin to cry. It was a regular occurrence and on many evenings he had seen the girls with Mickie in a pram, walking around waiting for their mother to calm down. He knew that the constant arguments weren't good for a small child.

Since the birth of Mickie to Megan, who had still been at school, their mother had refused to help with the little boy. Megan and Mali had managed to find a job they could share, each doing half of the day in a tea shop and the other half looking after the child, who was now aged two.

Hesitating to interfere, nevertheless once he heard the door slam behind their mother, leaving them standing outside trying to comfort the little boy, he called, 'Is everything all right?'.

'We're moving into a flat after Mam told us to go, and now, she's insisting we stay. But it isn't fair for this little love to put up with her temper, so we're leaving.'

'I just wish we had somewhere to go for the two weeks until the flat is ready for us,' Mali added. 'Mam is getting impossible.'

Henry hesitated for a moment then said, 'Why don't you ask Ruth if you can stay with her? Two weeks isn't long and she's hating living in that big house on her own. I'm sure she wouldn't mind, and anyway it won't hurt to ask her.'

* * *

Ruth had a rabbit stew cooking and, as the butcher had found her some suet, there were dumplings ready to add. She stared at the food simmering in the large saucepan and sighed. Once again she had made too much. When would she learn to cook small amounts and not prepare for a family?

The back door was locked even though it was day-time, and when she heard the knock she hurried to answer. Henry came in first and gave a brief explanation, then Megan carrying Mickie, with Mali following.

'We'll understand if you say no, mind,' Mali said, after Henry had explained. 'Our Mickie isn't the quietest lodger you could find.'

'Come, and welcome,' Ruth said. 'And look,' — she gestured towards the cooker — 'I must have known. Rabbit stew and plenty for us all.'

Over the next few days, ration books, temporary changes of address and the rest of the formalities were easily dealt with. Rota for using the kitchen was agreed, their contribution to the household, all were quickly arranged. The girls helped as drawers and cupboard space were cleared and three days later, with the shiny new lock on the front door and three lodgers in one of the big rooms at the front, Ruth gave a sigh of relief. Perhaps now she would sleep.

A week later, while the girls were out, Ruth climbed up into the loft to tackle the muddle of papers that had been thrown into a box to be sorted later. She slid down a box of papers followed by a large, ancient suitcase into which she intended to place the things she thought should be kept. The rest would go onto a garden fire. Lifting the battered box she tilted it and allowed the contents to flow like a river across the floor.

Much of it was family memorabilia. School reports hoarded by their mother, old photographs which she always intended to put in an album one day. There were also some insurance papers which must be of no value as everything had been sorted out at the time of their parents' deaths. She hesitated to throw them away. Perhaps, one day, a child or grandchild might enjoy perusing them, learning about their grandparents. She kept out one photograph to show the boys. It was of their grandmother Thomas and some people she didn't know. Distant uncles? Cousins? Why hadn't she taken more notice when her parents had been there to explain? There was no one she recognized, except Aunty Blod who didn't believe in living in the past, and would surely recommend burning the lot!

The gate opened and the two girls came in, a chattering Mickie between them carrying a small bag containing sweets, 'For after dinner,' he told her, giving her his wide smile. Ruth gathered the papers without sorting them and pushed them untidily into the suitcase. They could wait.

That evening there was a commotion at the front door then a banging on the back door. 'Oh!' Ruth gasped. 'I've forgotten to give the new keys to Tommy and Bryn!'

Henry, who was fixing an extra shelf in the kitchen laughed. 'Forgotten them? Thank goodness for that! It's a very good sign!'

Almost as soon as they were inside, Toni asked in her forthright way, 'Ruth, why don't you get a job? Getting out of the house for a while each day would be a good thing.'

'What would I do? I don't have any training.'

'Neither did we,' Bryn said, 'but Tommy and me, we have a nice little business. When we finished our two years in the army, we looked around and realized that gardening maintenance and garden planning was an increasing need, and we started small, helping out on farms with seasonal jobs as our experience grew.' He winked at his brother. 'We could give you a job if you like?'

'Yes, sawing wood, chopping down trees, mixing cement, carrying rocks, you'd love it.'

After they'd gone, and Megan and Mali were in their own room, Henry stood to leave. 'Toni has a point, you know. Now there isn't as much to do here, you could work for a few hours each day and still cope with everything.'

'I do have to earn some money,' she admitted. 'I've been trying to ignore it, although I have been looking in the paper for something that appeals. Without the boys contributing I'll soon be needing some.'

'Shops? Office work? Canteen assistant? What about cooking, like Mali and Megan? You wouldn't find that difficult after all the years you've fed the boys. Or you could learn to type, that would open many doors.'

She laughed. 'You've given this idea some thought, haven't you?'

'You need to get out and make a life for yourself.'

'I'm thinking about it but the idea is scary. I haven't mixed with many people over the past ten years, have I?'

'It's time you did.'

'All right. For a start, what about inviting Tabs and her father and the formidable Martha for dinner one evening? I'd like to talk some more about my family.'

'Tabs and George and Martha and all your brothers, I suppose.'

'No,' she said, changing her mind rapidly, 'just you.'

When they arrived on the following Saturday, Martha carried a large flat package which she handed to Ruth. It was a painting, not a very good one, obviously painted by a child and cheaply framed in wood that had been stained to the colour of dark oak. 'No letters. I must have thrown them away. But this was painted by your poor Uncle Ralph,' Martha told her, 'while he was still at infant school. Your mam kept it until she died. I don't know why, but I couldn't throw it away. There ought to be something for him to be remembered by.'

Ruth was staring at it. 'Thank you. I'll treasure this. I know nothing about my Uncle Ralph. So you rescued this? How d'you know it was Ralph's work?' She looked at it then said, 'It isn't signed.'

'Your mother told me. It was the only thing she had to remind her of her brother. When she and your father died and her things were sorted out, it was going on the back of the fire. I asked your brother Emrys if I could have it and he looked at it, saw it was of no value or interest and agreed. If you would like it back, it's yours. I don't know why I kept it, perhaps so I could hand it back to someone who might be interested.'

'I am interested. Thank you, Martha.' Ruth propped it up on the mantelpiece and stared at it for a while. 'Poor Ralph. I wonder what became of him?'

'Probably dead by now, poor dab.'

* * *

Henry's mother lived in the pretty seaside town of Penarth, and he saw her often. She ran one of Henry's shops in which she sold mostly old jewellery. She didn't do much business, but she needed something to fill her days now she couldn't get around very well. He was happy to keep it going and he encouraged her to buy as well as sell as she became more knowledgeable.

He lived above the shop that was the base for his antiques business, built up since the war. Tabitha, shy, nervous, yet extremely interested and with a basic information about many aspects of the business, helped by looking after the shop for a few hours each day.

Thinking of his mother, he went to a phone box and invited her out for a meal, with Ruth. When he went to unload the items he had bought, it was past 5.30 and he was surprised to find the shop open and his assistant still there.

'Tabitha? You're working late today. Have you been busy?'

'I've been waiting for you, Mr Owen.'

'Something wrong?'

'My father is marrying again and, he — she—' She began to cry. 'I'm sorry, Mr Owen, but I—'

'Come on, Tabs, I'll make us a drink and you can tell me all about it.'

She had calmed down by the time he handed her a cup of tea and she explained.

'They want me to leave. They're getting married in July and want the place to themselves. I don't blame them,' she said quickly, as he began to respond. 'They need time together without someone like me hanging around. I understand that, but where will I go?'

'Someone like you will have plenty of choices, Tabs. You'd make an excellent lodger if you fancy living with a family, or there'll be a room to rent somewhere that will make a comfortable home. Look, don't worry about it. I'll make enquiries and we'll have you settled in no time.'

'It's only April. They aren't getting married until July.'

'No need for you to wait for a formal goodbye and have them close the door behind you. You tell them goodbye, let them manage without you for a few weeks.'

'I couldn't do that, Mr Owen. Dad will need someone to look after him until Martha moves in.'

Henry chuckled and looked at her. 'What is it about me that I attract silly women?' Tabitha looked shocked and she half rose out of her chair. He touched her shoulder and pressed her gently back down. 'Silly because they are too kind, they worry too much about others and not enough about themselves. You and Ruth are so much alike.'

'Too kind, or too silly?'

'Both! Once you find a suitable place, don't wait, take it! It's what they want, isn't it? For you to find a place of your own? Honestly, Tabs, you mustn't allow them to use you until they no longer need you then tell you to go. That's silly. D'you see?'

'I'll look for a place in the local newspaper.'

'Good girl!'

'Hardly a girl,' she said sadly. 'I'll be twenty-nine soon.'

'All the more reason to get out and find a life for yourself. Honestly, you and Ruth, you both need a shove. Tabs, don't be sad, get excited. This might be the best thing that's happened to you.'

He discussed Tabs over the meal with Ruth and his mother. 'It's a pity there isn't a way to help her. She just lacks confidence. Can you suggest anything, Ruth?'

'Too busy!' Then she laughed and explained her flippant remark. 'It's Mickie! I didn't dream that two year olds could be such hard work. But he's a darling child, such fun. I'm enjoying having Mali and Megan staying at Ty Gwyn, I really am.' She added, 'I will think about Tabs, and there is a way I think might solve her problem. I'll tell you about it later.'

Ruth was pleased at the way Megan and Mali and little Mickie settled into life at Ty Gwyn. They went out a lot when they weren't working during the day, and took the little boy to parks and to the beach and for picnics in sheltered places on mild afternoons. He would come home happy and tired and slept easily from the moment he was put into bed. Megan and Mali both went out often in the evenings, to dances and to the cinema or simply to meet friends, but never together, they shared the care of Mickie completely and, listening to how they were with him, there was no discernible difference in the way he was treated.

They spent more and more time in the large, comfortable kitchen and would occasionally share their meal with her. In May 1954, fats and cheese rationing ended and they celebrated by making a supper of baked potatoes to which lots of cheese had been added, with piles more sprinkled on the top and melted under the grill with a crisp bacon garnish. Butter was thickly spread on bread and topped with jam, and they declared it a feast.

One evening when they were all in, Henry came, and to everyone's surprise, he brought Tabitha, his shy, nervous assistant. 'Tabitha's looking for accommodation,' he announced to the sisters. 'She's decided to leave her father now he's remarrying and, thank goodness, she isn't needed to look after him any longer. Wise girl, our Tabs, eh?' She was about to disagree with his reverse summing up of her situation, but he smiled encouragingly and she nodded agreement.

'Stay for the evening, Tabs,' Ruth invited, and ignored the girl's immediate attempt to refuse, took her coat and offered her a chair near the fire. Back in the kitchen, she said to Henry, 'It might be a good idea to break her in gently to leaving home by coming here for a few evenings to get used to people rather than go straight into a room with strangers and probably become a hermit!'

Tabs said very little but seemed to enjoy the company, as long as she wasn't given too much attention. She ate sparingly, as though convinced that everyone was watching her. She went into the kitchen to start on the washing up once the meal was over but was stopped by Ruth, who insisted that she was a guest.

Tommy and Toni, Bryn and Brenda called in and Tabs began to scoot away, reaching for her coat like a life-line, but she was persuaded to stay. For Ruth the evening was perfect, chatter and laughter and the house filled with people demanding food.

Although the evening was warm, Toni wore a loose coat that swung from her shoulders, which she seemed reluctant to remove.

'Cup of tea, Toni?' Ruth asked. Toni shook her head.

'Off tea she is,' Tommy said. 'Who'd have believed that, eh?'

With a twinkle in her eyes, Mali said. 'You've put on some weight, Toni. Being married suits you, doesn't it?'

'When's it due?' the more forthright Megan asked.

Into the sudden silence, Toni brushed the remark aside and she and the others didn't stay very long.

'Shy, is she?' Megan asked, when they stood at the door to wave them goodbye.

'Toni? Of course she isn't shy. She's as at home with me here as in her new flat.'

'Told you about the baby, then, has she?' Mali asked.

'What baby?'

'Come on! Putting on weight, wearing a coat that looks like a tent, on a mild day like today? Refusing a cup of tea? All the usual signs.'

'She can't be expecting. I'm the first person they'd have told.'

She went to Toni and Tommy's flat the following morning and found Toni there. 'No work today, Toni? Everything all right?'

'Yes, everything's fine,' Toni said, sitting down and pulling a cushion onto her lap to hide a pregnancy that was hardly visible.

'Why didn't you tell me about the baby?' Ruth asked softly. 'I felt such a fool, Mali and Megan guessing before me.'

'We had to get married and we couldn't tell you, it was too embarrassing, you being an unmarried sister. It sounds stupid but we hoped we could hide it until nearer the time so everyone would think it was a honeymoon baby, even if it comes suspiciously early.'

'You should have told me.'

'Why?' Toni asked in exasperation. 'You're only my sister-in-law and your opinion isn't our first thought.'

Ruth felt the shock of the unkind words and stood to leave.

'Don't go.' Toni sighed. 'Look, you have to face the facts, Ruth. You were wonderful looking after the boys all these years, but it's over and you can have your life back. Surely you want a life of your own? Or are you going to spend all the years ahead waiting for visits and cooking big-huge meals in the hope that someone will come and eat them?'

'You're so unkind.'

'If it's unkind to be truthful then yes, I'm unkind. But trying to make you see you have a life to live?' She shook her head. 'Who but you would call that unkind? You must know deep down in that coping, caring, motherly nature of yours that I'm right. Marry Henry, have babies.' She patted her barely visible swelling. 'This one will be needing cousins, won't he?'

Ruth was tearful as she walked back home, but by the time she had reached the house, and heard the sound of Mickie shrieking with laughter as he played ball with his mother, she had calmed down. Toni was right. It was a time to look for a new direction. Change was never easy, and change of attitude was the hardest of all. But marry Henry? She couldn't marry him simply because there was no alternative.

The first stage of this new life that beckoned, was a job, Toni had been right about that, too. She turned away from the gate and went to buy a local paper to look for the jobs vacant column. Today she would restart her own life.

Turning the pages carrying advertisements her eyes stopped at the accommodation required section. Perhaps she would see something suitable for Tabitha. Then her eyes lit up. *Her* life Toni had told her, then she could make her own decisions. She would invite Tabitha to come and live with her in Ty Gwyn. Whatever anyone said, it was what she wanted, the house filled again and with people she chose. New life, new attitude. If it was what she wanted, then that was what she would do. Tabitha would benefit from being there, seeing her brothers and their wives calling in, they'd ease her out of her shyness. She was humming as she hurried once more towards home.

She didn't go into the house but instead went to see Tabs. She asked her straight out, if she would like to come and live in Ty Gwyn and was surprised when Tabitha shook her head, her eyes wide in alarm.

'No, I couldn't! You're very kind but I'll manage, you don't have to put yourself out for me.'

'I'm not being kind, I would prefer not to live in that house all alone and Mali and Megan will be leaving soon to move into the flat they are renting. Please, Tabs, I think we'd get on very well. At least give it a try.'

A lot of persuading was required but Tabs finally agreed to move in — 'Just as soon as my father doesn't need me anymore. I'll have to stay until he and Martha marry.' We'll see about that, Ruth thought, having been told of the situation by Henry.

Henry walked into the shop later that day, stopped and stared in disbelief at the silver tea-set which Tabs had polished and which stood in the centre of the window. He picked up the teapot and looked at the marks and the unfortunate dents. Frowning, he looked at Tabs. 'Where did this come from?'

'I told you, I bought it on Friday.' She took out the form which the tramp had filled in and he snatched it from her.

'What have I done?' she asked. 'I rang Sergeant Miller, what else should I have done?'

'I gave this set to Ruth. How could she sell it?'

'It wasn't Ruth, Henry. A rather scruffy individual brought it in. I suspected there was something wrong, the way he looked, all nervous. But I checked and it was a good price and . . . Oh, I'm so sorry.'

'She might not have brought it in, but I gave it to her and somehow it ends up here.'

'I'm sorry,' Tabs repeated.

'Don't be. Could you lock up for me, please, Tabs? I think I need to go and talk to Ruth about this.'

'Of course.'

Henry took the silver and when he got to Ty Gwyn he unpacked it onto the kitchen table. 'If you hadn't wanted it you only had to tell me. I offered it but I wouldn't have been heartbroken if you hadn't liked it.'

Ruth stared at it.

'But where has it been? I thought you'd changed your mind and taken it back. I didn't accept it very graciously.'

'I left it here, on this table and the following Friday it ended up in the shop.'

'But how? I didn't see it after you'd gone and I presumed you'd changed your mind about giving it to me.'

'A man came into the shop and offered it to Tabs, who bought it, not knowing it was already mine.'

'Then someone must have taken it. Truthfully, Henry, I didn't see it after you'd gone.' She was alarmed at the expression in Henry's eyes. 'Henry, I don't know what happened. I only know I didn't sell it or give it away. I wouldn't. You must know me better than that. It must have been stolen the night I found the door unlocked. I thought at first I'd packed it away somewhere after another sleep-walking incident, but then, as nothing else was missing, I thought you must have taken it back.'

'Another mysterious happening in this house?'

'Yes, so it seems. It also seems that once again you don't believe me.'

'I do believe you. I'm trying to work out what could have happened.'

'Well, seeing you looking at me with such a suspicious, disbelieving expression, I wish you'd work out what happened somewhere else! Please go away!' She pushed him through the door and slammed it after him. 'So much for my happy fresh start,' she muttered. 'No Henry, no Tabs as a lodger and, from the smell coming for the oven, no dinner either!' She pulled the too large cottage pie out of the oven and sighed over its blackened edges and threw it outside the door.

CHAPTER THREE

Tabitha's father was trying to move some of the furniture out of the bedroom into which he was going to bring his bride. Martha Howard had made it clear that she didn't intend to move in and live amid the trappings of his previous marriage.

'A fresh start is what you deserve, George, dear,' she had explained, when he told her magnanimously that she could rearrange the rooms as she pleased. 'We need a complete change. After all my taste is different from your first wife's and poor Tabs doesn't have much idea about furnishing a room. With some new furniture and some cheerful curtains instead of those drab, heavy old browns, you'll feel like a young man just setting out on life.'

She had chosen the main bedroom and suggested the second bedroom would be perfect for the occasional guest.

'Tabitha — silly name, dear — can manage in the box room. There's plenty of room for her things and she can sit up there in the evenings for us to have some privacy. She'll be quite comfortable there with a chair and a small table.'

'But Tabs won't be here!' He smiled in expectation of her delight. 'Surprise, surprise, dear. She's moving out so we can have the place to ourselves. That's my special news,

Martha. The whole house will be ours, just like you wanted. We'll be starting out like two young newlyweds should.'

Martha hid her disappointment well. She had imagined that Tabitha would be running the household as she always had, leaving her to enjoy the freedom of not having to deal with the boring chores.

Later, after she had cooked George his favourite meal of liver and onions and given him a glass of beer, she broached the subject again.

'If Tabitha is leaving you without help, I hope you aren't expecting me to do all the housework as well as the cooking, George.'

'I thought you'd be pleased that I told Tabs to go.'

'I am, dear, it was a wonderful surprise, but if she leaves us, we'll have to have someone here to run things. I'll be concentrating on looking after you, won't I?'

What began as a discussion began to get rather strained and George considered the cost of employing someone to run the house and decided that wouldn't be possible.

He relaxed, confident that over the weeks before the wedding he would be able to persuade Martha that being on their own, with no interference from servants — which he couldn't afford — or his irritating daughter hanging around like a wet week, was the perfect way to start married life. Whenever he mentioned it her responses grew colder and he began to worry.

* * *

Jack gathered money from his various endeavours and bought a few decent clothes. As it was summer, a smart pair of slacks and a shirt was all that was needed to improve his appearance and he found a job in a green-grocery. His hands were still dirt-grained with the nails black edged with ground-in dirt from living rough but that would be put down to sorting out potatoes and the like. They would take a while to improve. A hair-cut and daily shaves improved his appearance and he soon had a regular group of admiring customers, attracted by his lively humorous chat and exaggerated flattery. With his wages safely hidden in his clothes, he slept out in abandoned barns and bus shelters for another week, then he found a room easily; there were many householders only too pleased to find a lodger to help pay their bills.

So far he hadn't been lucky. If this was the house his father had spoken about, then the family had vanished. He mentioned the name to several customers, but all he had was a frown and a shake of the head. Searching for his father's family and his inheritance was frustrating. He knew so little about his father's childhood and now he could no longer ask. This town had seemed likely to be the one as he had added the few clues and oddments of memory together.

He went into the antique shop and spoke, almost as a last hope, to Tabitha. She might be the lead he'd been searching for; he had seen her coming out of the house, the name of which he half remembered, several times, Ty Gwyn. The place was almost exactly as his father had described it to him.

There were fields around it, a church on the next corner and the oak tree in the garden. There was even a pond, now dried up but it was there, just like the picture that had been in his mind all these years. It seemed so right, but how was he going to find out? To do that he needed to get into Ty Gwyn and with time for a proper search. From the people he'd seen in and out of Ty Gwyn, Tabitha seemed the most likely to fall for his approach.

After a few questions about the shop and its contents, he asked about the house called Ty Gwyn and whether it was owned by a family called Tyler.

'Tyler? No, I'm sorry. The family there are called Thomas. I know them so would you like me to ask them whether the name is known to them?' She felt breathless with embarrassment and she hoped her voice didn't give her away. 'If it would help?'

'You're very kind, Miss—' His heart thudded similar to hers but for a different reason. This plain, boring-looking woman was someone he needed to cultivate. 'Miss——?' he invited again.

'Bishop,' she said, her face reddening with embarrassment.

'I'm Jack.' He offered a hand apologetically. 'Sorry about the state of them, but serving potatoes and cleaning up rotten vegetables makes a mess of them.'

'Is that what you do?' she asked hesitantly.

'Come out and have a cup of tea and a cake and I'll tell you all about me,' he said. 'We'll both be off at one, half-day closing. I've just been to the bank for some change,' he explained, 'and I saw your friendly face and just had to come in.'

At one o'clock she closed the shop and looked around anxiously. As she had expected there was no sign of the young man. She was about to turn the corner when a shout stopped her. 'Miss Bishop! Wait!' Jack ran to her and said, 'Come on. What's your first name? I can't call you Miss Bishop, it makes you sound like my aunty!'

'You aren't from around here, are you?' she said.

Laughing eyes looked at her. 'How can you tell?' he said. 'Is it the way I say "aunty"?' He pursed his mouth and said aunty in an exaggerated way and she laughed.

'I hate telling people my name,' she said.

'Tell me, it can't be worse than Miss Bishop!'

'Tabitha.' She waited for the exclamation of amusement or disbelief.

He looked at her for a moment then said. 'Yep. Tabitha is fine. Unusual, but not boring, in fact, it makes you sound interesting. Too much of a mouthful for me, though, so come on, Tabs, let's find a café that sells real creamy cakes.'

On that first date he didn't question her about the Tyler family. It was clear she was very unsure of herself and he could easily frighten her off, so he encouraged her to talk and, in a startling moment of realization she was aware of sitting talking to this handsome stranger and she felt embarrassment overwhelm her. She was talking too much, he must be bored, what was she thinking of!

She put down the cup she was holding, missed the saucer and spilt tea across the table. She gasped and went to stand up but he held her hand and beckoned to the man behind the counter. 'Give him something to do,' he whispered. 'He looks bored standing there. He isn't as lucky as me, having someone as exciting as you to share an hour with.'

She didn't believe him. He was being kind.

'I'm clumsy,' she said. 'I'm always dropping things and breaking things.'

'Not true,' he said firmly. 'That boss of yours wouldn't employ you in that shop if you were. So don't tell me porky pies. That's an expression my father used to use.'

'My father calls lies Tom Peppers.'

After the table had been wiped, he talked to her while she calmed down. He told her a little about his childhood — most of it pure fantasy.

'My father was born in Wales but his parents took him to England when he was very young. Just a baby I believe. I don't know anything more than that.' That wasn't true either but it was all she needed to know.

'So you don't know where your family are?' Her eyes were moist with sympathy.

'Or even if I have any.' He looked glum, but his eyes were twinkling as he teased, 'Sorry for me, are you, Tabs? Are you going to look after me to ease my loneliness?'

Tabs thought that was a role she would willingly accept.

They parted after an hour and she walked back into the house and hurried to her room. It had been such a remarkable day she needed to sit and think about it or she would imagine it had been a dream. She wondered whether she would see him again and began counting the hours until the shop opened and she could watch the door in hope.

Realistically she guessed she would be watching the door for many days until she had to give up.

* * *

On Saturday morning, Ruth went shopping and she expected either Megan or Mali to be there when she got back. To her dismay the house was empty and worse, the back door was unlocked. She went inside and stood listening for a long time before starting to look in the rooms. The silence was in her head like a hissing sound, and she imagined someone watching her as she forced herself to look in every room. Foolishly, she carried a teapot, the first thing her hand touched when she had put down her shopping basket.

The downstairs was empty and nothing had been moved, but she was still frightened as she slowly went up the stairs. Each room she checked was empty and showed nothing out of the ordinary. There was a muddle in Megan and Mali's room. The unused one looked the same as normal.

Her own, left until the last, was where she had the biggest fright. The wardrobe doors stood open and the clothes had been moved, slid along the rail gathered at each end. She looked around her half expecting someone to jump out and attack her. Then logic prevailed. Of course no one had been in the house. Who would want to look through her things? There was nothing in the house apart from oddments the family had gathered over the years. Personal things. Certainly nothing of value. Nervously she touched the few clothes she had and looked behind them before adjusting them so they were neatly spaced.

She must have closed the door carelessly, she told herself, a sleeve or the hem of a coat must have stopped it closing properly and a gust of wind or something would have been sufficient to allow doors to slide open.

She went back down only half convinced. The house had always been filled with people and nothing like this had happened before, or was she so tense that she noticed things more? She had told herself that the dressing table drawers being tipped out in her bedroom was due to her sleep walking, even though she had no knowledge of ever having done so since she was a child, and now she was telling herself she had not closed the wardrobe properly and given herself another fright. She went into the kitchen and turned the radio on very loud and sang along with Johnnie Ray, 'Walking My Baby Back Home'.

She told no one about the open wardrobe, gradually accepting that she had been responsible, but last thing at night when she was alone in the kitchen setting the breakfast table as she always had, she shivered and knew that the house was different, less friendly and she couldn't understand why. It hadn't changed, so she must have done. She needed to get out of the place, find something to keep her coming and going, in and out, then it would soon be as ordinary as it had always been. But she didn't want a job, she couldn't work. Not while there was a chance she might be needed by her brothers.

She took out her work basket filled with assorted cottons and with every colour of darning wools she had used for darning the boys' socks. The white wool wrapped in tissue looked out of place among the dark colours and she picked it up and began studying the knitting pattern for the baby's coat. She was unlikely to sleep tonight so she might as well do something useful.

When she went around to see Toni and Tommy on Sunday morning, Toni was on her own. 'Tommy and Bryn have gone to work,' she said by way of greeting. 'I'm going in later for an hour or two.'

'On Sunday? Wool shops don't open on Sundays.'

'I'm going in while the shop's closed to sort out the knitting patterns, they've got in a bit of a mess.'

'And Tommy and Bryn?'

'They're finishing creosoting a barn for one of the farmers they do occasional work for.'

'Why didn't you say? I'd have invited you for dinner.' She reached into her basket and handed Toni a tissue-wrapped packet. 'I've brought you this. I made it for the new baby, sat up half the night so my gift would be the first,' she said with a smile. 'Now, I want you to tell me how I can help.'

'We're managing fine, Ruth, but thanks.'

'Oh, I don't mean now, although I have a cake to bring over later, when I've iced it. But later on, you'll need lots of support when the baby comes and I want you to know that whatever you want me to do, I'll be happy to help. It's such an exciting thing, a baby in the family. I couldn't sleep last night, thinking about him — or her.' Well, that was almost true.

She looked at Toni's face and the young woman's expression shocked her. Tight-lipped and eyebrows almost meeting in a frown. 'Is everything all right, Toni, love?'

Then she saw the packet, lying still unopened on Toni's lap and thought, with a stab of pain, that she knew what the girl wanted to say. 'The baby, he's still all right, isn't he?'

'The baby is fine, we're all fine, but Ruth, this is our life now, mine and Tommy's and we'll cope with our baby when he comes.' She looked uncomfortable and her voice was tense as she went on, 'We appreciate all you've done, of course we do, but now you have to find a life of your own and leave us to deal with ours.' She was silent for a moment allowing Ruth to speak but Ruth just stared at her. 'You really need to get a job, Ruth, get out of the house for a while each day. We won't do things your way but we'll manage. And now, with all four brothers married, this is time for yourself. We're all settled and getting on with our lives, really we are.' She tried to smile to take the sting out of her words but it wasn't successful. 'Look, I'm not doing this very well, but your brothers are all really grateful for the way you've looked after them since your parents died and they always will be. You kept the family together. It's thanks to you that they've had a home all these years. But it's time now to let go, find a life of your own, they all want that for you.'

Seeing the shocked expression on Ruth's face, she reached out and held her hand, the tissue-wrapped packet falling unheeded, to the floor. 'Ruth, it's you we're thinking of as well as ourselves. We don't want to lean on you, you've done your bit and you've been wonderful, but we want to cope on our own, do things our own way, as new parents always do. You have to do the same, cope with the change in our lives, or you'll end up a lonely old woman. Tommy and Bryn, Emrys and Geraint, they don't want that and neither do I. Deep in your heart you must know we're right. Please believe me, it's best for us all.'

'Of course I understand. I'll be glad to be free, it's about time, isn't it?' Ruth heard the words and could hardly believe they came from her own lips. The voice didn't sound like her own. She wanted to shout and rail at the hurtful words. How could her brothers discard her on the word of someone who had been in the family for such a brief time? She had been mother, father as well as sister to them and now, because Toni thought they should, they were brushing their hands together dusting off ten years of loving, unselfish care.

She picked up the tiny coat she had lovingly made during the night when she couldn't sleep and offered it again to Toni. Her newest and most outspoken sister-in-law opened the tissue paper slowly, and tearfully said, 'It's beautiful, Ruth. Thank you very much. I will treasure it. Our baby's first gift.'

'I'll—' Ruth was about to say she'd make more but she stopped and instead, said. 'If you'd like any more, just ask.'

'Yes, please,' Toni replied at once. 'We'd love more as lovely as this one. Thank you, Ruth. I know how lucky I am to have you for a sister-in-law,' she added, as Ruth stood to leave. 'Tommy and Bryn told me how clever you are at handiwork. You used to knit them beautiful jumpers. Complicated cable patterns and Fair Isle, wonderful work.'

'Yes, I did, but that's all in the past now, isn't it?'

Ruth went back to the house and lifted the rugs and heaved the furniture around and scrubbed the kitchen floor. It was what she always did when she was upset, scrub and clean until she felt calm again.

* * *

Henry went into the shop, surprised that it was closed. Tabitha, his assistant, was normally so reliable. She didn't work full time at the shop selling antiques, it wasn't the kind of business that filled the shop every moment of the day with customers queuing for assistance. Henry advertised the hours he opened and when he wasn't there, Tabitha usually filled in. For her not to be there as promised was unusual and he wondered if she was all right.

Tabitha, at the age of twenty-nine, was very unworldly and even a stranger smiling and greeting her with 'good morning' made the colour rise in her cheeks sending her hurrying away like a frightened goose — one of her long-standing nicknames. She was a very nervous person, constantly criticized and often humiliated by her father. After years of his taunts, she accepted his low opinion of herself. Following the death of her mother, she had automatically left the factory where she worked as a cleaner, and stayed home to keep house for her father. Gradually she had been allowed to help out at Henry's shop, and she loved it.

Her knowledge and interest had surprised him and he was pleased to be able to discuss his purchases with her. She agreed with his estimated value on most things. After a short time he allowed her to buy if she saw something they could re-sell, and until the silver tea-set, which remained a mystery, she had never been wrong.

Her father had begun to go out in the evenings more frequently over the past months. She didn't ask where he went, presuming it would be the local club of which he had been a member for many years. She was just pleased to have time on her own, without his constant criticism, although she rarely did anything more exciting than listen to her favourite programmes on the wireless. She made very few decisions and when Ruth offered her a room she presumed she hadn't really wanted her there. It was only when Henry added his persuasions, promising her that if she was unhappy he would find her something more suitable that she accepted gratefully. Another decision avoided. Decision making was something of which she had very little experience.

An only child, she had always known she was not wanted. Her father constantly told her how her arrival had ruined their lives. She often wondered whether they had given her such an unusual name out of spite. Besides being shy, her mother's choice of dress, long shapeless skirts and blouses that were too large, and shoes with ankle straps like those worn by small children, added to the impression that she was a little odd, even simple, although she was neither.

Teasing had been a daily agony at school and the unusual name was a gift to her tormentors. No second name, just Tabitha Bishop, so the few friends she had made in her sad life called her Tabs. Many of the girls she knew had earned nicknames, a sign of affection, and she longed for someone to call her something different, but apart from 'scaredy cat', and 'goose', and even by some, 'the idiot girl', she waited in vain.

Being introduced to her father's 'intended' had been a shock. She wondered how she would cope with another woman in the house. Martha would probably treat her in the same way as her father, but she couldn't think of anything she could do to change things. Leaving her home was the last thing she expected to do and her father telling her she must, gave her nightmares. But Henry had helped to reassure her that it would be a good thing to break away.

She was very grateful but apprehensive about moving her few possessions into Ty Gwyn. It was such a large and imposing place with its huge porch and solid oak door with the beautifully designed stained-glass window, and standing in its own garden made it seem far more important than the houses close by. She didn't see the shabbiness, the need for paint and repairs after years of neglect.

Her own home had been the middle of a terrace of neglected houses without front gardens so the door led straight in from the street and behind the house was only a cemented yard.

She set off to talk to Ruth but walked around the block twice, attempting to summon the nerve to lift the heavy brass knocker on that impressive door. When she did walk up the front path she lost her nerve and went around to the back and tapped timidly, wondering where she would go if no one answered.

The door was pulled open abruptly and she backed away expecting a complaint, but the face that appeared was smiling and a hand came out to take her bag in a friendly way.

'Tabs, come in. Why did you come to the back? I thought you'd use the front door.'

'I'm sorry I thought . . .' Words failed as Ruth ushered her inside and she saw the kitchen with its fire burning brightly and the comfortable couch on which a very fat cat was sprawled.

'It's I who should be sorry! This isn't a good first impression, coming through our tatty, old-fashioned kitchen. I thought I'd be showing you the best room first.' Ruth laughed. 'We talk about improving it, making it into a proper kitchen, but nothing happens. It's the most popular room in the house, and no one really wants it changed.'

'It's lovely,' Tabitha said, staring about her in awe. 'Such a friendly room. I've never seen a more — happy place,' she finished in a whisper.

'I'll show you your room and the rest of the house soon but first we'll have a cup of tea.'

'Thank you.' Tabitha sat on the edge of the chair Ruth pulled out for her and clutched her handbag tightly.

'I'm glad you're coming to stay. I've looked after the house ever since my parents died,' Ruth explained. 'My four brothers have been my life since then and now they're all married and I don't like not having other people around. I rattle miserably in all these empty rooms. Mali and Megan Grange and young Mickie are only staying for a few weeks, until they move into their flat and they have one of the big front bedrooms. The other room at the front is yours if you'd like it.'

'Any room will do, certainly not one of the best ones!' Tabitha looked horrified at the thought of such special treatment. 'No, not the best room. One of the back ones would be fine.'

Ruth looked at her pale, thin, anxious face and thought that if she offered a cupboard on the landing the poor girl would gratefully accept. 'The best room is yours,' she promised. 'I like it in my small back room and I don't want the bother of changing.'

* * *

Moving in was simple, Tabitha carried all her worldly possessions in a couple of paper carrier bags and once installed, the room looked exactly the same as before. Ruth put a few cheerful cushions on the chair and some flowers on the window sill — which Tabitha immediately knocked over. She seemed afraid of being seen, and during those first few days, she unknowingly acquired a new nickname.

'She's like a little mouse,' Ruth told Henry. 'She creeps about so afraid of being a nuisance I hardly know she's there and when we do meet she appears to be walking backwards in case she's in the way. Poor little mouse.'

'She'll open out to you, I'm sure of it. Her father has never done much to encourage her to think good of herself. According to what I've learned, he wasn't much kinder to his wife, either.'

'I'm glad to have people living here again, but I still feel as though I'm alone. Mali and Megan stay in their room, only appearing when they need to use the kitchen, and the little mouse, she's more like a shadow than a real person. D'you think it would be wrong to ask her to help with a few chores? Better than her staying in her room, hiding away like a prisoner. Perhaps if I could persuade her to talk, she might be willing to share meals with me. It seems sad, both of us having to make our meals separately.'

'You're enjoying this, aren't you?' Henry was smiling when she looked up expecting to see disapproval on his face. 'You like looking after people, so why don't we marry and start a family of our own?'

They were sitting on the couch near the slowly dying fire, and she moved slightly away from him, leaning forward, staring at the grey ashes. 'I miss looking after the boys, but before I start thinking of marriage, I want to do something on my own, find out who I really am. It was something Toni said that made me realize I've done nothing except look after the boys and keep this house going for them so they have a home. I want to find out who I am. Does that sound stupid?'

'No, I think that's a good idea, just as long as you don't allow your search to take you away from me.'

As though she hadn't heard she went on, 'Tommy's Toni has really unsettled me. She's very outspoken and says I should get a job, forget the years I sacrificed — her word not mine — caring for the boys, and do something I really want to do.'

'And what do you really want to do?'

'That's the trouble, I don't know. I've run this house for the family for so long that if I thought about it at all, I'd have imagined that it would go on in much the same way for ever.'

'What about collecting insurance, door to door, would that suit? A friend told me about a vacancy and it hasn't been advertised yet. I could put in a word for you? You'd enjoy getting out each day, at least for a while, until you decide what you really want to do. I'll buy you a bike!'

She hesitated. 'Henry, I don't know. With Mali and Megan and now Tabs, I might find it possible to manage. They all pay me a little rent and it might be enough. With Toni's baby on the way, I might be needed there too. I wouldn't like to let them down.'

As though she hadn't spoken, Henry stood up, then leant down to kiss her before saying, 'You have an appointment to speak to a Mr Burrows tomorrow at 10.30.'

'What d'you mean? I haven't said I want a job yet!'

He handed her a piece of paper on which he had written the address and, kissing her again, he picked up his coat and left before she uttered another word.

It was Wednesday and she expected Tabs to be home before two o'clock and had waited so they could eat lunch together. By three o'clock she gave up and ate one of the sandwiches she had made. When Tabs came in a five o'clock she had a glow to her face that Ruth hadn't seen before. Surely Henry wasn't the cause? Tabs was unlikely to have found a boyfriend.

Tabs went to her room and changed her clothes from those she wore for the shop. She was so excited she knew people had stared at her as she walked alongside Jack, and on the bus journey home. He had been waiting when the shop closed and walked with her to a café where he bought her a cake, which she dropped, and tea which she spilt. He laughed, dropped his own cake before asking the counter assistant to hand him a cloth and dustpan and brush. 'I'm so clumsy, it's this girl,' he told the counter assistant. 'Got me in a real state she has.' Which increased her embarrassment even more.

A miracle had happened. She had met Jack, a young and very good-looking man seven years her junior and he enjoyed her company. He didn't find her boring and when she dropped something or spilt something, he just laughed and helped to clear it up. It wouldn't last; she wasn't stupid enough to think it would. Once he had given up looking for his family he wouldn't stay. He'd move on and she'd be on her own again. Meanwhile she'd store memories and mementoes, like the bus tickets, and a stolen menu from a café. She would savour the moments like jewels; admired, borrowed, then returned to their proper place.

* * *

Ruth didn't sleep that night. She could hardly explain, but walking back into the house when there was no one there was something she still found very difficult. Mali and Megan were out for part of each day and she could usually arrange to go out at a time when she was sure there would be someone in when she got back. A 10.30 appointment was not a good time. She'd be back about twelve, long before anyone else. She knew this was becoming an obsession, timing her shopping to coincide with her lodgers. Tabs had said she would be going to Henry's shop later, and Megan and Mali were out all day, alternating shifts and looking after Mickie.

She finished clearing up after breakfast and stared at the note. Her first instinct was to telephone this Mr Burrows and cancel, but, as she turned to reach for her coat to go to the telephone box, she bumped straight into Tabs who had entered the room silently and was standing trying to pluck up the courage to announce herself.

'Oh! You gave me a fright, Tabs! How long have you been standing there?'

'I just came to ask if I could make a cup of tea. I haven't bought my food yet. Martha promised to get me some, but she didn't and—'

'Tabs, you can make tea any time you want. But now, you must have breakfast. Will some cereal do you? Or would you like some toast? There's marmalade, or jam?'

'No, don't go to any trouble,' Tabs said.

'I'm not! You can make it, I've got to go out. I've shown you where everything is and tomorrow we'll sort out a shelf in the pantry for your own things. Right? Unless — what do you think of sharing our shopping? It will be easier, won't it?'

'If you're sure, I'd like that.'

'Tabs, promise me one thing.' The shy woman nodded anxiously. 'Promise me that you'll believe that if I say something, I mean it. I won't try to be polite by saying something I don't mean, and hoping you'll disagree. Remember that and we'll get on fine.'

Tabs smiled and reached out for the kettle and pushed it closer to the fire. 'Just tea, I've had breakfast.' She opened her bag which she carried everywhere with her and showed Ruth. Inside was a bag of biscuits. 'I brought these so I didn't have to bother you until I do my shopping and pay you some rent.' Her eyes were wide as though expecting Ruth to be angry.

Ruth lifted the paper bag out and put them on the table. 'Put them in the tin with the others. From today we share everything. Right?' She watched as Tabitha spooned tea into the pot that stood warming on the hearth and reach for the holder before lifting the kettle and pouring the boiling water onto the leaves. 'I'll be back in an hour and we'll have coffee with condensed milk, my favourite,' she said as she went out.

* * *

Mr Burrows was in his late fifties, balding and with the newly scrubbed complexion of the fair skinned. Ruth noticed only his friendly smile as he gestured for her to sit. He was behind an impressive kneehole desk on which there were piles of papers, files and a telephone. 'Henry tells me you're looking for work after years spent looking after your brothers,' he began.

'Yes, they're all married now and apart from staying in the house so they still call it home, they don't need me anymore.'

'Are you excited at the prospect of going out each day and taking home a wage each week?'

'Yes,' she lied. 'It's time I had a life of my own.'

'And selling insurance, collecting the weekly payments, it appeals?'

She decided that honesty was the wisest route or she would become entangled in her own lies. 'I confess I hadn't thought of a job like this one, Mr Burrows. I hadn't really thought about what I'd like to do. It all happened very suddenly you see. Two brothers and their wives finding flats and all moving out at the same time, it left me with nothing to do and I can't just drift, hoping they'll come for a meal sometimes because they feel sorry for me.'

'Is that what you've been doing, Miss Thomas?' he asked softly.

'Yes,' she admitted.

'Then you're very wise to realize it and decide to do something about it.' He smiled then and said, 'If you would like to give it a try, I'll get one of the other agents to go around your route with you for the first week, and then, if you decide it's for you, you can start a week from Monday. Will that suit you?'

'Thank you very much.'

Sick with a mixture of excitement and dread, she went to a telephone box and phoned Henry's shop to tell him.

'Ruth, I'm proud of you,' he said.

'Don't be. Not yet. After being shown what I have to do — including book-keeping and making sums add up, I might not be taking the job!'

He just laughed. 'See you tonight and I'll bring fish and chips to celebrate.'

'Better make it for three then, the mouse and I have decided to share everything.'

'Everything? Does that include me?'

'She wouldn't dare!' They were both smiling as the telephones were replaced.

A few days later, Tabitha had settled into a routine and if she did more than her share of the cleaning, Ruth said nothing, afraid of embarrassing her. Time to sort out a few rules to balance things out later.

Tabs decided that working a few hours for Henry wasn't enough to pay her way. She didn't want to stop helping in the shop but needed something more. She so enjoyed talking to Ruth, listening to her stories about her childhood and of the antics of her four brothers. Her own experience of family life hadn't been anything like the life Ruth described and she knew she would never tire of hearing about childhood in Ty Gwyn. Her nightmare was being told to leave.

For a couple of weeks she did a poorly paid job in a newsagent's shop, getting up very early and marking the papers and putting them into the bags ready for the boys to deliver them. After they had gone she sometimes earned a little more by doing some housework for the wife of the shop owner. One day, the newsagent hurt his hand and asked if she could possibly fill in the outgoings and income for the week. Her handwriting was neat and the books were updated efficiently. When the newsagent realized how clever she was with figures, he found someone else for the morning tasks and asked her to do the book-keeping instead. Fast and never making a mistake, she was taken on permanently and given a small room at the back of the shop as her office. She loved it.

One of the first things she did was read through the names and addresses of customers and she found two families called Tyler. These she handed to Jack when they next met. To her alarm he kissed her, right there in the street, for anyone to see. Laughing at her confusion, he led her behind a hedge in the park and did it again.

'Did you find out anything more about where you're staying?' he asked.

'Ruth doesn't know anything about her grandparents except what Dad's wife-to-be Martha has told her. But she has a pile of papers to look through, old forms, insurance books, school reports and ancient bills all jumbled up. When she looks through them there might be something helpful.'

'Thanks. Tabs. I don't know what I'd do without you and I hope I never find out.'

With feigned reluctance he left her, after kisses that left her breathless, and more flattery. 'I'll be away for a while but as soon as I get back I'll come and find you,' he said, adding huskily, 'Tabs, I can't wait to get back to you.' He waved until she was out of sight then ran to the railway station. First a train, then a bus, it was time to get back to his other life.

* * *

Jack telephoned Abigail, thankful that she had a telephone. 'Abi, love,' he said,' I'm on my way home.' Abigail gave a sigh of relief when he called to say he was on his way back to her. When he went away to search for his family she never knew how long he would be away. She met him at the bus stop and they walked, arm in arm, stopping for an occasional kiss.

He loved walking beside her, she made him so proud. She was slim, elegantly dressed and never without a matching hat, turning heads of both men and women.

Their reunion was affectionate, and as they ate the meal she had prepared, they began exchanging news. She laughed at his stories of surviving without spending any money, determined to add to their savings. He explained in light-hearted fashion the menial jobs he had done, but told her nothing about his thieving, as he handed her all he had brought to add to their savings.

When they prepared for bed she became serious and said she had something important to tell him.

'Jack I'm going to have to give up my job.'

'Why? Been given a better offer?'

She shook her head. 'I'm going to have a baby. I won't be able to dress like a mannequin and parade around in beautiful clothes for much longer.'

He hugged her to hide the shock his face must show. 'Darling Abi, I'm so thrilled. It's exactly what we need. I'll give up searching for my inheritance at once and stay here to look after you.'

'There isn't enough saved to start a business like we planned. I haven't been very sensible with money,' she admitted. 'I've bought so many clothes; there's the car, the holidays we've enjoyed, and everything in the flat is the best I could find — now I wish I'd been practical. When you earn a lot of money as I've done, you treat it as normal, convinced that it will go on for ever. You never think there'll be a time when it isn't there. This has been a shock and I honestly don't know how we'll manage. I have to find a cheaper place, one where Mum will be comfortable. She's important. I have to consider her before myself.'

'Me, too. She has to live in a place where she's truly content. Don't worry, we'll find a place easily. Leave it to me. I'm your man and I'll look after you. You'll miss working, you love it, but you and our baby come first. How long before you have to give up your job?'

'A few weeks before clothes start looking as though they were made for someone else. I've already given notice on this flat.' She looked around her. 'It will be a long time before we can live in a beautiful place like this again.'

'Not that long. If only I could find the family that owes me my inheritance. We could certainly do with it now.' He looked at her hesitantly. 'I might be close to finding them, d'you think I could have a little while longer to try and find them?'

Abigail smiled and agreed. Whatever Jack wanted was fine with her. A week later he went by bus and train back to a cheap bed-sit not far from Ty Gwyn, and asked for his job back in the green-grocery.

* * *

At Ty Gwyn, life settled down into a pleasant routine. Collecting insurance was something that Ruth found she enjoyed. Meeting people, discovering mutual acquaintances and even a few people who had known her parents, and remembered her and her brothers as children, made many visits into social occasions that took longer than they should as kindly people insisted on making her tea and it was difficult to get away after writing the transactions into their books.

Once a month a few farms were included on her round and she loved walking into the huge farm kitchens with the tables neatly spread with a white cloth and plates ready for the men to come for their food. She looked forward to the next visits with happy anticipation. Henry came with her once, driving her around and talking to the farmers, listening to their stories about the wildlife they saw and sharing descriptions of favourite walks. One young farmer, Ted Wills, became a friend and he sometimes joined them on walks, inviting them back to the farm for tea. Ruth and Henry had always enjoyed walking in the countryside and were quite knowledgeable about the flora and fauna of the area. Ted added a lot more to their knowledge and interest.

Walking back into Ty Gwyn was no longer a fear and there had been no further worries about things being moved or searched. Gradually Megan and Mali came more often to the kitchen and even Tabs relaxed and no longer asked before making tea or a sandwich or helping herself to a cake.

Tabs and Ruth sometimes went to the pictures and Mali and Megan invited Tabs to go with them to a dance, which she quickly refused. The sisters never went together, one of them would always be with Mickie. Ruth offered to look after him so the sisters could go together.

'No, thanks. Mali and I promised each other that no one else would look after the baby and it's a promise we'll keep until he's old enough to go places on his own,' Megan said firmly. 'Besides, I think Mali likes to see a certain trumpeter without my playing gooseberry,' Megan teased. Ruth learned to her surprise that Mali sang with the local dance band in which the trumpeter Kenny played.

Ruth wondered what would happen when one of the sisters found a serious boyfriend. It hadn't happened so far. Then, Megan came in with a young man called Sam. To Tabs's embarrassment, Mali gave her sister detailed warning to, 'Be careful, Megan, our Mickie might not be ready for a brother or sister just yet.' Then, after a whispered comment shared by Ruth, they all began to giggle. Tabs didn't think it funny.

'We aren't flippant about having a baby, Tabs; we're just picturing our Mam's face if we told her Megan was expecting again!' Hesitantly, imagining her own father's reaction, Tabs tried to laugh with them, but failed.

Sam soon faded from the picture, but there was always excitement in Mali's face when she was brought home from the dance by Kenny, the trumpeter in the band.

* * *

Ruth planned to say farewell to her lodgers by inviting her four brothers and their wives for a picnic lunch in the garden, a prospect that frightened Tabs and made her disappear for a whole day trying to think of an excuse not to be there.

Guessing her fears, Ruth told her she could spend the day in her room if she wished, but she hoped she would be there to help serve the food. "Specially as you'll be helping me to make it!' she hinted.

Tabs prayed to be struck down with a severe cold that would give her a genuine excuse to stay away from them all. She was used to Megan and Mali now and she loved the little boy, but sharing a day with eight strangers? How could she possibly cope with that? She stared at herself in her small handbag mirror and wondered why she was so stupid. She also wondered if she would ever be any different and thought not.

Ruth invited Aunty Blod too and tried to use that invitation to encourage Tabs to be there. 'She's a little unsteady on her feet, see, and I'd appreciate you being there to keep an eye on her and look after her.'

'All right, I'll stay for a while, but only to get the food set out, then I think I'll go for a walk.'

'Thanks,' Ruth said, as she thought up ways of making the anxious woman stay, believing that if she did she would enjoy the day and benefit from it.

A few days before the picnic lunch, Tabs came to Ruth and told her she would have to leave.

'Tabs, why? Have I upset you in some way?' Tabs seemed unable or unwilling to explain and Ruth said, 'I'm sorry if I've hurt you. I promise you I haven't meant to.' Still no explanation. 'Is it the party? You don't have to stay, really you don't.'

'It's my father.'

'I thought he was getting married and wanted the place for himself and his new wife?'

'Now he wants me back.'

'Can you tell me why? Is it something we can sort out?'

'Martha Howard isn't happy about running the house. He wants me back to look after it all as I did before. Then stay out of their way between meals, I'd imagine,' she added sorrowfully.

'And you? How d'you feel about going back home?'

'Having two people telling me how useless I am? One was bad enough. No, I want to stay here, but I can't, can I?'

'You're old enough to make you own decisions, Tabs.'

'I can't refuse. She won't marry my father unless I go back. She didn't expect to have to run the home without me there.'

'I'll come with you. You can explain that you want to stay here. He won't upset you if I'm there. I promise not to say a word, mind. I'll just be there.' She crossed her fingers as she promised.

It took two days to persuade her, but with coaxing from Henry, as well as Megan and Mali adding their opinions, Tabs and Ruth eventually set off to confront Mr Bishop and his 'intended', Martha Howard.

Tabs gave in almost straight away, nodding and agreeing without saying a word. As she was whispering, 'All right, I'll come back', and despite her promise to say nothing, Ruth overrode her submissive replies and insisted that she needed Tabs at Ty Gwyn.

'Besides being my friend, she has a responsible job as an accountant at the newsagents.'

'An accountant? Rubbish!'

An argument ensued during which Martha shouted, then cried, then started a fresh argument with Tabs's red-faced father.

'I'm your father and you'll do what I say!' he said, his face close to Tabs's, his expression threatening.

'No she won't,' Ruth replied for her. 'And that's an end to it.'

'Get out of my house! This is nothing to do with you. She's coming back home where she belongs.'

'No, she is not!' Ruth replied with irritating calm.

Wide eyed, Tabs looked from one to the other and began wailing in despair. Ruth shoved her back away from her father who was trying to wear her down by glaring at her.

'Come on, Tabs, we're going home.'

'This is her home and this is where she'll live!' George Bishop shouted, while Martha's large brown eyes swivelled from one to the other.

Ruth had always considered herself a placid person. She had never felt strongly about anything and her life had been trouble free, but listening to this man demanding that his daughter give up a life she was just beginning to build, to move back home to his domination, because her prospective stepmother was lazy, was too much.

'Very clever she is, our Tabs. And I respect her brilliance with figures and so does the newsagent. She's a valued friend and I won't hear of her coming back to be an unpaid housekeeper. There! That's the situation. Come on, Tabs, we have to get back or the casserole will be ruined.'

Tabs stood undecided, staring at her angry father and a tearful Martha Howard until Ruth grabbed her arm and pulled her from the house.

They didn't go back to Ty Gwyn but instead went to the shop to find Henry. When they told him of what had occurred she and Tabs were laughing and soon all three were enjoying the surprising end to what had been intended as a polite discussion explaining why Tabs wasn't going back home.

It was a changing point for Tabs, albeit a small one. She was still very unsure of herself in company, but together with the job she had found and the growing friendship of Ruth, she found a confidence which she would never have found at home.

'D'you know,' she said one evening, when Ruth and Henry were entering payments into Ruth's weekly statement book, 'I'm grateful to Martha Howard. If she hadn't agreed to marry Dad, I'd have still been that frightened woman nicknamed the goose. Or mouse,' she added, admitting she knew of Ruth's nickname for her. 'I'm still a bit of a mouse,' she added as they smiled at her, 'but a bit bolder, don't you think?'

'Is there still going to be a wedding?' Henry asked.

'I haven't heard any different, but I don't think Martha will want me there, do you?'

* * *

In her father's house Martha reluctantly agreed to continuing with the wedding plans on condition she would have a cleaning woman twice a week.

'Sorry Tabitha's let you down,' George Bishop said. 'I don't know what's got into her. She's been so difficult since she met up with that Ruth Thomas.'

'I'll remind Ruth of the part she played one day,' Martha said. 'I could tell a few tales about that family that Ruth wouldn't like broadcast around the town. How that poor Ralph was treated, it was a disgrace.'

'I've never heard of Ralph.'

'Not many remember him now. But I do. Sent away he was, poor dab, hoping the shame of what he did would remain hidden, but my memory's long and one day I'll tell her what happened to her Uncle Ralph.' She smiled, wondering what she could invent that would embarrass poor Tabitha the most.

George was hardly listening. 'We'll invite Tabs to the wedding, won't we?'

'Well, I did expect us to have a rather grand reception. She wouldn't feel very comfortable, scared goose that she is. Capable she might be, but I can't imagine her coping with a wedding like ours will be, can you, dear? Kinder if we don't ask. Better we forget to post her invite, don't you think?'

So relieved that the wedding was back on track he could only agree.

CHAPTER FOUR

Tabs's father turned up one day and at once, Ruth went to stand by her in a protective manner.

'Hello, Dad. Arrangements going all right, are they?' Tabs asked nervously.

'No thanks to you!'

'I expect you've brought the invitation to the wedding,' Ruth said politely. 'It's next month, isn't it?'

George Bishop ignored her.

'I want you to reconsider,' he said to his daughter. 'Take no notice of Ruth. She doesn't know about family loyalties. Can't help it, mind, her not having parents to teach her. But you know how I rely on you and Mrs Howard expects the same.'

Ruth made a low growling sound in the back of her throat as Tabitha began to reply.

'Sorry, Dad, but I've left home and I enjoy living here with Ruth. And I'm really enjoying my new job.'

He argued for a while, glaring at Ruth between attempts to persuade his daughter to return home, then he left.

An hour later, Mrs Howard knocked the door. As soon as Ruth opened it she pushed her way in and demanded to speak to her future stepdaughter. 'Where is she? Tell her I want to speak to her.'

Ruth gave a tight smile and said, 'I'll see if she's in and if she wants to talk to you.'

Instead of calling up the stairs as she usually would, Ruth went up the stairs and to her irritation, Mrs Howard followed.

'Which is her room?' she demanded when she stood on the landing. Wordlessly, Ruth pointed with a thumb to the relevant door, and Martha walked straight in.

'Tabitha, my dear,' she said, before slamming the door closed against Ruth's attempt to follow. Shamelessly, Ruth put her ear to the door and listened. 'I'm disappointed you won't be sharing the home with your father and me. Friends I thought we'd be. I haven't come to persuade you where your duty lies,' she added with a hint of a sob. 'I just wondered if there were any special things you'd like to take from the house now you've left home. Little things that have some sentimental value, you know what I mean. Come one afternoon while your father's at work and we can look through the drawers and cupboard to see what there is.'

Ruth could imagine Tabs frowning as she thought about some of the treasures she had left behind.

'No, there's nothing, except one or two pieces of my mother's jewellery. Not that there was anything of value, but I'd like a necklace she wore often, and one of her rings, just a few mementoes.'

'That might be awkward, my dear. Your father offered some of the better items to me and, as I don't want to start my marriage wearing things he'd bought for your mother — you understand I'm sure, dear — we sold them. There isn't much left. In fact, we sold some of the pieces so he could buy me this beautiful engagement ring.' She held out her hand for Tabs to admire.

'Then there's nothing I want, but thank you for offering,' Tabs replied sadly. 'I did love the opal ring that had once belonged to my grandmother. I'd have liked that.'

'No, I couldn't have let you wear that! I made sure that was sold.' She gave an elegant shudder. 'Unlucky things, opals.'

'But so beautiful.' Ruth heard the disappointment in Tabs's voice.

'Well, dear, I wish you'd change your mind about sharing our little home. If you do your father would be delighted. Loves you, he does. And he misses having you around. He was only saying last evening how lost he is without you to chat to. Even me moving in won't change that,' she said, with another hint of a sob.

'Perhaps I should—'

Ruth opened the door and said, 'Tea anyone?'

'I was just telling Tabitha how much her father misses her,' Martha said. 'Loves her he does.'

'But once you and he are married he won't be lonely then, will he? And we all know what they say about two women in a kitchen,' Ruth spoke breezily, as she coaxed Tabs out of the room. Martha tried to hide her fury as she followed them down the stairs.

In the kitchen she noticed the child's painting. 'Oh, you have Ralph's picture on show. He would be pleased.' She stepped closer to Ruth and whispered, 'Better than anything Tabs can do, mind, even though he was only a child. She does have a false idea of her abilities.' She leaned closer and waited until Tabs had moved away. Behind a hand she whispered, 'Tell the truth, her father is worried about this job she's so proud of. She isn't capable of something like accounts. I mean, where would she have learned about something like that? The poor man will find out when she gets everything in a mess.'

'How can you say such a thing? Tabs is clever and it's taken all these years for anyone to realize it!' She pushed the woman aside angrily and opened the door. She stood as Martha left without another word. She turned to where Tabs was beginning to set out cups and saucers, and forcing a smile, said, 'Tabs, I'm proud of you for not giving in to that woman's false affection. Come on, take the kettle off the gas, I'm treating you to tea in the café. Right?'

* * *

Jack saw Henry leave the antique shop and drive away. He opened the door and slipped inside. 'Tabs, I had to see you. I saw Henry leave and I couldn't resist coming in. I miss you and want you so much.' He locked the shop door and pulled down the blind on which a notice said 'Closed'. Between kisses he said, 'Once I've found my family, nothing will keep us apart, my beautiful, wonderful Tabs.'

'Jack, I have to open the shop! Someone might tell Henry I closed up!' Her protests became less and less urgent as other concerns awoke in her body. He led her up the stairs and she guided him into Henry's living room, where she surrendered to a passion that engulfed her. They lay for a while, calm after the storm that had overwhelmed her and she marvelled at the realization that she was in love and this fascinating man loved her, something she had never imagined happening to her.

She went to tidy herself in the bathroom as Jack said a reluctant goodbye, promising to meet her the following day in the park. She went to the kitchen and made herself some tea, dawdling dreamily, almost unaware of what she was doing.

She was still glowing with happiness when Henry returned. He saw at once that several small and valuable pieces of silver were missing from the cabinet. She looked horrified when he showed her. Had she spent too long in the kitchen? Someone could easily have stepped inside and taken them. The cabinet wasn't locked as Henry had never thought it was necessary. Foolishly, she helped his search, even though she knew exactly where they had stood.

Henry noticed the rosy cheeks and the glowing eyes and wondered about Tabs's boyfriend. Could she have been day-dreaming and got careless? It wasn't very likely, but love can do strange things, especially to someone as inexperienced as Tabs. She admitted being out of the shop for a while and he wondered if the boyfriend had distracted her. There had been a cushion out of place in his flat. Tabs being used as an accomplice to a thief? Surely not.

Tabs had a moment's doubt about Jack. He was the only one who could have taken them, the shop bell would have told her if someone else had entered and there had been a delay before he left. But she brushed the disloyal thought aside. Not Jack; he wouldn't have risked compromising her by taking anything from here.

Henry informed the police and explained that fortunately he had photographed the items that were missing. Something he did occasionally, taking a snap of a group of pieces in case there was a problem of ownership. He was able to check and assure an enquirer that the pieces hadn't passed through his hands. Occasionally members of a family sold something without the agreement of others.

Tabs was afraid; the small doubt about Jack wouldn't quite go away. He was in the park the next day, joining her as she sat eating her lunch, and she told him about the theft. He suggested possibilities: regular visitors who rarely made a purchase, someone slipping in while she was in the kitchen. 'I know what you Welsh girls are like for your cups of tea,' he teased.

'You think it was my fault?' She looked tearful.

'You aren't in the shop all the time, silly girl! Henry is there too. Why couldn't it have been him? I bet you didn't notice whether the things were there or not when you and I got together, did you?'

* * *

Ruth had been sad to see Megan, Mali and Mickie leave. They hadn't been there long, but Ruth had been glad of their company, especially the lively little boy and she would miss them. Henry had helped them to transport their belongings to the flat they were renting and to everyone's surprise their mother was waiting outside with a few cardboard boxes. 'Food to fill your pantry,' she told them, gruffly. 'And a card to wish you good luck.' She dropped the last of three boxes near the gate and pushed the card into Mickie's hand, picked him up and hugged him, then hurried off before the girls were able to think of a word to say other than 'Thanks, Mam.' Mali called after her mother asking her to 'Wait, don't you want to see the flat?' but their mother didn't turn around.

Megan opened one of the boxes to see packets of basic dry stores. Another held tinned food and a third contained perishables like bread, cakes, pasties and pies, with some fresh salad items wrapped untidily in newspaper and sprinkling the rest with soil.

'Fabulous!' Megan said. 'Kind, wasn't it? We'll go tomorrow and thank her.'

'Kind? Maybe. Or making sure we didn't go back home!' Mali said. 'She's still ashamed of our Mickie and I'll never forgive her for that.'

'Yes, you will,' Ruth said. 'She's your mum and that will always make her special.'

Mali picked up one of the boxes. 'She could have carried them in for us,' she said, 'instead of dumping them on the pavement!'

On moving into the new flat, the complaints began in earnest. Their radio, early morning noises, the sounds of Mali and Megan playing lively games with Mickie, but mostly Mickie. Ruth called on the neighbours and explained that she had had them as lodgers for a few weeks without any problems.

'You don't have to get up early and go to work,' one of them retorted. When she explained that she did in fact have a job, the reply was that it wasn't an important one. She gave up and crossed her fingers, hoping the little boy would win them over and the complaints would die down.

* * *

'Your father's wedding is tomorrow, isn't it Tabs? What time is the ceremony?' Henry asked, when they were both at the shop sorting some new acquisitions. 'Have you bought anything special?'

'I haven't had an invitation,' she replied. 'Dad doesn't want me there.'

'Nonsense. It must be an oversight. Of course you'll be there.'

'I asked once and they were both vague about the time and place, and evasive about the invitation. No, it's Martha's day and she doesn't want me spoiling things for her.'

'You don't sound very upset?'

'I'm not. You know how I hate formal occasions and dressing up and all that sort of thing. No, I've promised to go and help Ruth sort out some papers she brought down from the loft. She thinks her brothers might like some of it and the rest will be thrown in the ash bin.'

'That sounds more boring than your father's wedding!'

She laughed and pointed to the pile of plates she was unwrapping. 'Talking about boring, if I unwrap many more of these I'll throw them in the ash bin too!'

Tabs left the shop at five o'clock, but she didn't go straight back to Ty Gwyn. Jack had promised to meet her at the café on the corner and she waited outside, too embarrassed to walk in alone. Standing on the street corner was difficult enough and she walked a little way and stood instead looking at the children playing in the little park.

The curtains were pulled down on the shop window and Henry had gone up to his flat. She hoped he wouldn't see Jack arriving. She didn't want to explain; that would almost certainly lead to teasing, something with which she found difficult to cope. To her relief Jack arrived quite soon and she didn't see Henry watching them as he took her arm and led her out of sight around the corner to the café entrance.

Jack and Tabs both began to talk as soon as they were seated and had given their order to the waitress.

'Have you got any further in your search for family?' Tabs asked.

'I still haven't excluded Ruth's family, even though they all seem to be called Thomas. I'm thinking of such a long time ago.'

'I might be able to help you there, even if it's only to take them off your list of possibilities. Ruth has a huge pile of papers, all stuff belonging to the family and she wants to sort it out, throw away anything useless and just keep a few things to pass to her brothers.'

'How can I get to see it? I can hardly ask. There'll be questions I'd rather not answer.'

'I offered to help her look through them, so anything I think might be relevant I'll hide and give it to you to look at. How's that?'

He reached across the table and kissed her. 'You are amazing. How lucky I am to have you in my corner.'

Her colour increased but she didn't seem as unhappy about being seen as the first time. Encouraged, he did it again.

'I don't want to sound mysterious, Tabs, but don't talk to anyone about me or the family I'm hoping to find. They might not want me to find them. After all, it would sound suspicious, me turning up out of nowhere and telling them I'm a long lost distant cousin twice removed or something.'

'I don't see why. Surely there isn't really likely to be an inheritance? That only happens in fairy stories.'

He shared her laughter then he said, 'Please, Tabs, love, I'd rather no one talked about why I'm here.'

Talking about Jack was the last thing she wanted to do; how embarrassing that would be! She assured him that their friendship would be a secret shared by only the two of them. 'Not a word,' she promised.

'It's unlikely Ruth and her brothers are part of my family, that's too much to hope for, so best if we don't get them involved. They might not like the intrusion, and who would blame them, having a stranger coming and asking questions and maybe unearthing some family secrets?'

* * *

The few people who knew Tabs and were aware of her father's wedding asked about it: what she would wear, where the happy couple were going on honeymoon, what changes had been made in the house, and she evaded their questions hoping they wouldn't guess that she didn't know the answers. She felt sad about not taking part in the occasion and it was on her mind that day.

Ruth suggested they went to the church to see them coming out as man and wife but Tabs insisted she was working and had no intention of bothering her boss by asking for time off. In fact it was an afternoon when she would be at the antique shop and Henry had already offered to stay while she attended.

'You can't disappoint them,' he'd said. 'You'll be given a place at the top table as daughter of the bridegroom. An empty chair would be an embarrassment and your father would be hurt. You have to go, Tabs.'

'I haven't had an invitation,' she said, her voice quivering a little.

'An oversight, surely. Come on, Tabs, it isn't like you to be childish.'

'No oversight. When I asked about the arrangements Martha didn't tell me the date or the time and made it clear I wasn't included.'

'In that case, go and embarrass them, they deserve it!'

At lunchtime, a couple of hours before the wedding, she went into the park with sandwiches she had brought from home and sat on the seat in the sun. At least it could have rained, she thought. That was childish, but she didn't care, just wishing for rain, hail, thunder and lightning made her feel better.

Jack came before she had started eating and he carried a flask. 'I thought I'd find you here,' he said, giving her a light kiss on her cheek. 'Tea and a couple of doughnuts to extend the feast. Have you got a sandwich to spare for a starving man?'

'There's plenty,' she said, opening the package wrapped in grease-proof paper.

'Eat up and we'll go and look at the dolled-up woman who you have to call Mummy,' he joked.

'I'm not going to the wedding,' she said calmly. 'I wasn't invited and I won't stand with the rest of the gawpers, watching and saying "oooh" and "aahh".'

'Just a peep? We could stand at the entrance to the sweet shop next to the church and no one would see us.'

'I couldn't go like this,' she said, waving her arm at her long navy skirt and plain cream blouse.

'You bought something to wear, didn't you? When you were expecting to be invited?'

'No, I did not.'

'Not even a hat? With feathers and a couple of roses?'

'Nothing.'

'Then something better than what you're wearing now. Tell you what, I'll go back and fetch the suit you wore when we last went out. Green, I think it was. Tell me where it is and I'll be back in half an hour and you can change in the shop.'

Encouraged by his enthusiasm, she agreed and handed him her key, with instructions about where to find her suit and high heeled shoes. She was smiling as he set off at a fast rate, stopping twice to wave.

* * *

At Ty Gwyn, Jack knocked and waited a while before letting himself in. He quickly found the suit and shoes then he looked around the other bedrooms. The suitcase from which letters and papers fell in a frozen waterfall was in the middle of one of the back rooms and he began to move them, his eyes skimming them without reading, in the hope of seeing the name Tyler. He glanced at his watch. This was hopeless, he had to look through them properly before abandoning the hope of there being a connection with himself. Reluctantly he gathered up the clothes and hurried back to the park, but on the way he stopped and had an extra key cut. It was certain to be useful one day.

Tabs and Jack watched as onlookers gathered. She saw Ruth and Aunty Blod, Mali and Mickie, and several people she knew from the antique shop and the newsagent's. They hid in the doorway of the sweet shop and watched as cheers announced the appearance of the bride and groom coming out of the church.

Martha was dressed in pink. A dress reaching just below her knees, layered and decorated with sequins which sparkled in the sun. Her headdress was made of tiny feathers and she carried a bouquet which also included feathers. Tabs stifled a laugh when she head the voice of Aunty Blod carry across the heads of the crowd, 'Pink's too risky at fifty.' A murmur of laughter echoed her own. Jack squeezed her arm as he, too, chuckled. Someone in the crowd added, 'Duw, there's a laugh! Fifty? She won't see sixty again!'

That evening Ruth and Aunty Blodwen talked about the wedding, asking if Tabs had heard any reports about the reception.

'No, but perhaps I'll be sent a slice of wedding cake,' she said with a smile.

To everyone's surprise, a boy delivered a note signed Martha Bishop, inviting them all to go to a party a week later, on the newlyweds' return from honeymoon. A chance to celebrate their wedding among friends, the note explained.

'She's hoping for a few more presents!' Ruth said unkindly.

'I'll have to go,' Tabs told Jack later.

Thinking of the empty house, with Ruth and the rest going to the party, Jack turned the newly cut key in his pocket and agreed.

* * *

The August evening was warm and still. 'I'll leave the windows open,' Ruth said, as she began to close the doors. 'We'll be back in a couple of hours.'

'I'll see to the doors, leave them open for a bit,' Aunty Blod said. 'I'll follow you later, our Bryn is giving me a lift in that old van of theirs. Sitting among the garden tools won't hurt. It isn't far and easier for me than the bus.'

Ruth, Tommy, Toni and Brenda strolled through the streets to where the newlyweds were waiting and Blodwen dozed as she waited for Bryn to come. Jack was watching and, as he heard the van turn into the road he dashed into the house and ran softly up the stairs.

He listened as Bryn helped Blodwen from the house and into the van. He heard the key turning in the back door and the van driving away. Then he went to where the suitcase had been and it wasn't there.

Frustrated, he looked in the other rooms then went back to the first room and looked inside the wardrobe. It was there and the work of only a moment to drag it out and open it. Carefully, he began looking through the untidy assortment of papers.

* * *

Tabs had been asked by her father to go to the house at four o'clock, hours before the guests were due to arrive and, as she had guessed, Martha was dressed in her finest, sitting on the armchair, waiting for her to set out the food. There wasn't enough, Tabs could see that immediately, and glancing at the clock, she reached for flour and fat and other ingredients and began cooking. Scones, and sausage rolls and small cakes as well as sandwiches to add to the few Martha had prepared began to fill plates. Hot and flushed by her efforts, Tabs stood in the kitchen watching the last batch of cakes cooking, as they stood to receive their guests.

Many were people she didn't know, friends of Martha and some of her father's acquaintances from the club where he had always spent his evenings. No one introduced her and she stayed in the kitchen, handing people plates piled with food to take in, while her father dealt with drinks.

It was a relief when Ruth and her family arrived, closely followed by Aunty Blodwen and Bryn. Ruth stayed in the kitchen when it was clear that Tabs had no intention of moving. Then Henry turned up and pulled Tabs into the crowded room. The moment she was free from him she darted back into the kitchen. She reached for her coat and left.

'Go after her, Henry,' Ruth said, as she saw Tabs's hasty exit. 'She deserves better than this. I'd like to bang her father's head against the wall.'

Henry ran out of the house and saw Tabs leaning against the wall of the house further along the street. He walked up to her and put an arm around her shoulders. She remained stiff and upright, unwilling to accept the comfort his arms offered.

'What is it about me that I always settle for the role of idiot slave?'

'Your father trained you too well. It was the way he brought you up, convincing you that you were unimportant. Just an unimportant addition to his life, accepting your exceptional skills and capabilities without thought. He should be so proud of you. You are a remarkable woman, Tabs, and it's about time you realized it. Once you do, then others will too. I know how fortunate I am to have you for a friend.'

She didn't reply but she relaxed from her stiff refusal to be comforted and he felt her fall softly against him. He put a second arm around her and they stood there without talking for a long time, his hands slowly stroking her back and shoulders, soothing his face against her hair.

'Come on,' he said at last, 'I'll walk you home.'

* * *

In Ty Gwyn, Jack was sitting on the bedroom floor surrounded by piles of papers. From what he could see they were mostly school reports and out-of-date receipts for things like coal, electricity and gas, plus a few accounts from the local grocer. None of it went far enough back to be any help to him. Nothing bore the name Tyler. If they had lived here once they were long gone and there was no way he could find out where.

Slowly he returned the papers to the suitcase, shuffling them about a bit from the neat piles he had made. He put the case where he had found it and, as he began to walk down the stairs he looked up at the entrance to the loft. That was the place where things no longer used were stored. Things that people hesitated to throw away were put up in the loft and forgotten. He needed to get up there, but how? He sat on the top stair feeling dejected but determined to check as carefully as possible before giving up and moving on. Another town, another family maybe called Tyler, it seemed hopeless, but he wasn't going to give up while there was another place to search.

With Tabs's help he had to make absolutely sure that these weren't his people, before going back to a boring job and an abysmally low wage. Not when he might find his inheritance which his father referred to as his treasure. Well, it would be his now, if only he could find the family. Better try a while longer before giving up and moving on from this area. He had a strong feeling that this was the place where he'd find it. The memories passed on from his father seemed to be linked with this town. Certainly more than with any other town he had explored. Places he'd mentioned as he'd reminisced were recognizable: the house and the church, the pond and the tree — surely it was too much of a coincidence not to be the house he'd been looking for? But people moved and there was no certainty that the family living there was the one he wanted to find. Oh, how wonderful it would be to find them, claim his inheritance and have money in the bank. He wondered if he had missed his chance. So many years had passed and he had so little information. He couldn't remember whether he had really heard his father mention the name Tyler, or if it had simply slipped into his consciousness from somewhere else and had lodged there, a false memory with no basis in fact.

* * *

It was as the town hall clock was striking ten that Tabs and Henry passed through the town square. 'Will there be anyone home?' he asked.

Tabs shook her head. 'Not unless they invented an excuse to leave early and have overtaken us.'

'I wouldn't blame them, but I bet they'll enjoy your food before that happens. You'll be all right on your own?'

'Of course. Thanks, Henry. You shouldn't have walked all this way. I'll be all right now. Will you go back to the party?'

'Not unless you've changed your mind and want to stick it out until the others leave.'

'No thanks! I might be an idiot but I'm not a martyr! A cup of tea, then I'll go to bed with a book.'

'A much better choice.'

They walked to the gate and she opened it and turned to him. 'Thanks.'

He gave her a brief hug and turned to walk away. 'See you tomorrow.' He waved and was gone.

Jack heard the sound of the gate and jumped up in alarm. He ran down the stairs and out of the back door, not stopping to close it, and hid in the bushes. The August day had been bright and sunny and the late evening was still light. He held his breath. If she had turned towards him she was bound to have seen him, but she opened the door and disappeared inside. He released his pent-up breath and hurried away.

Tabs went in but she didn't go to bed. She made herself a sandwich and a cup of tea and sat near the fire and waited for the others to return. She didn't have to wait long. Just before eleven o'clock she heard the sound of laughter and happy voices. She opened the door and they came in chattering and laughing. Bryn and Tommy were singing in harmony. The tune she recognized but the words she did not. They were making up the words as they went, and her stepmother's name featured prominently.

'Where did you get to, Tabs?' Toni asked, as she heaved herself awkwardly into a chair. 'Any chance of a cup of tea? Bryn brought me back in that old van and I'll never recover.'

'Where's your Aunty Blodwen?' Tabs asked. 'Surely she didn't walk?'

'Bryn's going back for her,' Ruth said. 'When we left, Martha was trying to wake her and get her ready, but our Blod was unmovable and I think they might have to leave her there until morning.'

'Mrs Martha Bishop won't like that!'

'Neither will Blod if she misses breakfast!'

Tabs went to the fire where the kettle simmered and began to make a pot of tea. Ruth took the pot from her and said she'd deal with it. 'You've done enough today,' she added. 'The cheek of that Martha. Inviting you just so you could deal with the food.' She turned then and asked, 'Where's Henry?'

'He walked me back then I think he went home.'

'He promised to walk me home later.'

'I don't think parties are his favourite way of spending an evening.' Tabs said. 'He likes people and gets on with most, but he'd rather see people individually and not have to make up false conversation.'

'Me an' him both.' Tommy muttered.

'Go back to sleep,' Toni said.

With the twins being guided by their wives, they all finally left.

The house was quiet by midnight, and as Tabs locked and bolted the back door she frowned, suddenly remembering that the door had been open when she got back. Aunty Blodwen must have forgotten to lock it. Best not to tell Ruth; she didn't want to get the old lady in trouble. And nothing had been moved, so far as she could tell. She checked the bag containing Ruth's cash and payment book were still in the dresser drawer with the cutlery, but nothing had been disturbed.

* * *

Ruth went to see Henry the following day. She had been surprised that he hadn't returned to the party after seeing Tabs home. He had always been most attentive and his abandonment of her was hurtful, even though she knew his concern for Tabs had been justified.

'Where did you get to last night?' she asked, when she went into the shop. She kept her voice light as though amused rather than angry. 'Thanks for looking after Tabs. Isn't that father of hers awful? He treats her like his servant, and even now, with a wife to look after him, he wants her back as unpaid housekeeper.'

'You didn't bang his head against the wall then? Thank goodness for that.' He put down the brass poker he was polishing and took off his gloves. 'Give me a minute and I'll make us a cup of tea.'

'You finish what you're doing and I'll make the tea.'

'What, and have you accuse me of behaving like George Bishop?'

'Just try it, that's all,' she warned, running up the stairs to his flat.

She looked around after putting the kettle to boil. The flat was large and comfortable. The living room was spacious, with large armchairs arranged facing the fireplace, and a table and chairs at one end where you could sit and look out at the park across the road. It was fully carpeted and the furniture was polished Welsh oak of the finest quality. Mostly eighteenth century she had been told. Another room which Henry used as an office overlooked the garden at the back. A wooden beautifully carved staircase led up to three bedrooms and a bathroom above. This was Henry's home and he wanted her to share it. She loved the way it was arranged and didn't think she would want to change a thing. It was a dream of a home and she knew that with Henry she wouldn't want for anything. She'd be loved, and cared for and life would be perfect, so why was she refusing him?

'Any sign of that tea?' Henry called, and she quickly lit the gas and set out a tray. A stray niggle of jealousy entered her mind and when she went down with the tea she asked, 'Was Tabs all right last night? She must have been very upset. How did you manage to calm her down?'

'I put an arm around her and talked to her. She's been treated so unkindly. The trouble is she accepts her father's low opinion of her.'

'Careful that she doesn't fall for you; she doesn't want to be hurt even more, even if it is intended kindly.'

Henry laughed. 'No chance of that. She has a secret boyfriend and I think he's making her happy. It's only her father and his new wife who make her miserable.'

'It's true, then? Tabs really has a boyfriend?'

'I saw them meeting after the shop closed and she'd added a touch of lipstick and combed her hair and fixed it with a new Alice band.'

'I'm so pleased. Good for her!'

'Not a word, mind.'

'That will be difficult. I hope she tells me soon or I'll burst with the effort of keeping quiet. Tabs with a young man! What was he like?'

'I can't tell you. He grabbed her arm and whisked her away.' He thought of the missing silver but said nothing of his suspicions. Tabs was naïve and probably gullible to the man's flattery, but until he was sure, he couldn't say anything.

'Taking her home might not have been a good idea, though.' Ruth said, bringing his thoughts back to the present. 'Better if you'd found her a taxi.'

He looked at her then, an eyebrow quizzically raised. 'Not jealous, are you?'

'No, of course not . . . Yet!'

'Marry me.'

She slipped into his arms, but the reply never came. She couldn't imagine herself as his wife, yet the thought of him being attracted to someone else was unimaginable. So what did she want? She wished she knew.

When Tabs entered the shop after lunch, she coloured up, aware of how Henry had comforted her the night before. She wondered if he was embarrassed too. After all, he was sort of engaged to Ruth Thomas who had been left at the party. She didn't know what to say, so she said nothing.

'Were the others late getting home?' he asked, as he picked up the tray to take it to his flat.

'No, most of them walked. Bryn did two journeys bringing Toni first then going back to bring Aunty Blodwen. She wasn't too keen to leave apparently,' she said with a smile. 'I gather she was hoping to stay the night, but Bryn whispered about the big breakfast Ruth had planned and she was convinced she'd be better off at Ty Gwyn!' Their laughter eased away any embarrassment and the day progressed happily.

At lunchtime the next day she went to the park and was joined by Jack. After asking about the party and commiserating with her about the presumption that she would be chief caterer and not chief guest, he led the conversation to the search for his own family.

'I don't think your Ruth and her brothers are anything to do with me,' he said sadly.

'Then you'll be going away?'

'I'll have to move on, try another town.'

'But you aren't certain? I mean they might be the family you're searching for, mightn't they?'

'I bet the clues to the family history are in that loft. If I could get up there and look through the abandoned rubbish that families keep, I could be sure. Oh, Tabs, wouldn't it be marvellous if they were my family, and I could stay here for ever? But without telling them why I'm here and probably putting them off helping, I don't see how I can find out. Thanks to you, I've done all I can.'

'But if you could get up in the loft? Is there a chance you might find what you're looking for?'

'A chance, but how can I, without anyone knowing and sending me on my way?'

'I could help, Jack. I'll choose a day when Ruth is at work on one of her country routes. Aunty Blod is going home in a couple of days. The house will be empty during the day and you'll have time for a proper search.'

'You'd do that for me?'

'I'll even buy you a torch!'

He hugged her and, when she went back to the shop, Henry again noticed the rosy cheeks and the glowing eyes. So she had been meeting this secret boyfriend, that much was obvious. Without any reason except a cautious need to protect her, he decided that the following day, when she was again working at the shop, he would try to get a look at the man and maybe find out something about him. Someone must know him and a good look at him was the first step.

* * *

Ruth went to Henry's shop the next morning and asked if he would like to meet her between calls on her insurance round, and maybe have lunch together. He declined and although she asked, he seemed unwilling to tell her why.

'An appointment?' she asked. 'Buying? Selling?'

'Not really, just something I'm doing for Tabs.'

She waited, but he didn't explain further. 'It doesn't matter,' she said airily. 'I don't really have the time anyway. Tommy and Toni are coming at four to pick up a nursing chair that Aunty Blod is giving them.'

'Good,' he said vaguely and she suspected he hadn't really listened to what was said. Surely Tabs wasn't a rival? That idea was ludicrous.

She left feeling slightly uneasy without understanding why. She and Henry had been loving friends for so long and there were never any secrets. It was rare for either of them not to know the whereabouts of the other. Whatever he had planned, she was clearly excluded. She decided to go home and eat before setting out to finish collecting. Aunty Blod was pleased to see her and she made a snack, prepared vegetables ready for the evening and then stayed a while to help Blod with her packing.

'I'll go to see her tomorrow evening,' she told Tabs. 'I've booked a taxi for her for mid-morning, but I'll go later to make sure she's comfortable. She can manage, I don't want her to think that she can't, and Mrs Harrison is a kind neighbour, but I'll feel better if I make sure she's all right.'

'Tomorrow is your long day, isn't it?'

'Yes, and I invited Henry to join me on my round so we can have lunch together, but he's busy.'

'Will you be out all day?'

'Yes. It's a long day. No chance to get back between calls as the farms are a long way off. I'll go to Aunty Blod's flat straight from work. I'll take a couple of sandwiches with me, although I get offered food everywhere I go so I won't starve,' she added. 'I really enjoy the country round; the people are so kind and it's very interesting.'

'It's my half day, so I'll get a meal ready. I'll make some cakes too, shall I?' Tabs offered. 'I'll be glad of something to do, being on my own in the house all afternoon.'

When Tabs went out to post a letter, Jack was waiting as arranged and she assured him that, from eleven o'clock, when the taxi came for Aunty Blod, the house would be empty. 'I'll be back at one o'clock,' she added.

He was there soon after one and they hugged each other, laughing like the conspirators they were. Tabs told him where to find the ladder and he pulled himself up into the loft space with ease. She handed him two torches and went back down to begin the cooking she had promised Ruth she would do.

* * *

On her third call, Ruth had filled in the books and was talking to the farmer, Ted Wills and was on the point of leaving, when the house phone rang. As she waved goodbye his wife called her back. 'Ruth, it's for you!'

'For me? How can it be?' She took the receiver and listened for a while then, stared in disbelief. 'It's my Aunty Blodwen. She's had a fall and the ambulance men spoke to my boss and asked where I'd be. I have to hurry home!'

Ted Wills put on his boots, and reached for some keys. 'Come on, I'll take you, the bike will fit in the back of the truck.' Ignoring Ruth's protests he lifted the bike into the truck and they set off.

* * *

Jack was still in the loft and Tabs had handed him a cup of tea when they both heard the sound of the truck at the side of the house.

'Quick, get downstairs,' Jack hissed.

'I can't leave you here!'

'You have to. Get moving, you can let me out later!'

Tabs scrambled down the ladder after closing the trap door, and she was struggling down the stairs with the ladder when Ruth came in.

'It's Aunty Blod, she fell and hurt her leg,' Ruth explained, then she saw the ladder. 'Tabs? What on earth are you doing?'

'A spider, up in the corner of your bedroom,' Tabs said. 'I put it out of the window on a duster.'

'I have to go to the hospital. I'll be back as soon as I can.'

'Don't rush,' Tabs said.

'Why don't you phone the hospital first?' Ted suggested. 'She might already have been sent home.'

Nervously, Tabs disagreed. 'Best you go straight there. She'll want to see you.'

The sound of another car broke the brief silence and there was a knock at the door.

'Miss Thomas? I have your aunt in the taxi, all right to bring her in?'

Tabs glanced up the stairs towards the trap door and wondered when she would be able to release Jack from his prison.

Blodwen wasn't seriously hurt and although the hospital would have preferred to keep her in overnight, she had insisted she would be better off with her niece. Ted left after profuse thanks, and there followed a frantic hour sorting out a bed on the ground floor for Blodwen, and making sure she had everything she might need, close at hand.

Ruth flopped onto the couch in the kitchen. 'I feel like I've been chased by a maniac with an axe! I'm so tired. It must be the shock. Thank goodness you're making the meal, or I think I'd forget eating altogether!'

'Oh dear,' Tabs said, shamefaced. 'I forgot all about it. Beans on toast all right?'

Ruth sent a neighbour's son to Tommy and Bryn's flat with a message to tell them what had happened and the four of them came at about 7.30 with flowers and some sweets. Toni was made comfortable in the carver chair at the table, as getting out of low armchairs was difficult now her pregnancy was in its seventh month.

Henry, who had spent the lunch hour watching the park in the hope of seeing Tabs and her secret boyfriend, called at nine. While Tabs and Ruth were in the kitchen, he spoke to Tommy and Bryn and their wives about the house.

'It's all too convenient for people to use Ruth like this. She doesn't mind, but I do. She uses their emergencies as an excuse to delay marrying me. Why don't you sell the place? I spoke unofficially to an estate agent and it would be a couple of hundred pounds for each of you. When you're ready to buy, you'll be able to use it as a deposit. Isn't that what you want, houses of your own?'

'We've suggested it,' Tommy said.

'And she turned the idea down,' added Bryn.

'I agree with Henry,' Toni said. 'Ruth would be much happier once she gets over the shock of knowing we don't need her anymore.'

Ruth came in with some cakes and tea followed by an anxious looking Tabs. 'You're all looking serious,' she said with a smile.' Don't worry, Aunty Blod will be fine after a bit of spoiling.'

'Trouble is,' Blod replied, 'I don't want to go back to the flat. I need a few days to get strong again. If you sell up, where will I go if I'm poorly?'

'What are you talking about? Sell this house? It's the family home. Why would we sell it? There's nonsense you talk sometimes. Sure it was your leg and not your head you hit?'

'But the boys are talking about you selling and sharing the money so as they can buy places of their own. Henry says, it's for the best.'

'Oh. Henry does, does he?'

'I agree,' Toni said quickly.

'Out of the question,' Ruth said sharply. 'Now, pour the tea before it gets cold, will you, Tabs?' She turned to look at Henry who was staring at her in a curious manner.

Tabs went to the door with Henry and, as he was leaving, she put a hand on his arm. He was surprised and pleased. Contact was something Tabs found difficult and this was a sign that she was becoming less inhibited. A fleeting thought that the mysterious boyfriend might be the reason, quickly faded and he smiled. 'Now I'm the one needing comfort,' he said, patting her hand then walking away.

'I think you should go after him, Ruth,' Tabs whispered, when she went back inside. 'That was very hurtful. He wants what's best for you. There isn't any other motive.'

'And what's it to do with you?' Ruth was so angry she couldn't hold back the words.

'Nothing, except I like you both, and hate seeing you unhappy.'

The others stood to leave, Blodwen nodded off to sleep in her bed near the dying fire. Tabs excused herself and went to her room, hoping that the house would soon become quiet and she could rescue Jack from the loft.

Ruth stayed up for a while then dampened down the fire and went to her bedroom and thought about what had been said. How could she leave this place? Why couldn't Henry understand? It was the place everyone called home. The flats where Bryn and Brenda, Tommy and Toni lived were convenient places where they could display their different ideas of what a home should be, but when anything important happened, it was to Ty Gwyn they came to find sympathy or to celebrate.

* * *

In the loft, Jack sat on some old clothes, convinced he would have to stay there until the next day. In the fading light from the torches he had looked through a few shoe boxes which were mostly filled with old letters. One gave him a frisson of excitement and he read and re-read it several times before putting it in his wallet. It was signed Gran and he knew it must be either from Ruth's maternal grandmother, or her paternal grandmother. If it was her mother's then the author of the letter might not be a Thomas but how could he find out? There was no address on the letter and no date. It was only the state of the paper and the faded writing, that made him think it was old. There were other letters, some written during the war but all signed with Christian names only, none signed Tyler. He put the other letters in his pocket. It was worth having a more thorough look.

At three o'clock in the morning Tabs went down and with great difficulty managed to get the ladder up to the landing without it touching anything and causing a noise. She opened the trap door cautiously, and in silence, stifling nervous laughter, they closed the trap and took the ladder back outside. They passed Aunty Blod who was snoring peacefully. Nervous laughter was imminent, but they got outside without disturbing the old lady and put the ladder back in the shed making very little sound.

'I mustn't stay. I'll meet you in the park at lunchtime,' Jack said, kissing her, holding her close. She waved him off and set off up the stairs to dream of his kiss and his love and revel in wonderment that she had found someone like Jack.

Ruth awoke as Tabs was closing the trap door. The minimal sounds as the ladder was brought down the stairs, made her aware of something happening. Her senses heightened as she heard footfall and breathing, the sounds stopping and starting, with even a whispered comment she might have heard or might have imagined. But they were so faint she tried telling herself they were just the movement of the old building. Then the sound of the back door opening was clearly recognized and she sat up and listened with increasing fear.

Footsteps were now coming up the stairs, there was no doubt now. Someone had entered the house and was heading towards her. She opened the door a slit and peeped through. A figure, unrecognizable in the almost complete darkness was passing her door and she watched as the shadowing figure went into Tabs's room and closed the door. She listened for a moment then followed. She heard the creak of the bed springs and then a slight cough as Tabs settled into bed.

Sighing with relief she knocked on the door. 'Tabs? Are you awake? Was that you wandering around?' She leaned over Tabs and switched on her bedside lamp.

'Sorry, Ruth, I wanted a drink of water,' Tabs said. 'Sorry if I woke you.'

Tabs was snuggled right down in the bed clothes and to save her disturbing herself, Ruth apologized and leaned over again to put out the light. Tabs wasn't completely hidden by the blankets and she saw that Tabs was dressed, not in her nightdress, but in outdoor clothes.

* * *

Martha and George were leaving friends where they had spent the evening. George was trying to drive but he was having difficulty after too much to drink, and it was Martha who was steering the vehicle as they went slowly along the road. They were both laughing. Common sense prevailed when they brushed against a hedge and almost frightened a stray cat hiding there, and they eventually parked the car and began to walk, still laughing.

Approaching Ty Gwyn they began talking about his ungrateful daughter, Tabitha. Stopping for a rest, they saw someone coming out of the house. A man, but unrecognizable. He stopped once to turn and wave at someone standing at the open door. Martha and George sobered up and stared at each other.

'Someone is visiting Ruth! Miss perfect Ruth Thomas that must have been, standing at the door in the middle of the night and waving goodbye to a man. And it wasn't Henry Owen!'

CHAPTER FIVE

Martha was busy sorting out the lumber room, usually called the box room. The smallest of the three bedrooms, it had always been used to store items that were rarely used. Suitcases, boxes of out-of-season clothes, oddments of furniture, and lots of books, many from Tabs's childhood. Some of the contents belonged to Martha, brought there when she and George married. She now had to decide what, if anything, she would keep.

At the time it had seemed important to keep mementoes of her life before George, but seeing the pile of assorted oddments, she wanted to open the window and throw the whole lot out. She wasn't so anxious to keep memories of her previous marriage This one was going to be very different. One box she decided she would keep. It was filled with old letters, and birthday cards she had particularly liked. She sat on a suitcase and browsed through them. Cards from school friends, many more than fifty years old, she put on one side. A few love letters from her first husband and previous boyfriends. Those she would keep. It was unlikely she'd have any more and it would be nice to dream about those happy, innocent days, when she remembered being beautiful.

One letter puzzled her and she pulled open the envelope to find it was a note from an ex-neighbour and grandmother to Ruth Thomas. Tabs had asked about the family recently so she hesitated. It was only a note asking her mother to look in and feed the cat, as she would be staying in Bristol for a few days. That can't possibly be of any interest. She threw it onto the pile destined for the ash bin.

Giving up on her day-dreaming, the room was soon emptied. The new furniture had been chosen and would be delivered the following week. For this tiny room she had bought a second-hand bed and a chest of drawers and a few hooks for clothes, a chair and a tiny table. It would be a squeeze but once George had painted it and they'd spent a little on a new rug, Tabs would fit in there quite comfortably, leaving the other bedroom with its new furniture and quality bed-linen ready for her new arrangements.

She set off for the hairdresser an hour later and on impulse, decided to call into the newsagent's to tell Tabs about the letter. 'Hello,' Tabs greeted her nervously, expecting her to start once again on pleas for her to go back home.

Martha told her about the letter. 'I'm only mentioning it because you were asking about the family recently. No interest though, just a note about feeding cats, so I threw it in the ash bin,' she said. 'From Ruth's grandmother it was. Neighbours we were, us and Ruth's family.'

'I think Ruth would like to see it,' Tabs said. 'She's interested in anything relating to the family. Her mother died when she was only seventeen and there are so many questions she had no chance to ask.'

As though she hadn't heard, Martha went on, 'Oh yes, I remember that lot really well. I can tell you all about the trouble they had; perhaps I will one day.'

'Trouble?' Tabs queried, but Martha shook her head refusing to be drawn. 'Best you come away from Ty Gwyn. Things are happening there that a decent girl like you wouldn't believe! Men wandering about where they shouldn't. Worried about you, we are.' She leaned closer to whisper. 'There's a criminal streak in that family, and things go on at night that I don't think you should be involved with. You'd be safer back home with me and you father.'

'I'm very comfortable there,' Tabs assured her. 'Ruth is so kind.'

'There's a side to her that you don't know about. She isn't as innocent as people think — men,' she whispered.

Tabs felt her heart lurch. Had she and Jack been seen? Was this what Martha was hinting at? Presuming it had been Ruth out there last night? She smiled inwardly. Having a reputation for being boring and a little stupid might be useful. No one would believe she had been creeping around in the middle of the night with a man.

'I wish you'd come home, dear,' Martha went on, tearfully. 'Your father misses you something terrible and I still hope we'll be friends. Won't you think about it?'

Tabs half promised, in her usual non-confrontational way, and Martha left, blowing a kiss from her heavily lipsticked mouth as she departed.

Getting a taxi home was an extravagance, but after visiting a few shops she had several things to carry. The new rug for the room which she hoped would be Tabs's and some china dishes she had bought cheaply. The curtain material was chosen and a neighbour would make them. All she had to do was place a few advertisements for summer visitors and persuade the irritating Tabs that her place was back home. The prospect of a small business of her own was very exciting but she felt exhausted at all it would entail without Tabs there to do most of the work. Once the tiresome girl was back home it would be easy to encourage her to stay in her room when there wasn't any work to do. George's boring daughter wouldn't be too difficult to cope with. The alternative was too much work and that was something she didn't want.

* * *

Ruth was curious about the noises during the early hours of the morning and finding Tabs fully dressed. Why hadn't she confronted her at once? She admitted to herself that she'd been too cowardly, but, as the hours passed, she thought about it more and more and there seemed no other explanation apart from Tabs having a visitor. And it had to be a man; a girlfriend she'd have been told about. But a man? Meeting a man in the park, that's fine, but bringing him here at night? It seemed so unlikely she tried to convince herself it had been a dream, that she had been mistaken. Had Tabs really been wearing something other than the pink nightdress that appeared on the clothes line regularly? She shook her head. No, it couldn't have been a mistake, or a trick of the light. It had definitely not been a pink nightdress, what she had seen was the rough tweed material of an out-door coat almost, but not quite, hidden by hastily pulled up bed covers.

She finished her collections by half past three. It was one of the easier days; fewer places where she stopped for a chat and a cup of tea. This was mainly because many of the calls were to houses where no one was in, and she had to pick up the money and book from the garden, or a shed, and in several places, lift the window and take the money from the windowsill, replacing the book receipted in her neat writing. From her last call she cycled straight to Henry's shop where he was serving a customer with an inexpensive vase. She waited until the woman had left.

'I won't get rich on customers like that one,' he said smiling at her. 'She's a sweet old lady and I rarely make any money out of our transactions. I tell her a price higher than I expect to get and let her believe she's beaten me down and got herself a bargain and she goes home happy.'

'You like people, don't you? You always have time for them and think the best of them.'

'I suppose I do. I like seeing you best of all though. But today you look worried. Is there a reason you're here, apart from wanting to see me?'

'Henry, what do you know about Tabitha?'

'Tabs? What is there to know? She's lacking in confidence, mainly due to her father's selfish way of treating her, and that's a pity because she's very knowledgeable about this business. If her mother had lived I imagine Tabs would be a very different person. Still quiet, still a bit old-fashioned, but probably less afraid of offering her opinions. She might even have had a business of her own.' He frowned, then asked, 'Why do you ask? Is something wrong?'

'I don't know, Henry. In fact the more time that passes, the greater my doubt whether I saw what I think I did. It seems so unlikely.'

'Now you have got me intrigued!'

She had thought a great deal about everything she had heard and seen, and the events were now clear in her mind. 'Last night, about three o'clock, I was woken by some noises. I listened and it sounded like something being moved, then footsteps going down the stairs, slowly. I think there was something being carried. I heard the sound of something knocking on the banisters. I thought it must be Tabs getting a drink but I heard whispering and once a low chuckle of laughter.

'I got out of bed, wondering whether I should risk confronting a burglar, then I heard the back door open and something banged against the window of the door, then more giggles.'

'You must get a phone installed, Ruth. You'd have been able to call the police.'

'Hardly; I was upstairs and if I had a phone it would have been in the hall! Anyway, I went to the window and looked out. There were two figures, one taller than the other and I feel sure that one was a man. They went towards the shed carrying something but I couldn't see what. A torch flashed weakly once or twice but only for a moment. The back door closed a few moments later and I hesitated. I didn't know what to do. If I put lights on, they — whoever they were — could come back. So I waited. Then footsteps came up the stairs, they were so quiet I wasn't sure they were real and not a part of my imagination. Then, and this is the puzzling bit, I went into Tabs's room and she was awake and I switched on her bedside lamp and in the light of it I saw that she was wearing outdoor clothes. It must have been she who woke me; she'd had a man in the house.'

'Are you sure?'

'Henry! What a ridiculous thing to say! Of course I'm sure!'

'Have you found anything to be missing?'

'No, and apart from a few scratches in the varnish on the banisters and a couple of marks on the kitchen wall, there's nothing to prove what happened. But it did, Henry. Tabs was fully dressed under the bed covers and I saw her and a man, taking something to the shed. Please don't insult me by saying I dreamt it.'

'But Tabs? Bringing a man into your house? It is hard to believe, isn't it?'

'So you don't believe me! Right!' She began to leave and he held her arm then pulled her against him.

'I believe you, Ruth. Of course I believe you. What I find difficult is it's just so out of character for someone like Tabs.'

'She's fooled us all. Obviously.'

He continued to hold her and she relaxed. 'What shall we do?' he said and she gave a sigh of relief. He hadn't said, what will you do, he'd said we.

'I thought you'd believe her and insist I was inventing it or dreaming after too much supper!'

'You come first, Ruth. You always will. But what are we going to do about Tabs?'

'She can't stay. If she can bring a boyfriend to her room, allowing him to creep in at night without telling me then she can't be trusted and she'll have to go.'

'Her freedom from her father and meeting this man must have changed her personality completely. It's very odd.'

'You've seen him?'

'She's been meeting someone in the park at lunchtime. I'm curious enough to have tried to see him but I've had no luck so far, apart from a distant glance. He was too far away for me to be able to recognize him again.'

'I'm telling her to go. I have to. I wouldn't feel safe at the thought of men I don't know wandering in at night. But I don't think we should do anything more than that. It isn't our business.'

'Right. Then will you find another lodger, or will you marry me at last?'

She looked at him, smiling. 'Henry, your proposals are becoming more mundane, I'll have to think about them carefully before they dry up completely.'

'Please do, Ruth. Time is passing. I'm thirty-four in a month's time.'

'I'll have to think of a special present.'

'The only present I want is for you to say, yes.'

The following day Henry went out to attend a house sale in a village the other side of Cardiff. He didn't wait to see Tabs and ask for her explanation of the visitor. He had to wait until he and Ruth were together and question her carefully, just in case there had been a mistake, although Ruth had seemed quite clear about what she saw and heard and she wasn't one for flights of fancy.

At the newsagent's it was almost lunchtime and Tabs was locking everything carefully before closing the shop when her father and Martha arrived.

'Hello, dear,' Martha said. 'We were wondering if you'd like to come home and have lunch with us. Lovely it'll be to have you there for a little while. I can show you the changes we've made. We'd value your opinion, wouldn't we, George?'

Tabs glanced at her watch, thinking about Jack, who might be waiting in the park, even though the weather was not really warm enough to eat outside and rain threatened. It was never easy for her to lie but she shook her head. 'Sorry, Dad, but I have to go on an errand for Henry. Another day?' She glanced at her watch again.

'Why don't you come this evening, then?'

'Good idea,' George said with a smile. 'Because you choose to live away from home, that needn't mean we never see you.'

'Sorry, Dad, but not tonight.'
'Something special planned?'
'Not special but I can't change it.'

When they had gone, Tabs hurriedly closed the shop and ran across the road to the park. It was a dull day and there were few people about. She went to where she could see the bench where they habitually met but it was empty. Holding the pack of sandwiches, cake and fruit she had brought for their lunch, she walked disconsolately on and sat near their usual place from where she could see the entrance.

George and Martha watched and Martha nodded wisely. 'She's meeting someone, I knew it. The way she kept looking at her watch, the extra care with her hair and lipstick an' all. I knew it wasn't work she was worried about. Oh, George, dear! It couldn't have been Tabs we saw with a man at three in the morning, could it?'

* * *

Abigail's sickness was as unexpected as it was severe. She was ill every morning and although it eased, she was never free of it until the evening. A car coming slowly alongside hers at traffic lights, or seeing a movement of a sign swinging in the breeze, were enough to start her stomach churning. She called on fewer and fewer customers and her sales went down until she had to tell her boss that she was expecting a baby. With regret, they told her she had to leave.

It was several days later that she began to look at her finances and discovered how serious her situation had become. She had spent all she'd earned, confident there was plenty more to come. She was a very successful saleswoman, but, as her boss had pointed out, her skill in selling had a great deal to do with her good looks, her dress sense and her ability to model the hats and make people believe they would look as good as her if they bought one.

She went back to her attractively furnished flat and picked up the post. There was a letter, so beautifully timed, she thought sadly, reminding her of her arrears on the rent. If only Jack were here, she thought as panic rose. Why couldn't he forget the doubtful claim in some treasure his father had told him about and stay with her, help her?

She wasn't sure where to find him but perhaps she should try before the car was taken away, she had known for weeks that payments on that were overdue but had ignored the letters, convinced that she would be able to clear them, when she set her mind on it.

She talked to her mother, but kept from her the truth about their situation, only stating that as she and Jack were seriously planning to marry and settle down, they needed to move to somewhere cheaper, just until Jack got on his feet and found a proper career. They spent a miserable afternoon listing some of the best items in the flat and preparing them for sale. When they had sorted out their debts, there would be very little left to pay rent; they would be in a very lowly situation, unless Jack came home and stayed to help. The first thing she must do was to find a job, any job that would bring enough to feed them. How could she have allowed this to happen? And where was Jack?

* * *

Jack was in the busy market in Cardiff. Twice he managed to lift a purse from the top of a shopping basket. Fools, to make it so easy for people like me, he thought, as he threw the purses away and pocketed the money. Not much, only a little over two pounds, but enough to keep him going for a day or so.

He walked past Ty Gwyn late that evening and saw Tabs sitting at her bedroom window looking out. She waved and he waved back, pointing to the corner and beckoning her. Making the excuse of needing a walk, she quickly joined him.

'Martha found this.' She waved a handwritten note in front of him. 'Martha told me she'd found a letter written by Ruth's grandmother and I made some silly excuse about

Ruth valuing everything to do with her family and she got it back out of the ash bin.'

He read it and frowned. 'What's the use of this, love? There's no name on it.'

'She said the name Tyler, and that she was related to Ruth and her brothers. Her grandmother on her mother's side. Could she be one of the family you're searching for?'

'You, Miss Tabitha Bishop, are a very clever girl.' He put it in his pocket and hugged her. 'Come on, we'll go for a walk and I can show you just how much you mean to me.'

Martha and George called at Ty Gwyn and were pleased to learn that Tabs was out. They discussed what had happened during that night, George almost accusing Ruth of running a house that was far from respectable. Martha was tearful, insisting she was deeply concerned about Tabitha, her dear stepdaughter. Henry was saying little, being cautious and avoiding an accusation about Tabs. Ruth was angry and determined to get the facts clear.

They left before Tabs had returned from her walk and Henry waited with Ruth, reminding her that so far all they had was supposition, guess work. And a theory that didn't match Tabs's character.

* * *

When Tabs went back to Ty Gwyn a couple of hours later, Ruth and Henry were sitting beside the fire, Henry had his arm around Ruth's shoulder. Tabs felt her cheeks reddening as she saw them there. Ruth stared at her, disapproval and disappointment in her eyes.

Tabs knew her loving moments with Jack showed on her face. Besides her eyes, which she was sure would be shining and full of happiness, she had been wearing make-up and, if there was any left it would be smudged and telling a tale of love.

'Ruth and I have been talking to your father and step-mother,' Henry said. 'They are worried about you.'

'They want me to go back home, but only to be an unpaid servant,' Tabs said sadly.

'They saw someone coming from this house very late at night and thought it was Ruth and a mysterious man.'

'And was it?' Tabs's face was even redder and slick with perspiration.

'You know it wasn't,' Ruth said. 'You were the one wearing outdoor clothes in bed.'

'I wasn't . . . it wasn't . . . Please, Ruth. It wasn't what you're thinking.'

'I'm sorry, but I hate lies. And I hate being taken for a fool.'

'All right, I met someone. He came in but he didn't stay for long.'

'Who was he? What did he want in my house? What were you doing in my shed?'

Tabs looked down, her fingers fidgeting as though they too were involved in the fight with her conscience. 'I can't tell you. I promised.'

'Loyalty is a good thing,' Henry said, 'but you owe that to Ruth, don't you? She has given you a home where you can relax, be yourself, live your life the way you want to live, but in return you at least owe her honesty. You risked her reputation by what you and this boyfriend did. Rumours have grown from a lot less. Ruth doesn't deserve that.'

'I can't tell you,' Tabs whispered. 'I'll pack my things and tomorrow I'll go back home.' She ran from the room and up the stairs and they heard sobs before her bedroom door closed and shut off the sound.

'Ruth, we can't send her back to her father, we can't.'

'I'll talk to her tomorrow.'

When Ruth went downstairs at five the following morning, Tabs was already in the kitchen, her small suitcase near the door. She was nursing a cup of tea, the fire was laid and ready to light.

'If you'll be straight with me you can stay.'

'I'm sorry,' Tabs stuttered. 'I can't . . .'

'You have to promise not to invite strangers here.'

'That won't happen again. I can promise that but I won't talk about him.'

'Tabs, if you have a boyfriend, I'm delighted. Henry and I would love to meet him. Will you arrange for us to meet? Here would be fine, or a place where we can talk or have a meal. Just a brief chat so we know something about him, make sure he's a decent person.'

'It isn't your business,' Tabs whispered. 'I'm not a child who needs parental guidance. Certainly not from someone younger than myself.'

Angry, Ruth stood up and poured herself a cup of tea. 'Best you go then.'

'Can I stay for a few hours? Martha won't be awake and I can't go to the shop.'

Ruth threw the tea into the sink, muttering that it was cold and set the kettle ready to make a fresh one. When she turned around, to tell her she could stay, the suitcase was still there but Tabs had gone. She heard muffled sobs coming from her room when she went up to get dressed.

Following the sound she went to Tabs's room and went in without knocking. She didn't demand answers, Tabs had been right about it not being her business. Instead, she assured the unhappy woman that she was still her friend and would be there when she needed one.

Instead of setting off on her insurance collections, Ruth went with Tabs to her old home where Martha and George were just finishing breakfast. Without giving anyone a chance to explain, Martha urged them to go up and see the room she had prepared for Tabs. 'I knew you'd come back to us,' she said happily. 'Look, I've done this room ready for you.'

'I thought I'd have my old room,' Tabs said. 'This one is very small.'

'Come and see what we've done in your old room, dear.' There she proudly explained about her plans for accommodating summer visitors. 'Crying out for decent places to stay, they are. So I thought — your father and I thought — we could make ourselves a little extra money. Doesn't it look lovely? All new and so pretty and soon it will have new curtains and a fitted carpet.'

Ruth saw the stricken look on Tabs's face. A face that had changed back to how she used to look before leaving this house where she was treated so badly; a frightened, browbeaten child. She knew she wouldn't have a moment free from guilt if she left her there 'Come on, Tabs,' she said briskly. 'We've seen all we need to see. Now we're going home.'

'But I thought you were coming back,' Martha wailed. 'We've done your room out special.'

'No, she isn't staying.' Ruth didn't listen to any arguments, just pulled Tabs back to the front door, picked up her suitcase and marched her off.

'I won't talk about him, so please don't ask me.' Tabs looked defiant and Ruth nodded. 'I want to stay with you more than anything, but you must stay out of my private life.'

'All right. But if you're to stay in my house, there'll be no more midnight visits, right? Bring him home and introduce us when you feel ready to do so, but you have to promise never to bring him to Ty Gwyn without telling me and certainly not when I'm not there.'

Tabs tearfully agreed. 'Thank you.' Drying her eyes she went on, 'I'm sorry, but he doesn't want anyone to know he's here. He's searching for someone and that's all I can tell you.'

'Well he won't find them hiding in a shed!' Ruth said, and succeeded in making the tearful girl smile. She had agreed to forget the frightening incident but it was far from satisfactory.

* * *

Bryn and Brenda came that evening, invited for a meal. They arrived at the same time as Tommy and Toni, who was finding it difficult to sit on the couch on which the others sprawled, but instead sat on the carving chair near the table.

'We've got news for you,' Bryn said, when they began to eat.

Ruth looked, not at Bryn, but at Brenda.

'We're going to have a baby,' Brenda said. 'Sometime in March we think.'

'What kept you?' Tommy demanded, 'ours is due in October!'

'We didn't want to spoil your moment in the spotlight,' Bryn retorted. 'Ours will put yours in the shade soon enough.' The banter went on for most of the evening between the twins while the sisters-in-law chatted more calmly and shared information, promising support for each other.

Henry congratulated them and Tabs was so embarrassed she spent the rest of the evening hiding in the kitchen.

'Have you told Emrys and Susan, and Geraint and Hazel?' Ruth asked. 'We see so little of Geraint and Hazel I wonder if they've forgotten all about us.'

'London's a long way off, so we wrote to them with the news,' Brenda said. 'We haven't heard from them yet but I expect they'll be pleased that the family is growing. Emrys and Susan know; we went to Bridgend yesterday and told them. They were pleased at the thought of being aunt and uncle, twice.'

Hiding her surprise at being the last person to be told, Ruth asked, 'How are Geraint and Hazel? Their business keeps them in London working all hours but it's a shame they can't get down sometimes. We don't see much of Emrys and Susan either, and they're only in Bridgend. It's a long time since we were all together. I think I'll phone them tomorrow and suggest a family weekend.'

'What if we have twins?' Bryn said, so quickly that Henry wondered if he were forcing a change of subject.

Tommy stood up and glared at his twin. 'You wouldn't dare upstage me like that!'

The others laughed and the banter went on. But Ruth hadn't been distracted from the idea of a weekend with all the family.

The next morning she telephoned the office of the postal sales company in London, owned by her elder brother, and a secretary answered. Ruth asked the girl, Miss Collins, to leave a message for her brother and his wife inviting them to come to Ty Gwyn the following weekend for a family gathering. Miss Collins seemed a bit vague but promised to do what she could.

'Are they away?' Ruth asked. 'They didn't tell me anything about a holiday.'

'Leave it with me, and I'll make sure the message is passed on.' It wasn't a satisfactory reply but the pips were going again and she had no more change.

The bus took her to Bridgend and at the office of the building firm for whom both Susan and Emrys worked, she left a message for them. Putting aside the vagueness of the responses, she happily made lists, ordered food and prepared the rooms ready for the family to come home.

There was no acknowledgement from London or Bridgend but all eight of them arrived on Friday evening and the occasion began well. Emrys and Susan announced that they were buying a house. Geraint seemed rather off-hand but Hazel reacted with pleasure and promised them a few items of furniture they no longer needed. The two women discussed what Hazel had that was surplus and what Susan would be pleased to accept. The two men sat in silence half listening, Emrys smiling happily and his brother Geraint staring into space as though none of it concerned him. Henry studied the faces of Geraint and Susan and suspected there was another announcement to come.

On Saturday Ruth was up early and Tabs joined her to get the food preparations underway. The four brothers went into the garden and did a few jobs with which Ruth needed some help, cutting back dead flowers, trimming bushes and piling them in the garden ready for burning. In the evening they went for a walk by the sea, chattering and laughing, couples, including Ruth and Henry, strolling arm in arm, all except Geraint and Hazel, who kept changing places to talk to one or other of the family.

'They ought to come more often,' Ruth said. 'Look at the way they're going from one to the other, trying to catch up with all the news.' Henry said nothing but he wasn't convinced.

They stayed up beyond midnight, and on Sunday morning they slept late. As usual it was Ruth who went down first and set everything out ready for breakfast, so she was surprised when the back door opened and Geraint walked in. 'Good heavens, Geraint, Where have you been so early?'

'Ruth. There's no easy way to tell you this, but Hazel and I have sold the business and we're getting a divorce.'

Ruth sat down on a chair and stared at him. 'Come on, surely this is something you can work out? A divorce? But I thought you and Hazel were happy? Working together, a nice home, and successful business, what on earth more d'you want?'

'So you think it's my fault?'

'Isn't it?'

'Hazel has met someone else.'

'Never!'

'We've been living apart for three months and now it's in the hands of a solicitor.'

'But why didn't you tell me? There might have been something I could do?'

'What could anyone do? She's moved in with this man, Eddie Collins, and that is that. I wouldn't have her back now whatever happened.'

'Collins? Isn't that the name of the secretary I spoke to in your office?'

'It's her brother.' He shrugged as though to put aside the discussion and pointed to the food set out near the cooker. 'Is that breakfast? I'm starving.'

'You know you can come back here for a while, don't you? This is still your home.'

'We've sold our house and the business too, so I might do that when I move out. Just until I arrange my next move.' Movements upstairs stopped the conversation and Geraint picked up the newspapers from the hall and sat in the living room while a distracted Ruth began cooking.

When they were all squashed around the table, Geraint told the others and when Henry arrived later he, too, was told.

'It's a lot to take in,' Tommy said, reaching for Toni's hand. 'Bryn and Brenda's baby, Emrys and Susan buying a house and now this. A divorce. Are you two sure it's what you want?'

Hazel was about to speak, but Geraint answered first. 'I've never been more certain of anything in my life!' Hazel jumped up and ran from the room and Geraint put his head in his hands and stared down at the floor.

'You promised me,' Hazel shouted from the hall. 'You promised not to tell them until we got back.'

Geraint went out to where his wife was standing, reaching for her coat. The murmur of their voices was heard by the others until the door slammed shut behind them. They sat and stared at each other in disbelief.

'I thought they were happy together, building the business which is earning them enough money to enjoy themselves and have a decent home. What went wrong?' Tommy asked.

'Eddie Collins — whoever he is,' Bryn replied.

'No wonder they offered us their unwanted furniture,' Toni muttered.

Unable to think of anything to add, and needing to keep busy, Ruth finished cooking the breakfast. 'Go and see if they're coming back to eat,' she asked Tommy as she began putting food on plates. Henry smiled and touched her shoulder. 'Whatever happens in your little world, your first thought it to feed people.'

'Well, we still have to eat, don't we? Pass your plate, there are some tomatoes left.'

'Caring for people — that's how you should earn your living.' Still smiling, he offered his plate.

Tommy came back and explained that Hazel wasn't hungry and they were leaving as soon as they were packed.

'Oh no you don't!' Ruth went out to where they were still arguing. The words were softly spoken, only the tension in their faces showing their anger. 'Come on, we aren't going to join in your argument, take sides, but I'm not wasting good food, so come on, and eat up. Then you can get packed and go.'

The meal was eaten in silence, only the occasional word as someone asked for more bread or needed a tea cup re-filled. Still silently, Hazel nodded to excuse herself and went upstairs. The tension eased slightly as the men discussed which was the best route, Chepstow or Ross-on-Wye to get to Gloucester and on to London.

Henry stood up and helped Ruth with the dishes. 'I wish you hadn't invited Geraint to come back here,' he said. 'You aren't the mother, and he's old enough to sort out his own problems. It's time for you to make a life of your own.'

Ruth scrubbed the saucepans a little more vigorously. 'It will only be for a little while. He's terribly hurt and coming home offers comfort and gives a chance to heal.'

'Are you working tomorrow?'

'Yes, but I should be finished by three.'

'Then come to the shop. I have something to show you.' To his disappointment she didn't even show curiosity. 'Don't you want to know what it is?'

'Sorry, Henry, is it a new purchase? Something beautiful?'

'Yes. And no.' It was useless, she wasn't concentrating on what he was saying. If he'd said it was a pack of elephants she would probably smile and say, that's nice! 'I'll expect you at about half three, then.'

'Half three,' she repeated. 'Fine.'

Henry wanted to show her a house he was hoping to buy, a place on which to build their future. But she needed to see it and decide whether she could live there. He had to do something to move their relationship on or he might as well walk away — as his mother frequently suggested he should. Sometimes the thought was tempting, but only for fleeting moments. He loved her and knew she would make him happy. His doubts were whether she felt the same way. Confronting her with the house and his plans for it might make her feelings clear.

It was with more trepidation than excitement that he drove her through the terraced roads near the centre of town and onto the outskirts.

The house was overlooking a common, where seats and shady trees attracted people to walk with children and dogs, or to sit and admire the flower beds and the wild birds that were regularly fed there. It was double-fronted and set back from the road. He parked the car and opened the door for her. She hadn't asked a single question.

'What are they selling, silverware? Paintings? Furniture?'

'No, they're selling the house. I want you to look at it and decide whether it would be a suitable home for us and our children. I know you wouldn't want to live in my flat with its lack of a garden.'

She turned and stared at him and he watched the surprise, the doubts, then pleasure cross her face. 'It's beautiful.'

'Wait till you see inside.' He took her arm and led her to the front door, which was opened before he could raise the knocker.

'Mr Owen?' the man queried and held the door back for them to enter. Introductions followed and the man explained that, since the death of his wife he found the place too large. 'It's a place for a family,' he added. 'We had four children and were very happy. Now they've gone and I need to find somewhere smaller, a flat probably.' He went into each room explaining a few things they might have otherwise missed then went to sit in the garden allowing them to look around on their own.

The place was mature and comfortable with a feeling of warmth and contentment. Five bedrooms, all of which were large, three reception rooms, a garden, a large barn, a stream and behind all that, a small woodland that was a haven for birds and wild flowers.

'It's a beautiful house and I can imagine someone being very happy here,' Ruth said.

'Someone? Not you and me?'

'I don't know why you brought me here, Henry. I live in Ty Gwyn, it's the family home. I can't leave it.'

'Not even if your brothers want it sold?'

'They don't want it sold! How can you think such a thing?'

'Bryn and Tommy are both expecting their first child. Emrys and Susan are buying their first house. Geraint will need finance to help start a new business. The money is needed by them all.'

She waved and called thank you to the owner of the house and hurried through the hall and out. Henry stood for a moment, then went back to answer the man's call of 'What d'you think?' with a vague muttered reply that said nothing.

Ruth was sitting in the car and her face looked stony.

'If you don't intend to marry me, I think we should call the whole thing off. I don't want to waste any more of my life while you play at "being mother".'

'I'm not playing at "being mother"! I'm keeping the family home going. It's important to all of them. Geraint's need to come back home when he wants a place to lick his wounds and make decisions about his future just proves me right.'

He said no more. He stopped at the shop and watched as she picked up her bicycle and rode away.

Tabs was in the shop, cleaning some brass horses he had recently bought. She didn't look up or she might have seen his tense expression. 'I don't think we'll sell many more of these,' she said, rubbing furiously. 'Many went for scrap during the war and people wanted to replace them, but I think polishing brass is already losing its appeal.'

'Tabs, do you have to go anywhere this evening?'

'I haven't anything special planned. Why, do you have a job for me?'

'No, I'd like some company. Do you fancy going out for a meal? Down The Vale maybe?'

'I'd love to. I want to talk to you about a neighbour who has some china and cutlery she wants to sell, Georgian some of it.'

He smiled. Tabs was unusual in that her first thought hadn't been what would she wear. Then she looked shocked and said, 'I'll have to go home first, I can't go like this. I've got brasso stains all over my sleeves.'

'Give me that rag. I'll stain mine to match. Come on, let's just go.'

* * *

Ruth sat up thinking about what she wanted from life. Of course she wanted marriage and children but now wasn't the right time to move away from Ty Gwyn. Geraint needed a home more than he needed money. The others too looked upon the house as the centre of family life. It would be a useful sum though and she understood how it would help the four couples with their new commitments, but selling their home? Surely they didn't really want that?

Her thoughts danced about, from the idea of selling the house to Henry's remark about ending their plans for the future. As the fire burned low and the room cooled she shivered, but it wasn't the lack of warmth, it was the realization of what that would exactly mean. Could she face a life without him? The balance was between being here for her brothers, being on the periphery of their lives, taking what crumbs their wives offered, or marrying Henry and building a life of her own. Yet her commitment to being the mainstay of the family, its anchor, was hard to put aside. She did have a life and it was here, being custodian of Ty Gwyn, the centre of the family, its past and its future. Yet she still felt a little afraid of the empty years that threatened.

She heard a car approach and stop outside and recognized it as Henry's. Relief filled her. He had come back to make it clear he would never leave her. She stood up and ran to open the door. She had been foolish; they could marry but live here. That way she'd satisfy all her needs. Sure he would agree, she opened the door. Henry got out of the car, but before she could call out she saw him open the door for someone else. Tabs stepped out and he hugged her for a moment, before driving away.

Tabs came in laughing, her eyes bright and her cheeks glowing.

'You'll never guess where I've been,' she said, throwing off her coat and scarf. 'Henry took me out to dinner in Cowbridge then we went to Swansea and walked on the beach, in the dark, all on our own. It was such fun.'

'Tell me about it tomorrow, will you? I'm tired and I've got a busy day tomorrow. Aunty Blod isn't feeling well. I'll pop over and bring her back here for a few days. It always does her good to come home.'

She went to bed but didn't sleep for a long time. Had Henry meant it when he said they should end it? Had he already been thinking about Tabs? Someone who had abandoned all ties with her family and who understood his business and was interested in the same things he enjoyed?

She'd fill the house again, that was the best way of dealing with disappointment, making sure every moment of her time was filled with people who needed her, understood her and most importantly, valued her and appreciated having her in their lives.

* * *

While Ruth was clinging to her home, Abigail was walking away from hers. Being seriously sick during the mornings which eased slowly through the day, migraine headaches exacerbating the problem, she had tried and failed to find work. She only needed to work for a few weeks until Jack returned to look after them, but it was apparent to any prospective employer that she was not well enough to do any of the jobs for which she had applied.

She had no success, even when she managed to get further than a brief chat with someone who arranged an interview. Prospective employers were put off by her confident manner, unnerved by her attitude, unable to imagine her taking orders, afraid she would be after their jobs in a matter of weeks!

Two jobs she tried had ended after a couple of days and there seemed no prospect of even the poorest paid work until the sickness passed. And by that time her pregnancy would be showing and no one would employ someone and train them for what might only be for a few weeks.

After vacating the flat and paying the overdue rent, returning the car and settling that account, she had enough money to stay in an hotel for no more than two weeks. Everything worth anything had been sold. There were only the beds and an armchair left at the flat and, she thought sadly, if someone offered a few pounds they would go too. Someone told her about a bungalow which they admitted was rather a mess but which was cheap to rent and she took it unseen, grateful to have somewhere to go. Where was Jack?

She hired a van to take the few items they had left, mostly clothes which were wrapped in tissue paper and packed in three trunks. One day she would go back to what she did so well, selling beautiful hats and until then, she needed to keep her 'other self', her clothes and accessories and make up, as a talisman, a promise to herself that those days would return. Bedding and other necessities filled two more trunks. Not a lot to show for all the money she had earned, she thought ruefully. How stupid she had been.

She left messages for Jack at the flat and with her ex-employer and set off for a house they hadn't seen, in a village she had never heard of and hoped that somehow Jack would find them and look after them. For a moment, looking at the van with its sad contents, she had qualms of doubt but she smiled at her mother and promised her that once Jack came he would put everything right.

CHAPTER SIX

Ruth woke early and went downstairs with confused remnants of her dreams in her mind. She'd had fractured dreams of her wedding day with a church filled with her friends as she walked down the aisle with a beautiful dress floating around her, and Henry looking handsome beside her. Voices called good wishes and confetti showered on them and laughter filled the air.

Then, the scene distorted and became mingled with scenes of Ty Gwyn empty and abandoned, windows broken, grass growing on the paths and slates fallen from the roof. Another half-remembered scene showed strangers moving around its rooms.

Amid all these were pictures of Henry smiling down at Tabs after telling her their love-affair was over. That wasn't a dream, she thought, as she reached for the teapot and cups. It happened and I can't face it. Henry with someone else, with anyone else, was breaking her heart.

Abandoning the teapot and turning off the kettle, she grabbed a coat and went to talk to Henry. As she walked towards the shop she relived her dream. She didn't understand such things but it seemed to be telling her she had to choose, the family home or Henry. Henry meant a home of her own and that was what she wanted, but to abandon the house? To part with the place the family still thought of as home? How could she do that? Would her brothers let her give it up? Where would they meet without Ty Gwyn as a base? How would they stay in contact without that sanctuary, that place where news was shared, where arguments were resolved, where everyone felt safe?

Henry opened the door and she didn't know how to behave. Should she reach up and kiss him as she usually did, or did their last conversation mean that was no longer acceptable. To her relief he opened his arms and she slid into them and reached for his kiss. Relief that all was well made her tearful. Nothing had changed, yesterday's words were just that, words.

As she relaxed in his arms she thought about how rarely they had disagreed, apart from her hesitation to accept his regular proposals. Henry didn't argue, he just discussed things calmly and if he didn't convince her of whatever they had disagreed on, he just let it go, accepting and respecting her opinion. Sometimes, like now, she was grateful for his understanding but occasionally, when she was alone and thinking about their future, she wondered if his calmness might be one of the reasons why she couldn't make up her mind to marry him. His life seemed set to continue unchanged.

Dullness wasn't a word she could honestly associate with Henry but she could see a time, some distance in the future when her life might be just that, dull. She wasn't one to crave excitement, but she suspected that without an occasional spat and some change of mood, she might regret saying yes.

* * *

Abigail stared at the bungalow she had rented in utter disbelief. Semi derelict, even the roof didn't seem keen to keep its position as it leaned on the damaged guttering for precarious support, causing the chimney to lean at an alarming angle. Her heart raced with fear as she approached the door. Surely there was a mistake? This couldn't be the place? On the door there was a faded sign which announced the place as Heavenly View. Someone with a warped sense of humour she decided.

It was late, the day was ending and she was achingly tired. She would have to stay for one night at least. Tomorrow she was bound to find something better. Taking a deep breath she stepped inside.

The room smelled seriously of damp and the walls were patterned with the signs of its long term damage. She shuddered. She couldn't stay here. But her first impulse, to find an hotel for the night, was quashed. She had hardly any money until her final cheque at the end of the month, so she couldn't afford even one night.

After dragging their belongings inside, she built up the fire. At least there was plenty of wood around where gardeners had thrown their rubbish to join the rest, then made herself a bed of sorts wrapping herself in cushions and blankets. She lay there wondering how to start on the mammoth task of making the place fit for her mother and wondering when Jack would come to help them.

Allowing Jack to wander around the country searching for some imaginary treasure had been fun, a way of making people admire her tolerance, but now the joke had come back to hit her hard between the eyes. Within weeks everything had changed and she needed him here. In a way she could never have imagined, she had lost everything and she desperately needed his help.

She went each day on the bus, to see her mother and dreaded to be told she could come home. How could she bring her to a place like this? Working most of each day and half the nights lit by candles she had found in the dismal kitchen, she scrubbed and cleaned.

* * *

Two weeks passed before Jack came to find Abigail and Gloria. He was unclear about what had happened to make

Abigail leave the flat. Explanations had been vague but he learned that she had lost her job and that alarmed him. He had optimistically told himself there was plenty of time, she was sure to be offered work in the office when she could no longer trade as a saleswoman. She was highly valued, how could they tell her she must leave? He had no money to offer her, and without a job and with her extravagances, Abigail would soon be in difficulties.

He asked directions to the bungalow of a few people and was rewarded with curious looks and comments of surprise that anyone was living there. The place, which he had been told was next to a garage, was a shock. The garden was overgrown with mounds where grasses and wild flowers had covered piles of rubbish and abandoned machinery. More recent rubbish littered the area around the back door where it had been piled, presumably to allow access.

He stopped at the rusting old petrol pumps and looked behind the garage to where the bungalow stood. Tattered curtains blew at the window and smoke curled up from the precariously balanced chimney. Looking in at the muddle of bedding and half opened boxes, he began to walk away. This had to be a mistake.

* * *

Tabs was worried. She hadn't seen Jack for days and, not knowing where he lived, there was no way she could look for him. He had been evasive each time she had asked where he went when he disappeared for a few days, not exactly refusing to tell her, but vague and he managed to answer the question without actually telling her anything. She had been curious but not worried — until now. Now she badly wanted to see him, to be reassured that his love meant they would be together for always. That was what most people usually meant when they shared a moment of love and uttered those words, but she had an uneasy feeling that Jack might be different. No permanent address, unwilling to tell her about his family, not even telling her the real reason for his being here. Saying I love you might have meant something far less than it did to 'most people'.

He frequently disappeared for a few days without explaining. He'd describe places he had enjoyed; some to which he would take her. She never pressed for explanations. One day he would tell her everything and until then she would be patient. She mustn't pester him, that might drive him away. She couldn't bear that. He was the only person in the world who truly cared for her and far too precious to risk losing.

She sat on the park bench, their bench, and ate her solitary lunch. She had brought more than she needed, just in case Jack surprised her and joined her. She ate very little and spread the remainder on the grass for the birds.

* * *

Jack was some distance away, walking down an unmade up road following directions to the bungalow called Heavenly View once again. He had asked again at the flat where Abigail had lived and had been assured that the directions he had been given were those left by Abigail. There was no one around; this was no longer a highway. Traffic had once regularly passed the garage but came no longer. Grasses and weeds grew on the cracked surface of the road.

He stopped at the rusting old petrol pumps and looked behind the garage to where the bungalow stood. Forcing a smile, he pushed open the door called. 'Abigail? Gloria? Anyone home?' He went into what he presumed was the living room and looked around at the shabby furniture; the bed against one wall, a couple of armchairs beside the fire, a small table on which, incongruously, a vase of wild flowers stood. Surely this can't be where Abigail lived?

It had to be a mistake, the woman now living in the flat had given him the wrong information. A further search alarmed him even more, there were only three rooms and the building was in need of repair. A place like this called

Heavenly View? That must be a joke! He recognized many of Abi and Gloria's possessions; Abi's beautiful clothes were hanging around the walls protected with tissue paper, the boxes containing hats piled in one of the other rooms.

He looked in vain for a note, something to explain where Abigail and Gloria were. He sat down and prepared to wait. Abigail would be working, and Gloria wasn't able to walk very well although, she might have reached the bus stop, he mused.

He dozed for an hour and was woken by Abigail coming in. She gave a cry of pleasure seeing him there and ran into his arms. 'It's Mum,' she said, before he could comment on the place. 'She's in hospital, pneumonia they fear. It's this place, Jack. It's so damp and we've had nothing but bad luck since we came.'

He listened to her story, in which she admitted ignoring warnings from the bank and he blamed himself for not being there. He stayed overnight and the next day he spent some time fastening broken window frames and adding a stronger lock on the door.

Abigail went back to the hospital to see Gloria but Jack stayed at the bungalow, intending to make the place as safe as was possible. He bought tools and other things he needed and spent the day cleaning up and doing what he could. He chopped piles of wood and sawed through some trees he found nearby to make a reasonable pile of logs. He bought a couple of sacks of coal and helped himself to a second loaf when he paid for one, and took milk from the delivery cart while the milkman wasn't looking. He had done all he could for now but — as he looked around the room, so different from the beautiful flat, with its sad attempts at cheer where Abigail had polished an old table, added a bright cushion, or filled a couple of jam-jars with flowers — he felt ashamed and angry. He had to do something more than this, and soon. Abigail and Gloria deserved better than he had given them. But he might be close to getting the money he believed waited for him, so regretfully he left the bungalow and headed back to Tabs.

Sitting on the bus, he thought of Tabs. He needed to encourage her a little more, careful not to frighten her away; she had to be persuaded to help him. He desperately needed money. It was lunchtime and he guessed that Tabs would go to the park and wait on the bench, hoping to see him. Not today, but in a few days' time he wouldn't disappoint her.

* * *

Abi went with the crowd that surged forward as the ward doors opened. Her mother had a hand raised, anxious for that first glimpse. Abigail smiled at her mother, the relief showing so clearly in Gloria's expression. As if she didn't expect me to return, she mused. As if I'd let her down.

'Heard from Jack?' Gloria asked.

'He's been held up,' Abigail lied. 'Some problem with payment, you know how difficult it is sometimes.'

'They want the work done but argue about paying for it. I don't know why people are so mean. I think your Jack's too soft. Too nice for business.'

'You're right, Mam. He's so kind, often doing work and not taking the money when he thinks they can't afford it. Foolish, I know, but you'll never change him and I don't think I'd want to.'

'Neither would I. He won't stay away now, knowing how we need him. And once he sees his beautiful baby he'll never want to leave again. Lovely boy he is.'

Abigail glanced again at the door. 'Lovely he is, but I wish he'd come back. When you come out of hospital, I don't want you going home to the euphemistically named, "Heavenly View". It can't be healthy for you. It's so damp and cold. But I can't do anything for a while, I have to sort out my finances first.'

'We'll manage. It's just till Jack comes home and finds a proper job. All this travelling around from job to job isn't much of a life. He'll never want to go away again, fortune or no fortune, when he knows how we are fixed.'

Abigail smiled. She wondered whether there was anything she could sell, to buy some extra coal and logs. What Jack had provided wouldn't last long. A good fire and a pantry filled with nourishing food, that's what her mother would need in a few days' time, when they sent her home.

The bungalow behind a garage that had been closed for several years would never be a suitable place for someone who had been as ill as her mother. The pumps were still in situ but rusted, the glass over the circular gauges cracked and covered with dirt. The rent was nominal but no repairs had been carried out and Jack's temporary repairs wouldn't last long; the weather was a powerful enemy.

Jack had promised to make the place more comfortable and, for those few days, he had worked on it, mainly to make it weather-proof, but he hadn't quite achieved that aim. She went home every night after the hospital visit and more failed attempts at getting a job, and did what she could to improve the place. She worked during the day shutting her mind off to everything else. Thankfully there would be money at the end of the month and paying final instalments on the debts would leave her with enough to heat the place and provide decent food for a while at least.

It was such an isolated place and although there was nothing to attract a burglar, someone looking for a place to sleep might think it was unoccupied, and break in to shelter for the night. The thought made sleep difficult. Restless she got up several times and by the light of a torch made herself a hot drink, which she left to go cold as she dozed briefly. Then she was woken by a severe pain.

The pain increased and engulfed her and she knew that she was going to lose the baby. She wondered between agonizing cramps how she would manage if she couldn't work, ignoring the fact she no longer had a job. Then her thoughts were only on the pain, and the misery of her loss. An hour later she began to think about how she could get to a doctor. It was some time before she felt confident enough to walk to a phone box and call for a taxi.

The miscarriage was a nightmare. She wanted the baby and facing the loss, just as she was beginning to feel the excitement of becoming a mother, was cruel. The severe pains seemed to last for ever. Then, the attention of a nurse and reassurances from a doctor and she was left to sleep before going home. She realized that she was in the same hospital as her mother.

* * *

Jack jumped off the bus at the end of the road and walked towards the abandoned garage. No smoke from the chimney of the bungalow: did that mean Abigail and Gloria were out? Damn. He was hungry and he hated having to cook for himself.

He arrived at the same time as Abigail, meeting at the corner from different directions, Abi having travelled by bus, Jack on foot. They both gave a cry of delight as they hugged each other, Abigail tearful as she told him about their baby and her mother's continuing illness. Jack was ashamed that she'd had to deal with it all on her own. With promises falling from his lips, holding her close, they walked towards the door which, to her alarm, was open.

'Someone's been here!' Wide-eyed in alarm, Abigail eased herself away from his arms as they crept closer. Jack reached into his pocket for a weapon, a torch, which was all he carried. Looking inside Abigail gave a wail of dismay, Jack a growl of rage. The few pieces of furniture they had were broken, the half-burned wood on the fire that spilled out onto the grate and even the slate floor, evidence to their fate. A hasty look into the food cupboard and Abigail began to cry. 'They've taken everything. The food I'd been storing for when Mam gets home, everything.'

Jack looked around him after searching the other rooms. Everything had either been taken or destroyed. The bed was filthy, where various drinks and food had been spilt, thrown around and left in squashed lumps on the remains of the furniture, the torn bedding and over the floor.

'Where can we go?' Abigail whispered. 'Mam can't come home to this.'

Jack was white-faced with anger. Forcing himself to speak calmly he said, 'Do what you can to clean things up and I'll go and get what we need just for tonight. Tomorrow we'll decide what to do next.'

Like a zombie she filled a pail and found a scrubbing brush, and even some soap and bleach, and began scrubbing. The furniture that hadn't been burnt was filthy but she managed to set up a small table and a couch that she covered with her coat. The bed was unusable. The bedding once immaculate was now stained by heaven alone knew what; she could not allow her mother to sleep in it. Frustration giving her strength, she dragged it outside and set fire to it.

Jack didn't return. She sat up all night and waited, crying and dozing and waking to cry again. Everything had gone wrong since Jack had left on his search for an inheritance; what had been a prideful joke on her part was no longer an amusing story to tell people, it was a disaster. Having no money wouldn't make him leave her, she knew him better than that. He'll be back. She was torn between going to see her mother and staying put until Jack came and settled for waiting. Her mother didn't know about the miscarriage and wouldn't expect her until later. She'd stay and wait for Jack.

* * *

Jack was on his way to see Ruth. This was an emergency and Ruth had empty rooms. Pity about Tabs, but she'd have found out some time. It was early morning when he knocked on the door and as soon as Ruth opened it he began pleading. He calmly explained about the bungalow being robbed and the loss of everything Abigail owned, and about her mother due to be released from hospital within days.

'Who is Abigail? I thought you and Tabs were, well, more than friends,' Ruth queried. 'Does Tabs know about this Abigail? Have you been deceiving her? If so, I don't think I want to help, Jack.'

'An elderly lady with nowhere to go except a damp bungalow, without decent food and not even a dry bed. Please, Ruth. I'll talk to Tabs and I know she'll understand.'

'I hope so. She's coming any moment and before I make a decision you have to assure her. Then I'll listen. Right?'

'Thank you. I'll go and meet her now.' He went to the park and sat on the bench knowing Tabs would soon appear. Trying to think of a way of explaining Abigail and her mother that was close to the truth yet acceptable wasn't easy, but talking his way out of trouble was something at which he excelled.

She locked the shop and ran to where he was sitting. They hugged and she led him back into the shop, pulling down the closed sign on the door. He waited while she went up to the kitchen to make some tea and swiftly slipped out, muffling the bell and hid several easy-to-sell items in a garden nearby. When she came down again, he was wearing a serious expression.

* * *

Abigail was cold and she sat near the dead ashes as though they would offer comfort. She dozed often and awoke with a start and would step outside and listen for the sound of Jack's footsteps, then return to the stained and smelly couch which she had dragged as close to the fireplace as possible. Smoke infiltrated the room as the bed burned, until most of it had been consumed. The sound of the flames fell silent and even the cessation of that eerie sound made the loneliness more fearful.

Darkness was falling and she didn't know when Jack would return. She didn't have the strength to go back to the hospital, even though that offered warmth, for a while at least. Smouldering ash from the burnt bed drifted around as a playful breeze found it, dancing in the air like a flock of birds. One small spark created a flame as it touched a piece of paper and flared with renewed vigour.

* * *

Jack hadn't kissed her but Tabs thought nothing of it, apart from disappointment. From his expression she could see he was troubled. 'What is it, Jack? Are you ill?'

'No, but a friend of mine is and I have asked Ruth if she can stay here for a while. You wouldn't mind, would you?'

'Who is she, this friend of yours?'

'She's called Abigail and she and her mother, Gloria, have hit upon unfortunate times. I want to help but, with no home and not much money, I have to ask someone else to do what I want to do but cannot.'

'You haven't told me who she is, this Abigail.'

'Abigail Tranter was engaged to a friend of mine and because he and I were good friends when he died I promised myself I'd look out for her. Travelling as I do I'd lost touch and when I found them again, she was living in terrible circumstances trying to look after a sick mother.'

'Is that where you go when I don't see you for weeks?'

'Not really. I've been working, but I've called from time to time, trying to make the awful place where they live safer and buying a few things to help them.' He looked at her, his eyes looking into hers as though forcing her to agree to help by force of his stare. 'So will you help? Please, my love. Will you persuade Ruth to give them a room?'

She knew he wasn't telling her the truth. There was something about his expression that made that absolutely clear. But she nodded. 'All right, I'll talk to Ruth, but only if you agree to take me to this place when you go to fetch them. I want to help too.'

'Thank you, Tabs. I knew I could rely on you.' He kissed her affectionately and at the same time wondered if she wanted to help or to see for herself just how awful this place was and whether Abigail's mother really was ill. She was trusting but not completely gullible.

Then his kisses grew more urgent and between them he whispered of his love and his problem. 'I have to help Abigail to find a place to live and I'm desperate to get her settled so we can be together, you and me, Tabs, together in our own home planning our future. I need money to make it happen. Help me, please, my darling Tabs.'

'I'll ask Ruth if they can stay with her.'

'That's only a temporary arrangement, my love. I have to find them a place of their own, I promised my friend.' He hesitated, then went on, 'There is a way you can help. There must be plenty of stuff in Henry's shop, things he's forgotten about. We could sell it and make our dream come true much quicker.'

'I can't—'

'Can't wait? Neither can I, love. Do it for us. It isn't much of a risk,' he added quickly as she began to protest 'I want us to marry, live together and forget all about Abigail and her problems. Do this for us, darling, and it can happen so much sooner.'

The horror of stealing from Henry faded and she knew she would do as he asked.

Ruth agreed to Abigail staying, having learned more of the situation. Filling the house was what she needed to do, an excuse to avoid naming a day for her wedding or persuading Henry that it would happen soon. Fears of him taking a serious interest in Tabs had faded. Tabs's expression when she and Jack came to explain, showed her clearly that Jack was the one who had touched her heart. She was Henry's valued assistant, nothing more. Someone on whom he could rely but never more than that.

Henry drove them but, as they drew near to the disused garage, the place was hidden by smoke filtering through the trees and the road ahead. The sound of approaching fire engines overtook them and in rising panic, Jack urged Henry to hurry, afraid that, with no other buildings in the area, Abigail was in serious trouble.

He leapt out of the van leaving the door open, as soon as the van slowed down but he was stopped by a policeman's upheld hand. Tabs pushed her way forward and they both ran towards the building. Attempts were made to stop them reaching the blazing building but Jack ignored the warnings and Tabs followed.

Henry and Ruth got out and stared in horror at the flames stretching into the sky, silhouettes danced in front of the red glow, a parody of a bonfire party, but no laughter here.

Shouts were heard giving orders, men moved in haste, bringing hoses and other equipment and amid the chaos they saw Jack walking alongside a stretcher with a figure wrapped in blankets being carried by two firemen. They were running, and Ruth wanted to tell them to slow down, that the poor woman was being shaken by their haste. Instead, they were told to move back. Tabs stared after the stretcher and Ruth pulled her away and back towards the car.

'Get back! Right away from the area!' a policeman urged, beckoning them towards him. 'We don't know whether there's any petrol left in the tanks.'

'It could blow up! Hurry!' another shouted impatiently. Ruth and Henry held hands. Tabs followed and they ran back towards the car.

Behind the fire engine an ambulance had stopped and two ambulance men ran out to help the woman, and Jack, into the back of it. As Henry hurried Ruth and Tabs into the car and started the engine, the ambulance drove off towards the nearest hospital. Tabs was crying.

'Who was on the stretcher?' Henry asked her. 'Someone you know?'

'A friend of Jack, she's just a friend,' she added to reassure herself. 'He had to go with her; there's no one else. Only her mother and as you know, she's in hospital too.'

'You can phone tomorrow to ask how she is. Don't worry, I'm sure she'll be all right.'

'I hope she isn't burnt,' Tabs whispered, tearfully. She didn't think Jack would leave her if she was seriously hurt. She feared that this woman, Abigail Tranter, was more important than that. More than just the former fiancée of a friend. Jack's face, when he thought she was hurt, the way he had run towards the fire, gave lie to his explanation.

'Don't worry, their room is ready for them and it seems I'll have two patients to look after if they both come out of hospital at the same time,' Ruth said in an attempt to be cheerful. 'You and me to look after them, Tabs, both recovering in the happy atmosphere of our house.'

Henry said nothing, just increased his speed. He didn't stay once he had seen Ruth and Tabs back into the house. Ruth filled the kettle for the inevitable cup of tea but he had declined, nodded to them both and left. Ruth smiled but Tabs was staring into space, her arms wrapped around herself, her face a picture of — of what?

Ruth stared at her, her expression was of utter tragedy. She didn't answer when Henry left or when Ruth spoke to her. Ruth wondered why she was so distressed by the incident. Abigail was a stranger, and concern was normal up to a point but not as much as Tabs was showing.

* * *

When Abigail was well enough to leave the hospital, Henry agreed to fetch her but when he brought her to the house, he didn't speak a word to Ruth. He and Jack helped Abigail in and settled her in an armchair beside the fire.

'Can you tell us what happened?' Ruth asked, when Henry had gone.

'The burglary, the mess. I was so upset and I couldn't imagine sleeping in the bed those filthy people had used. I dragged it outside and set it on fire. Better to sleep on the cold slate floor than that. I didn't know where I'd find another one but I couldn't have let my mother sleep on it after the filth they had left. I propped it against a dead tree and it fell, caught the curtains alight — they had broken all the windows you see. And before I realized what was happening, the door was ablaze and I was struggling with the front door when the fire brigade arrived. Someone passing had seen the flames and called them.' She looked exhausted and they helped her upstairs and into the room prepared for her. She was asleep before they had left the room.

There was no sign of anyone when Tabs left for the shop the next morning. She called and no one answered. Unwilling to knock on the bedroom door and introduce herself so early, she went to the shop. At lunchtime she went home. She wanted to see the woman who was so important to Jack. He was sitting beside the pale, doll-like woman and he didn't move when she walked in.

'Hello, I'm Tabs,' she said, approaching the armchair where Abigail sat wrapped in blankets and surrounded by cushions. 'We didn't get the chance to say more than hello, yesterday.'

'Hello — Tabs?'

'Tabitha.'

'I'm so sorry to cause so much trouble.'

'Lucky Jack's here to keep an eye on you; it's one of Ruth's busiest days. Can I get us all something to eat? Ruth won't be back until teatime. Will a sandwich do?'

Abigail looked at Jack and waited for him to answer. Tabs tightened her lips. The expression was well known to her, she had been deferring to her father for the simplest decisions most of her life. But she guessed that Abigail's need for guidance wasn't out of fear, her eyes told her it was love and adoration. Shivers goosed her arms as she went into the kitchen. Abigail was more than the ex-fiancée of a friend, that much was clear. She was far more important to Jack than that.

Abigail's mother arrived two days later and again, it was Henry to brought her from the hospital. She was a lively character and when Aunty Blod came to meet the new arrivals the two elderly women were soon laughing and chattering like old friends.

Between working and providing food for them all Ruth was busy every moment of the day and when Henry called and asked her to go out with him for a meal and a chat she refused.

'If you want to tell me goodbye I'd rather you do it here, not far away in a strange place. Here is where I live—'

'—and it's here you want your memories stored? Saying goodbye to me is just another one, is that it?'

'No, Henry, it isn't. I don't want to say goodbye to you, not ever, but I could hardly argue about marrying you in a restaurant where we'd provide the cabaret, could I?' She smiled, persuading him to smile too but he shook his head.

'There is no reason to wait so unless you marry me before the end of this year I'll get out of your life. I want a wife, a home and a family. You can't want the same if you're content to stay here and prop up your brothers like an ageing aunt!'

That evening Tabs and Ruth went to the pictures. Neither became absorbed in the film, they were both worrying about the men in their lives.

'I'm very fond of Jack,' Tabs said, as they waited in a queue for fish and chips to take home for supper. 'But I think Abigail is more important than he admits.'

'Nonsense. He's a caring man and if he promised his friend he'd look after her, then that's what he'll do. You're lucky to have such a kind and loyal man.'

'If he chooses me,' Tabs sighed.

'I don't think Henry and I will marry,' Ruth said.

'But I thought you'd been together for ever? What's gone wrong?'

'Me. I've gone wrong. I've looked after my brothers for so long I can't stop. I've let Henry down and I think he'll walk away from me someday soon if I can't get my mind away from being a surrogate mother to four grown men. It sounds so ridiculous when I say it out loud, but no one understands how difficult it is.'

'Talk to your brothers.'

'I have and when I do they agree with me that the home is mine until I no longer need it. It's my home.'

'Then you're cheating them!' a voice behind them hissed and, startled, Ruth and Tabs turned to see Tabs's mother-in-law, Martha, smiling at them. 'You must see that the money would be handy. They all need it at the moment, but you're sitting on their inheritance when they all need it desperately.'

'I'm sorry, Mrs Bishop,' Ruth replied politely, 'but my family isn't your business. And I don't want my affairs discussed in a chip shop!'

'A divorce in the family I hear. That's expensive for sure. And babies on their way. Plenty to buy with babies on the way. One coming a bit too soon is what I've been told. Desperate they must be, longing for you to up stumps and move.'

Embarrassed by Martha's loud voice and the waggling ears all around them, Ruth dumped the money for their supper in Tabs's hand and walked away, her face red with shame.

'You shouldn't have done that,' Tabs told Martha, wanting to run after her friend. 'She's never done you any harm.'

'Maybe not, but I can do you a favour, my dear. We haven't let our smart new bedroom yet, so what if your father and I offer the room to the latest addition to Ruth's household? Abigail, is she called? And that mother of hers? Comfortable with us they'd be and if they came to us, we'd be doing you a favour, you being sweet on Jack. We can keep an eye on them, make sure there's no funny business between him and that Abigail. You can come home, Jack can visit you, and we'll be one happy family, us three and two ladies to share our happy home. Put it to them, why don't you, I'm sure they'd be pleased to get into a beautiful room like ours.'

'Next, please,' the woman behind the counter shouted, and Tabs was saved thinking of a reply as she gave her order and handed over the money. She hurried out with the steaming packages before anything more could be said. As she walked back she wondered how her stepmother managed to find out all that was going on. Her information was accurate and up to the minute. She must have a huge network of people spying for her. She imagined Martha sitting pondering over all she had learned and putting everything together like a general in an army, planning how she could use it.

She sat down on a garden wall and wished she had such an efficient network herself. She needed to know a way to find out, accurately, what Jack really felt about Abigail, wondering whether knowing would make her happier. Somehow she thought not.

Tabs told Ruth about Martha's offer in a tone that implied that the idea was too ridiculous to even consider. To her relief Ruth laughed and shook her head. 'I don't think that's a good idea, Tabs. Martha would have you installed in that tiny room and treated like a servant before they'd unpacked their belongings.'

Hesitantly, Tabs asked, 'What d'you think of Abigail, Ruth? Jack says she's just a friend he promised to look after, but is she more than that?'

'It's hard to say. They haven't been staying with us long enough, but if you're really fond of Jack, why don't you ask him?'

'I can't. I'm fond of him, very fond, but I don't know how he feels about me.'

Ruth hugged her and said no more, relief that it was Jack and not Henry who was causing her the concern that was making her more talkative than usual.

That evening Jack came to see Abigail and Gloria but he didn't stay long. Instead, he persuaded Tabs to go for a walk. 'I'll leave, then wait for you at the corner,' he whispered as she handed him his coat. 'Just you and me at last! I can't wait to see you without all the hangers-on.'

Trying to hide her excitement she made an excuse of needing some fresh air and almost ran to the corner where Jack was waiting. He held her close and kissed her passionately then with arms around each other they made their way to the park gates and slipped through. It was dark, the only street lamps too far away to shed light on the place, which was surrounded by old trees and overgrown bushes.

In the centre of the park was a small building that had once been used by a park keeper. Now it was neglected, park keepers a luxury no longer afforded. It was used occasionally to hold tools, but at that moment practically empty. Jack shoved against the door which opened silently and they kissed as Jack moved her into the greater darkness inside.

It was one of their regular places to sit, and make plans, to dream of a future which beckoned; to an escape from the misery of her father and Martha. The world as seen from the inside of the old shed promised a wonderful life with Jack. Making love quickly become an urgent need. For Tabs it was an inevitable extension of their growing love, as natural as breathing. Ignoring the cold, they slowly undressed each other.

***

As they walked back to the house Jack stopped and held her close. 'You know how I feel about you, don't you? I hate every moment we're apart. But I have to go away for a while. I've been promised a job in Norfolk.'

'Norfolk? But that's the other side of the country! Why do you have to take it? Can't you find something nearer than Norfolk?'

'I need the money to get Abigail and Gloria into a place of their own, just a couple of rooms, then I can walk away, leave them to sort out the rest of their lives, I'll have done what I promised.'

'Can't they stay with Ruth? When — if — I move out there'll be plenty of room and Ruth will value their company, she hates the house being empty.'

'Come on, Tabs,' he said sharply. 'You can't expect them to stay as lodgers for much longer. Abigail is used to better things.'

'How long with you be away?' She pressed her cheek against his, whispering the words, alarmed at the anger in his tone.

'How do I know? I don't have to report every move to you, do I? What sort of a life will we have if you treat me like a child, demanding a timetable of my day-to-day activities?'

Frightened by the unexpected and unreasonable anger, Tabs said nothing more. Jack increased his pace and removed his arms from around her. When they reached the gate they were almost running and she tentatively asked if he was coming in for some supper.

'What, to sit and smile for the others while you ask more of your inane questions? No thanks.' And he walked off.

She stood outside the house for a long time, trying to convince herself that he would come back, tell her he loved her. She waited for more than an hour but he didn't come.

She went inside and smiled at Ruth and the others, made herself a hot drink and was in bed when the horror of it struck her. The quarrel had been a deliberate set-up. He had wanted to quarrel. For whatever reason, he wanted to end their affair and had engineered the whole thing and immediately after making love in their special place where the night had been filled with promises and redolent with love.

She walked the streets the next day between the hours she worked and said nothing about it to anyone. The wandering was fruitless and pointless as she had no idea where he lived. Had he gone to Norfolk? How could she possibly get in touch with him if he was so far away? She wasn't even sure where Norfolk was, apart from knowing it was a long way off.

When she burst into tears one morning, Henry closed the shop, led her up to the flat and coaxed her to tell him what was upsetting her. When she explained about the quarrel and being unable to find Jack, and the presumption that he was in Norfolk, he smiled. 'He certainly isn't in Norfolk. I saw him yesterday.'

'Where?' she asked, relief causing the pent-up tears to flow.

'I'll show you where he was standing. I presume it was where he was living as he looked as though he had just stepped out of the front door. Quarrels can quickly be mended. Come on, wash your face and give it a smile.'

They searched for several hours, knocking on doors asking at the local shops but no one had seen him. 'As we've only our description of him and no second name, it's not surprising no one is able to help. Our enquiries sound weaker every time I offer them,' he said. 'But, Tabs, if you're seriously involved with this man, why don't you know where he is and at least have a name?'

'I daren't ask, I was so afraid of driving him away.'

Henry thought that might have been a good thing but said nothing.

They went back to Henry's flat where he put the kettle on and put out bread and some cheese. 'Hungry?' he asked. 'I am.'

She opened her bag and pulled out two packets of sandwiches. 'I make them every day, hoping he'll meet me in the park like he sometimes does,' she said, and the tears began again.

* * *

Ruth was not being kept up to date with Toni's pregnancy, no reports of mysterious twinges and false alarms, so it was with mixed feelings she learned that her baby was born. Ruth had visited as often as she dared — Toni still giving broad hints reminding her that she wasn't welcome at the flat too often — so the actual birth came as a complete surprise and a hurtful one. She had been expecting to be needed, to comfort Toni and to be there when the baby began to announce its arrival, but the first she heard was when Tommy burst in, closely followed by his brother, Bryn, shouting the news before the door was open.

'I'm a dadda!' Tommy shouted.

'It's a baby boy and he's beautiful!' Bryn echoed.

'Bloomin' marvellous she was, my Toni!' Tommy was still shouting, his face red with excitement. 'None of that screaming like you see in the pictures, We never heard a sound until Samuel cried to let us know he'd arrived!'

'Bloomin' marvellous she was,' Bryn echoed.

'Samuel, that's what he's called, Samuel Thomas.' Then they were both talking at once and it was some time before Ruth learned that Brenda and Bryn had been waiting at the hospital with Tommy until they were told the news.

Ruth almost demanded to know why she hadn't been informed, why she hadn't been there, at the hospital, one of the first to hear the news, but she managed to swallow her disappointment. Toni had made it quite clear from the beginning that family or not, a sister-in-law wasn't the most important person in their lives — by a very long way. 'So how soon can I see baby Samuel then?'

'Soon. And be prepared to be amazed. He's so handsome you'd never believe!'

Ruth hugged them all, made tea, brought out the cakes and biscuits and, when they had gone dashing off to tell their friends, she went to see Henry. At least she'd be the first to tell him.

To her surprise the shop was closed. Tabs had left for her work at the newsagent's that morning explaining that she wouldn't be home until 5.30 as she was working at Henry's shop in the afternoon, helping him to clean and sort some china and glassware he had bought. So where were they? She tried the side door which led up to Henry's flat and walked quietly up the stairs, part of her wanting to turn and run, afraid of finding them together.

To her shock and dismay they were together. She released a breath that was a sigh, an almost silent wail of disappointment. Henry's arms were around Tabs who was obviously crying. Ruth hesitated at the door unable to move. She wanted to run but her muscles had locked. Henry heard the small sound and gently turned Tabs and led her to a chair. He stepped towards her and said, 'Sorry, Ruth, but this isn't a good moment. Meet me in an hour and we can take her home together.'

She ran down the stairs and out of the door and, without stopping, ran blindly across the road. A car caught her swinging coat and she fell to the ground.

Henry's face appeared momentarily at the window as he looked to see the reason for the squealing brakes. Then he was there, holding her, persuading her not to get up until help came, and behind him, Tabs watched and blamed herself.

She wasn't hurt and after a visit to the doctor who advised her to rest and prepare for aching muscles, Henry took her home. There was no sign of Tabs.

'She's admitted she's been stealing from the shop,' Henry told her, when they were alone. 'Jack's influence, I'm sure of that.'

'Why didn't you call the police?'

'I don't know. I feel sorry for her. She'll do anything for this Jack. He's probably the first person to show her love.'

'What about me? Knowing she's a thief you say nothing and let her stay in my house? Where do I come in all this, Henry?'

'I don't know. You tell me where you come in my life.'

'Below thieves, con men and pathetic women like Tabs, that's where.'

'Then you'll tell her she must go?'

Her shoulders drooped. 'You know I can't. You might be a fool, Henry but I must be one too.'

He hugged her and held her for a long time without another word.

CHAPTER SEVEN

Ruth looked out at a dreary morning where dark clouds and drizzle looked set for the day. She gathered her rain cape and boots. Today's round was a long one, fairly spread out and she would be cycling all day in rain by the look of the sky.

'I wish Henry would appear and offer to drive me around,' she said, as Tabs was also getting dressed to leave. 'He sometimes offers but I can't rely on him being available.'

'Oh, he won't be free today,' Tabs told her. 'He's taking me to the dentist as it's a long way to walk from the bus stop.'

'Oh? That's kind of him.'

'He insists and I must confess I'll be glad not to get a bus and then walk in this awful weather.'

And it doesn't matter about me cycling around in it all day, Ruth thought, angry at Tabs's casual acceptance of Henry's help. Anger stayed with her and she finished the round earlier than normal. It had rained heavily all day and almost as soon as Ruth arrived back from her collecting, soaked through and feeling very cold, Henry arrived.

'Why didn't you phone? As it happens I was free today apart from one errand and I could have driven you.'

'Why should I bother you?'

Speaking quietly but with an edge of irritation, he said, 'I can't understand you behaving like this.'

'Can't you?'

'Ruth, this is childish, are you sulking because Tabs was upset and I was comforting her?'

'She was your errand today too.'

'Yes, she was.'

'She can't be trusted. And as for that Jack, who knows who he is? She invited him into my house at night, remember? I don't know anything about him and very little about Tabs.'

'I'm sorry I asked you to go away and come back in an hour. That was very rude. But Tabs seemed on the point of talking about something and I didn't want to discourage her. If I'd been given the chance I'd have explained,' he added pointedly.

'I'm tired,' she said petulantly, and he stood to leave.

'Please, Ruth, don't tell Tabs to leave. She'll go back to her father and stepmother who will ruin everything you and I have achieved. I have her word she won't do anything dishonest again. It was the fascination of this man, the first time a man has shown any interest in her. It was such a thrill and she just wanted to please him, couldn't face losing him. In some ways Tabs is still a child.'

'Money was missing from my collections on three occasions. I didn't say anything before, I was hoping against foolish hope that I was wrong.'

'What? That wouldn't have been Tabs! She wouldn't have stolen from you!'

'Then who? My brothers?'

'It can't have been Tabs. Besotted with this man she might be, but there's a limit to what she'd do to please him. If she does see Jack again he won't be able to persuade her to do anything as stupid. I pointed out that a gaol sentence could have been the outcome if I'd phoned the police that day and she knows that next time I will.'

'Will you?' She looked doubtful.

'I don't think she'll be employed by me for much longer so, hopefully, I might not have to make that decision.' Irritatingly he didn't tell her any more but quickly changed the subject.

'Whatever she's done, please don't tell her to leave here. You've helped her so much. Don't waste it.' He bent towards her as though to kiss her but instead he just patted her shoulder and went out.

She closed her eyes but not out of tiredness. She wanted to hide away, like an ostrich burying its head in the sand. She closed her eyes, screwed them up and wondered how she could ever put things right. She knew she had been childish and utterly stupid.

Tabs came in and nervously asked whether she had to leave.

Ruth's voice was harsh as she asked, 'Where will you go?'

'Back to Dad and Martha, I suppose. At least she'll be pleased.'

'You can stay, Tabs, but remember that this is my home and I have a say on what happens here and who comes in. Didn't you realize that you were risking having a criminal record? Jack obviously doesn't think very highly of you if he can put you in such a position. Forget him, Tabs. There are plenty of really decent young men out there, men who would appreciate all the good things you have to offer.'

Tabs wanted to argue, defend Jack, but she was afraid to say anything apart from 'Thank you'. From Ruth's expression she was likely to change her mind, and living here under sufferance was better than living at home with Martha.

Uneasy at the thought of Tabs's dishonesty and thinking about the missing money, Ruth decided to give up her job. Having money in the house might be one temptation too many. Despite Henry's trusting belief in her, it must have been Tabs or Jack who had taken the money from her collections.

She didn't want to start another argument with Henry, so she told him she was too busy to continue working. He didn't comment but waited for her to explain. 'Mr Burrows was disappointed but he's accepted my resignation with a month's notice. I'll finish at the end of the year.'

1955 would start with everything changed. She shivered nervously as she wondered whether her new beginning would include Henry, and what she would do if it did not.

Henry said very little, but thought the coincidence was surprising. He too had decided to change his life around and, like Ruth, he hadn't quite made up his mind where the next steps would take him, although an idea kept re-occurring.

* * *

Meeting Tommy and Toni's baby that evening took Ruth's mind off Henry and Tabs and her own idiotic behaviour. Tommy came in carrying little Samuel with Toni hovering close by. They were followed by Brenda, carrying a basket with all the myriad needs for a baby's brief visit. A space was cleared for the wicker cot, carried by Bryn, and the baby was ensconced on his new blankets to be admired.

A lot of teasing went on with Bryn reminding Tommy that he and Toni only had the limelight until March when his child would be born.

'Close enough in age to be friends,' Tommy said happily.

Toni had brought some of the cards they had received, including ones from Emrys and Susan, and from Geraint, with a separate one from his estranged wife, Hazel. After they had gone, a sadness overcame Ruth. Even with the new guests and Tabs still there, the place seemed empty after the lively visit. The house had always been so full of people: chattering, demanding food, creating laughter from everything.

She called to see Henry the following morning but when he invited her out for the day the following Sunday she refused, explaining rather weakly that Bryn and Brenda, Tommy and Toni might be coming. 'Glad of a meal made ready for her Toni will be. Having a baby to care for must be so exhausting,' she had said.

'You've invited them?' he had asked, and when she had shaken her head he had complained and they had argued.

She was standing outside as she said, 'I'll always welcome my family, but I am tolerating Tabs to please you, remember!'

'Ruth, you do nothing to please me, in fact, I wonder what you're doing here.'

'In that case I'll leave!' She ran along the street, not aware of the lady approaching from the corner.

Rachel, Henry's mother, was approaching Henry's shop when she stopped. Henry was outside talking to Ruth and, from their demeanour they were not happy. Ruth was exaggeratedly upright, looking slightly away from Henry. He was looking down at her, saying something Rachel couldn't hear and Ruth was shaking her head. Then Henry gave a brief nod and disappeared through the shop doorway. Ruth turned and ran away. With a sigh, Rachel wished it was Henry who was running away. There seemed little chance of a happy ending for them. She called and waved and he came towards her, smiling a smile that failed to reach his eyes.

'Hello, Mum, what are you doing around here? Coming to see me?'

'I had to call on someone the other side of the park so I thought I'd come and have a cup of tea.'

He led her to the shop and called to Tabs. 'I'm off to the café, Tabs. I'll be about half an hour.'

When they were sitting in the café with tea and toasted teacakes in front of them, Rachel said,' Henry, dear, why don't you have a holiday?'

'In November?'

'Why not? It's a change of scenery you need, not a warm sea to paddle in! You'd benefit from a few days away from the shop and the phone calls and the rest of it. Weather is secondary to all that.'

'What about the shop?'

'Couldn't Tabs do the extra hours?'

He hesitated a moment then said, 'Mum, Tabs has been stealing.'

'Then why is she still there? Didn't you call the police?'

'No. It was someone she loves desperately who persuaded her. I frightened her with visions of prison and I doubt if she'll be so stupid again.'

'Loving someone isn't an excuse for becoming a criminal, dear!'

He gave a twisted smile. 'I wish someone loved me half as much.'

'Ruth, you mean?'

He nodded sadly.

'Ruth loves you but her previous love keeps getting in the way.'

'That's too deep for me, Mum. What previous love? D'you mean her brothers?'

'Not exactly. She can't let go of the role she's played for so many years, the role of parent, housekeeper and all round good egg.' She said it lightly, watching his face to see whether she dare say more. Then she went on, 'She's seen the twins through from scraped knees and droopy socks, to handsome bridegrooms and proud fathers. They were only twelve when their parents died, remember. She coped with them through playground fights, stroppy, argumentative schoolboys, and through the difficult growing-up-and-knowing-it-all years and through the agonies of unrequited love. She did a wonderful job, but she can't see that her work is done, that it's time to let go.'

Henry declined to answer, instead he said, 'Tabs's love is very strong, even though it was misguided enough to lead her to behave stupidly. Jack is the first one and he came when she had given up hope of love and marriage.'

'And she was persuaded to steal for him?'

'She was desperate to please him, afraid of losing him, poor girl.'

'Ah, that's a different kind of love again. Poor Tabs hasn't had a very happy time, has she?'

'Her father used her to make his life more comfortable and then she meets a man who talks about love, and she'd do anything to prevent him leaving her. Anything.'

'He's using her too, but she can't see that. All she can see is the emptiness she'll return to if he goes, so hers is a desperate love.' Before he could comment she added, 'A sad parody of love. It's up to you to make Ruth see what real love is; equal, happy, fulfilling love, or, my dear, you must walk away.'

The coffee and the teacakes were cold, the butter congealed and they pushed them away. Henry went to pay for the uneaten snack and she waved and went out. She didn't want any further talk to take what she had said away from the front of his mind.

He went back to the shop but it was closed for lunch. Tabs had left a list of messages and people he needed to contact. He was glad to be alone; his mother's comments wouldn't leave his mind. He left a note for Tabs and drove to one of the lonely, rarely found beaches on Gower. There he sat in the car and tried to concentrate on where his next move should be. It was cold and drizzle covered the windows so he couldn't see ahead of him and that, he decided, exactly suits my present mood! He saw the woman with the dog, walking towards the beach but didn't call. He enjoyed her company and would have been glad to lose his worries for a while in pleasant conversation, but decided not to inflict his company on her while he was in such a morose mood. He sat for a long time before driving away.

* * *

Tabs was in the park, oblivious to the biting wind of that November day. There was no sign of Jack. She spent most lunchtimes sitting on 'their' bench and watching the path in the hope of him appearing. Her feelings were confused. She longed to see him again, to feel his arms around her, to lose herself in his kisses, but the remembered sensations were tinged with guilt: she had been persuaded to steal from Henry and Ruth who had both been so kind to her.

Yet she still couldn't really blame Jack. Guilt for her own share of the criminal acts was a continuous ache. She had been so easily persuaded that there must be something bad at the core of her being. Perhaps her father had been right to keep her from leaving home, perhaps he knew how evil she really was and had been protecting her. Her self-esteem dropped lower than it had ever been and she wished she could run away, and never ever come back. How could she continue to face people, decent people, after what she had done?

* * *

When Ruth went to Tommy and Toni's flat with the excuse of taking them a cake and some pasties, Tommy was at home and Bryn was with him. Toni nodded a greeting of sorts but made no effort to appear welcoming. I suppose I'll just have to get used to it, Ruth thought, forcing a smile for her sullen sister-in-law.

'Finished early,' Tommy explained. 'Working in the park we are, and one job was done and we didn't want to start another. What you got there, Sis? Starving I am.' When they were sitting down, having unpacked the food, Tommy said, 'We saw that bloke today, the one Tabs sees now and again. Jack something or other.'

'Tabs will be pleased he's back,' Ruth said with a frown, 'but I'm not! She told me he was working somewhere far away. Where was he?'

'Up at Johnson's farm looking for work. Didn't get any, mind. There's a hedge wants digging out and some ditches cleared, but he wasn't very keen. He doesn't look the type for heavy work.'

'Too idle for any honest work if you ask me,' Bryn muttered.

While she was at Tommy and Toni's flat, Megan and Mali called with little Mickie. After hearing that the flat they had moved to was not ideal, that the other tenants were still complaining about the child, insisting he was noisy, Ruth left them to their baby talk and went home, relieved to get away.

As usual, Toni had remained edgy, making it clear she wasn't welcome to stay any longer.

That evening she told Tabs that her brothers had seen Jack. Later that evening, covered by a pretence of posting a letter, Tabs went out. She had to find him, talk about things, make sure he understood that she wouldn't help him steal ever again. Her heart was racing. Would he walk away from her? That would prove he had been using her and the loving was nothing more than convenience. Deep down she knew that was the case but the flicker of hope stubbornly remained.

She walked around the places where they had spent some time but there was no sign of him. As she walked she rehearsed what she would say although she knew without doubt that when she saw him every carefully planned word would vanish from her mind.

While Tabs was out on her futile search, Ruth told Abigail and Gloria about her new nephew, boasting about him, and she told Abigail how well Toni and Tommy were coping. To her alarm she suddenly noticed that Abigail was quietly crying. Tears ran down her cheeks and her mother handed her a handkerchief to wipe her face.

'What is it? Are you ill?' Assured she was not, by a concerned Gloria, Ruth asked, 'Have I said something to upset you? I'm sorry.'

'It's all right, Ruth, I'll just get her up to bed.'

'Can I do something?'

'No one can,' Abigail said tearfully. 'I had a baby you see, and talking about your baby Samuel, and Mickie, memories suddenly overwhelmed me.'

'A baby? What happened?'

'He died. I was obviously not a suitable mother and I lost him.'

Ruth glanced at Abigail's hand although she knew full well there was no wedding ring there. Seeing the automatic gesture, Abigail said. 'We weren't married but we love each other and one day we'll be together and then we'll have other children and maybe the pain will ease.'

'Of course,' Ruth said. 'Your husband-to-be, he lives a long way off? He'd have been here when you were in hospital if he'd been able, wouldn't he?'

'He came as soon as he could.' There was hesitation and a slight alarm in the young woman's eyes and at that moment Ruth suspected that the man who had fathered the child was Jack. She hurried out of the room apologizing for asking too many questions and filled the kettle noisily and rattled the tea cups and banged cupboard doors, singing to herself, hoping Abigail hadn't see the expression of horror that must have shown on her face at the thought of Tabs, poor silly Tabitha, being fooled by Jack. Tabs, who at this moment was probably day-dreaming about him, a man for whom she was prepared to steal from friends, a man who was a cheat of the worst possible kind.

Tabs came in, made an excuse about reading in bed and went up. Ruth went into the kitchen to prepare the breakfast table without another word. If only Henry were here. She needed to talk about this but there was no one else she could tell. Suddenly she felt irrational fear, she was alone with only Tabs and two strangers for company and her footsteps echoed as she walked across the kitchen floor. She was a stranger and no longer belonged in the hollow-sounding house.

She took her tea and went to bed to read her library book, hurrying up the stairs as though ghosts were chasing her. The house wasn't her own anymore and she wanted it back, just as it used to be, a place loved by the family. Somewhere safe and friendly, not this place filled with other people's problems making her walk a tightrope of caution every time she opened her mouth.

There was a light under Tabs's door and unreasonably, she blamed Henry for the change in the atmosphere. Why had he persuaded her to let Tabs stay after he'd caught her stealing from him? Why hadn't he called the police? Being completely alone couldn't be worse than this.

The next day, Ruth was writing her weekly letters to Geraint and Hazel in London, and to Emrys and Susan in

Bridgend, describing her nephew with fulsome praise. She usually began the letters at the weekend then waited until Wednesday, when she received theirs, before finishing off and posting them. That way the day-to-day news filled the pages and the replies to their questions and comments were quickly added. So when the post fell onto the mat she went to pick them up, expecting the usual accounts of their week. In Geraint's letter was a request to phone him that evening at nine, a very unusual request; they normally communicated by letter.

Armed with a handful of small coins, she went to the telephone box on the corner. It was very cold and she shivered as she ran towards the lighted box. The night was dark and she wished she had remembered to pick up a torch. She rang the number and Geraint answered at once.

'Geraint? Is anything wrong?' she asked.

'Wrong? Not really, but can I come and stay for a few days?'

'Of course you can, silly. It's your home, isn't it?'

'That's what I want to talk about.' Before she could add further assurances, he went on, 'Look, Ruth, I can't talk now, but I'll see you on Friday. All right?'

She came away from the phone box wearing a frown. Something was wrong, something he couldn't talk about over the phone. She went through all the possibilities. A re-think about the divorce? Confession about an affair? News that he was seriously ill? Then she wondered whether he was about to ask if he could come back home permanently. The frown left her face, her heart raced with joyful excitement and the night became less dark. Friday seemed a long way off.

She stopped before going inside, savouring the thought of being needed again. The night wasn't really dark; the sky was lit with the glow from the street lights in the town, and several windows nearby were un-curtained, allowing early Christmas lights to shine out, and the air was no longer chilly, but crisp with the feel of the season and tinged with happiness.

As she went into the house she wondered if Geraint's visit would justify planning a family Christmas party. The house would love a party, she thought fancifully. It always seemed different when the rooms were filled with people celebrating something; cosy, warm, well used and loved. The house needed people as much as it needed a strong roof.

It was very late on Friday when her brother finally arrived, almost eleven o'clock. To her surprise, Tommy and Bryn were with him and, as she was about to close the door, she was even more surprised to see Emrys coming in behind them.

'Don't tell me you all want to stay,' she said with a laugh. 'I'm definitely not the one who'll be sleeping in the bath!' She hastily set the kettle to boil and took pasties out of the oven. 'Not many,' she said gesturing towards them. 'I didn't expect all of you.' They all looked serious as they found places around the large kitchen table and she felt a growing fear. This was a parody of the party she had imagined, and she couldn't begin to guess the reason for it.

Her hands were shaking as she poured tea for them and her voice, when she spoke, sounded strange. 'Come on then, let's have the bad news.'

Geraint spoke first, while the others lowered their eyes, concentrating on the cup of tea in front of them. 'We want to sell the house.'

'But we can't. It's our home, all of us.'

'Toni and I want to buy a place and selling this would give us a deposit,' Tommy said.

'Me too,' Bryn added quietly. 'The flat isn't big enough now we have a baby to consider.'

'What about Aunty Blodwen? You know how she loves to come here. She needs a break from that tiny place of hers sometimes and it was her home, where she was born and brought up.' No one spoke and she added, a little angrily, 'What about me?'

'That's what we're here to consider,' Geraint replied. 'We're so grateful to you for being there when we needed you, but now things have changed and we all want to go our own way, build a new life.'

'Without me.'

'No!' they all chorused.

'We want you living close and being a part of our lives just like you've always been!' Tommy added.

Ruth stared at him. 'Not any more, not since you and Toni married.' She calmed her voice and added untruthfully, 'I can understand Toni wanting things her way. But she reminds me at every opportunity that I'm no longer needed and it hurts. Now this. I don't know what I'll do if I have to leave here.'

'Marry Henry?' Emrys queried.

'Because it's convenient for you?' she demanded.

'Because it has always been convenient for us to have this place, somewhere to come back to, and have you here for us, but now it isn't convenient any longer,' Geraint said, his voice sounding harsh and even irritable to Ruth's sensitive mind.

'We've all enjoyed having this place as the centre of things,' Bryn said more softly, 'but now it's time for change, you must see that. We're all settled, Ruth, we've all made lives for ourselves, we have homes of our own.'

'We're well aware of how much we owe you.' Tommy added. 'You were so good to us, giving up years of your life to care for us.'

'You did a wonderful job,' Emrys added, 'but it's over and now you're free to do what you want.'

'What I want is to stay here,' she whispered.

'Sorry, Sis, but we think it's for the best, for us all,' Geraint said. 'Including you.'

'And what about Abigail and Gloria? They don't have anywhere else to go.'

'Then they must find somewhere. They aren't part of our problem,' Geraint responded firmly.

'But I am?'

'Of course you are. We have to consider you first of all.'

The one consoling thought in it all, she decided as she went up to bed, was she'd be able to tell Tabs to leave.

The following morning Geraint explained that he would like to stay and do a few repairs and some decorating. Ruth knew it was spiteful, and was ashamed afterwards, but at breakfast time, she told Tabs to leave. 'Geraint will be staying for a while and it won't be convenient as he'll be decorating the rooms, starting with yours,' she said.

Tabs turned away and stared into the fire. Where could she go? This was the worst possible time to be friendless and homeless. Controlling her panic, she said, 'I understand, Ruth and I'm grateful that you allowed me to stay this long. Especially after my stupidity. Really grateful.'

How Ruth hated that word. 'Grateful' sounded as though she did everything grudgingly, 'grateful' was when you did something you didn't want to do and although that might be true in Tabs's case, it certainly wasn't true about the care she had given to her brothers and sisters-in-law or Aunty Blodwen. They were family and she cared for them out of love. Tinged with duty, maybe, but still out of love.

She heard Tabs running upstairs and being sick and guessed the shock had been more than she had shown. She really was a mouse, she thought guiltily and I should have told her in a kinder way. But I've made excuses for her, forgiven her for her actions and she deserved to be upset. Then compassion returned and she went up to see if there was anything she could do.

After dealing with breakfast, she decided to swallow her pride and go to see Henry. She felt completely alone, all her brothers and their wives were against her and she had to try and put things right between herself and Henry, and explain to him why she had asked Tabs to leave.

She stayed less than two minutes. When she told him of the brothers' ultimatum, he told her he knew what they were planning, but was asked not to say anything. She shouted at him and ran out. In the whole, big wide world there was no one on her side.

* * *

Abigail couldn't see her way out of the mess she had created. They needed a home and to achieve that she had to work. But she couldn't work and leave her mother to be cared for by Ruth, who was out at work for most of the day anyway, and without working she couldn't get them a home. Round and around the problem went until she was exhausted with the search for a solution. She had applied for her job back but without a car and the loss of several big customers due to her absence she was refused. Someone else had stepped in and was doing good business and they saw no reason why they should ask the new employee to leave. She knew she had let them down by leaving without notice and without keeping in touch more regularly but her mother's illness and her own miscarriage, followed by the fire that might have cost her her life had been so frightening she had no thought for how much they needed the coverage in the areas she had built up and had so enjoyed.

* * *

Henry had been considering a change. Nothing was right. The business wasn't making him happy any more: it was growing, and recently he had met a man who was approaching retirement but was looking for work in the business he knew best. He had run an antiques shop in a small town outside London for many years and, after selling it and returning to South Wales, had found retirement less than enjoyable.

They had met at an antiques fair, spent a lot of the day together and Henry learned that Peter James's knowledge of furniture was impressive. Henry didn't want a partner; he enjoyed being independent and making his own choices, but he offered to sell the business and Peter looked at the books and the properties and accepted without hesitation.

Henry hadn't mentioned his decision to Ruth. Each time they had met recently she had been on the defensive and any discussion had been impossible. Besides, Henry thought about his mother's words and began to wonder if she had been right, and his wisest move was to walk away.

Ironically, Ruth heard about the shop being offered for sale, not from Henry as she might have expected, but from Tabs. That made the news even more difficult to accept. There was something in the old saying, 'Don't shoot the messenger', as her anger was as much towards Tabs for telling her as towards Henry for not.

She went to the shop when she finished her collections but he wasn't there. She badly wanted to talk to him but in this instance was glad he wasn't at home. She would have made a difficult situation much worse by walking in and complaining at being excluded from such an important decision.

She calmed down and rode back to Ty Gwyn. It was time for her to decide what she wanted from life and whether she could imagine living a life without Henry. She wondered where he was and mused sadly that until recently she would have known exactly what his plans were.

Henry was on the way to Rhossili. He stopped at the house where Lillian lived and knocked on the door. She came around the side of the house, holding a heavy raincoat around her shoulders explaining that the front door was stuck again.

She invited him into a room that was beautifully decorated with holly and ivy and strings of Christmas cards, and he handed her a box of cakes he had brought.

'Problems, Henry?' she asked, placing the cakes onto a plate.

'I've sold the business. All three shops and I'm not quite sure what I want to do next,' he told her.

She laughed. 'You're certainly a man of surprises. Well done. I'm all for having fresh horizons to yearn for.'

'I don't know what horizons I'm looking for, at least, my ideas aren't exactly firm.'

'What about Ruth? Doesn't she have an idea of what she would like? You must have discussed it before taking such a drastic step? I presume this is partly to find something you can both share.'

'Ruth knows the shop is sold and unfortunately she found out from Tabs before I could talk to her. It happened very suddenly, you see.'

'That was unfortunate.' She refilled his teacup and patted his shoulder. 'If Ruth is to be a part of this new stage in your life, you must talk to her. Involve her in every stage. Take her somewhere quiet and explain how you feel.'

'She is as slippery as an eel when I try to talk about our future.'

Lillian thought it wise not to offer her comments on what seemed to be an obvious move — saying goodbye to a woman who can't or won't make up her mind! Instead she asked, 'Where will you live after the shop is sold?'

'There's a house which I took Ruth to see a few months ago and I think it might be perfect for the idea I have in mind.'

'When you're ready to talk, come and I'll listen,' she promised.

He didn't drive straight back to the shop, instead he went to the house on the common he had shown to Ruth and spoke to the owner, who was still looking for a buyer.

* * *

Geraint had begun the work on the house, Tabs was packing ready to leave and, ignoring them both, Ruth began to prepare for Christmas. She was being stupid, she knew that. Over the Christmas period she would be sitting in the house alone, while her brothers and their wives celebrated in their own way.

Geraint had told her he would be going back to London to see about starting up his new business; Toni and Brenda, Tommy and Bryn had their plans made. Susan and Emrys asked her if she'd like to spend the few days with them but Ruth declined. 'I'll be needed here for Aunty Blod, and several friends will be popping in,' she lied. 'But I'll help with some cooking if you like.' She knew as she spoke those words that she had laid herself open for another rejection. Smiles, apologies and that word 'grateful' were repeated, but, 'no thanks' was the message.

She sat in the silent house while Geraint was out buying more supplies and Tabs was at work and she listened to the silence around her, and the emptiness filled her with dread. This was her life from now on into the empty years ahead. Wherever she lived, in this house or another, or a soulless flat somewhere, she would face every day alone.

Her job would finish in a couple of weeks and she knew she had to get another. That might open up her life a little, but the truth was that she didn't want her life opened up to other people. She belonged here, in this house, providing a base and security for her brothers and their families. She ignored the small voice within her that warned her the role she envisioned playing didn't exist anymore, and maybe it never had. Her position had always been temporary, so why couldn't she accept that and move on?

She told Henry that she would miss the farm visits. Talking to the people who lived and worked in the country had been a joy, her interest in the wild flowers had increased and the sights she had been shown of some of the shy animals that lived their secret lives alongside man had been fascinating. She and Henry had spent hours walking the cliffs and fields and their knowledge was growing, adding to the pleasure of the walks. But those outings were rare now, since her inability to accept change had spoilt so much between them. Perhaps, once the house was sold and she was settled in wherever she decided to live, she and Henry would revert to the loving friends they had always been. She admitted to herself that most of the change had to come from herself, and wondered if Henry still cared enough to give her a chance. Telling Abigail she and her mother would have to leave was more difficult than telling Tabs. She guiltily admitted to herself there had been a certain glee in telling Tabs she must go, but Abigail seemed so frail and helpless, depending on Jack to help her.

'Do you have any idea where Jack can be?' she asked Abigail, after explaining about selling the house. 'Or when he'll be back?'

Abigail shook her head. 'He travels around getting work wherever he can, trying to raise money to help us. But we can't rely on him now. I don't know how to get in touch with him and after Tabs persuaded him to steal from Henry he can't come back here, can he?'

'Tabs persuaded him? I understood that he persuaded her!'

'Jack works hard, but he's never been dishonest, until he met Tabs.'

Ruth was confused, and couldn't accept what Abigail was saying, she disliked Tabs who had let her down so badly but she was such a mouse, how could she have found the courage to steal from Henry? She must have been persuaded by Jack. She said nothing more. Gathering the plates and cutlery from the dresser she set the table for lunch.

'I have found a job,' Abigail told her then. 'But I don't know whether I can take it, and I don't know how we'll manage if I don't.'

Ruth sat at on the couch and waited for her to tell more.

'I can't do the job I was doing before. I let them down, you see, with Mum being ill and . . .'

She hesitated and Ruth said, 'The loss of your baby.'

'But I've been offered a position as sales lady in a fashion shop within a large store and I can't take it unless someone will look after my mother and there's no one. I don't know when Jack will be back.'

'Does she need looking after? What will happen when you find a place of your own?'

'It's just for the next few weeks. Until I feel sure she's fully recovered. Then, with a flat nearby where I can see her every lunchtime, I'll be happier leaving her.'

'All I can do is say you can stay with me until the house is sold. After Christmas I'll be here all day. If that helps?' The woman thanked her profusely with relief showing on her smiling face. Ruth wondered how Henry would react and thought a smile unlikely. Or, that little voice whispered, perhaps he will smile, if he no longer cares.

* * *

Tabs moved back to her father's house, the worst possible place for what she had to deal with over the next few months. She squeezed herself and her few belongings into the small cramped room. She was determined not to become Martha's unpaid housekeeper but soon found herself preparing breakfast for the three of them and on occasions for paying guests too. It would soon be Christmas and she imagined herself sitting alone in her over-filled room except when Martha asked her — oh so politely — to help with something. It was a small defiance, but she went out every evening before the dishes were cleared and walked around the town. If it rained she went to the pictures, if not, she would dress as warmly as possible and walk around the places where she had seen Jack. One day he would reappear, she was sure of it.

* * *

Three days before Christmas, Geraint went to do some shopping. He bought a gift for each of the family he expected to see on Christmas Day. Ruth watched indifferently as he placed them under the tree. There were very few parcels there, where usually everyone placed their gifts ready for the grand opening session on Christmas morning.

For the first time she could remember, Aunty Blodwen wasn't coming to spend Christmas with her. Aware that the boys were all going elsewhere, Blod explained that she would stay with a friend. 'I thought Geraint was decorating the room I usually have and I didn't want to be a nuisance,' she had explained on a brief visit. 'I'm grateful for all the Christmases you've looked after me,' she went on.

There it was, that word again!

'I want you here,' Ruth insisted.

Blodwen shook her head. 'Tommy's wife explained how we were all taking advantage of you, so I've arranged to spend the day with my neighbour Mrs Harrison.'

'Our Christmas is nothing to do with Toni!'

'I know, dear, but she was only thinking of you, being kind.'

Ruth's first instinct was to tell Henry but she stopped the thought as soon as it begun. She had quarrelled with Henry. She had made it clear that he was less important that her absentee family. She was on her own. Then, to her surprise she had two invitations. One came from Mrs Harrison, Aunty Blod's neighbour. She invited her to spend the day with her and Blodwen, but before she could consider how to reply, Henry came.

He knocked on the door and walked in, and handed her a card which also held a note. He waited silently when she read it. 'It's from your mother, inviting me to spend Christmas with her.' She stared at him in surprise. He quirked an eyebrow in a silent question. 'But I can't,' she said.

'Why not?'

'I can't leave the house, the others might come for a meal, or — I just can't. Sorry. Will you explain to your mother?'

'Can't, or won't?'

'Oh, don't start all that again.'

'I'll call for you at eleven on Christmas morning.' As she began shaking her head again, he added, 'Be ready, unless you really want to spend Christmas Day alone. You have a choice — this year. Next year you might not.'

Was that a warning of his intention of saying goodbye? She watched him go and with tears in her eyes glanced at the calendar. It was ominously empty of any star markings, denoting visits.

* * *

Tabs stood watching Ty Gwyn, wishing she was still living there. Curiosity had brought her there. She was doubtful of Jack's story of helping a friend. She could see the silhouette of someone inside, walking backwards and forwards, then the figure could be seen slipping into a coat, and winding a scarf around her neck. She recognized Abigail and she was obviously going out. At this time of the evening, there were only the public houses or the chip shop to entice someone to brave the bitingly cold wind. She shivered as she watched the door and waited.

She was rewarded a few minutes later by seeing Abigail come out, almost unrecognizable in the heavy coat and the thick scarf, lumbering along on thick fur-lined boots. She followed her without difficulty and groaned in disappointment when she went into a bus shelter at the edge of the park. There was no way she could follow her on a bus without being seen.

To her relief two buses passed and she realized that she wasn't getting on, but waiting for someone to get off. Jack! As he jumped off the bus and walked towards Abigail, Tabs didn't know what to do. She couldn't continue to follow; Jack only had to turn round and he would see her. Better then, to go up to them straight away, and see what Jack had to say. But she hesitated before moving towards them and Jack put his arms around Abigail and they kissed. Not a kiss between friends, but a loving, passionate kiss of lovers. Stifling a sob she slowly and cautiously moved towards them, bushes around the bus stop gave her shelter and she was able to stand close enough to hear what Jack was saying.

'I have to see Tabs again, Abi, love. We need her for a while longer. I feel something positive about Ty Gwyn, I'm disturbed by distant memories; things my father told me. This is the place where I'll find my inheritance, and my family. I'm so certain this is where I'll find my inheritance, my father's treasure, if you can be just a little more patient. Darling, I know it's asking a lot but we'll be fine once I get what's mine.'

Tabs couldn't hear Abigail's reply but Jack protested and his words were clear. 'Abi, love, I promised you there wouldn't be anything but an occasional kiss and I've kept my word. You are my love, my only love.'

Tabs's hands moved to her belly where she knew Jack's child was growing. She must have misunderstood; it wasn't easy to hear their words with their faces muffled by their clothes. She tried to change the words she had heard, distorting them, making them say something different, Jack must have been telling Abigail that she — Tabs — was his one true love. It had to be a mistake. How could she cope if it weren't? A baby with no one in the world to help her?

She was shivering with shock and cold and she was afraid to move. She couldn't confront them, not now, she needed to prepare. She would wait, then try to find Jack and tell him about the baby. He wouldn't let her down, not when she had done so much to help him. She saw Jack dig in his pockets and hand something to Abigail.

'Only twenty-two pounds, love, but I'll get some more in a week or so. I'll be back and we'll be together for always.'

Tears slid down Tabs's face, she hadn't misheard that. She stumbled as she tried to move away and she waited, shivering with shock and misery.

Jack kissed Abigail but as he did so, his eyes moved to the bush behind which Tabs was hiding. She couldn't see his eyes or she would have been afraid of the anger they showed. She froze and sighed with relief when he didn't come to investigate. He kissed Abigail again but his eyes were searching the darkness of the bushes wondering who was there. Could it be Tabs? Could she have heard?

Tabs waited until the couple moved away, arms around each other, walking across the road where a bus stopped and hid their goodbyes. Then Abigail hurried back to the house and, stiff with cold and misery, Tabs followed.

Jack hadn't got on the bus and he ran softly across the road and watched as Tabs walked away.

It was late, almost eleven o'clock, and Tabs knew her father would be worried, but she didn't go home. Her unhappiness led her to Ruth.

The house was dark, Ruth's bedroom window showed a glimmer of yellow light behind thin curtains and Tabs guessed she was reading. Almost without thinking, she knocked on the door and called. The lights came on but the door didn't open until Ruth had asked who was there and Tabs sobbed her name and asked to come in.

The fire was still glowing and seeing that Tabs was shivering Ruth added some sticks and fresh coal before putting the kettle to boil and setting out cups and saucers. She didn't ask any questions until Tabs was beside the fire, snuggled up in a blanket and with a hot-water bottle wrapped in another blanket, near her feet.

'Jack, I presume?' Ruth said, as she handed the still shivering girl a cup of cocoa.

'He doesn't love me and I'm going to have his baby,' Tabs whispered.

Ruth felt a twist of pain at the thought of the baby. Tabs didn't deserve a child after the way she had behaved. Surprised at her reaction she wondered whether a desire for a child was dormant in every women, even if they didn't realize it.

'Why were you so stupid?' she asked gently 'He was using you, couldn't you see that?'

'I didn't want to see it,' Tabs whispered.

'Well, what are we going to do now? You'll need help, so will your father support you?'

'Support a daughter who's having an illegitimate baby? I can't see that happening, can you? I'm on my own with this.'

She finished the hot drink while she told Ruth how she had followed Abigail, then she seemed to be suddenly aware of her surroundings. 'Ruth,' she gasped, beginning to rise. 'I'm sorry! I had no right to bother you with all this. I'll go. My father will be worried and — my feet just brought me here, I'm so sorry. So sorry—'

Ruth interrupted her and pushed her gently back in the armchair. 'You're not going anywhere.'

'But my father—'

'I'll phone Henry, he'll tell your father where you are.'

'I'm such a nuisance.'

Ruth went to the phone box and spoke to Henry, who promised to go straight away and tell Tabs's father she was safe and staying with Ruth. 'I'll see you in the morning, and thank you,' he said before ending the call. 'Thank goodness he didn't say he was grateful', she muttered, as she went back to the house.

Tabs was curled up in the swirl of blankets and fast asleep on the couch. It seemed a pity to wake her to put her into a cold bed in a cold room, so she left her, added a little more coal to the fire and settled herself in the chair opposite, wrapped in blankets from her bed, and she too slept.

CHAPTER EIGHT

Tabs rose early and she folded the blankets in which she had been wrapped, and went into the kitchen to make some tea. Ruth was still asleep in the armchair opposite and she placed the tea beside her and prepared to leave. She scribbled a note of thanks and was just opening the door when Ruth awoke. 'Tabs? Stay and have some breakfast, you can go straight to work then.'

Tabs shook her head but she hesitated, not relishing the thought of going back to face Martha. 'I should get back to explain to Martha and Dad.'

'Breakfast first or you might not have time to eat and you have to be sensible now.'

Uncurling from the gloriously warm bedding, Ruth reached for a dressing-gown hanging over the door and padded into the kitchen carrying her tea and sipping it as she went. She drank her tea then began getting out what she needed to cook breakfast, as always, happy to have someone to cook for, but before the pan began to sizzle Tabs came out and said, 'Thanks, Ruth. You're very kind, kinder than I deserve, I know that. But I won't stay. I'll go to the newsagent's early and perhaps leave at twelve instead of one o'clock.'

When Tabs reached the newsagent's, trying to force her unhappy thoughts aside and concentrate on her morning's work, she saw Jack waiting for her.

'Tabs, love,' he whispered as he reached for her hand. 'I've got myself in a bit of a mess.'

'The police?' she asked coldly.

'It's Abigail. I've been helping her because she was the fiancée of a friend, but she's become too fond of me. I'm so embarrassed but I don't know what to do.'

'Kissing her doesn't help!'

'I've kissed her often but it's suddenly become serious and I don't want to hurt her feelings. Please, love, meet me this evening so we can talk about it. I need your help to sort things out without causing her more embarrassment.'

She didn't believe him. Those kisses he shared with Abigail hadn't been friendly pecks on the cheek. Nor were they instigated by a desperate Abigail towards an unwilling Jack. But she desperately needed to talk to him so she agreed to meet him at lunchtime. 'On our very, very special bench,' he said, staring into her eyes. She tried not to be affected and shrank away from him; could she believe anything he said? But she had to talk to him. He had to be told about the baby. Time was passing and soon people will guess. Before Martha found out, she wanted to be able to tell her herself and explain that Jack was supporting her. Surely he would get a job, somewhere to live and marry her once he knew about the baby? She knew she was dreaming, lying to herself, and how pathetic was that?

* * *

After Tabs had gone, Ruth listened to the silence for a few moments then stared at the calendar. In two days' time it would be Christmas Eve 1954 and, so far, there was no one coming to spend Christmas with her except two strangers, Abigail and her mother, Gloria, and they would probably spend much of the time at the new home Henry had found for them, which they were at that moment negotiating to take. They were already gone from her in spirit. How could it have happened? She ruefully counted the invitations she had received by touching her fingers, one by one. Emrys and Susan, Mali and Megan had asked her to spend the day with them and Mickie, and Henry's mother had invited her too. Even Toni had asked her to call in on Christmas evening.

How foolish to have refused them all. She had been so confident that everything would continue this year as in the past ten, that she had turned them all down. Surely her brothers would change their minds? Persuade their wives that this was where Christmas should be spent? Or could it be a joke? Would they come in at any moment, laughing and telling her they had been teasing her? Would this Christmas suddenly rearrange itself and be like all the rest, with four brothers, four sisters-in-law and Aunty Blod filling the house with their chatter and laughter, and demands for food? This was the baby's first Christmas and she should be spending it here, in the family home.

She remembered then that even Aunty Blodwen had declined the invitation that had previously never needed to be sent. There had never been any need to ask any of them, it was a natural occurrence, taken for granted. Christmas was spent here, with her, Ruth Thomas, organizing everything from the turkey and crackers to the bedding and potato peeling. Unreasonably, she blamed Toni.

She put on a coat and scarf, built the fire with damp small coal to persuade it to burn slowly while she was out, and picked up her handbag. She would ask Aunty Blod herself. Aunty Blodwen would surely prefer to come home, rather than spend part of the time with a neighbour? Of course she would. Toni must have convinced her that changing the routine of years was a kindness to her, Ruth, who loved every moment the family spent with her.

She wondered whether to invite Tabs. Surely she would prefer to be away from her stepmother for a few days?

Before opening the door she looked around the house, listened to it. The rooms already felt cold, hollow, as though accepting the changes that she could not. She locked the door behind her and set out for the bus.

* * *

Tabs was in the park, where she and Jack had arranged to meet. Henry saw her there and felt a surge of pity. He took a flask of tea, went out and offered it to her.

'Drink this, Tabs. Although I think you should go home. It's very cold for you to be sitting here.'

'Thanks, but I'm all right. Jack will be here soon. We arranged to meet here at one.'

'But it's only half twelve. At least come and wait in the shop.'

She shook her head, and assured him she was, 'just fine'. How could she tell him that they had arranged to meet at twelve and that Jack obviously wasn't coming?

At two she gave up and went home to where Martha had left a meal congealing on the top of a saucepan of now cold water. She scraped it into the rubbish bin. Still shivering with cold she went out again, this time to see the doctor.

Waiting in the surgery she watched a girl, several years younger than herself, nursing a small baby. Could she do that? Care for a small, helpless, dependent child? The child began to cry and the mother took out a cloth-wrapped feeding bottle, fitted the cloth beneath the baby's chin as a bib and offered the teat to the rosy little mouth. The baby began feeding, frowning with concentration, and the girl looked down at the child with such a loving expression on her face that Tabs wanted to cry.

Her pregnancy was confirmed and Tabs was given several leaflets, a few words of advice and told to make another appointment with the receptionist before leaving. 'If you have any concerns, please come and see me,' the doctor said kindly, aware that Tabitha Bishop was unmarried and with a father not known for his compassionate nature, if the care of his deceased wife was anything to judge him by.

* * *

Ruth knocked on the door of Aunty Blodwen's flat and it was a long time before there was a response. Limping badly, Blodwen smiled and opened the door wide for Ruth to go inside. 'Why didn't you use your key?' Blod asked, heading for the kitchen.

'Forgot it, Aunty. I was in a hurry to see you, hoping I can persuade you to change your mind about coming for Christmas.'

'I think we've scrounged on you for long enough, it's time you did something for yourself. Christmas seems a good place to start. I know Henry's mother has invited you and we think you should go.'

'Toni's idea?' Ruth asked, putting out cups for the inevitable tea.

'Not only Toni, we all think the same, dear.'

'But Toni thought of it first?'

'Maybe, I don't remember. Last week it was. They all called to see me. Tommy and Bryn and Emrys, and their other halves. Brought cakes they did. Hang on, I think there are some left.' Avoiding looking at her visitor she delved into the pantry and brought out a memorial tin of King George and Queen Elizabeth's Coronation and took out a few Welsh cakes.

Although Ruth stated her case, lying a little when Blodwen asked how many were going to be there, her aunt insisted that this Christmas, Ruth must please herself and stop allowing others to dictate her plans. 'If it doesn't stop now, dear, you'll be slipping into old age as the favourite aunty with time for looking after nephews and nieces and no life of your own. Marry Henry before he gives up and looks elsewhere.'

'I can't do that! Marry Henry as the alternative to an empty old age?' The oft repeated protest sounded false. 'That's insulting to Henry as well as me!'

'You don't love him enough then, or those things wouldn't matter, or even enter your head. If that's the case, let him go, dear, give both of you a chance to find the right one.'

Calmer, Ruth asked. 'You've never married, Aunty. Was there ever anyone you loved?'

Blodwen chuckled. 'Quite a few! Too many and too easily forgotten.'

'No one special?'

'No one special.' The sad, nostalgic, expression on her aunt's face made Ruth want to ask more but decided now wasn't the time.

'So,' Ruth said, sipping her tea and reaching for a cake, 'Christmas. Are you sure you won't change your mind?' She wanted to admit that there was no one coming, that she faced a few days with nothing but memories to keep her company but she didn't. It would sound so pathetic, a kind of emotional blackmail, forcing her aunt to change her plans. Life was changing and she'd just have to find the strength to deal with it. Once Christmas was over she'd do just that. Get a job, find a flat, and build a life without using her family as a prop. If she could get through Christmas she'd cope. It would be over in a week, she told herself — knowing it would be a very, very long and empty week.

Blodwen hugged her as she left. 'You must come and visit, mind. Mrs Harrison will be pleased to see you. Remembers you as a baby she does, and talks a lot about your mam. You'll enjoy that.' She closed the door and stood for a long time, listening to Ruth's footsteps fading. She wasn't sure they were doing the right thing, even though it was with the best intentions.

Ruth went home and put the finishing touches to the trimmings, as the decorations were locally called. The tree stood in a corner of the hall, it's twinkling lights ready to greet anyone who called. Branches of fir trees partly sprayed with silver, hazel twigs painted white, holly with plenty of red berries, and a selection of artificial flowers filled every available shelf. Cards fastened to ribbons showered down the walls. It was beautiful but it made Ruth want to weep. She began making mince pies, weighing out a pound of flour. Surely someone will be here to eat them, she thought, and defiantly added a second pound of flour to the bowl.

A knock at the door made her wipe away the tears and answer it. 'Henry! Why didn't you walk in?'

'You locked the door,' he said, smiling. He reached out and put an arm around her shoulders. 'The trimmings look lovely. You've been very busy. Mam has been doing the same. She has decorated every room, including the bathroom would you believe. Won't you change your mind and come, at least for Christmas Day?'

Stupidly, she shook her head. 'I have to be here. The boys and the others are bound to call in sometime during the day and I don't want to be out.'

He pointed to the pile of gift-wrapped parcels under the tree in the hall. 'Shall we go tomorrow and deliver them?'

Again she shook her head. 'If we do that I won't see them being opened.'

'It's all part of life's changes.'

'We'll leave them where they are.'

He nodded and without another word he left.

Abigail and her mother came in, their faces rosy with excitement. 'I've got the job,' Abigail said. 'And unbelievably we have somewhere to live! The rooms Henry found for us are perfect and at a rent we can afford. The landlord has agreed to a small deposit and the rent being paid at the end of the month when I get my first wage. Isn't it amazing how from the depth of despair things can suddenly turn around?'

Ruth agreed but wondered if Henry's reason for helping them had been to make sure she didn't use their lack of somewhere to go as an excuse not to leave Ty Gwyn.

Tabs was the next visitor and she carried two parcels. 'I've brought one for you and one for Henry,' she explained, adding them to the pile. Then she admired the trimmings and sniffed appreciatively at the smell of mince pies cooking.

'I expect Martha's busy too,' Ruth said, taking the first batch of mince pies from the oven. 'Her first Christmas with you and your father — the first one is always special.'

'Very special,' Tabs replied sadly. 'They're going out for the day.'

'Oh? That'll be nice for you.'

'For them, yes. I think it's a lovely idea.'

'Just them? What about you?'

'Oh, I'll be fine. It's just a few hours.'

'I might be on my own, just for a few hours, so if you would like to eat here . . . ?'

Arrangements were made and Ruth felt even more depressed after Tabs had gone, telling her how grateful she was. If she heard that word again she would scream!

The postman brought a pile of Christmas cards and one, in spidery writing was addressed to Aunty Blod. Ruth put it on one side, and when the cooking was done, took it around for her.

* * *

Blodwen stared at the letter that had been enclosed with the card. There was no signature, just A FRIEND written in capitals. Apart from that there was just a brief sentence asking her to meet someone in a public house called the Yeomen's Arms on Friday 18 February, and not to tell another soul. She screwed it up and put it in the bin. Some prankster, or someone mistaking her for someone else.

Then she took it out, smoothed it and reread it. The envelope was addressed to her, Miss Blodwen Tyler, and the address where she had lived as a child, was correct. She read through the brief note several times but there was no extra information to be gleaned. Again she threw it in the bin, but for some reason, she marked the date on next year's calendar.

Turning back to the December page she stared at Friday 25th, Christmas Day. Could she really leave Ruth alone on that day? No matter how many times Toni and Brenda insisted it was for the best, she knew she couldn't.

She knocked on the wall — a regular way of contact, then she and Cathy Harrison opened their adjoining front doors and greeted each other. As she began to speak, her friend interrupted. 'It's all right, Blod, I understand. I knew you wouldn't really come here for Christmas. You couldn't leave that girl thinking she'd be on her own. Stubborn she might be but there are better ways of persuading her than this.'

'Cathy, d'you know where the Yeomen's Arms is?' Blodwen asked.

'I think it's the one near the prison. Why? Not taking to drink are you, Blod?'

'No, I just heard the name somewhere and wondered where it was, that's all.'

She patted her friend's arm. 'Thanks for not being miffed about me changing my mind. I'll go and tell Ruth I'll be there on Christmas Eve with my little overnight bag.' As she fastened her coat and shut the door behind her, she stopped and went back inside. Taking the creased envelope and letter from the litter bin, she smoothed them again, re-read them and with a frown, put them in her kitchen table drawer, hidden by a chopping board and the clutter of letters that she never managed to sort out. The Yeomen's Arms near the prison? Who can it be and why choose that place?

* * *

Ruth went to the shops after speaking to Blodwen and came back loaded with food. Tabs and Aunty Blod. Abigail and Gloria. It wasn't the same as having the family filling the house but it made the days ahead manageable. Pushing aside thoughts of all the Christmases to come, when Tommy and Bryn would have their babies, and their own celebrations to plan, she began filling tins with cakes and pastries, topping up the dishes of nuts and sweets, and making lists of things to do. It was the same as she always did but this year it had an air of artificiality. She was playing a stupid game of make believe, pretending that this Christmas would be a family time just like the rest. Defiantly, she opened the boxes of crackers and spread them around the room.

* * *

Henry went with a large beribboned box of expensive chocolates and left it in Lillian's porch. Leaving the van parked on the road nearby, he went for a walk. The weather was cold and a gusting wind made him hurry to keep warm. At the point overlooking the beach, he stepped down and found a sheltered spot to sit and watch the birdlife at the tide's edge below him. He took out a notebook and added names to the list he had previously made, making a note also of the date of the entry. He had been filling notebooks like this for years, helped by Ruth. Flowers, animals, insects and birds had been a lifelong interest for them both until she had become so obsessed with caring for her family she no longer had the time. When he returned to Lillian's house, her dog, Sally, was sitting beside his van, watching the road and when she saw Henry, she jumped up and came to greet him.

Lillian waved from the doorway and he called to her, inviting her to go with him and have some lunch. As they sat enjoying the warmth of the restaurant watching the increasingly wild wind outside, he told her of his plan.

'There's a house I've decided to buy,' he began. He described the house to which he had taken Ruth and added her reaction to it. 'But now she knows she really has to leave Ty Gwyn and perhaps will think more positively about what she wants,' he added. Lillian waited silently for him to continue.

'Behind the house is a long garden and beyond it a small woodland with a stream running through it. If I buy the lot, it would make a wonderful place for people to come on holiday. I'd need to take on one extra knowledgeable person, and between us we can take them on walks to see the variety of wildlife and flowers that many pass without noticing. Experts too would love visiting such a place, with Gower on our doorstep and so many beautiful places to visit.'

Lillian didn't say anything and he asked, 'So, what d'you think of the idea?'

'Where does Ruth fit in? You have discussed it with her?'

'I've tried but she's not in a very receptive mood at present.'

'But you want her aboard?'

'Definitely. I hope she will be housekeeper and cook. Feeding people is what she likes best.'

'If she goes into the thing whole-heartedly, you can't fail. It's a wonderful, exciting idea. But you have to talk it through with her now, before everything is underway or she'll feel like an afterthought. Don't wait until it's all arranged and then be surprised when she isn't exactly enthusiastic.

'Difficult,' he said ruefully. 'I've already bought the house and land.'

'Oh dear.'

'It was taking Ruth on her country round and visiting the farmers that gave me the idea. Some of the people I met have agreed to help with expertise and advice. In fact I have already ordered some bird nesting boxes and feeding stations and mapped out some of the walks.'

'Henry. You can't fail!'

* * *

Christmas Day was strange, with episodes of lively chatter as her brothers and sisters-in-law came and went, interspersed by miserable silences with Geraint sitting at the table and eating, then disappearing upstairs to his room. He appeared briefly when his brothers came to exchange gifts and managed to smile as he handed Ruth a parcel containing three hand-embroidered cushion covers. They were beautiful and Ruth was delighted, until he spoilt it by saying, 'I thought they would be nice for your new home.'

None of them stayed long, and Blodwen put on some records of favourite music, Tabs showed them some card tricks and brought out the draughts board. Ruth built up the fire and drew the curtains early, to try and create a cheerful atmosphere but she found herself watching the clock, longing for the day to end.

She thought it was much the same for Abi and Gloria. Christmas was just an interlude before moving into their flat and returning to the life they had lost. Not with as much money, but from what she had been told by Abi, that had been criminally wasted anyway. Every time she glanced at them she had the feeling they were ready to spring up and go. Whereas for her, she wanted to tie herself to the couch and refuse to move.

Each time she passed through the hall she glanced at the parcels still sitting beneath the Christmas tree. They seemed to be glaring at her with disapproval. One from Henry and one for Henry. They could be there until Easter, she thought, although if Geraint had his way she and the parcels would be long gone before that.

As one record ended and Blodwen rose to select another, they became aware of a strange sound. Ruth went upstairs and was angry to discover that Geraint was removing wallpaper from his bedroom ready for re-decorating.

'What are you doing? It's Christmas Day! Are you in so much of a hurry to sell my home?'

'Sorry, but I can't sit and do nothing. Hazel wants everything settled. She and this Eddie Collins are buying me out of the business and it seems she can't wait to get me out of her life.'

'Just like you can't wait to get me out of this house!' Ruth stamped down the stairs and told the others what Geraint was doing.

'Terrible hurt he was, with that wife of his carrying on and having to get out of the business an' all,' Blod said. 'I don't agree with the way he's rushing you, but you have to feel some sympathy.'

'Do I?' Without warning, Ruth burst into tears. 'Everyone has an excuse for behaving badly except me! I'm Ruth, everyone's shoulder to cry on and I don't count!'

'I'd better go,' Tabs said. She put her arms around Ruth and hugged her. 'Can I come again tomorrow?'

'Sorry about this display of temper, but my brother is so selfish.'

Tabs gathered her coat and her gifts. 'I'll see you tomorrow and thanks so much for today.' Abigail and Gloria went to their room.

Upstairs the scraping sound continued.

* * *

There was no friendly greeting when Tabs walked in to see Martha sitting beside the fire and her father handing her a cup of tea.

'Threw you out, did she?' her father muttered.

'No, I thought I'd spend the rest of the evening with you.'

'Glad I am to see you,' Martha said. 'You'll make the casserole for tomorrow, won't you? I'm that tired you wouldn't believe. There's a lot of chicken left and plenty of vegetables.'

'I thought you were going out for Christmas dinner?'

'Changed our minds. Your father wanted to make our first Christmas together special.'

So the day out had been nothing but an excuse to get rid of me, she thought. Without a word she went into the kitchen where used dishes were spread over the table and draining board. Her father followed and nodded towards the bread bin.

'There's plenty of bread, you can make a bread and butter pudding, too. Martha's favourite that is. We're just popping next door for an hour.' He stopped at the door and said, 'There's tea in the pot if you want a cup.'

She thanked him with exaggerated emphasis but her sarcasm was wasted.

At eleven o'clock when the food was cooked she went to bed and tried to read. Like Ruth, it was time for her to rebuild a life for herself. Knowing Ruth and Henry had made her a bit stronger, a little more confident, but the thought of stepping out into the world and soon to have a child to look after, was nothing less than terrifying. She knew nothing would change unless she left this house where was treated like a servant, where she seemed unable to resist their demands. But what alternative was there that might not be worse?

She had reread a page for the second time, forcing herself to concentrate, when there was a knock at the door. Apprehensively she went down, her dressing gown held tightly against her.

'Who is it?' she demanded.

'It's me. Jack. Please don't walk away, I have to talk to you.' As Tabs made no move to open the door, he whispered, 'Tabs, I have to talk to you, I need your help.' Still no movement. 'Tabs, I love you, please open the door.'

The key turned and before she could work out what to say, how to act, she was in his arms and he was moving her towards the stairs.

His love-making was exciting and she succumbed without hesitation, or guilt. His lips worked their magic and even when she heard the door open and Martha call, she didn't react, so wrapt in the happiness of belonging to the man she so desperately loved. His explanations of the conversation she had overheard didn't enter her mind until long after passion faded and a quiet perfect calm filled her with content.

They were silent, smiling like conspirators in the poor light from the street outside, uncomfortable in the narrow bed now their need of each other had eased. They heard Martha and her father come upstairs and go into their own room and they waited a while before Jack whispered, 'I'm sorry about the mess I've made of helping Abigail, but remember, Tabs, it's you I love.'

'Jack, we're going to have a baby.' She felt the jerk as his body reacted to the shock. 'I wanted to tell you before but I waited in case I was mistaken. But now it's definite, I've seen the doctor and it's true. Jack, I'm so happy. You and a child of our own. It's a dream come true.'

'Tabs, that's wonderful.' If his voice sounded flat she wasn't aware of it, so joyful did she feel, with Jack here holding her in his arms and telling her he loved her.

'One of the best parts is being able to walk away from this house where I'm treated like a stupid servant,' she told him. She talked dreamily of their future for a while with Jack adding a word occasionally, holding her close, kissing her cheek but staring into the darkness with panic-filled eyes.

'Tabs, I'm so happy being here with you, holding you in my arms. Listening to your wonderful news was a dream come true for me too, but I have to go. I don't want you having to face your father if he finds me here.'

'Stay. I wake early and I'm always the first to get up. I'm expected to take tea in for Martha. Please, Jack. Let's spend a night together.'

Jack hugged her. 'Darling, I'd love to, but if I sleep for six or seven hours on this damned uncomfortable bed, I won't be able to make my escape in the morning!'

He pretended to succumb to her whispered pleading, promising to stay until morning and lay there wide awake, trying to think of a way out of the mess he had created, until she was asleep. Then he gradually eased himself away from her. He felt his way downstairs and into the kitchen but couldn't find the key to the back door. He tried the front door but that was also locked and the key hidden. Eventually he opened a window, slipped out and pulled it down after him.

* * *

Ruth dismantled the tree and pulled down the trimmings on the day after Boxing Day, far earlier than usual. She had always left them up until Twelfth Night, then they were parcelled up and packed away carefully ready for the following year. This time she pulled them down roughly and stuffed them carelessly into flour sacks given by the baker. Then she went outside and tipped them into the ash bin. So far as her family was concerned, Christmas was no longer a family celebration.

The rooms looked so bare without the artificial brightness. She always hated the moment when the house was stripped of its temporary splendour. Dusting surfaces untouched since the first cards were placed was always the first job but she threw the duster aside and sat listening to the hollow emptiness of the house. Upstairs, Geraint was painting skirting boards and window frames. The wallpaper he had bought was in the smallest bedroom ready for the next stage. She picked up a duster to begin polishing surfaces that had been covered with greenery but again she threw it aside. She couldn't do this. Not today. Tabs was back with her parents, Aunty Blod had gone home to spend New Year with her neighbour. Abigail and Gloria were at their new flat. She was alone apart from Geraint, who came down occasionally to make tea and hardly spoke a word.

She put on her warmest coat and a new scarf she'd been given and went to see Henry. The shop was closed, although most businesses opened for the period between Christmas and New Year. She knocked on the door of the flat but there was no reply. She didn't feel able to go to his mother's home so she walked dejectedly through the park.

Most windows were still lit with coloured lights and occasionally doors opened and laughing groups of people emerged, calling greetings to everyone, including herself. She responded, but believed that the coming year would be the worst year of her life.

It wasn't particularly cold but she snuggled down into her scarf, bending her head as though fighting a chill wind, so she didn't see Henry until she almost bumped into him. 'Henry!'

'Where are you off to?'

'I've just called at the flat but you weren't there and I'm, I don't know, just walking off some of the excess food, I suppose.'

'The van is round the corner; come and see Mum. She'll be pleased to see you and to thank you for the musical box you gave her.' She hesitated almost from habit and he said softly, 'Unless you have some people to feed?'

'No, there's no one home except Geraint and he can jolly well feed himself!' She said nothing more, took his offered arm and walked with him to where the van was parked. She wouldn't talk about Geraint's thoughtlessness! She wouldn't! But she did.

'You'll never believe this, but Geraint has spent Christmas decorating!'

'I know,' Henry said, 'but don't let's talk about it now, let's just have a pleasant hour talking about other things.'

She was immediately on the defensive, ashamed of her weakness in blurting it out moments after promising herself she would not.

'It's all right,' she retorted in a tight voice. 'I know how unimportant selling my home is to you.'

He stopped the car and, when she expected an argument ending with her walking off, he pulled her towards him and kissed her. 'Now we both know Christmas was a disaster so shall we forget it and think of a New Year and a new start instead?'

She stared at him, then reached up and kissed him again.

Rachel Owen had decorated the hall as well as the porch but had used very few decorations around her pleasant room but, Ruth admitted to herself, the effect was perfect. 'Mrs Owen, this is lovely,' she said and meant it.

'I'm sure yours were even better,' Mrs Owen said with a smile, offering a glass of sherry.

She wouldn't tell Henry's mother that she had thrown away everything, an end to family celebrations. She wouldn't. She wouldn't!

'Henry tells me you have some decorations that come out every year, a sort of tradition. That sounds nice, dear.'

She wouldn't tell her, she wouldn't. 'Oh, I've thrown them all away,' she said casually. 'No one wants them anymore.' She turned away. Brave words but not such a brave face. She felt Henry's hand on her shoulder, squeezing, comforting, and fought back tears. She shouldn't have come, this was a mistake. She was better off on her own, wallowing in her misery.

To her surprise Rachel went into the hall and came back carrying Ruth's coat as well as her own. 'Come on, dear, Henry wants to take us for a walk.'

They went in the van, Ruth curled up in cushions in the back with an apologetic Rachel in the passenger seat. Henry drove them through some pretty villages and then on to Penarth, a charming town with its Victorian pier, interesting shops and ice-cream parlours. They had tea at a café then stood and watched the sea, where gulls and wading birds waited patiently for the tide to recede and offer a few hours' feeding time. Afterwards Ruth and Henry took turns to look through binoculars and commenting on the species present. 'Have you got your notebook, Henry?' she asked. 'We could make a list as we're here.'

This was the time to tell her about his plan for the future but he didn't know where to begin. Rachel walked to the railings and threw bread for the gulls to catch, laughing at the noisy protests from those who were unlucky.

While they were alone, Henry said. 'It's time for us both to make plans, and I want you to listen to what I have in mind.'

'I'm so confused, Henry. I'd never have believed that my brothers would turn on me like this after all I've done for them.'

'Change the wording. Tell it without the melodrama.' He smiled to take the sting out of the words. 'They haven't "turned on you", they are grown men, no longer needing your care and they want to make their own way. You did a remarkable job, bringing them up and you not much more than a child yourself. They know it and understand how hard this is, but it has to happen, for your sake as well as theirs. You can't see it now, but you will. Soon.'

'You look serious,' Rachel smiled as she returned.

'We can't decide whether or not we have room for an ice-cream sundae,' Ruth said with mock seriousness. They walked back to the largest ice-cream parlour and studied the list of choices.

When he drove her back to Ty Gwyn, Henry told her about his friendship with Lillian. She immediately thought the worst. He was about to tell her goodbye.

'Oh, it's nice to meet new people,' she said calmly.

'She's very easy to talk to. And you have to admit that you and I don't find that easy at present.'

'I'm sorry,' she murmured, still waiting for the words that would shatter her life into pieces.

'I have an idea of how I want to spend the rest of my life, and until you calm down and are prepared to listen, I have to depend on outsiders, strangers, to hear what I have planned.'

'That sounds as though your mind is made up, so what's there to discuss?'

'Your part in it.'

'Not now, Henry. Let's just go home. My life is in such chaos and I can't take on any more. It's like I'm standing on a cake walk at a fair ground,' she told him. 'Our house for sale, and Geraint's surly presence changing the house into a place I don't know. Tommy and Bryn house hunting and their wives treating me as a nuisance to be tolerated for a while now and then. And me, not knowing which way to go.'

'It's time you started looking for a place to live.'

* * *

Geraint was still decorating and, when they had no work, Tommy and Bryn helped too. Ruth hadn't thought of what work she would like to do or where she would live and, unable to make plans, she began helping Henry in the shop. Business was quiet and she spent time familiarizing herself with the stock and his book-keeping.

An offer of possible accommodation offered itself one day. Mali and Megan, with Mickie trotting behind them, walked up the path and knocked on her door.

'Is it true you're leaving this house?' Mali asked, grabbing a poker and putting it out of Mickie's reach. 'Rumours say your brothers want to sell and you need somewhere to live.'

'Unless you're going to marry Henry Owen at last,' Megan added, quirking an eyebrow.

'Yes, and no,' Ruth said with a smile. 'Yes we're selling and no, Henry and I haven't any plans to marry.'

'We have to get out of the place we're living now. As you see—' she shouted as she and her sister ran to where Mickie was climbing up onto the dresser, 'he's a bit of a handful.'

'How can I help? I don't know how long before the house is sold but I doubt it'll be very long.'

'We think we can help you!'

Mali took up the tale. 'There's a nice little bungalow down in the old village and it's for rent. If you don't mind sharing a home with this scallywag, then what do you think of us renting it between us, all paying a third of the rent and basic expenses? It won't be very much. What d'you think?'

'It sounds a good idea, although I have to get a job before I commit to paying anything.'

'You have to live somewhere. What's the alternative?'

'Sleeping on Aunty Blod's couch!' Ruth said with a chuckle.

They untangled Mickie from under the table, where he had made himself a nest with the cushions, and went to see the place. 'It's a bit run down but there's nothing that a paintbrush won't sort out,' Megan said encouragingly.

'I don't think it will suit me,' she told them after they had looked around the building and the garden. 'Besides, I don't know how long the house will take to sell. But what about Tabs? She could afford it and I'm sure she'd be happy sharing a home with Mickie. But there are problems which you must discuss with her,' she said, thinking of Tabs's pregnancy.

'What problems?' they demanded. So she told them about Tabs's pregnancy and at once they offered support and began to get excited at the prospect of Tabs and another child in the house. Ruth left them discussing who would have which room and promising to get a room painted for Tabs to move in within the week, if she agreed to sharing with them. Ruth left them, happy that she had done the best for Tabs.

Tabs was approached and, after nervous hesitation, unable to believe that they really wanted her to share, she accepted. The decision made, they approached the agent and began making arrangements. Lots of lists were written regarding what furnishings they would need and Ruth knew that practically all they wanted could be provided by her.

After making the required checks and getting references from several people, they signed the necessary forms and were handed the keys. Golden Grove was theirs.

Two weeks later they all moved in.

'What about you?' Henry asked, after congratulating her on getting Tabs free from her father and stepmother. 'Have you thought about a job, or will you listen to what I have in mind?'

'I haven't thought about a job yet, I've been too busy getting the house cleared. The shed is full of clutter that I can't find a home for and a few items of furniture are ready for the second-hand dealer. Everything else has gone. All the contact with my parents will go when the house is sold; I'm parting with everything I've known all my life.' Henry made no comment and she added, 'I know I have to find work soon though. I realize that.'

Once more she's ignoring any plans of mine, Henry thought with a sigh.

* * *

Tabs had waited in the park at lunchtime day after day but there was no sign of Jack. It was early in February and she was worried. Her pregnancy was beginning to show and even the loose clothing she now wore wouldn't keep the gossips at bay for much longer.

She stared around her at people scurrying past hugging themselves against the cold. Once or twice she thought she recognized Jack and her heart leapt, but moments later she realized her mistake and she shrank back into her clothes and gave a sigh of disappointment. Her feet were stiff with cold and she wished she had worn boots. To warm herself she walked to the edge of the park and looked around, then she saw him. This time there was no mistake.

She ran, awkwardly at first as her ankles were stiff from standing so long in the cold, then faster as she saw him disappear around the corner She called and she saw him increase speed. He must have seen her, but why didn't he wait?

Jack had seen her at the edge of his vision and, instead of passing Henry's shop he turned away from the road and walked swiftly around a corner, then into the lane at the back of the row of shops. Fortunately a gate which led into a garage was open and he darted through and pushed it, almost closed, behind him. He saw Tabs come to the end of the lane, hesitate, then walk back the way she had come. He waited a moment then slipped out and ran to the end of the lane and back to where Abigail and Gloria now lived.

Tabs was walking in the same direction, her footsteps dragging. What could she do? The baby was a fact that wouldn't be denied and she had to make plans. She would have to tell her father. She doubted whether that would solve anything. He wouldn't be sympathetic, in fact he was more likely to tell her to stay away. He'd be embarrassed once the neighbours became aware of her situation. On second thoughts she had better not tell him until she had some plan in place. But what plan? Who could she turn to and expect help? Only Ruth — and she didn't really deserve any help from someone she had cheated and deceived.

'Hi there,' a voice called and she turned to see Abigail waving to her from across the road. She smiled and was about to turn away, but Abigail ran after her. 'Got time for a cup of tea? I've got such exciting news to tell you.'

Abigail was the very last person Tabs wanted to see, believing that she was the woman Jack truly loved, but she waited until the young woman caught up with her. 'I'm sorry, but I have to get back,' she excused, moving away.

'You look frozen! Come on, just a cup of tea, or hot chocolate, how does that sound?'

Reluctantly Tabs followed her to a small café, its steamed-up windows promising warmth to soothe her chilled and aching body. Nothing was said until they were served with their hot drinks and a plate of Welsh cakes, but Tabs guessed from the shining eyes of her companion that the news would not be what she needed to hear.

'Jack has a job! It's in a green-grocer's, a job he's done before, deliveries and counter hand. He's always refused to stay until he earned enough to keep us and now he does,' Abigail said. 'He's moved out of that awful room and has moved in with us. We're going to be married at Easter and I'm so happy.'

Tabs pressed her hands against the bump that was Jack's child and wanted to tell this girl she was wrong, that Jack couldn't marry her, that he was going to be a father and his place was with her and their baby, but she was struck dumb. She picked up the cup with hands that shook and hid her face behind it and muttered something, she couldn't remember what, before making her excuses and hurrying back out into the cold street.

She went to see Ruth, who was packing boxes with spare bedding and labelling them to either herself or one of her sisters-in-law. 'Jack is marrying Abigail!' she burst out as soon as Ruth opened the door. Tearfully, she told Ruth all that had happened, owning up to her dishonesty again and telling her that Jack believed he was related to Ruth's family in some way. 'I must have been out of my mind to believe what he told me.'

'He thinks he is related to us? I don't understand. We don't have anything valuable, we certainly don't have much money.'

'Someone told him that there is an inheritance waiting for him, his father's "Treasure" with a family called Tyler and your mother was a Tyler before she married. I'm sorry, Ruth, but I've been helping him. I let him search through drawers and cupboards in your house. I'm so ashamed. He looked though papers in the loft and when you saw me with the ladder, I was rescuing him after I'd locked him up there when you came home earlier than expected. I've behaved like an idiot and you've been nothing but kind to me.'

'Why does he think this — inheritance — is here? We don't have any secrets.'

'There's nothing except the name. He wouldn't give up and I thought it was because he loved me and was using the search as an excuse to stay. But it's Abi he loves.'

Ruth was frowning, it was such an odd story. Then she looked at Tabs's unhappy face, tears running down her cheek making her look like a child. 'I can understand how flattered you were. He's an attractive man and—'

'And I was convinced I was ugly and stupid and would never find love so I ignored my doubts and convinced myself he really loved me.'

'The thing is, what do we do now?'

'We?'

'Yes, Tabs, we have to think about what happens next. I presume you haven't told your father about the baby?'

'How can I? He and Martha will be horrified and I very much doubt if they'll help me.'

'That will be the biggest hurdle so we'd better do it straight away. Come on, I can finish packing later. I'll come with you and we can face Martha's outrage together.'

* * *

'You're what? You, expecting a baby? How on earth—' Martha turned to Tabs's father. 'She must be dreaming! The girl must be demented.'

Slowly, Tabs removed her coat and showed her swollen body.

'Who took advantage of you?' George demanded.

'No one.'

Martha turned to Ruth, 'It's living in your house — that's where she learnt to misbehave. It's your fault for bringing this decent family into disrepute: this is down to you!'

Ruth and Tabs stood together arm in arm and allowed the tirade to continue, then, as George and Martha paused for breath, Ruth said quietly, 'What do you want her to do? Now this has happened do you want her to come home?'

'Get out,' George said. 'I don't want her bringing her shame to this house.'

Without a word of reply, Ruth guided Tabs around and out of the door. 'You are coming back with me,' she muttered, as Tabs began to sob. 'Mali and Megan know about the baby and they'll welcome you and care for you. I'll help. Henry will help, you'll be fine, I promise.'

Tabs stayed with Ruth that night. She had the one remaining bed and Ruth settled on the couch. In a strange way it helped her, aware of how empty the house had become that she didn't even have a spare bed to offer. The decoration Geraint had done looked alien: out of tune with the rest, nothing like she would have chosen. Perhaps leaving would be a relief compared with living here with all its changes, the disappearance of all that was familiar.

She added a few more coals to the fire and put up the spark guard. She didn't think she would sleep for a while. An hour later, Tabs tiptoed down and joined her. They sat together on the couch, drinking cocoa and eating toast like delinquent children and it was well after midnight before they slept.

CHAPTER NINE

The For Sale board went up that morning and Ruth stared at it in disbelief. Suddenly it was really happening. She had carried a hope deep within her that something would happen to change her brothers' minds, but there was no longer any doubt. The house was being sold, the family it had protected for so long was abandoning it. She knew she was being melodramatic and didn't care, it was how she felt. Two people knocked at the door that day and asked about price and details of the accommodation. Rudely she referred them to the agents and swiftly closed the door. She knew she was behaving like King Canute, trying to stop the tide coming in and she gave a weak smile. It wasn't possible to stop the sale, but she wasn't going to make it easy!

She began to list in her mind all the things she could point out to viewers that needed attention. If she could delay for a while at least, give herself time to adjust to living somewhere else, that was all she could hope for. Aunty Blod had agreed she could stay with her for a while and she was grateful for that. The flat was small and some of her valued pieces would have to go into storage until she had a place of her own. Her bank balance wasn't large and certainly not enough to buy. She didn't have a job and that was something she had to attend to without delay. Living in Aunty Blod's small flat would only be a temporary arrangement.

* * *

Blodwen sat in the bar of the Yeomen's Arms, tucked in a corner, watching every new arrival. Lunchtime had been stated on the mysterious letter asking her to meet 'a friend' there, so she had come at midday and promised herself she would leave at two o'clock.

The place was quiet at first, with few people coming in and out. Two elderly men sat in a corner playing dominoes, the clicking of the pieces loud in the almost empty room. A man came in and asked for change of a ten shilling note for his bus fare. A woman came and sat in a corner sipping a cider and staring at her. A man opened the door without coming in, stared around then left. Was he looking for me, Blod wondered? But he was a stranger and she didn't go out and look for him. She sat nursing a drink and watched the doorway for — she didn't know who.

The place filled up as several men, workmen by the look of them, came and ordered drinks to go with their packed food. At half past one, she felt conspicuous and gave herself another ten minutes, then she left.

Across the road a man watched her leave, then he followed her. He got on the same bus and got off when she did. He noted the flats into which she disappeared then wandered off. He walked slowly and paused now and again to catch his breath, he had a sickly pallor and his clothes were a size or two too large for his wasted frame.

He went into a boarding-house a few streets away and rested on his bed for a couple of hours. Perhaps he had left it too late. He doubted whether he would have the strength for long enough to complete his task.

* * *

Curiosity got the better of Blod and at three o'clock she went back to the Yeomen's Arms, but by this time the place was closed so she couldn't go inside. It was already getting dark and she knew she couldn't stay long but she sat on a garden wall and wrapped her coat and scarf tightly around her and she waited.

She soon became chilled and having spent half an hour either sitting or walking up and down, decided that five more minutes was as long as she could — should — stay. No point in getting cold and becoming ill. Whoever had written the letter couldn't expect more. Besides, it might have been a joke. She stared around her as that idea took hold, imagining someone watching and laughing, and wondering what she would say if someone she knew had been playing an unkind trick.

About to walk away, she saw someone walking towards her and she stopped and waited in case it was the person who wanted to talk to her. It was Jack.

'Hello, Miss Thomas. Waiting for someone?'

'What d'you know about who I'm waiting for?' she asked suspiciously, ignoring his use of the wrong name.

'I don't know. Why should I? You ought to get home though, it's very cold to be standing about.'

She hesitated, then asked, 'You didn't write to me, did you, some kind of joke?'

He shook his head. 'What d'you mean? Did someone write to you?'

She touched the letter in her pocket but remembered the request to tell no one and kept her hand, which was stiff with the cold, in her pocket, and moved on.

'Come on, I'll walk with you to the bus stop; I think you should get yourself home, or you'll be ill again.'

When she got back to her flat she stared at the letter crumpled in her hand for a moment, and this time, when she threw it into the bin, there it stayed.

* * *

Tabs was delighted with the room she had been given in Mali and Megan's bungalow. It was hardly any larger than the one she had just left, but she thought it was heavenly. It had bright yellow walls that were helped by the sun giving its deceiving winter glow, she felt a surge of happiness as she walked in, something she hadn't experienced for a long time.

She continued to work for the newsagent, whose wife was sympathetic to her condition and frequently fed her at lunchtime before she left for home, and was even knitting sweet little garments for the baby. She missed Ruth but was grateful for the way her life was changing.

The thought of having a baby to care for was still frightening, fear of the responsibility was always her last thought each night before sleep claimed her, but watching Megan and Mali with Mickie slowly increased her confidence. If only she had a sister, how perfect life would be. But she knew how fortunate she was to have friends like Ruth and Henry, and now Mali and Megan.

It was a lively house but she soon became comfortable with the friends who popped in and stayed for a cup of tea and a chat. Mali and Megan went out a lot, taking it in turns to stay with Mickie, who called them by their first names having given up sorting out which one was his mam.

The sisters went to dances and on occasions invited Tabs to go with them, but she declined. She had come a long way from being that frightened mouse, but she'd never be that brave! The cinema was different. Tabs often joined one of the sisters to see a film she wanted to see. She also went to films she didn't particularly fancy, knowing that too many refusals might end up with them not bothering to ask. She missed Jack and longed for him to come back, still half believing that, one day, he would.

One evening, after much persuasion, she braved it and went to the dance with Mali. She hid herself in a corner, not because she expected someone to ask her to dance, she knew that was unlikely, but because she felt unable to talk freely to strangers. To her surprise, Mali walked onto the stage and sang with the band and Tabs was amazed at the quality of her voice and her confidence as she moved to the music and sang. The crowd loved her and she sang once more later in the evening. Tabs went the next day in great excitement to tell Ruth and beg her to go to the next dance, just to hear her.

* * *

Not wanting to stay in the cold, empty house, Ruth got into the habit of joining Mali or Megan with Mickie, and sometimes Tabs, for the lunch hour. With little to fill her time she was soon helping at the bungalow by doing the odd chore, and she slipped into the role of cook and general organizer with ease, as though it had been planned. She was soon in charge of cooking the evening meal at which they all sat together in the kitchen and shared news of each other's day, before she left to spend the rest of the evening in the cold and no longer friendly Ty Gwyn.

Ruth sometimes went out with one of the sisters, and once, to the weekly dance, where Mali left the dancers to sing with the band. And whenever Tabs had to attend a clinic she always went with her. It was Blod who warned her that she was taking on a role very similar to the one she had left. Ruth joked about it and said it was only until she had decided what she wanted to do.

'It's only on a temporary basis, Aunty Blod,' she assured her. 'Just until Tabs settles in. I don't want her to automatically fall into the routine of being housekeeper for the sisters as she had for that father of hers.'

She left her aunt's flat where already some of her things were stored and went back to the house, which still stood unsold, and spent time there, huddled near the fire and tried to make plans for a future that looked bleak and lonely. She hardly saw Tommy or Bryn. The house was effectively empty and without that centre, that base, there was no natural meeting place and the family was disintegrating as she had guessed it would, and there was nothing she could do to stop it.

Two couples came that weekend to look at the house and she showed them around with indifference, answering their questions with little enthusiasm. It would sell, she knew that. Like King Canute she couldn't halt the inevitable, but she was determined not to help.

Tommy and Bryn had called at Blodwen's flat on their way back from work a few times in an attempt to remind her she wasn't forgotten. They called once when Ruth was there and greeted her enthusiastically, and asked about the prospect of a sale. They begged a cup of tea from Aunty Blod, but it was difficult: the flat was too small for visitors. Blod didn't have the endless supply of food that Ruth had always been able to provide and too many people around tired the old lady who was used to a quieter life. Ruth knew it could never replace the house that had been the centre of the family all their lives.

* * *

Henry was far from happy. He needed to change his life too and it was proving difficult to make a decision. The most important decision was being made for him, with Ruth avoiding him and refusing to talk. Twice, he had taken a book and a snack and driven to Rhossili to spend an hour with the sound of the sea for company. Early in March, Lillian's dog darted out barking and causing him to brake. He opened the van door and said, 'Sally, you silly dog. It's me; surely you haven't forgotten me?' The dog jumped into the van and settled on his lap as though preparing for a ride. He was laughing when Lillian came out, apologized and invited him in for a cup of tea.

'Once the stupid dog knows you, she might give up attacking your van.' She smiled and added, 'She only might give up; Sally's a bit stubborn, I'm afraid.'

Henry parked the van amid excited barking and much tail-wagging from Sally and followed the lady around the house into the back garden.

'This is a heavenly place,' he said. He stood and stared over the low hedge to a view of the beach far below, with its towering rocks creating arms to encompass the huge breakers hurling themselves at a sandy cove. 'But I'll be glad to get inside out of this cold wind.'

After a pleasant hour during which they shared information about themselves and he learned that she was a widow, who had spent most of her life in London, where her husband had been a doctor, she asked if any progress had been made between himself and Ruth.

He shook his head. 'We're more and more like strangers these days.'

'You've told her about the new business?'

Again he shook his head. 'I've tried, but she refuses to listen.'

'But it will be starting soon. You'll have to say something then, unless,' she added softly, 'unless you plan to walk away from her completely?'

'April is when we open for business and if she isn't interested, I'll be looking for a cook-cum-housekeeper and a part time handyman-gardener. It shouldn't be too difficult to find suitable people. I don't want to employ anyone yet. I still hope to persuade her to join me, if only as a paid member of staff.'

'Good luck, Henry.'

'I'll need it!'

* * *

Jack still worked at the green-grocery and on Fridays and Saturdays he was given the task of delivering the weekly orders to customers. The pay was abysmal and trying to keep Abigail and Gloria comfortable was almost impossible, until he hit on a plan.

* * *

A few customers paid at the end of the month, going into the shop to settle the four or sometimes five weeks' bills.

Most customers paid on delivery and from these he made a small profit.

He would knock at the door and stand smiling, with the box of vegetables in his arms, they would ask how much they owed, and, without offering the invoice, he would tell them an amount just a little bit higher than the total. Still not showing them the invoice he would take their money, sometimes even letting them off a few pence, and would leave happy customers thinking what a lovely, polite young man he was.

It was a lady called Miss Farr who spoilt it all. She had bought a few things for a 'bring and buy' sale and wanted to know the prices of the items. Jack pulled out a pocketful of invoices and, apologizing, promised to bring it next time.

Mrs Farr went to the shop and explained her request to the shopkeeper. When she was shown the copy of the invoice she was surprised as the total was one shilling and sixpence less than she had paid.

'It must have been a mistake,' he said apologetically and handed her the difference and a couple of oranges as compensation.

He didn't think any more about it until a few days later when another customer remarked that her regular order had increased by two shillings and asked what item had been the cause. She explained that she hadn't been given the invoice so was unable to check for herself. He then picked up the invoice book with its copies of orders delivered and called on a few customers. He soon realized what had been happening.

Sacked and with no reference, Jack knew he'd got off lightly. But with no wages, and no work, how was he going to look after Abigail and Gloria?

He explained his difficulties to Gloria with a few imaginative changes to the facts and she and Abigail wrote out false references for him, hoping that a prospective employer wouldn't bother to check.

His next employment was a casual arrangement that suited him perfectly. He occasionally helped with deliveries of furniture and heavy items for a second-hand shop. It wasn't much but at least there would be enough to buy food. And he was still adept at lifting the odd purse.

Abigail's job was a success. Her skills as a sales lady with her beautifully modulated voice and elegant appearance were soon noticed by the manager and she was transferred to the large hat department where she was an even greater success. Jack knew they could manage, but if he could find the family he'd been searching for, there was the promise of enough money for a good start in a place of their own.

He knew he was lucky that even after all the disasters, Abigail still insisted on him continuing his search. He would make it up to her when he found his inheritance, but he wondered how much more time he could spend looking for it. With what Tabs had found out and his own gut feeling, he had been so sure Ty Gwyn had been the place.

There was no way he could find out if they were the family he was seeking without revealing the reason for asking, and they would wonder why he had been so secretive. So much time had passed since the days his father had talked about and he knew that he would have to give up soon, but not yet. He wasn't ready to give up on an inheritance. His father's treasure was somewhere and he wanted it. Perhaps he'd wait for the summer then try somewhere else, some other small, seaside town. He had to find them, they owed him!

* * *

Ruth was passing Henry's shop when the van stopped and he got out. He was carrying a box containing carefully wrapped vases which he had bought. He didn't invite her upstairs, but put the box on the counter and asked if there was something wrong.

'No, but I wanted to tell you that my moving in with Aunty Blod won't work. She can't cope with the boys visiting and I want—'

'Ruth, I have something to tell you. It's important and I'd like to know what you think.'

'I'm sorry, Henry, but this is important too. The family is falling apart and I need to find a place they can treat as their home, call in and expect meals. Aunty Blod isn't up to it and—'

'I'm sorry, Ruth, but I haven't time for this!' She was startled by the anger in his voice and stared at him. 'When you have time to listen to what I have to say,' he added, as he opened the door for her to leave, 'if you ever have time to listen, perhaps you'll let me know!' He opened the shop door, gesturing for her to leave, and its bell tinkled cheerfully as, with a gasp of annoyance, she went out.

She didn't go upstairs to sleep after eating a snack supper beside the fire. The couch in the cosy room was impossible to leave as night fell. The stairs looked dark and uninviting. The fire was banked up and would stay in all night, she had no one to please but herself, so why move?

Geraint had arranged for a telephone to be installed and it sat on the dresser. Beside it were notebook, pens and pencils so any appointments could be written down. There had been surprisingly few since a busy period after the For Sale board had first been displayed and those who had come, had been discouraged by her pointing out all that needed to be done, rather than telling of its best features. The large house with a roof needing attention and in need of paint seemed too much of a commitment for the young couples who came, and one elderly couple were convinced that the place was unsafe when Ruth pointed out a small crack in one wall that wasn't even a part of the house, but a separate outhouse where the washing boiler had once lived.

Ruth had taken down the last of the pictures and mirrors, and darker patches in the colour of the walls revealed their absence like guilty secrets. There was nothing structurally unsound, except in the doubts she placed in viewers' minds.

The place did need money spent on it. Ruth hadn't noticed how shabby it had become, but now she felt a sneaky, guilty pleasure and hoped it would never sell. It was an excuse for not starting to make plans, or to look for a place of her own, although she knew that once summer came and everything looked brighter, it would have more appeal. She wouldn't necessarily be given much time to make arrangements. Although, even then, she told herself, there was always Aunty Blod.

To her dismay, there were two appointments made during that morning and she reluctantly prepared for them. Hostess skills couldn't be ignored and she made cakes in case they had come a long way, the kettle simmering on the cheerful fire. The first couple were not impressed and spent the time criticizing everything, even the friendly kitchen, which they said would have to be ripped out as it was impossible to use in its present state. The lovely room where the family met and talked about everything? Ripped out? Ruth rushed them through the rest of the visit and slammed the door before they had taken two steps away from it. How could she give the place to strangers, people who didn't appreciate its wonderful warmth, its spaciousness, and who lacked the imagination to see themselves living there happily as she and her brothers had done?

* * *

Blodwen received another letter. As before it went to Ty Gwyn and Ruth gave it to her. 'It's from an old friend,' she told her. 'Lost my address she has, and I haven't written back. Shame on me,' Blodwen muttered, stuffing it in her handbag.

The letter was unsigned like the first one and it apologized for not turning up as promised. It went on to explain that he, or she, had been in hospital but was now well again. There was another date, this time in two weeks' time and curious about it, Blodwen marked the date on her calendar.

When the day came, she was sitting eating her breakfast and wondering what to wear as the sky looked dark and rain threatened, when there was a knock at the door.

Bryn was there and his white, anxious face made her immediately think something terrible had happened to Brenda and the baby.

'Aunty Blod, can you came and stay at the flat for a few hours? Brenda's in hospital and I want to be near so I get the news fast. Damn me, I think we ought to get one of them phones.'

'What's happened?' Blod asked. 'Calm down and tell me what's happened, boy.'

'Fell, she did, and I called the doctor and he sent her to hospital. She might be having the baby, now this minute! Tommy and Tina are away, visiting her parents, and they've taken the van. They'll be back soon and they'll wonder where we are. Stay, will you, till they come, so you can tell them what's happening?'

'Go you, give me a key and I'll wait for them. Why didn't you tell Ruth? She's closer than me and she's got a phone.'

'You know what she's like; she'll be fussing and Toni has convinced Brenda she'd be better without her. She doesn't want anyone else there, just me nearby, waiting for the news and being the first to see the baby. It's a special time, see, and we don't want to share it.'

'You can't be so unkind, Bryn! Ruth looked after you all for years. At least phone as soon as you've seen the baby, she deserves that.'

'I will. I promise. It's just that, well, Toni isn't used to close families and—'

'Oh go back to your Brenda, or the news will be in the local paper before you know yourself!'

She glanced at the mark on the calendar and shrugged. Whoever this mysterious stranger was, the unknown friend who wanted to meet her, he was going to be disappointed. She picked up her coat and set off for the flat, while Bryn ran to the bus stop as though wild animals were in pursuit.

Brenda gave birth to a son and they had already chosen the name, so Bryn phoned Ruth and told her that Joseph Thomas was seven and a half stone and beautiful.

Laughing she asked, 'I presume you mean seven and a half pounds, Bryn.'

'Beautiful he is. I got that part right.'

'Bryn, I know you don't want me interfering, but would you like me to go to the flat and get it ready for when Brenda and Joseph come home?' Bryn didn't argue.

After phoning to tell Henry the news, she rushed over carrying a bag of cleaning materials. Opening the door of the flat was a shock. It was crammed full of things for the baby, plus some boxes and small pieces of furniture which she guessed they had bought ready for the house they would buy as soon as Ty Gwyn sold. She could hardly move. Better if they had stored the excess in Ty Gwyn; when the house was sold would be the time to take it away.

Carefully she rearranged the clutter and managed to make room in the bedroom for the cot beside the bed and a cupboard of the baby's things close by. Really, they should have stayed in Ty Gwyn, not squashed themselves into this tiny place. But, as she worked, she felt a growing guilt. They shouldn't have had to manage like this. If she had been more helpful when viewers came to look at the house, it would have been sold by now. She worked hard. Beside cleaning the place thoroughly, she dealt with the laundry and cleaned windows and washed the kitchen curtains. When she had finished, the place was clean and organized but it didn't look like Bryn's and Brenda's home any more.

Anxious, in case she had overstepped Brenda's wishes, she left a note and explained that she had moved a few things for her to come home to and knew they wouldn't be permanent changes. She offered her help if it was needed, and hoped Brenda wouldn't be angry.

She went there again on the day mother and baby were due home and took cakes and pasties and did some shopping. As soon as they came, she hugged them all, eulogized about the baby and quickly left.

Later that evening, Bryn rang and thanked her for sorting out the muddle. 'Brenda intended to do it but our Joseph came earlier than expected and, well, thanks Ruth. Brenda and I are really grateful.'

At least Brenda wasn't as unfriendly as Toni, thank goodness, Ruth thought.

* * *

A week later a young couple came and looked at the house and, smiling widely, said they loved it and would buy it as fast as their solicitor could make the arrangements.

Ruth showed them around, her mind filled with the difficulties Bryn and Brenda, and Tommy and Toni were facing in their tiny accommodation with their new babies to care for. She liked the look of the young couple and showed them the rooms politely and with encouraging comments. She made them tea and offered cakes and concentrated on the wonderful life they had enjoyed there. Two days later she was told that it was sold. The new owners would be taking possession in the middle of April.

Geraint sighed with relief when she telephoned him, Emrys wrote back and congratulated her, the twins were jubilant, Blodwen was sad, knowing it was the end of an era and nothing would ever be the same again. Ruth went to see Henry, and cried.

'With the house sold and only a few weeks to get out, there's so much to do,' she told him. 'Geraint and Emrys are coming to help with the final clearing and they'll need feeding. There are decisions to make. You've no idea what this move entails, Henry. It's the family home and that's different from selling a business.'

'Of course, my moves are nothing compared with yours.' His sarcasm was wasted. 'What will you do?'

'The furniture that's left will go to a second-hand dealer, except the couch. I know you'll think it silly but I want to keep that. I've arranged for it to go into store.'

'I can store it for you if you wish.'

'How can you keep it? Have you found a place to stay?'

'I've bought a house and there'll be plenty of room for your couch.'

'You've bought a house? Why didn't you tell me?'

'I tried. You've been so obsessed with your decision making, you haven't had time to listen to mine.'

'I'm sorry, but it's been a difficult time for me.'

'Yes, for you, always you, Ruth.' He stared at her disapprovingly, and as she was about to speak he went on, 'Don't worry, I do have someone who listens. Lillian is a good listener and she's also very wise.'

'You told this — Lillian — and not me? Have we drifted so far we aren't even friends?'

'Sad, isn't it? And all because you won't accept that nothing is forever, that life has to change.'

'Where is it, this house of yours?'

'You've seen it, although you might not remember. It's the beautiful house on the common, with a small woodland behind and large enough for the new enterprise I am starting in May or June.'

'A new business? Not antiques?' Her voice was low and she stared at him as though she didn't know him, which was how she was beginning to feel.

'Not antiques. When you have time, I'll tell you about it. Maybe before I open for the summer season.'

'Henry! Stop it! Tell me what you're planning.'

'Not planning. It's already planned. Lillian and I went to see the council and every detail was considered and approval given. Lillian made other suggestions for the winter months and they too have been given the necessary permission.'

'Summer plans, winter plans? What sort of business is it? Not an ice-cream stall on the beach I hope.' She smiled but he remained serious.

'I'll take you there on Sunday morning and you can see for yourself.'

'Sunday, but I can't, they might be needing Sunday lunch.' Too late she realized she had given the wrong answer. 'But I can leave sandwiches and cook in the evening.'

'No, don't change your plans just for me.'

'All right,' she said, suddenly angry, 'take this Lillian with you! She understands you better than I do.' She knew her anger was against herself for her stupidity and not Henry's fault at all, but he had walked away and it was too late to take back her foolish words.

On Sunday, she left messages at the flats to tell Tommy and Bryn and the others that she would be out all day, and went to find Henry. It was still early, not yet nine o'clock, and she hoped he would still be at the flat. Although she still had a key, she knocked and waited for him to respond.

'Can I still come with you to see the house?'

He stood back and allowed her to enter. On the table she saw what looked like a diagram of a building and went to look at it. He picked it up and folded it away. 'Better you see the actual building rather than architect's plans,' he said. Ruth took a deep breath and swallowed her sharp retort. This wasn't going to be easy.

They went in the van that still showed the name of the antique shops he owned. Soon the logo would be changed, but to what, she had no idea.

She was silent as they drove to the house and she stepped out and looked at it with curiosity. It was larger than she remembered, but she hadn't seen it all, her lack of interest had been obvious and he hadn't insisted. What could he be planning? Something of which she wouldn't approve? Was this the reason he had been less tolerant of her need to care for her family lately? Or was this a home he had bought for himself and this — Lillian?

The owner wasn't there and Henry took her straight into the lounge which looked towards the road. Pleasant, but dark as it faced north, she thought. The other rooms were explored and with five bedrooms, all of them large enough to be called doubles, she decided that it was far too large for two people, but Lillian might have children, and that thought was more painful than the rest.

In what was apparently the dining-room, he took out the architect's plan and spread it on a table. 'This,' he told her quietly, 'will be a holiday centre. I will invite guests to come on walks to explore the area and most walks will be aimed at one particular aspect of wildlife or flowers. Insects too, and fungi and farming and sea life.'

'But how will you start? How will you find people interested in what you offer? Who will cater for them?'

'Questions at last!' he said with a smile. 'Remember Ted Wells, one of the farmers on your insurance round? He will guide some of the walks and there are others who will come when needed and, unbelievably, and thanks to Lillian and her suggestion of early advertising, we already have several bookings.'

'But what made you decide on such a complete change?'

'Our walks, mainly. I enjoyed them and believe you did too. We can't be the only people to get pleasure out of our countryside, so I began to research the idea and when I saw this house I knew it would be perfect.'

He led her outside and showed her the long private garden and the woodland, and the stream gently flowing across the property.

'You're right, it's perfect,' she told him Then she asked about the large barn halfway down the garden. 'Is that yours too?'

'All the outhouses are part of the deal. The owner told me he and his wife used to rent it out for barn dances. Lillian thinks it might be possible to use as a dining-room for large groups once it's restored.'

'Clever Lillian.'

She thought she would scream if he mentioned the woman's name once more. Regret was an ache in her heart. Henry should have waited until she was ready, she should have been involved in the planning, not this hateful woman who was stealing Henry from her.

'Well, I think it's a wonderful plan, but I'd better go. You'll need to get back to Lillian and I've got to cook for my brothers,' she lied.

'Yes, I'd better get back to Lillian,' he agreed and she glanced at him. Was that a smile he was trying to hide? His eyes looked full of amusement too and she decided he was laughing at her. Leaving her for this Lillian and laughing at her. She went through the house and got into the van and didn't speak another word about the house, just filled the air with trivia all the way home.

She was glad not to be on her own. The four brothers were there and she helped with the final cleaning and cooked a meal, while they talked cheerfully about their future plans. As she listened to their chatter, she realized that they weren't dismayed at leaving Ty Gwyn. The likely disintegration of the family by its loss wasn't real to them. And she admitted for the first time that they didn't see her as a victim, as she was having a share in the proceeds too.

When Tommy and Bryn left, Geraint and Emrys went with them for a few hours and Ruth sorted through the piles they had left to go onto the planned bonfire. The picture painted by her uncle when he was a child was thrown with the rest. It wasn't worth anything, the frame was poor and the glass had a crack across one corner, but some last moment of sentimentality called to her and she lifted it out from the rubbish and put it with other pieces she had saved.

Once she set about the final clearance, the house let her go; the memories were hers to keep but the place was no longer hers and the pull of sentimentality was gone. Perhaps this was because her mind was filled with regrets. Why had she been so obsessed about parting with the place and refused to allow her brothers to leave to begin lives of her own? She had left herself with nowhere to go. Henry had left to make a life of his own as her brothers had done and it was her own fault.

She needed to see him, to tell him she didn't want to lose touch. She had to make him promise to remain her friend, him and this Lillian. She went to the shop, which was closed. There was no van outside and she began to turn away, then she saw Henry leaving by the door to his flat. 'Henry? I thought you were out, there's no van outside.'

'It's gone for repainting, with Peter's name. I've bought a small bus,' he told her casually. 'Lillian pointed out straight away that we'll need transport for the guests if we're going to take them further than the garden.'

'That's obvious,' she muttered.

'Did I tell you my mother is moving there too? The shop being sold means her flat is sold too. She's very excited about the project. She's chosen a room and she'll help with the telephone and bookings.'

She waved goodbye and hurried back to Ty Gwyn. She had been unable to talk to him about her own plans, which were abysmally vague. 'Perhaps I should go and ask Lillian!' she said petulantly to Tabs, who laughed rather than sympathized. Tabs had too many problems of her own.

* * *

Tabs knew Jack was working in the town but she rarely saw him and when she did, he was always in a hurry to be gone. When she tried to talk about the baby, he said all the right things, that as soon as he could he would get them a place and he'd look after her, but she no longer believed him, the words were almost a chanted, rehearsed response with no substance.

Seeing Abigail and her mother was a painful embarrassment. It was obvious to them now that she was expecting a child, but she couldn't tell them that Jack was the father. The confrontation was too much for her to consider; she was chilled by the thought of speaking the words to Abigail and Gloria and the exchange of looks that would clearly show she was not believed.

She tried to see her father on three occasions and each time Martha sent her away. The third time Ruth went with her but the result was the same, with Martha adamant that her father didn't want to see her. 'It's Martha, not my father. Dad wouldn't throw me out like a heroine in a Victoria melodrama,' she said to Ruth. 'It's she who doesn't want me to be seen, but where she thinks I'll hide the baby when he comes I don't know. Shooing me off like a flock of geese won't work then, will it?'

'Have you seen Henry, lately?' Ruth asked her. 'The shops change hands next week and he'll be leaving.'

'I know and isn't it wonderful? The place he's going to run is called Country Walks Centre and I know it will be a success.'

'You've see it?'

'Twice. I went over yesterday to see how the alterations are progressing.'

Ruth listened to Tabs explaining how some of the bedrooms were being divided into two, and about the extra bathrooms that were being installed. Already the barn was cleaned and would be ready to use for parties and barn dances by the end of the summer. She listened and nodded, pretending she knew all about it. Inside she ached with misery.

When Henry called at Ty Gwyn on the day before she was finally leaving, she invited him in wondering what he had to tell her. She dreaded hearing the name Lillian, afraid Henry was more than her friend.

'I have a problem,' he began and she frowned, expecting the name Lillian to be a part of the next sentence. 'I have seven guests coming in two weeks' time and I haven't found enough staff.'

'Can't Lillian help,' she asked, and immediately regretted the childish response. 'I mean, doesn't she know anyone who needs work?'

'She thought of you. How do you feel about helping, just for a while. I need a cook and someone to take charge of the cleaners and the waitresses.'

'Why me?'

'You can cook and you need a job.'

There was that suspicious hint of amusement in his eyes and she hesitated. Humiliation faced her if he and this Lillian had fallen in love. Yet even in such circumstances she was curious.

'I don't know what my plans are yet, but I don't mind helping for a week or two.'

'Thank you. We'll expect you on Saturday, we'll have a week to get ready for the first group.'

Awkward to the last, she shook her head and said she'd be there on Sunday.

She moved into Aunty Blod's flat with as few possessions as possible, aware that there was very little room to spare. Some of her things were in store, the rest she stored in the bungalow with Tabs, Mali and Megan.

Sharing with Blodwen was difficult. Aware that her aunt was used to living alone, she tried to avoid disturbing her routine. Meals were a problem too as she couldn't take over in her usual manner, she had to wait and find out what and if she could do anything to help.

Henry called for her early on the Sunday morning and she was dressed smartly, determined to outshine the dreaded Lillian, but she carried a bag filled with older clothes more suitable for sorting out the kitchen which she could hardly remember, except that it looked small.

She was thinking about the large room in Ty Gwyn with its fireplace and the old couch when she stepped out of the car. The door opened before they reached it and an elderly lady stood there. She was small and she walked with the aid of a walking stick. She was smiling and the pretty face with its surrounding white curls was welcoming. Ruth smiled at her and reached for the offered hand, wondering where this charming lady fitted into this new household.

'Hello, Ruth,' the lady said. The smile deepened as she added, 'I'm Lillian.'

CHAPTER TEN

The surprise at meeting Lillian must have shown on Ruth's face, as both Lillian and Henry began to laugh. 'I think Ruth was expecting someone younger,' Lillian said. 'Have you been teasing her, Henry?'

'I didn't expect someone so pretty,' Ruth said, recovering. 'I've been so busy clearing the house and all that entails we haven't had much time to talk.' She turned to glare at Henry but he had gone inside and she and Lillian followed.

She was led into a room in which work had been completed. Henry's mother wiped a few cups which had been wrapped in tea towels against the dust that was everywhere. She unpacked sandwiches and cake and said, succinctly, 'Lunch.' They found seats and ate, the two older women working happily together as food was offered and tea poured. Ruth could find little to say. All this was Henry's and nothing to do with her, all she could do was ask questions and she didn't feel able to do that.

She had barely looked at the house when she and Henry had come months ago and now, as she was shown around she looked at every room with great interest, surprised at how large it was. 'How did you think of such a grand idea?' she asked Henry.

'From you partly.'

'Me? I'd never have thought of running a Country Walks Centre.'

'The walks we enjoyed, the places we visited, the enjoyment of watching wild life and searching for rare flowers, made me think that perhaps others would enjoy them too. It grew from there, and when I saw this house and its extensive grounds I knew I'd found my dream.'

'You didn't tell me that at the time.'

'The time wasn't right,' he reminded her.

She watched as workmen dragged out a piece of lino, dust flying up as it shed cement and oddments of rubble. 'It looks more like a nightmare than a dream at present,' she said.

The place was one large mess with work in progress in almost every room. Shelves and walls pulled down, and others added. An extension was being made to the kitchen, which had been rather small, and three of the bedrooms were being divided to make two where there had been one.

Gradually, Henry explained what he was doing and after showing her the house, he led her to the barn, where work was almost completed. It was a large space and apart from one small dividing wall in a corner, planned for a kitchen and serving area, the room was to stay the same. The walls were lined with plywood and windows had been installed. 'This,' he told her proudly, 'will be the dining-room when we have a full house and in the winter, we'll be having barn dances and parties. What d'you think?'

She made some comment about how well he had thought everything out, but couldn't really tell him what she was thinking. The truth was she felt cheated somehow, left out, and she knew the reason had been her own insistence that her problems were paramount. She knew she had ignored the times he had tried to tell her about this, his dream, all this planning and organizing about which she had known nothing.

He talked about the grounds and the safety plans so children could stay and they talked about the walks he was including, the arrangements already made with several local farmers, including several she knew.

Lillian called them and they went back into the least messy room, where she and Henry's mother had set out tea and biscuits. Rachel took out notebooks and swatches of material and the three women discussed colour schemes while Henry went to help with the work in the kitchen.

'Surprised at my son's change of direction?' Rachel asked, as they spread out the sample squares of colours in an experimental fan.

'I had no idea,' Ruth said, then added, 'I've been so busy, with the family and the house sale.'

'Yes, dear, you've told us,' Rachel said, with just a hint of disapproval in her gentle voice. When Lillian left, Ruth said she was ready to leave also. 'I promised Aunty Blod we'd go to see Mali and Megan,' she explained. It wasn't the truth; she was feeling uncomfortable, an outsider, in the presence of Henry's mother and his friend Lillian. They disapproved of her, and she felt she didn't belong, she was an interloper in the new life on which Henry was embarking. Henry nodded, stopped what he was doing and prepared to drive her back to the flat.

After taking Lillian home they drove back to where Aunty Blod was impatiently waiting to hear about the project. Before Henry left to return to the new place, he said, 'I know you're busy,' which to Ruth sounded like a criticism, 'but if you'd like you can come over and discuss what equipment we need for the kitchen, Mum and Lillian would be grateful for any suggestions.'

'"Grateful" — if you only knew how I hate that word!'

'Mum is marvellous, but I need some advice on the kitchen layout from someone who knows. Feeding all your family is good training for a project like this one.'

The weeks before the first visitors arrived at the centre were very busy and despite her determination not to become involved, Ruth increased her visits until she was there every day, helping to clear up after the builders at first, and discussing with Rachel the arrangements of the rooms. Although a room had been offered to her, Ruth went back to Aunty Blod's flat every day, either Henry or Rachel driving her.

Although Henry's mother was dealing with the furnishings, she was willing to listen to Ruth's suggestions and ideas, and indeed encouraged her to take part when they discussed the way the place was set out.

'It has to be comfortable but simple,' Henry had told them. 'Cleaning will have to be considered so there won't be too many frills and fancies.' Both Ruth and Rachel agreed and together they chose curtains and bed covers and rugs that would make the rooms look homely but with material that was not difficult to launder.

'The kitchen is where we need your expertise,' Rachel told her firmly. 'I can't think beyond white walls and yellow curtains! Henry wants to leave the planning of what goes where, and the best equipment to buy, to you.'

Pleased to have been asked to contribute, she spent the next few days gathering information and prices of kitchen equipment and drawing a plan of how it should be set out. She tried not to imagine living there and sharing the dream with Henry. That was no longer a possibility; her involvement with her family had meant the project had happened at the wrong time, the opportunity was gone.

* * *

Jack was surviving without a permanent place to sleep and without a job. He saw Abigail and Gloria often but he couldn't stay with them as they had only two rooms in someone else's house. He hadn't tried for another job either. Word got around between business people and, as last time, it wouldn't be long before someone passed on the warning that he was a thief.

He was on the point of moving right away, to another town that might be the one he sought, but each time he made plans to leave something stopped him, usually lack of money. He saw Tabs one morning as she was on her way to the newsagents and he stepped out and without giving her the chance to move away, he held her and kissed her.

'Tabs, love, I've missed you. You living with Mali and Megan there's no chance to see you or talk to you and I've been so miserable.'

'You want to know how I am?' she asked with gentle sarcasm 'Whether the baby is all right?'

'Of course.'

'We are both fine.' There was an edge of disappointment in her voice. 'Ruth comes with me when I go to the doctor or the clinic. She's been wonderfully kind, considering how you persuaded me to let you into her house and search through her things.'

'I'm sorry, love. I shouldn't have involved you. You were so good to help me as you did.' He lifted her arm to see her watch. 'Any chance of coming to the café for a cup of tea? I've got two shillings and seven pence in the whole world and I want to spend it on you.'

She smiled. 'I'll meet you at lunchtime when I finish at the newsagents and I'll treat you to a hot meal; it sounds as though you need one.'

He was waiting outside when she left and he kissed her on the cheek and led her to a café in a road off the main street and found them a table. The menu consisted of an assortment of choices all served with chips. She ordered a full plate for him and a snack for herself and sat watching as he ate hungrily.

'I'm thinking of moving on,' he told her, 'but,' he added quickly, reaching out to hold her hand, 'I'll keep in touch with you. It's just that with the house being sold, and no chance of finding the Tyler family that I'm looking for, I want to go somewhere and find a decent job. I have to find a way of earning some money so I can look after you and our baby.'

'I don't want to be left on my own — couldn't we marry? At least that would stop some of the wagging tongues.'

'I don't want our marriage to be a sordid affair, performed in secret, just so we can convince the small-minded that we've been married since last year.'

'No one will believe that. Not now. But our son, or daughter would know they weren't illegitimate,' she whispered.

'Please, can we wait? I know that if I can only find the money owing to me, we can do it all properly. That's what I want for you.'

'Where are you staying?' she asked.

'Nowhere at the moment,' he said 'I left the place I stayed until last night as it wasn't very clean. Don't worry about me. I'll soon find somewhere that's cheap and cheerful.'

'With two shillings and seven pence?'

'I lied,' he said ruefully. 'I have enough for a few nights but I daren't spend it. You don't want me sleeping in the fields, do you?'

She left him to go back to the bungalow and he went to where he'd been promised a few hours work cleaning in the cellar and yard of a brewery. There were a couple of empty stables in the yard and if he was careful, he might be able to sleep there that night. It was warm up in the loft where the hay used to be stored.

Tabs went home in a confused state of mind. She didn't know if she would see Jack again and the future looked even more uncertain now he had made some more of his false promises.

* * *

One by one, Ruth's friends and family came to see what Henry was doing. Tabs came with Mali and Megan one Sunday morning and they had brought food in the hope the weather was kind enough for a picnic. The woods beyond the garden looked inviting. On their way to look around it, Mickie ran straight into the stream, but he was firmly held on his reins and Megan had prepared for it and dressed him in waterproofs and Wellingtons; he thought it great fun. The fence and a strong gate would be installed before the first visitors arrived, as day-visitors had been invited to bring children.

'You've thought of everything,' Megan told Henry.

'Except where to find someone to run it,' he said.

The girls had come by car and the driver was sitting in the car waiting for them. 'Who is he?' Henry asked. 'Why don't you invite him in?'

'Kenny,' Mali told him. 'He's someone I know from the Saturday dances.'

'He's a musician,' Megan added.

'He plays with the dance band when he can and he drives buses,' Mali told them.

Kenny came in and was introduced. Mali looked happy and Kenny was attentive and it looked likely that the two would soon be more than friends. A glance at Megan's face showed a frown and Ruth guessed she was wondering how she would manage to work and look after Mickie if her sister married. Yet that was something they must have discussed often.

Abigail and her mother called and they brought a house sign they'd had made as a moving in present with the name of the establishment and, in smaller letters, Henry's name as proprietor.

'Visitors are fine,' Rachel said with a sigh when everyone had gone, 'but it slows down the work and there's plenty of that here. When the work is finished there's still the problem of finding a cook and housekeeper.'

With a show of reluctance she didn't really feel, Ruth agreed to take on the cooking. 'Just until you find someone suitable,' she told Henry. Then she wondered why she was being so stupid. Cooking for a crowd of people was something she enjoyed and adjusting to varying numbers wouldn't worry her at all. Working beside Henry in this new career would have been perfect, if she hadn't spoilt it all by her stubbornness. She watched as he walked down to check the measurements for the new gate at the stream, and felt a powerful burst of longing, wondering whether they would ever go back to the love they had once known.

* * *

Tabs stopped outside the shop that had been Henry's and looked at the window display. It wasn't centred properly and looked lop-sided, and a display of Georgian silver wasn't shown to best advantage. It needed to be higher, where it would catch the eye of passers-by. The shop door opened and she backed away, but a voice called her and she turned to see the new owner, Peter James, beckoning to her.

'Come in, Miss Bishop, if you have a moment.'

'I was just going to the shops,' she said, edging away.

'Time for a brief chat, surely? I'd like to hear what you think of the way I've rearranged the shop.' He took her arm gently and guided her inside.

The counter had been moved back against the far wall, new lighting had been installed and the walls had been given a coat of bright yellow paint. Wall cupboards were also now lit, brightening the shop even more.

'It's wonderful,' she told him, looking around and smiling with pleasure. 'I can't believe the difference. Henry will be very impressed, I'm sure. But be careful to keep the shop window locked,' she said. 'Now it's unprotected by the counter and customers can walk up to it, it will be easier for someone to steal from it.'

'Thank you for that, but I've put another lockable bolt at the bottom, can you see?'

She smiled and looked around. 'It looks more cheerful, and welcoming,' she said.

'If you're looking for a job, would you consider coming back?' he asked. 'I need someone while I'm away at fairs and sales. What do you think?'

'I was sacked.'

'I know. But I don't think you'd do anything so foolish again. So, what d'you think?'

'I won't be able to after the next few months,' she said, stuttering in embarrassment.

'I know about that, too. But you still have your expertise and we can worry about the later stages of your pregnancy when we come to them. So, will you think about it?'

She didn't need to think about it; she desperately needed the money. 'Start tomorrow,' he said and didn't ask for references or discuss wages. She was too relieved to be earning to argue, she would accept whatever he paid her.

Strangely, it was Henry she wanted to talk to. There was no one else. Then she remembered that wasn't true; she was no longer friendless, there were others who cared. Ruth for one, who remained her friend despite her past behaviour towards her: allowing Jack to search Ty Gwyn and, she suspected, steal from her. Mali and Megan were well aware of her problems and sensible in their attitude to life. Feeling less alone, she was feeling almost happy as she went home to tell them about Peter James's offer.

* * *

The first visitors to the Country Walks Centre came by various means. Four in cars, two on bicycles and two by bus and on foot from the nearby youth hostel.

Rachel and a girl they had employed as a vague general help, showed them to their rooms and gathered them in the lounge where Henry gave an introductory talk. Ruth was panicking in the kitchen where she was setting out trays of tea and sandwiches, and preparing a supper of roast chicken and vegetables. On another table was a tray ready for an omelette and salad for the two vegetarians. 'That's all right for the first day,' she had said in alarm when she had been told of their preferences. 'But a whole week of vegetarian food? Help!'

By the end of that first week she felt able to deal with anything. She told Rachel that the job no longer held fears for her. 'It's much the same as feeding my brothers. One doesn't like this, another won't eat that, but it levels out. Is Henry pleased?'

'With the cooking? Delighted.'

'But?' Ruth waited for the criticism that hovered.

'We've spent too much money.'

'I haven't wasted much and practically everything was eaten. What more does he expect?'

'More economical meals, dear. If you feed them like kings, we'll be paupers before the end of the season.'

It took a while to convince her, but Ruth eventually listened to the advice of Rachel and Aunty Blod, who had worked as a cook for most of her working life, and a new menu was prepared.

The breakfast plate held less of the more expensive food and was filled by the addition of a few fried potatoes, and triangles of fried bread. 'They like a filling start to the day, these outdoor types,' Rachel assured her, and the breakfasts were accepted with delight.

Ruth went on a few of the walks with Henry, leaving Rachel dealing with the preparation of the evening meal and she listened with interest as he talked to the group. 'Take note,' he said. 'You never know when I'll need someone to help out.' She shook her head.

'Kitchen — that's where I feel at home,' she reminded him.

Some of the walks were at night where they waited for the badgers to appear, on fortunate occasions standing silently and watching the beautiful creatures in awe, most never having seen one before.

Ruth thought less and less about Ty Gwyn and the family, immersing herself in the new world of holidaymakers and the renewed joys of the surrounding countryside. The weeks passed and the summer drifted on.

* * *

Blod had almost forgotten about the mysterious letters and was surprised to receive another after months had passed. This one was similar to the other two as it gave no indication of the reason the friend wanted to meet her. The only difference was the addition of a plea and telling her that time was short and he needed to see her with some urgency. Another date was given and this time, she showed it to Henry.

'I think you should go,' he said, 'but not unless I go with you.'

It was another false alarm and again, no one approached her, even though Henry sat some distance away from her. They were laughing as he drove her back to her flat.

'It's obviously some poor soul who's bored and likes a joke. Probably watching from somewhere and wondering whether he can try it once more.'

'If you hear from him again, please tell me,' Henry said and he looked worried, glancing around him before he followed Blodwen into her flat 'And if you see someone hanging around, tell me straight away. Promise?'

'I promise. Hey, this is exciting, isn't it?'

'Yes, just someone having a laugh at your expense, but anything suspicious, tell me. Not that I think you need be afraid,' he added quickly. 'I'd like to catch the person and give them a good telling off, that's all.'

* * *

Tommy and Toni were considering buying a small, two bed terraced house. Toni had found it and was encouraging Tommy to take it, but Tommy was hesitating. Toni liked it and knew they would be happy there and she also knew why Tommy hesitated to make the decision. Until the twins found houses near to each other neither would move.

Bryn and Brenda were having the same discussions about a house that was at the end of a terrace but at least twenty minutes from the house Toni had found. They all needed to move to somewhere larger than the small flats they rented but it wasn't going to be easy to find somewhere to satisfy the brothers. Toni and Brenda knew it was futile to argue, they wanted their husbands to be happy and living no more than a few yards apart was essential to that.

It was Mali and Megan who found the solution. They were told about the house Toni liked and knew one of the neighbours. When the neighbour told Megan she was going to live with her daughter, Megan contacted the landlord and asked if he was considering selling.

In great excitement the two girls and Mickie went to see Tommy and told him about it. A hasty conference, a viewing and the twins went to see the owner and negotiated a price.

When they went to Aunty Blod's flat to share the news, Ruth showed none of her previous offence or dismay at not being told about the previous viewings. She had come to realize that their lives were not inextricably involved with hers and she greeted the news with delight. Perhaps because of this change of heart, Toni said at once that she must come and see the houses, and this was arranged.

The two houses were just two houses apart and they were identical, with two bedrooms, two living rooms, a tiny kitchen and long, narrow gardens, where the twins were already planning their vegetable plots.

When they went into the second bedroom of the house that would be Tommy's, they had a shock. The room wasn't empty like the others. There was a pile of sacks and a grubby blanket in a corner and a supply of half-eaten food. Spread carelessly around the floor was a loaf, pulled apart, tins of sardines, a half full lemonade bottle and a few apple cores.

'Damn me, we have a lodger!' Tommy gasped. Bryn stood on the banisters and pulled himself up to look into the loft but that was empty. They locked the door firmly and went to see the estate agent to report their find and were assured that the litter would be moved. Ruth wondered whether it was Jack, who, from what she'd learned from Tabs, was surviving on very little money.

From a nearby garden, Jack watched them go and gave a sigh. The empty house had been a comfortable place to stay but now he'd have to find somewhere else. A job in a public house had lasted no longer than the job with the furniture removers. Someone had told the manager about his thefts from the green-grocer and he was told to leave. He couldn't tell Abigail. He had told her the same as Tabs, that he was travelling further west where he'd heard of another family with the name he was convinced held the key to his treasure, but he was still around, stealing small amounts that so far hadn't resulted in the police being told, small amounts that people thought might have been a mistake on their part, and certainly didn't seem worth the trouble of calling in the police.

He called on Tabs at the antique shop a week after the house was no longer available to him for night shelter and at a time when he couldn't face another empty, filthy old barn.

'Jack! I thought you'd moved on,' she said.

'I did, but I came back. I'm worried about you, and I have to try and stay around here so I can see you, convince myself that you're all right.'

'What will you do?'

He began to cough then, and he was breathless when he calmed down. 'I've been ill,' he said, 'but once I'm all right, I'll try again to get work. This time I'll work so hard they'll never get rid of me. I hate asking you, Tabs, but could you lend me some money to tide me over till I get a job?'

'I can't spare any, Jack. Don't ask me to take from the money I've saved for when the baby is born, please.'

'It's only a loan,' he said, forcing excitement in to his voice. 'It's just a short loan. You won't believe this, Tabs, but I think I've found my family! Isn't it amazing? I've found them and as soon as the solicitor gets confirmation, the money will be mine. We'll be rich, Tabs, and we can be together, just like I've always dreamed.'

She didn't believe him, but she wanted to. She hesitated, and he kissed her, caressed her swollen body and said, 'Our baby, Tabs, we'll be so happy if you can be patient just a while longer.'

'Abigail loves you and believes you love her,' she said, trying to be strong. 'She says you and she are getting married.'

He shook his head. 'Perhaps she does love me, but she isn't carrying my child. You are where I belong, darling Tabs.'

'All the money is in a post office account. I'll need a few days to get it.'

'Thank you, my sweet, wonderful girl.' He turned the shop sign from open to closed and after a few moments of declaring his love for her, his kisses filling her with a longing to believe him, he left, slowly, reluctantly, coming back twice to kiss her again, and she was almost convinced.

She couldn't find Mali or Megan who were out for the evening at a children's party with Mickie, and Ruth was too far away. She had to talk to someone. So she went to see Aunty Blod, intending to wait there until Ruth came home. Within moments of arriving, she told Blod what had happened.

Blod listened carefully then told her she mustn't believe him. 'Can't you see how he's using you?' she said gently. 'Why hasn't he told Abigail that it's you he wants to be with? She truly believes he will marry her. Can't you see that it's lies he's feeding you? Shy you might be, young Tabs, but stupid you're not, so why are you pretending to yourself?'

'I don't want to upset him and maybe lose him. If I'm patient and understanding, he might—'

'Does Abi know it's his child you're carrying?'

'No, and I won't tell her until Jack says I can. She won't believe me and he'll be angry that I'd upset her. He'll tell her when he thinks the moment is right.'

'At least pretend there's a delay in getting the money. You need everything you have for yourself and your baby. At least agree to that.'

Tabs agreed. 'But only for a while. I'm sure he'll return it and I want to help him.'

'He's a thief. Even you can't deny that, dear, so what makes you think he'll return the money?'

'I don't. I just hope he will.'

Three times over the following day when she saw Jack approaching, she closed the shop door and turned the sign around and hid in the back room. She felt guilty and very foolish but she had to be honest, Blod had been right about her needing the money and she couldn't face Jack and tell him she couldn't help him. She saw him five times and after three days she saw him no more and wondered where he had gone. And whether she would ever see him again.

She had found Peter James a considerate man to work for and happily stayed longer than the hours for which he paid her. She had nothing else to do. She rarely went out, self-conscious about her now clearly visible pregnancy that attracted comments, many overheard and many more just imagined. Mali and Megan pleaded with her to go with them to the dance.

'Not to dance, we know you'd hate that, but can't you come and watch from a safe corner? It's such fun and we know you love the music,' Mali pleaded, one day in late August.

On Mali's promise not to try and coax her out from the darkest corner, she agreed. Wearing her largest dress and draping a large scarf around her shoulders to hang down in front of her she went. Her first surprise was Megan being with them, Abi having agreed to stay with Mickie for a few hours.

She recognized Kenny, playing trumpet with the five-piece band on the stage and her feet were soon tapping with the rhythm of the melody, then the singer appeared. There, in a shimmering dress, in front of the microphone was Mali. She sang two songs and the compère announced that she would be back later in the evening with two more.

'Isn't she's wonderful!' Tabs said to Megan.

Mali had often left the audience to sing but this was different. She wore a beautiful long gown that glittered, and the spotlight was on her. She was a part of the entertainment as never before. 'I knew she could sing, but it's such a long time since I heard her perform. This is more wonderful than I imagined.'

'Your sister is a star!'

'They love her, don't they,' Megan said proudly. 'I think I'll be losing my lovely sister before long; either Kenny or her talent will take her away from me.'

'Are you worried?' Tabs asked.

'Not as long as you'll stay with me, for a while anyway, until romance takes you away too.'

Thoughts of Jack came immediately to Tabs's mind and were pushed away. That scenario was no more than a cruel joke.

* * *

Ruth was walking towards Ty Gwyn one afternoon and she saw a young woman walking down the path near the front door brushing up leaves, watched by a baby in a pram. Beside them, a boy of about five was struggling with a large and boisterous dog. She stopped and smiled. The house was certainly being lived in, she thought and realized that she felt little of the regret and sense of loss she had once thought would never leave her. She saw the carefully gathered leaves scattered by sudden exuberance on the part of the five year old, and watched as the mother laughed and pretend to chase him with the witch's broom. An idea came to her and she stood a moment longer wondering whether Henry would be interested when she heard a car slow and stop. She was about to move on and she turned to see Henry frowning at her from the driver's seat.

'I was just thinking—'

'Don't tell me. I don't want to know,' he said irritably.

He started to move off and she shouted at him, 'I was just thinking that we could have a Halloween party in the barn!' She turned and hurried off in the opposite direction. By the time he'd turned and followed she would be out of sight. Just as well or they'd have an argument.

Footsteps behind her made her turn and she saw Henry running to catch her up. She took a deep breath and prepared for battle. He caught hold of her arm and smiled. 'Brilliant idea, I can't think why I didn't think of it!'

She felt her shoulders droop from the position of defence. 'You think it's possible?'

'Just what's needed to bring the place to the notice of the local people. Country-wide advertising is essential, but this first winter we'll need something more. Will you help?'

'I've planned quite a few for the—' She hesitated, then said defiantly. 'I know you don't like me mentioning them, but I arranged all sorts of parties for my brothers and their friends, so your Country Walks Centre won't faze me for a moment!'

'Your expertise has never been in question. It's your temper: you're more stormy than the weather.' He was smiling and she looked away, not wanting to back down.

'We can discuss it when I come tomorrow,' she said, beginning to walk away.

'Why not now? There isn't much time, is there, if we're going to get the event advertised.'

She walked back to the car and he held the door for her. They drove to the edge of town, and parked outside a restaurant.

'I can't stay long,' she warned.

'Why? Who are you feeding now?'

'Aunty Blod will wonder where I am.'

'All right, just a drink and I'll drive you back.'

She took out a notebook and began to write a list as he went to buy tea and cream cakes. When he came back she began to discuss the ideas she had noted. She looked up as he made no comments and saw that he was again, smiling.

'I wish you'd stay at the centre, or will you learn to drive so you can get there easier?'

'Drive?'

'Yes, a motor car. You know, you must have seen some about the place,' he said, clearly amused.

'What are you laughing at?' she demanded. 'Have I got cream on my face?'

'You. The way you question everything I say, with such suspicion. And yes, you've got cream on your face.' Now she was laughing too.

They discussed the ideas she had written and agreed to make a firm plan on the following day and get the advertising underway. As it was the end of their first summer, Rachel suggested the profits should be given to a charity to encourage more supporters and they decided on a charity for sick children.

'I walked past Ty Gwyn yesterday,' Ruth told Rachel, 'and I was surprised at how I have become accustomed to seeing a new family there. A young woman was in the garden brushing up leaves with a witch's broom and the children and a huge dog were hindering her efforts and she was laughing. It seemed so right to see them there. Isn't it strange? I thought I'd be unable to see strangers there.'

'I'm glad, my dear,' Rachel said. 'Change is good for us so we don't get too complacent, too satisfied with what we have, not realizing we can have so much more.'

* * *

Blodwen had been to the morning market in a nearby village and she had missed the bus back. Knowing she would have to wait for an hour for the next, she began to walk, confident that the bus would stop for her if she was between stops, if she waved her stick. A man approached and she stopped to stare at him, unsure at first, then she recognized Jack. He was in filthy clothes having just finished cleaning a yard for a farmer. He hated jobs that left him dirty but he didn't refuse any opportunity to earn a few shillings. Seeing Blodwen made him wish he could turn around and walk in the opposite direction, It was too late, she had recognized him and was watching him, disapproval on her wrinkled face.

'Missed the bus?' he asked.

'You won't be allowed on a bus looking and smelling like you do!'

'I'm walking through the fields. It isn't far, come if you like.'

She shook her head. 'I'll wait.' He shrugged and she saw him squeeze through a hedge and disappear in the direction of the town.

* * *

Jack, cleaned and wearing freshly laundered clothing, gathered from where he hid them, saw Abigail as he was about to walk through the park, presumably on her way back to work after the lunch break. She was passing the antique shop and, when he saw her cross the road as though going to see Tabs, he ran, calling her name, thankful he was tidily dressed. Tabs turned the corner and was about to open the shop door. He didn't want the two halves of his life to become close friends.

If Abigail learned the truth about him being the father of Tabs's child he would never see her again and that was too awful to contemplate. He loved her and if only he could solve the mystery of his inheritance, or forget all about it, he'd settle down to concentrate on looking after her. She had been so wonderfully understanding, accepting that he needed to find the truth, content to give him time, but even he knew he couldn't ask her to wait much longer. 'Abi,' he shouted and she turned as her hand was about to touch the shop door handle and walked towards him. He quickly led her away. Tabs was inside, taking off her coat and didn't see either of them.

'Jack. Just the person I want to see,' she said, and he was alarmed to see a frown on her face.

'Is everything all right, love?' he asked. He put an arm around her waist but she slid away from him. 'Abi? What's wrong?'

'Are you the father of Tabs's baby?' She looked at him, her eyes cloudy with doubts.

'What? Me and Tabs? Who's been talking rubbish? I love you, Abi, and you only have to look at Tabs to know there's no chance me doing anything more than a kiss to keep her sweet. I needed her help, you know that, but a baby? Abi, how can you think such a thing for a moment.' He pushed her gently into the doorway of an empty shop and held her close. 'Look in a mirror and you'll see a beautiful young woman, then compare yourself with poor Tabs. She'll never find a man to look at her with anything more than pity.'

Slowly convinced she asked, 'Do you know who the father is?'

'Yes, I know, but I can't tell you. Too many people will be hurt if the truth comes out.' His eyes slid in the direction of the antique shop and back to her face. 'I can't tell. Not even you.'

'Henry!' she gasped. 'It's Henry Owen, isn't it?'

'Don't make me say it, Abi. Please don't make me say it. Think of Tabs and Ruth and Henry's mother. So many people being hurt.'

'I'm so sorry, Jack. Mum really thought—'

'That I could lead the poor girl on and risk losing you? How could I look at anyone else when I have you?'

'Come with me now and talk to Mum. She's in the café waiting for me. Make her see she's mistaken.'

Gloria was not swayed by anything he said. 'He might convince you, Abigail, but I'm not so easily fooled. Haven't you realized how much time he's spending with Tabs? Face facts and tell him to go,' she said, staring into her daughter's eyes desperate to convince her.

'Leave it, Gloria,' Jack said wearily. He turned to face Abigail. 'You have to believe me. How can you think even for a second that I'd leave you? And with that poor Tabitha? Tabitha Bishop?'

She shook her head dejectedly but didn't offer him any assurances.

Late as she already was for work, Abigail waited until Jack had gone then went to see Tabs. 'Keep away from Jack!' she shouted, as she opened the door.

Tabs lowered her head. 'So you know then, about the baby? That it's Jack's?' she spoke in a whisper. 'Don't worry,

I won't ask for anything from him. I'll manage somehow. I'm not the first nor the last to find myself abandoned.'

It was true. The quiet conviction of Tabs's words was far more telling than her mother's outrage. Abigail stared at her for a few seconds, then ran off in tears.

'About time the truth was out,' Megan said, when Tabs told them.

'Glad I am, if it makes Abi come to her senses,' Mali added. 'She's put up with him wandering around the place not attempting to support her, believing he'll marry her next Easter and all the time, you and he . . .' She shrugged.

'Best without him, both of us,' Tabs summed up, brushing her hands together as though wiping the past months out of her life.

News sped around the town in days. Jack was shouted at and rudely pushed aside by men and women as he walked along the street. Martha and Tabs's father stopped him in the middle of the town and demanded to know what he was going to do. 'You'll pay for this,' George Bishop shouted and a crowd gathered. 'Taking advantage of poor simple Tabitha. You'll pay for this.'

Jack tried several times to talk to Abigail but she refused and eventually warned him she would talk to the police and tell them he was threatening her. Tabs ignored him when they met and he was in despair. The money was what he still hoped to find. If he had money he'd persuade Abigail to come back to him. Then he saw the To Let notice appear in the window of the flat above the antique shop. Henry had definitely moved out and Tabs was working for the new owner. He waited until he was sure Peter James was not there and went into the shop and locked the door.

'Tabs, please don't tell me to go away. I want to forget Abigail and stay with you. I'm longing to see our baby and if you'll come back to me, make a home for us all, I know we'll be so happy. I was caught up in affection for Abigail but it's you I love. I tried to look after them as I'd promised my friend but it all went wrong.'

She went to the door and opened it wide and stood there silently until he left.

* * *

Gloria went to the market the week following Blodwen's visit, to buy vegetables and a new frying pan. As she sat waiting for the bus, on impulse she decided to walk. It was a brisk autumn day and she felt so well after all the illness of previous winters that the prospect of a walk cheered her. She knew the route through the fields and it was only midday, there was plenty of time.

She hadn't bought much, so carrying was easy at first, but after a mile she began to regret her decision. She was on the point of hiding her shopping for her daughter to collect later, when Jack appeared. She adjusted the shopping bag on her shoulder and hurried on.

'Gloria, don't run away. I'm not angry with you any more, you were right to tell Abigail, I know that now. If I'd told her the truth instead of lying she might not have been so hurt,' he said catching her up.

She didn't deny his assumption that she had told Abi about Tabs's baby. It wasn't important what he thought of her. 'Go away. You've ruined her happiness and after she trusted you and allowed you to go off chasing rainbows and fantastic day-dreams. Evil you are and I don't know how you persuaded my daughter to believe you for so long.'

'She knows I love her and no one else,' he said. He took the shopping from her and carried it.

'And Tabs's baby, is that a fantasy too?'

'No, that's real. I was a fool. Just one mistake, that's all. I needed her help, see, and it all got out of hand.'

They crossed three fields, edging around a field of lively young cattle, and walked through a patch of neglected woodland. At the stream he jumped across then pointed further upstream to where a bridge stood.

'Just leave my shopping on the bank,' Gloria said. 'I don't want people seeing me walking through the streets with you. They might think I've forgiven you, and that I'll never do.'

He put the shopping on the grass a few yards from the stream and began to walk away. He was debating how he could find the money to go far away, forget the inheritance and Abi and Tabs and start again among strangers, when he heard a shout. He turned and there was no sign of Gloria. He ran back and saw that she had slipped on the mud at the edge of the stream and was lying half in the water, below a slide of mud marking her fall. He pulled her out of the water onto the opposite bank as the nearest was too steep, and sat her down to lean against a tree. He hoped she could walk. She was heavy and he wouldn't be able to carry her.

'Gloria, what happened?'

'I looked down at the swirling water and lost my balance and slipped on the mud.' He tried to help her up but she fell back with a shout of pain. 'You'll have to go for help, Jack. I can't walk, my leg won't hold me.'

He took off her coat and wrapped it firmly around her, then unpacked the shopping bag and used that to cover her legs. 'Not much help but it's the best I can do,' he said anxiously.

On the way back to the town, running to find a telephone box to ring 999 he saw Tabs. He was about to tell her what had happened but something held back the words. This was perhaps his last chance to persuade her to listen to him, make her see that she needed to help him. She had money and the possibility of a flat. Gloria wouldn't come to much harm in a few extra minutes. So he slowed his pace and walked back with her to the bungalow she shared with Mali and Megan. He believed that pleading his case was having some effect, he could see by her face that she wanted to believe him.

He stayed talking to her when they reached the bungalow and he was beginning to feel that there was some hope for him. He was about to leave her and get help for Gloria when he remembered the flat over the antique shop and he at once begged her to take it.

He tried with all his persuading skills to make her agree and when he glanced at her watch, he was alarmed to find that two hours had passed since he had left Gloria alone by the stream. Abigail would never forgive him if her mother became ill because of him. More alarming, it was already getting dark. As he went to call the police panic filled him. She'd be ill and he would be blamed.

'Where did you leave the lady?' the constable asked him and he pointed vaguely towards the fields behind the houses of the town. He didn't mention the stream, it wouldn't be so bad if he just mentioned her injured leg and said nothing about the fall into the water. He'd easily convince them it must have happened after he left her.

He went out with several others to where he said he had left her, but of course she wasn't there. She was sitting in wet clothes beside the stream two fields away.

A search of the area drew a blank and he was wailing his dismay, 'She's a lovely lady, better to me than a mother could be and I can't find her and it's dark and cold and it's all my fault.' Several people comforted him and said she must have managed to walk, and tried to get herself home. More guilt and more comforting went on through the night.

Abigail had been told about her mother being lost and she too joined the searchers. She didn't speak a word to Jack.

'See, she blames me, everyone will blame me,' Jack told the police loudly. 'I love Gloria. I wouldn't do her any harm.'

It was as dawn was breaking that they found her, still sitting against the tree at the edge of the stream, exactly where Jack had left her and a long way from the area he had described to the police.

Ambulance men carried her to the road and she was admitted to hospital semi-conscious and suffering from hypothermia.

CHAPTER ELEVEN

Abigail was waiting near the ambulance when the ambulance men carried her mother from the fields and down the narrow road. She stared in disbelief when she looked down at Gloria's unconscious face, looking so old she was almost a stranger. How hadn't she noticed how small and weary her mother had become?

The police were questioning Jack but she was hardly aware of what was being said.

'She hurt her leg and I came to the nearest phone box and rang for help,' Jack told them.

'Did you try anywhere else, were you delayed in any way?'

'No, I came as fast as I could.'

'Your friend Tabitha says you met her and walked with her for a while.'

'Yes, I met Tabs, but I didn't stop. I talked as we walked. I was frantic with worry.'

'Tabitha told my colleague that no, you didn't mention Gloria when you talked and no, you didn't seem in any hurry.'

'It's her condition, see, I didn't want to upset her.'

'Your child?' the constable asked.

Jack shrugged. 'That's what people believe.'

'The mud slide where she apparently fell into the water, it's not on the side from where she clambered out.'

'No, the bank is steep on that side, the opposite bank is easier to climb.'

'You noticed that, did you, sir?'

'Yes. When I saw the place where she was found.'

'Her hands were clean, no mud. If she'd clambered out that's surprising, isn't it? They'd be covered in mud, wouldn't they?'

Jack raised his voice and demanded, 'What are you implying?'

'Nothing, sir. Yet.'

Those were the words in Abigail's mind as she went into the ambulance and sat beside her mother.

She went with her to the hospital and it was as though time stood still, first as she walked up and down in the waiting-room, then after her mother was put into a ward, sitting beside her willing her to recover.

'Your mother had become very chilled,' the doctor told her.

'But she couldn't have been there very long,' Abi said. 'How could it happen so fast?'

'She must have been there for longer than you realized. Probably an hour or more. How far did the person who found her have to go for help?'

'Ask him, he's in the waiting-room,' she said. 'I know he wouldn't have delayed. He loves my mother.'

'I'll leave all that to the police,' she was told.

Tabs went to the hospital and asked whether she could see Gloria. She felt an odd connection with Abigail, probably because they had both loved Jack and had now both been let down by him. Jack's insistence that he had hurried to get help for Abigail's mother had been untrue. The reasons behind that lie were impossible for her to understand, but without knowing what he had told them, she had made it clear to the police that he was lying. Abigail came out and at once Tabs began to move away. 'I'm sorry, I shouldn't have come, but I wanted to see you, tell you I'm sorry I told the police what I did. I hadn't had the chance to speak to Jack, to know what he was going to tell them.' She was relieved to see that Abi looked worried and not angry.

'You told the truth, Tabs. He left my mother knowing she'd fallen into the stream and was sitting there soaking wet and very cold. How could he do that?'

'Perhaps he'll explain; perhaps it wasn't like it sounds. He loved her, didn't he? He wouldn't do anything to harm someone he loved.' And that excludes me, she thought sadly.

'Will you stay with me for a while?' Abigail asked.

The pregnant 'other woman' didn't seem appropriate company, but Tabs followed her back into the ward. They sat together, talking to Gloria although she was unconscious; they didn't know whether or not she could hear them.

So Tabs was with her when Gloria died. She sat beside her as the formalities were dealt with and then Henry came and took them both home.

Abigail found it very difficult to go into the rooms that from now on, would be empty every time she returned. No mother and at this time when she needed someone so badly, there was no Jack either, and never would be again.

* * *

Tabs went back to the bungalow and at once began to feel strange, niggling pains. She stood up and the pains began to sharpen. Megan saw her expression and held her. 'It's all right, Tabs, just try to relax. We'll get you to the hospital when things are underway.'

'Thank you. I don't know how I'd cope with all this without you and Mali,' she said.

Three hours later Tabs was back at the hospital and a few hours after that, gave birth to a daughter. 'Melanie Ruth Bishop,' she told Megan and Mali when they came to see the new infant.

'As he calls you Aunty, she's a sort of cousin for our Mickie,' Megan said happily.

* * *

Abigail couldn't decide whether she wanted to see Jack at the funeral or not. It was a very small affair, they seemed to have gathered very few friends and she was grateful to see that Ruth and Henry and their group were there to swell the congregation.

Afterwards, cars took them to Megan and Mali's bungalow where food was set out and they hovered a while but soon dispersed.

'I'm off to see Tabs and the baby, and tell her about it,' Megan said.

'I'll stay with Mickie.'

'I'd like to come too,' Abigail said. 'I know it's odd, under the circumstances, but it's Jack who's to blame here, not Tabs.'

When they reached the ward they were told they couldn't go in as there were already two visitors at the bedside. Curious, they peered through the small window in the door and Megan gasped. 'It's her father and that wife of his! I hope he isn't upsetting her, I'll box his ears if he's come to cause trouble.'

George and Martha Bishop gave them a brief nod as they left the ward and they hurried to where Tabs was sitting up in bed, smiling, and holding a five pound note.

'He didn't upset you then?' Megan asked.

'Lucky for him,' Abigail warned, 'Megan was going to box his ears!'

'He looked at the baby and he wore such a gentle expression. He said he'd help with money each month. I can't believe it.'

'And Martha? Was she in agreement? Or is she expecting you to work for it?'

'She looked about to explode!' Tabs was laughing, and then her face softened as they all admired the baby and she looked as near beautiful as they had ever seen her.

Smiling at her, Abi said affectionately, 'Motherhood suits you.'

* * *

Blodwen spent a few hours several times a week at Henry's Country Walks Centre and twice, when they were particularly busy with day visitors as well as residents, she stayed over. So she hadn't checked her post for a few days when she saw another letter from the mysterious stranger who had asked her to meet him then had failed to turn up. She almost threw it aside unopened but curiosity got the better of her once again and she read that he was very sorry he couldn't make it last time, but will she please try again. 'I promise I'll explain everything when we meet. Until then I would ask you not to say a word to anyone. Time is running out and I do need to talk to you.' A time and date were given and to her alarm she realized today was the date given. She looked at the clock. She had just two hours to make up her mind and no time at all to get in touch with Henry. If she went she'd be on her own.

She was there half an hour before the time stipulated and sat where she could watch the door. The day was cold and overcast, the door wasn't left open as on previous occasions and the room was gloomy. Every time the door opened, she looked up, screwing up her eyes wondering whether the newcomer was the person whom she waited for. Exactly on time a thin, sickly looking man came in. He looked around then went to the bar and asked for a glass of stout. Carrying it, he walked across to her and said 'Hello, Sis, it's a long time since we met.'

She screwed her eyes even tighter, 'Who the 'ell are you?' she asked, clutching her handbag protectively.

'I'm your brother, Ralph. Blodwen, don't you recognize me?'

She stared in disbelief for a long moment, but something about the eyes, the angle of the jaw, that long thin nose . . .

'Little Ralphy? You never are! Where have you been? What have you been doing? Why the secrecy?'

'You've put on some weight, Blod,' he said, smiling at her.

'You haven't! Skinny beyond you are and look as much use as a piece of chewed string!'

He sat down beside her and stared at her. 'I have a photograph of you and me and Hilda, want to see it?' He felt in his pocket and brought out a wallet from which he took a small, black and white photograph. 'Taken in the garden of Ty Gwyn,' he said. 'We had a party for my twelfth birthday, but I don't expect you'll remember that. But turn it over.' On the back was a childish scrawl saying, 'The three musketeers.'

'That's what we called ourselves,' she said softly, and stared at him again. 'It's really you?'

'It's really me. Now, tell me what you've been doing since we last met.'

'That's a lifetime, Ralph. It won't take much telling, mind. I never married and I worked as a cook most of my life. Hilda and William were killed but they had five children. Geraint, Emrys, and twins, would you believe, Tommy and Bryn. And a daughter, Ruth, who looked after them all till they married.'

'Still living at Ty Gwyn?'

'It's been sold and the money divided. Oh! I suppose you're entitled to some of that. Heck, that'll take some sorting, the twins have used their share to buy houses, Emrys too. And Geraint, he's in London licking his wounds after a divorce and starting up a new business.' She looked at him. 'What happened to you? Where have you been all these years? Did you go to Australia like Mam said?'

'Tell me about the others first.'

They talked for a very long time and he looked exhausted after two hours. Blodwen was tearful as they parted, proposing to meet very soon and introduce him to the family he had never known. He again begged her to say nothing until he could meet the family and explain things himself.

Blodwen found it difficult to keep quiet about her unexpected meeting with a brother she had presumed must be dead. She broke the promise once, by telling Henry, and he agreed to say nothing. 'There has to be a strong reason for his secrecy,' Henry said, 'and we might spoil something very special to him if we tell anyone he's back.'

'He's very ill. Not long for this world if I'm any judge.'

'Then perhaps that's why he wants to wait until everyone is present, and not tell his story many times.'

The days passed slowly as she waited for their next meeting, this time in a café in Cardiff. Two days before the arrangement a letter came. The handwriting was more shaky than before and in it he apologized but couldn't meet as planned. He explained that he was in hospital once more and would write when he was well enough to meet her. She whispered her disappointing news to Henry and waited patiently each day for the postman.

* * *

Tabs was surprised when her father became a regular visitor. He brought presents, nursed the baby and seemed genuinely thrilled with his granddaughter. Tabs was reminded by Mali and Megan to be cautious.

When Melanie was three weeks old, he came with Martha. A look at Martha's face was enough to tell Tabs that her stepmother was not ready to be impressed with her new and beautiful step-grandchild. She handed Tabs a hand-knitted coat in an off-hand way then sat, her shopping bag clutched on her lap in a very un-relaxed attitude and waited impatiently to leave. Megan was there with Mickie, and she deliberately ignored George's hints that she should leave them to talk in private.

'We've been talking about things, Tabs,' her father began. 'This isn't a time for you to be with strangers. Why don't you come home where you belong?'

'No, I'm never coming back.'

'Don't say that! I'm your father, you belong with me.'

Her heart beating fit to burst, Tabs picked up her daughter and said, 'I want Melanie to enjoy a childhood without criticism. To grow up confident, happy with who she is.'

'How can she do that? She's illegitimate! You won't be able to hide that!' Martha said, ignoring George's attempts to stop her. 'Illegitimate she'll be and everyone will know it.'

'She'll be told when she's old enough to understand, and by then she'll be strong enough to cope.' Tabs spoke in a quiet but confident manner and, glancing at Megan, she saw her cheering, out of her parents' sight and smiling widely.

'Sorry, but we have to ask you to leave,' Megan said then. 'It's time for Tabs to feed our Melanie.'

'Don't worry, we're leaving!' Martha stood up and gestured to her father. Tabs was pleased to see some, albeit slight, hesitation by her father, a final look at the baby before he stood to leave.

Before they were out of the room, Megan picked up Mickie who had been drawing on a blackboard with coloured chalks, and said,' Look, Aunty Tabs, isn't Mickie the cleverest boy?' She and Tabs discussed the artistic achievements of the three-year-old as George and Martha left.

'Pity about that,' Tabs said with a sigh. 'I don't suppose Dad will send us any more money now.'

* * *

The note Blodwen had been waiting for came at last and she went into Cardiff to meet her long lost brother. Ralph looked slightly better, there was a little colour in his cheeks and his eyes were brighter, sharper, as he watched her approach, leaning on her stick, then waving it, to the alarm of passers-by soon as she saw him. They ordered lunch but Blod noticed that Ralph ate very little.

'What is wrong with you?' she asked.

'Prison pallor,' he said grimly. 'That and a chest problem that is very unlikely to get better.'

'Prison?'

'It's a long story and I'll tell you when I meet the rest of the family.'

She didn't ask any more questions, just answered his — and there were many. He wanted to know all about their sister Hilda and William's children. 'I hope I stay well enough to meet them and get to know them,' he said sadly.

'What about you, Ralphy? Did you marry? Do you have any children?'

He shook his head. 'Not a single person in the whole world.'

She looked at him. It was obvious he was seriously ill and, determined to be cheerful, said, 'Why don't you come and stay with me? My flat is small but then, you aren't very big, are you?' she teased. 'Our Ruth is there at the moment but she can easily stay at Henry's place.' She had to tell him again, who Henry was and how he fitted into the family circle.

'D'you mean that?' He stared at her his eyes bright, almost feverish, she thought in alarm. 'You'd really look after me, someone you don't know? Someone who's been in prison?'

'Just so long as it wasn't for murder,' she said cheerfully.

'It was debts,' he said. He looked away, wondering how much to tell her. He still needed her to say nothing and the more she knew the more likely she was to talk about it. But she deserved to know some of the story if she was inviting him to share her home. The decision made, he asked for reassurance that she would tell no one until he was ready and said, 'I had a good business, selling newspapers, cigarettes and sweets and a few gifts. It was a perfect spot where people passed on their way to work or the shops or to school. It was a good living but I had to close when some nearby buildings were demolished and the bus stop was moved and fewer people passed.'

'And that's when the debts began?'

'Not exactly.' The expression on his pale face showed pain and sadness and something more. He patted her hand and began to rise. 'Time to go.' It was obvious he wasn't going to tell her any more.

'Think about what I said about coming to stay, Ralphy. You'll be all right with me, I'll soon fatten you up. If there's one thing the women of our family can do it's cook! Me, our Hilda and Hilda's Ruth, all good at feeding people. Oh, she'll be so pleased to see you. A great one for family, our Ruth.'

Blod was filled with excitement and again broke her promise and talked to Henry. 'If I don't tell someone I'll explode!'

He listened to her and asked a lot of questions to which she had few answers.

'Are you sure he's your brother?' he asked her.

'No doubt at all, and it would hardly be a stranger trying to steal my money, would it? I haven't any!'

It was difficult to be patient but she managed to say nothing to Ruth. Instead, she began writing down anything that came to mind that Ralph might like to know. After so many years there was a very long list.

* * *

Henry decided that the Halloween party would be used to advertise the centre and he invited several people from the town and reporters from the local newspapers. Tabs and Megan dealt with the decorations which included silhouettes of witches, cats, bats and owls, and all kinds of weird and wonderful models of castles. Moonlight artificially produced from lanterns lit the scene, low light bulbs were placed behind cut out figures of mysterious creatures adding to the eerie effect. The path down the side of the house to the barn was lined with jam jars each with a candle to light the way.

Ruth and Aunty Blod organized the food with Rachel and Lillian helping. Henry had bought trestle tables which groaned under the weight, and an unexpected delivery brought a piano, which Henry said would be useful when they arranged further dances and parties. Three musicians were booked and the music was already underway when the first guests arrived.

Megan and Mali were there with a very excited Mickie, and Tabs's baby girl was put to sleep in a cot which had been provided for visitors. Watched over by Blod and Rachel, she slept contentedly throughout the evening.

The party was a great success and stories about the evening were on everyone's lips over the next few days. 'If we've made a loss it would still have been worth it for the publicity,' Henry said, as they cleared away the last of the dishes left by the happy crowd. When they worked out the profit, Henry hugged Ruth and for a moment she relaxed in his arms, but then he released her and they stepped away from each other, embarrassed and sad.

* * *

Abigail didn't go to the party, she found it difficult to cope with the loneliness of being without her mother and happy crowds would have been hard to take. The landlord had removed one of the single beds out of her room to give her more space but that had made it worse. She moved the solitary bed to various angles, trying to hide the vacant place but nothing eased the pain of her loss.

She was successful at work, making an effort when people came to choose hats for special occasions, mostly weddings, as well as suggesting dresses and accessories from other departments of the shop. She was only twenty-one but decided that marriage wasn't going to be her future. She'd been such a fool, encouraging Jack to follow his dream, trusting him, wasting all the money she had earned. He had let her down so badly and, even though she had forgiven Tabs and become her friend, Jack's dishonesty and his culpability in her mother's death would never be forgiven. She had thought she'd known him so well. How could she ever trust someone again?

* * *

Henry went into the barn one morning to wash the floor and someone ran out. He gave chase and caught Jack, who was carrying a bucket in which there were apples, left from the party, and a few cakes.

'I'm sorry, Henry, but I'm broke and starving hungry. I was only taking stuff you would have thrown away.'

Henry took the bucket from him and urged him on his way. 'You won't get yourself out of your mess by stealing,' he said angrily. 'Find honest work. You're young and strong and many worse off than you manage to avoid stealing from others. Get out!'

Jack left, grateful for the apples and Welsh cakes he'd managed to hide in his pockets. He ate as he walked down to the town, cutting across the fields, stopping to drink the fresh clean water from a spring. He tried to forget Henry's words but they kept coming back and he knew he was right. Wasting all these months searching for an inheritance that probably didn't exist, he'd been a fool. He'd narrowly escaped arrest over the death of Gloria, although he had been warned that the case was not closed. Worst of all, he had lost Abigail.

He counted the money in his pocket, enough to travel a few miles and try to start again. Thoughts of another family called Tyler who might hold the key to his treasure were swiftly pushed aside. He'd start again; he was smart enough, once he could forget searching for the mysterious 'treasure' waiting to be claimed, and then, when he was firmly back on his feet, he'd come back for Abigail. Whistling cheerfully he went to where she worked and waited outside for her to come out for her lunch. He'd just tell her what he was planning and then leave.

She saw him straight away and turned in the opposite direction. When he caught up with her she stepped into a shop and he followed. She left and went into the shop where he had worked and from where he had been sacked and he waited outside. When she came out the owner of the shop was with her and he stood until Jack gave up and walked away. Curious despite her determination to forget him, Abigail followed and watched as he walked to the railway station, paid for a ticket and stood on the platform until the sound of the engine could be heard. She stood out of sight as he gave one last look around then got on the train. She brushed away tears and told herself she was pleased. With him out of the town she could really believe that he, with his tainted love, was gone for ever.

* * *

Jack found a seat on the train and sat there filled with a mixture of remorse and excitement. He didn't really believe he had lost Abigail for ever, one day he'd come back and find her. He'd be successful, and would have money honestly earned, would have put aside his dishonesty and convince her he would look after her for ever. It sounded so simple and, really, it was. All he had to do was get a decent job and work hard at it, and stay out of trouble.

He'd stay away from other women and forget the foolish search for an inheritance. Resolution swiftly faded when on the train he noticed the name Tyler, written on a letter held by another passenger.

'Excuse me, sir,' he said politely, 'but do you live in this area?'

'Not any more,' the man replied. 'But not far away. Just outside Dinas Powys. Why do you ask?'

'I'm distantly related to some people with that name and wondered if you were connected. I've lost touch over the years and would like to meet them again.'

'Sorry, but I don't think we'll be your missing relatives,' he said firmly. 'We're a very small family and so far as I'm aware, we haven't lost anyone,' He smiled and stood to get off at the next station. Moving swiftly down the train, Jack jumped off and followed him. London could wait.

In Dinas Powys, he found a job in a shop, this time giving his real name and making everything official. There was a pretty girl working beside him, called Winnie and he flirted a little; life, he told himself, doesn't have to be completely boring. He invited her to the pictures but wryly admitted that their date would have to wait until pay day. Unfortunately the film she chose was in the town he had just left, but Tabs wouldn't be going out, not with the baby to look after, and Abigail rarely enjoyed a trip to the cinema, as she preferred the theatre. Taking a chance on being seen added to the excitement and they went.

* * *

Mali always had a special glow after meeting Kenny, and Megan and Tabs discussed the possibility of Kenny proposing. Mali sang with the band in which he played trumpet and with so much in common, it was no surprise that love had grown between them.

'What will you do?' Tabs asked, as she helped Megan clear away Mickie's toys.

'I'll stay here as long as you stay with me, I suppose. Then find someone else to share.' She looked at Tabs and smiled. 'Sorry, that sounded as though I expect you to go. I really hope you'll stay. We get on so well, but I don't want you to feel you have to.'

'I can't imagine leaving here. I love Mickie and I'm so happy here with you and Mali. Motherhood wouldn't be so wonderful without you two sharing it. If you are happy to help with Melanie, as you suggested, I think I've got an evening job. Nothing exciting, and if I get it I'll tell you all about it.'

'A pub? Café?'

'I'll tell you later,' Tabs said, smiling.

'Marvellous news. You with a job, and Mali happy with Kenny, we'll have to have a celebration.'

'Maybe we should wait, we might be planning an engagement party soon,' Tabs added.

As though continuing with their conversation, Mali came bursting in, her eyes glowing, her cheeks rosy with happiness, and told them Kenny had asked her to marry him.

When they had calmed a little from the congratulations and hugs and details of how and when he proposed, Megan asked what their plans were.

'I don't know. We didn't get that far, just said we loved each other and want to spend our lives together. The details will come later.'

They stayed up late discussing the possibilities, including what kind of wedding and whether their mother would like to be involved, and it was when Mickie came out of bed to see what the noise was about, that they reluctantly postponed further discussion and went to bed. Tabs lay awake day-dreaming of a wedding with herself as the bride and Jack as her groom, but even a dream without substance couldn't stop her feeling happy for Mali and Kenny.

Mali didn't see Kenny until the following Saturday when it was her turn to go out. They met at the dance, and during the interval they talked about their love and a little about the future. It was as he walked her home that Kenny told her about a job he had been offered.

'It's with a much bigger band and a wonderful chance for me. You too,' he added. 'They've heard you sing and want to include you in their next programme.'

'You won't give up your job though,' she asked. 'It's too risky to take a chance on a band you haven't played with before and we'll need steady money, won't we?'

'I'll get another job easily when we get to Newport.'

'Newport?'

'Yes, Newport. I'm so excited. We can marry and find a place and I can get started with a proper band and who knows where it will lead? I could get work in London! You'll have to work too. We'll need plenty of money. I'll need new clothes and probably a better instrument.'

'What about Mickie?'

Kenny frowned. 'He'll stay with his mother of course.'

'Megan and I have agreed we share responsibility for him and he's only three.'

'She can't hold you to that. Not if we're getting married. She'll manage. This is a wonderful opportunity for me, Mali.' As an afterthought he added, 'For you as well.'

'Of course,' she said quietly. 'But I can't come with you. Mickie is far too important to me and how would Megan cope? Without me there she wouldn't be able to work.'

'Free from Megan and her son, you'd be able to work full-time and we'd need your money for a while. I'm relying on you, Mali — don't let me down for the sake of your sister's mistake.'

She pushed him away and went home.

When she reached the bungalow, Tabs and Megan saw at once that something was wrong. Mali gave them a brief resumé of the conversation and they listened in silence.

'With Tabs here Mickie and I can manage. Don't worry about us,' Megan said.

'And I'm not going anywhere,' Tabs added. 'I might have a job and . . .' Aware that she was not contributing to the household expenses and knowing she couldn't continue at the antiques shop for much longer, Tabs had discussed the possibilities of sharing the care of Melanie and Mickie with the sisters, and had found herself a job three times a week at the local cinema.

'Go with Kenny and be happy,' Megan urged.

Mali shook her head. 'Everything he said included the word "I". He's doing this for himself, not me. And if he doesn't understand how I feel about you and Mickie, he doesn't know me at all.'

* * *

Tabs was standing, holding a torch to see people to their seats in the cinema when Jack walked in with the pretty girl on his arm. Tabs guided them into seats in the back row. Jack didn't look at the young woman holding the torch and settled into the seats putting a proprietary arm around the girl's shoulders. Later, when she was guiding people into seats near them she saw, to her pain and misery, that they were kissing. When she saw Ruth a few days later, she told her she had seen Jack, but they agreed not to tell Abigail what she had seen.

* * *

Ruth had continued to stay with Aunty Blod and she made her way to the centre by bus, but this morning Henry wasn't there. A glance at the rota showed he was out with a party. His mother was in the kitchen, already beginning to prepare food for the party of eight who were there for the day. 'They've taken a lunch pack,' Rachel told her, 'and they'll be back for tea at four, and supper will be at seven.'

Ruth began sorting out the meals, writing down the costs in a notebook she habitually kept so Henry and Rachel could make sure they were profitable. She looked at the booking forms and saw that already there were several parties already marked for the following year. 'Mostly repeat visits,' she remarked to Rachel.

'And what about you, Ruth, dear? Will you be here for the next season?'

Shocked by the question, Ruth said, 'I don't know what I want to do. It's been so busy here I haven't had time to think about it.'

'Henry needs to know he has staff he can rely on.'

Did he really think of her as staff she wondered in disbelief. 'So you think I should leave to give him a chance to find someone permanent, get them trained ready for the spring?'

'Only if you aren't certain of staying.'

So Henry wants her to go and he had left it to his mother to tell me, she thought as she pummelled the dough to make the bread rolls for supper. As soon as Henry appeared she said, 'I'm going to ask Mr Burrows for my job back. I don't want you to delay in finding staff you can rely on.'

'What are you talking about?' he asked.

'Talk to your mother,' she said and, reaching for her coat, she ran out just in time to get a bus back to Aunty Blod's flat.

'Insurance, it's quite an interesting job,' she explained to Blod. 'And with the money from the sale of Ty Gwyn I can afford a car to make it easier. I'll go and see Mr Burrows tomorrow. He said I should talk to him if I ever wanted my job back.'

Blod said very little but she went to the phone box and told Henry he was a fool before slamming down the receiver.

Ruth didn't talk to Mr Burrows. She spent some time with Abigail, and with Megan and Mali and Tabs, but refused to talk about what had happened. She missed her family, wished they were still together, at least Tommy and Bryn. Risking a rebuff, she went one evening to see first Bryn and Brenda, who seemed very content in their little house and hinting that a second baby might be announced soon. A few doors away the reception was different. Moving to a house hadn't changed Toni, she thought, as she was shown into the cold, neat front room, with its crimson velvet curtains and matching three piece suite. Tommy wasn't his usual ebullient self, quietly listening to her news and Toni sat, straight shouldered, in an upright chair looking as though she were timing her visit. Ruth wondered if they had been quarrelling, or whether it was her arrival that had caused such chillness.

'Toni wants us to move again in a month or so,' Tommy said eventually, as Ruth was beginning to make a move to go. 'She wants something a bit smarter.'

'What about Bryn and Brenda?' was Ruth's first question. 'They seem very content here.'

'That's always the problem,' Toni said. 'We don't have to do everything Bryn and Brenda do. I'm more ambitious than they are. We need to live in a better area, with decent neighbours. Somewhere our children can grow up with people in common with our tastes and aims.'

'Staying together is the same with Mali and Megan,' Ruth said calmly. 'But the reason they want to stay together is Mickie. When Megan decided to keep him, not have him adopted like her mother wanted, she and Mali promised to bring him up together.'

'More fool Mali! I hear she turned down a proposal of marriage to stay with her sister. It's ridiculous.'

'If you don't understand about Tommy and Bryn, how important they are to each other, you don't know Tommy at all,' she said, repeating Mali's words to Kenny.

'Rubbish.'

'Separate Tommy and Bryn and you'll regret it,' Ruth whispered as she left.

Ruth went home feeling dejected. It was ages since she'd heard from her older brothers. Emrys and Susan weren't that far away, yet an occasional letter was all they managed. Geraint, in London, had written to tell them that his wife had left the man for whom she had ended her marriage. 'But,' he had told Ruth when she had phoned him, 'the divorce will still happen. I could never trust her again, and going through this misery once is quite enough for one lifetime.'

'I knew this would happen, Aunty Blod,' she called, as she went into the flat, but there was no reply. Puzzled she looked for a note. She was probably visiting her neighbour Mrs Harrison, she thought, and set a tray for tea for when she returned.

* * *

Blodwen was at the hospital. She had heard from her brother and he had told her where to find him. She went on the bus and waited outside the ward with other visitors, aware that they all carried some small gift and bags of what appeared to be freshly laundered clothes. She wished she'd brought more than a small bag of fruit. But how could she know what he needed? Next time she'd do better. She mentally made a list of items to bring on her next visit.

Ralph was sitting up in bed, his face rosy with the heat of the ward. He greeted her with pleasure but his first words were, 'You haven't told anyone I'm here, have you?' She shook her head, kissed him lightly and offered the fruit. 'Sorry I haven't brought anything useful, but tell me what you need and I'll bring it next time.'

'No need, Sis. I'm leaving here tomorrow. I'll be in touch, but I don't want to come to your flat just yet.'

'What's your story, our Ralph? Why the secrecy? I'm bursting to know.'

'Patience for a while longer, please.'

They talked for the rest of the time about their childhood, bringing to mind things long forgotten. Blod was very thoughtful as she went home. When she went into the flat, preparing the lie about where she had been, she heard voices.

'Tell me why you've suddenly decided to leave the centre. I thought you were happy there. To go back to selling insurance? Not much cooking and caring there and that's what you're good at.' Blod put a hand over her mouth to stop calling. This might be important. She quietly slipped into her bedroom and sat on the bed.

'Your mother made it clear that I should leave to give you time to get proper staff before next season,' Ruth told him. 'You couldn't even tell me yourself!'

'But I haven't discussed you with my mother. I don't want you to leave. I — I depend on you.'

Ruth frowned angrily. 'Depend? That sounds worse than grateful!'

'I need you, Ruth, and I always will. I thought we'd build up this business together. Please stay.'

Spoken as a grudging favour to hide the relief she felt, she agreed.

'But first,' he said, standing to leave, 'first I must talk to my mother.'

* * *

Abigail bumped into Jack, literally, as she turned the corner of the street near the bungalow where Tabs now lived with Megan and Mali. He smiled at her. 'Abigail, love, I didn't hurt your mother. I'd never have done anything to harm her. I loved her too. Please tell me you believe me.' How she wanted to take those extra steps and feel his arms around her. But she pushed him aside and ran to the bungalow and knocked on the door, which was opened by Tabs.

'Was that Jack?' Tabs asked. 'What's he doing around here? Not coming to see me, I hope.'

'You don't seem too surprised to see him? I thought he'd gone to London,' Abigail said.

'I saw him in the cinema. I actually showed them to their seats. I didn't want to tell you in case you were upset.' Abigail wanted the whole truth so she also told her about the girl he was with. 'Young and very pretty.'

'Thank goodness we're both free of him. He'll never be loyal, or honest. It isn't in his nature. It's a pity it took so long for me to learn that.' Tabs went into the kitchen to make tea and Abigail followed her.

'I feel at least partly responsible for the way he's behaving,' Abigail murmured.

'How can you blame yourself for a man like Jack?' Tabs protested.

'He believed an inheritance was waiting for him and it ruined his life. When we first met he had a good job, well paid, and it was me who encouraged him to leave everything and go off to find the family who owed him a fortune. Once I'd heard about the inheritance, the "treasure" that had been stolen from him, it sounded so romantic, finding a family lost to him for most of his life I begged him to find them.' She smiled sadly. 'I was so young and earning a lot of money to which I could see no end. I gave him money, there was plenty more where that came from. I was never one to save for a rainy day. It was so easy to persuade him and once he began, he couldn't give up.'

'You weren't the cause of him stealing, or for him using me to try to find this imaginary inheritance.'

'I don't think he'd have tried if it weren't for me.'

'Bringing out his greed and making him steal from friends who trusted him? That is Jack. No one made him that way.'

'One day I might believe that,' Abigail said sadly.

CHAPTER TWELVE

Ruth was edgy when she went back to the centre. She was unsure of how Rachel would behave. To her surprise Rachel came out to meet her, and hugged her. 'I'm sorry, Ruth. I had no right to interfere. I just wanted you to think about what you wanted, before Henry depended on you absolutely and you left us with a serious gap in the team.'

'I do know what I want,' Ruth told her, 'and it isn't working here as a general fill-in until Henry finds someone experienced and trained in the running of a place like this.'

'You are trained and certainly experienced. I'm very sorry, dear. Henry couldn't find anyone better. Now, can we please forget my stupidity in mentioning the possibility of your leaving?'

Ruth smiled at her but she wasn't convinced. Was Henry just making use of her until he found someone suitable? Would he then tell her to leave? She found that hard to believe. But, she admitted to herself, we have drifted so far apart, it wasn't impossible.

Christmas intervened and she didn't embrace it with her usual enthusiasm. Last year it had been a disaster and this year, with the absence of her brothers and sisters-in-law, it was likely to be even worse. She made no suggestions, just waited for instructions from Henry and his mother. She baked mince pies, and a Christmas cake and filled the pantry with extra food but it was Rachel who cooked the dinner.

The days passed quietly, leaving her almost unaware of the special occasion apart from exchanging gifts and eating the meal which didn't taste as good as her own would have been, although, she admitted to Tabs later, that was mainly sour grapes. The truth was, she felt as though she were among strangers. She wasn't involved. This wasn't her Christmas, she was a guest at someone else's.

Lillian was in North Wales visiting her son. Aunty Blod was back at her flat sharing the time with her neighbour, Cathy Harrison. They were few in number and that made it even more difficult for Ruth, who regretfully left the meals for Rachel to arrange.

Unknown to Ruth and the others, Blod visited Ralph in the bed-sit he rented and gave him a parcel of food to cheer his Christmas Day. 'As soon as you tell the others you're here, we'll have a second Christmas and celebrate in style,' she promised.

* * *

Tommy and Bryn and their families brought gifts but stayed away for the important days. Tabs, Mali and Megan and the children spent the time in the bungalow. Abigail was alone, having refused the invitation to join them. Christmas was a sentimental time, a time for memories, and she wanted to wallow in her misery of missing her mother — and Jack.

Mali had seen nothing of Kenny since she had refused his proposal and she watched passers-by hoping he would come. She knew she wouldn't change her mind, but saying goodbye to someone she loved was hard. Surely he wouldn't leave without saying goodbye?

While she and Megan and Tabs were playing hide and seek, with Mickie a very excited seeker, screaming in excitement when he found one of them, Kenny knocked the door but no one heard. He went around to the back and peered through the window. Bottoms were sticking out from under the table, Mickie and Megan were creeping up on them and when they tapped them more shouts and laughter filled the air. He walked away.

Tommy and Toni went to Bryn and Brenda's for Christmas dinner but Toni was clearly there on sufferance and kept looking at the clock, willing the time to pass so she and Tommy could leave. Brenda was not very organized and the meal was late and some of the vegetables were cold. Next year, she promised herself, she would do things her way and show Tommy how well they could manage without his twin brother's family dragging them down. She felt as much an outsider as Ruth.

* * *

Kenny had been at school with Tommy and Bryn and, unsettled and utterly miserable, he walked to where Tommy and Toni lived. He knocked on the door, convinced he would be invited in to share an hour of pleasant reminiscences, but although Tommy threw open the door and welcomed him, Toni was less enthusiastic. The place was immaculate, with only a bowl filled with holly branches to suggest that it was Christmas. Armchairs and a couch held cushions that appeared never to have been dented by anyone. There weren't even any cards on display.

The table was set for a meal, with serviettes and glasses for wine and he hesitated. 'Sorry, you're just about to eat.'

'No, it's all right,' Tommy said. 'We won't eat for an hour yet. In fact, why don't you stay?' But a look at Toni's disapproving face made Kenny give his excuses and leave. 'I only wanted to say Happy New Year. Perhaps we can meet soon, go for a drink, eh, Tommy?'

Toni said nothing, and an embarrassed Tommy showed him out.

A few doors away Bryn was opening the front door and putting milk bottles on the step. 'Hi, Kenny, got time for a drink?' he called, and Kenny followed him in.

The difference between the two houses made him smile with relief. There were clothes everywhere; drying on racks, piled in a basket ready for washing and a quantity of freshly laundered baby clothes in another, identical basket.

'The baskets were Toni's Christmas present; she thought it would help us to tidy up, I think,' Bryn said with a laugh. 'No chance of that, until this little one grows up, eh, love?'

'He's such fun we spend too much time enjoying him,' Brenda said. 'I can't see it changing for a long time. Daft Bryn's already bought him a football!'

'It's a lovely home and you, Bryn Thomas, are a lucky bloke.'

'And I know it!' Bryn agreed.

He handed the baby to Kenny who took him nervously. 'Coming to see your Uncle Kenny then, Niblo?'

When he left Bryn and Brenda's, Kenny walked back to the bungalow and this time he knocked. Tabs answered and called, 'Mali, it's Kenny.' She left him waiting at the door until Mali joined him.

'I'm not going,' he said at once. 'I want to stay here, with you.'

Joy flooded through her but caution quickly followed. 'For how long?' she asked. 'How long before you get itchy feet again, Kenny?'

'I know now I'd have been unhappy, trying to live a different life, when everything I need is here. I've just been to see Tommy and his ambitious wife, and Bryn, whose wife knows what happiness it. She enjoys what they have and doesn't waste today dreaming of a wonderful tomorrow that could turn out to be so much worse.'

'That's very philosophical, Kenny.'

'I've been thinking a lot about what I want from life. Living here with you is all I'll ever want. Marry me. I want a home and a family just like Bryn and Brenda.'

'And Mickie?'

'Mickie will always be a part of it.'

Behind the door, Megan and Tabs were leaning forward unashamedly listening, with crossed fingers held high.

* * *

Toni was already discussing with Tommy how they would arrange Christmas for the following year, in the elegant new house she planned to buy up near the park. Getting Tommy away from his cloying family had not been as easy as she'd expected. She couldn't understand it, when what she offered was so much better. Once Ty Gwyn had been sold she had expected the family connection to end, but Tommy and Bryn were still inseparable. That would have to change when they moved among more suitable neighbours. 'Tommy,' she called to where he was standing looking at the garden, 'will you open the wine, it needs time to breathe.'

Tommy raised his eyes to the sky and did what she asked.

* * *

It hadn't taken Jack very long to realise that the family referred to by the man on the train wasn't the one he was seeking. They were from the north of England and had no connection with the area in which he believed his family would be found. He went out with the young girl a few times but found her rather boring. She stared at him adoringly and uttered agreement to everything he said. There was no sign of any interest in her life except, he suspected, marriage and children. Not mine, he muttered, on their final date.

Regretfully, he left the job that was to have been the base on which to build a new, honest future, and went back to the town were Abigail lived. Work was hard to find so he returned to the casual work and occasional theft to survive. He watched Abigail as she went to work and at lunchtimes when she sometimes went out to do some shopping, and once he had knocked on her door.

'Go away, Jack. I don't want to see you. I'm sure you can understand.'

'I didn't neglect Gloria,' he pleaded. 'Please listen and I'll explain exactly what happened.'

'Guilty or not in law, I believe you were culpable. Whatever you say won't change that.' She closed the door firmly and ignored his continued knocks. She leaned against the back of the door until she heard his footsteps walking away. She wanted so much to call him back. Anything would be better than this loneliness.

He came the next evening, and the next. When he made his fourth visit it was in a snow storm and he was drenched and looking so ill she let him in. 'Just to dry off, then you have to leave,' she said.

'Thank you, my darling Abi,' he said 'I knew you wouldn't let me down.'

'You aren't staying,' she retorted angrily. 'Dry yourself, have something warm to eat, then you go.'

* * *

The centre attracted a few guests, even in the coldest months and even snowfalls added to the delight of winter walks along the lanes and through the fields. It was a gift to photographers. The guests were mostly bird-watchers, interested in the winter visitors and enjoying the extra visibility with the trees bare of their leaves.

Rachel felt the cold and stayed in her room. Ruth and Henry plus two staff managed well enough, until one, then the other phoned to tell Henry they were ill and wouldn't be in. It was difficult, as besides cooking and checking the rooms, Ruth also had to cope with the cleaning. Henry took the groups out on walks but had to rise early to get wood chopped and coal brought in and two fires lit. Paths had to be cleared of snow, which returned in fury and had to be moved again. Clothes and boots worn by the visitors had to be dried which added to the task of dealing with the laundering of bedding. It was frequently after midnight before they went to their separate rooms, and six a.m. when they met in the kitchen for a cup of tea before beginning their daily tasks.

Henry contacted a part-time assistant who worked only during the summer months, and to their relief she agreed to help, but then she called them back to tell them she too was unable to come as promised due to another heavy fall of snow.

Henry said, 'D'you think we should cancel next week's bookings?'

Ruth shook her head. 'All we need is someone to help with the fires and the snow clearing. We'll manage the rest.'

Henry rang several people he knew to find someone to help them but no one was available. He even asked his mother and Abigail if there was someone near where they lived who might be willing to work for a few days but no one came. Then Jack arrived.

'I hear you are looking for some help for a few days,' he said, as Henry opened the door.

'Not you, thanks,' Henry said, beginning to close the door.

'I'll work hard and you won't find anyone else willing to come out in this weather.' Jack stood and watched as the door opened again.

'You can sleep in the barn but you're not to come into the house.' He offered the sum he was willing to pay, knowing it was generous. Jack nodded, and Henry began to lead him towards the wood pile and asked him to saw some logs and chop some kindling.

'It's all right, I know where the tools are,' Jack said, and walked off insouciantly to leave Henry frowning suspiciously. Then he went to tell Ruth what he had done.

Three days passed and Jack did all they asked of him, sleeping in the barn with the fire burning to keep the place warm. Ruth washed his clothes replacing some with a few of Henry's cast-offs.

On his final day, when the permanent staff returned, and the snow was disappearing under heavy rain, Henry paid him and he gathered his bag of freshly laundered clothes to leave. The next day he returned asking for a jumper he'd left behind. He packed it into his bag and said, 'Sad about your Tommy, isn't it?' He slung the bag onto his shoulder and began to walk away.

'Tommy?' Ruth frowned. 'What's the matter with Tommy?'

'Had an accident, didn't he? How will your Bryn manage without him? I'm just off to see if I can help.'

Ruth had a word with Henry and, leaving the others in charge, he drove her to where Tommy and Toni lived. They could hear the baby crying as they knocked on the door, and Ruth called through the letter box. 'It's me, Toni. Is everything all right? Only we heard something about Tommy being hurt.'

The door opened and Toni stood there in a dressing-gown, holding the baby. Her hair hadn't been combed and she wore no make-up and looked distraught. Seeing her like that worried Ruth more than the words spoken by Jack. She went in and Henry followed.

'Stupid man,' Toni began tearfully. 'This will ruin our plans. He just doesn't think.'

'Tommy isn't hurt then?' Ruth asked.

'He's broken a leg and won't be able to work for weeks and weeks. He might not ever go back to the work he and Bryn do.'

'Come on, broken bones heal,' Henry soothed. 'But what happened?'

'He was lopping branches from a tall sycamore tree. They were over-hanging the road and they were going to deal with them later, when the weather improves, but your Tommy couldn't wait. Bryn had gone off to price another job and Tommy decided that, snow or not, he could climb up and deal with it himself. His foot slipped on an icy branch and he fell.'

'Where is he? Can we see him?' Ruth asked.

'At the hospital, where he's joking and making them laugh at his description of his acrobatic fall,' Toni said bitterly.

'When did this happen?' Ruth asked.

'Three days ago. He'll be home tomorrow, when the swelling's gone down.'

'Three days ago?' Henry said, reaching for Ruth's hand. 'Why didn't you tell Ruth?'

'She wasn't my first thought!' Toni snapped. 'I was shocked, frightened, but I didn't feel the need to run to Ruth. I've been worrying about how we're going to manage while Tommy can't work.'

'Come on, Henry, let's get to the hospital.' Ruth walked to the door without another word.

'You're too early,' Toni called. 'They won't let you see him until visiting time and that's not for a couple of hours.'

At the hospital, Tommy was sitting in the waiting-room, his leg in plaster above the knee reading a newspaper. 'Tommy? Are you all right?' Ruth asked, running towards him.

'Where have you been?' Tommy demanded. 'Why haven't you been in with grapes?'

'We were only told an hour ago. Jack told us.'

'Waiting for the ambulance to take me home I am.'

'Coming home? Does Toni know?'

'Yes, they told her yesterday.'

Ruth and Henry exchanged looks. They asked questions and learned more about the accident, which wasn't an impulse or a careless climb. It had been arranged for him to start the preparations while Bryn went to look at another job.

'It hurt more than I'd have expected,' he said ruefully. 'But they tell me it's a clean break and I should be as good as new in a few months.' He patted his leg, 'I'm not allowed to climb trees until the plaster's gone, mind,' he joked.

'Why did Toni tell us to wait before going to the hospital?' Ruth asked Henry. 'We'd have missed him if we hadn't gone straight away.'

'She's determined to separate Tommy from the rest of the family.'

'Why?'

'I don't know, but she wants to move up socially and you and the rest of us don't fit with her vision.'

* * *

Toni sat imagining her savings dwindling while weeks passed with Tommy inactive. She knew she had to do something. Next year they had planned to move to one of the better houses near the park, a detached house, with a proper garden. She had worked out the finances. It would be tight but would be worth it once they'd recovered from the initial expenses of moving and they'd be so happy there among more ambitious people. Now they'd have to forget it all, unless . . . She began to look through the advertisements in the local paper. There were jobs she could do and if Tommy couldn't earn then she'd have to. She was writing a list of possibilities when the ambulance men brought him in.

'I'm going to find a job,' she told him as soon as they had gone.

'Hang on a minute, first we have to decide what Bryn will do. This affects him and Brenda as well as us, remember.'

'Oh, they'll manage. They aren't planning to move, are they?'

* * *

Ruth was surprised when, a few days later, Toni came to see her. She had come by bus and on foot, with the baby in her push-chair.

With only a brief greeting, she said, 'Your Tommy won't be able to work for months and I'll have to. So if you will look after the baby for us, we'll cope somehow.'

Ruth stared in disbelief. 'You want me to look after your child while you work?'

'I've asked nothing of you since we married, so I didn't think you'd mind. I know how you feel about families.'

Henry stood near, putting away biscuits and cakes left from afternoon tea and he said nothing. But he was tense, wondering how Ruth would react and how he would deal with it if she agreed.

'I'm sorry, Toni, but I can't possibly help you. I'm needed here and I won't let Henry down.'

Henry's shoulders sank to a more normal position as he was filled with relief. When Toni left, he put an arm around Ruth's shoulders. 'Thank you. I know how hard that was for you.'

Ruth moved away reluctantly and began filling the sink with hot water ready for the teatime dishes. 'Toni has always made it clear she can manage without me, hasn't she?'

'Is that why you said no?'

'Henry, you and this place are my priority now. I want it to succeed.'

He smiled. 'Things have certainly changed, haven't they?'

'We all grow up, eventually,' she replied, taking the plates and putting them into the sudsy water to wash.

When Toni reached home Bryn and Brenda were standing at their door talking to someone carrying a bag across his shoulders. Bryn called to her. 'I want to talk to Tommy, all right if I come now?'

Toni nodded, irritated at being addressed so loudly across the road. She went in and Bryn and Brenda and their baby followed.

'I've tried everyone I can think of but no one is willing to work for us,' Bryn said, 'then along comes Jack.'

'You don't want someone like that working for you,' Toni called from the kitchen.

'We haven't any choice.' Brenda replied.

'He said he's worked for Henry and our Ruth, so if they trusted him — and he's promising to be honest if we take him on. What d'you think?'

'Like you said, we haven't any choice,' Tommy said. Toni's disagreement was noted by saucepans banging about and Tommy cringed jokingly, grinning at Bryn.

'What puzzles me,' Ruth said, when she and Henry were told, 'is how Jack knows what's happening. He knew about

Tommy's accident before I did, and before that, he came here, knowing we needed help.'

Toni found a neighbour willing to look after the child and went back to work in the wool shop.

'Should I do the same?' Brenda asked guiltily.

'No, we'll manage, love,' Bryn said. 'We aren't as desperate as Toni. It would serve her right if she gets pregnant with triplets!'

Tommy got around easily and he dealt with the books, and went out pricing jobs or dealing with the occasional complaint. He went on foot with the aid of a stick and by bus, occasionally being given lifts by Henry. Jack worked hard and caused no trouble, but where he lived and how he spent the time between jobs they didn't discover. He was careful not to give them any information and after a while they no longer asked. He did what they asked of him, there had been no complaints about his work, and they left it at that.

* * *

On one of their rare free days, Henry and Ruth went out for a drive. Henry wanted to take photographs of some of the beauty spots for a new brochure. The weather was fine and the winter scenes and the few spring flowers emerging made every view perfect. Before going home, Henry decided to check on Lillian's house as she was still in North Wales with her son.

Ruth hadn't seen the house before and she was as enchanted with it as Henry had been. 'I think I'll take a photograph of the view from the garden and enlarge it as a surprise for her. She might like to send it to her son to show him what he's missing,' he said. They gathered the post, which included several Christmas and New Year cards and put them on the hall table. Then Henry opened the door of the lounge to show Ruth the beautiful view. He stood to let her go first and, expecting a cry of delight, was shocked to hear her scream. 'Henry! The place has been burgled!'

Henry telephoned the police and explained why they were there. Then they sat and waited until the police arrived. While some officers looked around they were questioned for a long time and then waited until Lillian was contacted and assured the police their presence was not suspicious.

'I'll come tomorrow morning and drive you back,' Henry said to Lillian. 'You're upset and it's too far for you to drive after a shock like this.'

Ruth spoke to her and invited her to stay at the centre until the place was restored to its usual harmony.

They drove back in a sombre mood, both wondering whether Jack was responsible. He could have heard them discussing Lillian and noted her absence. It wouldn't be the first time he had broken into a house to steal. Abigail knew of his dishonesty, and told Ruth what she knew of his crimes, adding the suspicion that he had neglected her mother after her fall, and had caused her death, something about which the police were still unsatisfied.

Henry drove to North Wales and brought Lillian back. She visited her home which had been cleaned and tidied by Ruth, and talked to the police. They had no suspects and it seemed unlikely that the criminal would be found. Henry had added stronger locks, blocked the side entrances to make things more difficult, but she came away wondering if she would ever be safe there again.

When Ruth and Henry took her back after a few days, they avoided talking about the burglary, they just said, 'Cheerio' and 'See you soon' and went away as though nothing untoward had happened.

Lillian drew the curtains, and looked in every room before locking herself in and after three days, during which she determinedly went in and out frequently, her fears had eased and it was her home again. But she wondered whether she'd be brave enough to visit her son again over the Easter holiday. She had to go back soon to retrieve her car.

* * *

Ruth hadn't seen Abigail for a while and not wanting to lose touch with her, she knocked on her door one evening, carrying some cakes she had made. The door opened, very slightly and stopped her walking in as usual. Through the gap, Abigail said, 'Hello, Ruth. Nice to see you, but d'you mind if I don't invite you in? I'm in the middle of something important. Tomorrow perhaps?'

'Not tomorrow, we have people leaving and more coming,' Ruth said, stepping back from the door. 'I'll write a note suggesting a time, shall I?'

'Thanks.' The door was swiftly closed, leaving Ruth feeling surprised and curious.

'There was someone with her, I'm sure of it,' she told Henry when she got back.

'A new boyfriend? I hope he's an improvement on Jack!'

In the small rooms she still rented, Abigail smiled at Jack. 'I'll have to tell people soon, but let's have just a little more time together, just the two of us, before I admit to forgiving you and having to listen to their warnings about loving you, shall we?'

* * *

Mali and Megan invited Ruth one evening to talk about Mali's wedding. 'We want to book your barn,' Mali told her. 'And we want you to do the catering.'

Tabs at once began talking about pretty drapes and wall decorations and the lighting they could hire.

'As you gather, our Tabs is already in charge of the setting,' Megan said with a laugh.

Notebooks were filled with lists and although the wedding wouldn't take place until the following spring, every detail was discussed. More seriously, when they put the lists aside, Tabs said, 'You'll want me to move out, won't you, so Kenny and Mali can live here?'

'No,' Megan said. 'They'll find a place nearby.'

'My father heard about your wedding plans and he wants me to go back home.'

'No!' Ruth, Megan and Mali shouted in chorus.

'What about working with Henry and me at the centre?' Ruth suggested. 'A room of your own, and you'd be able to arrange help with baby Melanie.'

Tabs thanked her, touched by the offer, but she declined. 'We get on so well, Megan and me, and the children are safe with the arrangement we have. I don't want that to change,' she said.

Mali added, 'Megan and I will still work at the café and share the care of Mickie. Nothing will change.'

'Perfect,' Ruth said happily.

A few days later Ruth called to see Aunty Blod, but when she went to open the door, the key wouldn't turn. It was locked, bolted, and the kitchen blind was down.

'Aunty Blod?' she called. It was only at night that Blod locked her door. Perhaps she was out for the day. She was just turning away when the key turned, the bolt was pulled back and Blod beckoned her in. 'You'd better come in — and prepare yourself for a shock.'

A man was sitting on the couch and, when she entered, he stood and offered his hand.

'Hello, you must be Ruth. I've heard so much about you so it's wonderful to meet you at last.'

She shook his hand and looked at her aunt for an explanation.

'This is your uncle Ralph, the one we thought must be dead. Your mother's little brother.'

'Uncle Ralph? But you can't be!' she sank into a chair and stared at him. 'Not after all the years that have passed without a word. Where have you been? Why didn't you find us before?'

'It's a long story, but do you mind if I wait to tell you? I want the family to gather together and then I'll tell you everything.' He sat back down and she saw then that he was ill. 'I don't have much energy, you see. In fact, if you don't mind, I'll go and rest while my sister explains as much as she can.' He walked slowly from the room, stopping at the doorway to turn and smile and wave.

She stared at Blod. 'Well?'

'I don't know much, just that he's been in prison for fraud, and has had to live by finding poorly paid jobs when he once had a successful business. He'll tell you when he's ready. Until then, please, Ruth, it's important to him that no one knows he's here. Will you promise to say nothing? He doesn't want rumours to spread before he tells his story and he wants to tell it all just once. As you see, he is very tired and too many explanations will exhaust him.'

'I can tell Henry, can't I?'

'Henry knows.'

'What? He knows that an uncle we thought was dead has turned up, and he said nothing?'

'He promised.'

'But he should have told me! D'you know, Aunty Blod, Henry knowing about this and not saying a word is more of a shock than seeing Uncle Ralph!'

'Don't take it so personally. Ralph's been through so much and we have to respect his wishes. He's a very sick man.'

'But Henry knew! I really thought that Henry and I would rediscover our love for each other, that my future was with him and this Country Walks Centre. But this puts me firmly in my place, doesn't it?'

'Don't be angry.'

'Angry? I'm destroyed!' She fought back tears. 'I have to leave. How can I continue working for him? I'm just an assistant, that's all I am. I can't stay. Not after this.'

She walked back to the centre the long way. Not wanting to go inside and face Henry, knowing how little he cared for her, how impossible he found it to trust her with a secret she would certainly have shared with him.

He was talking to Lillian when she eventually went into the kitchen. Before she could tell him how she felt about his deceit he said, 'I'm taking Lillian back to North Wales to pick up her car early tomorrow. You'll be here all day, won't you?'

'I suppose so. I'm always reliable, aren't I? Someone you can trust?'

'If it's a problem I can easily go by train,' Lillian said, aware of the tension in Ruth's voice. She began edging towards the door. 'Please don't change any plans you have, Ruth.'

'No plans. I've just been to see Aunty Blod and met someone there whom Henry knows but declined to mention.'

Henry frowned, guessing what had happened, then said, 'We'll talk about it later.' He drove Lillian home then returned to where Ruth was sitting exactly as he had left her.

'How could you meet my lost uncle and not tell me?' she demanded as soon as came in.

'For some reason which I didn't ask, he wanted to wait perhaps until he felt well enough to face you all. Perhaps he didn't want half-truths and gossip spreading through the family before giving us the facts. He's ill, as you'll know if you've met him.'

'But you and I, we used to tell each other everything. My first thought when I met him was to tell you.'

'And I'm glad of your confidence in us, but this is an exception, you'd have been wrong. I don't know what he has planned, but a meeting with the whole family and telling his story is very important to him. I didn't want to risk upsetting him in his fragile state. That should have been your thought too.'

'No, any secret was shared with you. You were always a part of everything in my life, Henry.'

'I hope I still am, but we have to wait. When we know what he has to say, we can decide which of us was right.'

They sat for a moment, each waiting for the other to speak but there was nothing more to say and they went to their rooms in silence. The next morning she went down to see that breakfast was set out ready to cook, the tables were laid for the guests but Henry wasn't there.

'Henry left very early. He's driving Lillian to North Wales to collect her car,' Rachel told her.

'I know that, but he didn't tell me what arrangements have been made. Who is leading the walks?'

'Ted Wells is coming for the day. Both walks are in his area and he will get them back at the right time for meals.'

'When will Henry be back?' Ruth asked. 'He should have told me.'

'I expect he forgot, there's so much going on with eight guests. He hopes to be back by nine or ten o'clock.'

'I'll start the breakfasts, then I'd better ring Ted to make sure he knows. If he forgot to tell me, he might have forgotten Ted Wells too,' she explained.

'Oh, I doubt that, dear,' Rachel said. 'He's very organized where the business is concerned.'

And that's put me in my place again, Ruth thought sadly.

* * *

Tommy was gradually able to help Bryn again, only light work at first, but as he grew more confident and the doctors gave him encouragement, he was dealing with more than the paperwork and things looked hopeful.

Toni insisted on keeping her job at the wool shop. 'The extra goes straight into the house fund,' she said happily. 'We won't have such a long delay if I keep working, even having to pay someone to look after Dora Jane.'

'You are sure about this move, are you?' Tommy asked.

'Of course.'

'I'm not. While I've been laid up, the neighbours have been so kind, helping us in a dozen ways. I don't think we'll find that where you want to live. Detached houses, curtains drawn, I don't think there's much coming and going in a place like that.'

'There certainly isn't! That's what I want to get away from.'

'I don't. I like people popping in and checking when there's trouble. I want our Dora Jane to grow up surrounded with people who care.'

'Tommy, you've been talking to that boring brother of yours again. I just know it.'

'Bryn and Brenda are happy.'

'And so will we be, once we get away from this place.'
'Then you agree that we aren't now?'
'Stop complaining, Tommy. I know what's best for us.'

* * *

Blodwen did as Ralph asked her and after talking to Ruth, she wrote to invite Emrys and Susan, Geraint, and the twins with their wives to the centre for a family conference. Ralph knew his health was precarious and he left an envelope for Blodwen to open, should he not be there.

At the centre Ruth looked at the booking forms and noted that they had all agreed to come. She wished she hadn't met Uncle Ralph in Blod's flat that day. It had led to yet another disagreement between her and Henry, and with him leaving for North Wales without discussing his plans, it seemed likely to be the final one.

The guests sat in the lounge until eleven p.m. talking, playing board games. She sat in the kitchen listening to the murmur of voices and the sporadic laughter wishing they'd go to bed. The days were long, starting before six and, when Henry wasn't there, without a break during the afternoon. When the last one had called 'Goodnight', she didn't go to bed herself. She sat and waited for Henry.

At two o'clock she began to doze, but roused herself with a cup of tea. Few cars passed along the road and each time she heard the distant sound she stood and listened for its approach. At four worry made sleep impossible. Foolishly she went out into the dark night and watched and waited, as though that would make him come back sooner.

Scenes of accidents flashed through her mind, Henry injured, in hospital, on a deserted road, unconscious and alone. She couldn't stand it any longer, and at six o'clock she woke Rachel and told her Henry hadn't returned. Rachel hurriedly dressed and joined her in the kitchen where she was already preparing breakfasts and packing lunches for the all-day walk that was planned.

'Did he tell you he was staying overnight? You should have told me if that's the case. I've been imagining everything. I've been sitting here all night, waiting for him.' She saw the fear on Rachel's face and was immediately sorry for her outburst.

'He said he'd be back by ten,' Rachel said in a small voice.

'I think we should call the police, don't you?'

'No. Not yet, that will make it serious, hopeless. Please, let's wait for a few hours.'

* * *

Lillian left to drive back to South Wales very early but Henry left a few hours later. He was always curious to explore a new area and, borrowing maps, he walked around the area, making notes and promising himself that one day he would come back and explore further. The journey home seemed very long and he was tired. There were several detours as, lacking his usual skills through fatigue, he lost his way. A road blocked by an accident caused further delays.

He stopped to rest several times and drank from the flask he'd filled with coffee. When he was close to home, instead of driving to the centre, he went to Rhossili to deliver the reading glasses and a purse Lillian had left behind. Leaving the package in her porch he turned the car and, seriously lacking in concentration he went too close to a ditch and the back wheel slid into it. He closed his eyes and surrendered to sleep.

Lillian had heard the car. She went out, shook him awake and led him indoors to give him coffee and a brief rest. He sat on her couch and rolled into a comfortable position and immediately slept. Promising to telephone to tell Ruth first thing in the morning, presuming she would now be asleep, she covered him with blankets and let him sleep. Unfortunately she too overslept. The garage sent a pickup truck and extricated the car from the ditch which took some time, then Henry set off back home.

* * *

At nine when Ruth's hand was about to lift the telephone, she and Rachel heard his car. He walked in, unshaven and with eyes that were still red and strained. 'I'm sorry,' he said, 'I fell asleep and both Lillian and I overslept.'

The phone rang then, before either of them could ask a question.

'It's Lillian. I've had to find a phone box as mine isn't working. Is Henry home safely? I hope you didn't worry, but I thought it safer to let him sleep on my couch, he was so exhausted. He'd put the car wheel into the ditch.' Still confused by what had happened, Ruth thanked her and rang off.

'I was so afraid you were hurt. Or,' she admitted in a low voice, 'that you'd left me.'

He held her close. 'I'm sorry you were worried, I just couldn't drive any further last night. Lillian's phone didn't work and—'

'I'm sorry too. I overreacted when Aunty Blod told me you knew about Uncle Ralph.'

He kissed her and behind them Rachel left the room. She was smiling, and she hid by the door until she heard them say, 'I love you.' At last. Now she could go back to her own life, and leave them to get on with theirs.

* * *

Ralph arrived in a taxi accompanied by an anxious Blodwen. Ruth found him a comfortable seat on the old couch that had survived the move and was in the living room Henry and the staff used. Geraint had booked a room in a nearby hotel, Emrys and Susan drove from Bridgend after lunch and they stared at Ralph in amazement after being introduced. The twins came in and, after marvelling at the unexpected addition to the family, were soon boasting about their children. In a remarkably short time they were comfortable with each other although they each had a dozen questions hovering on their lips.

'First of all,' Blodwen said, 'Ralph wants you to know why, at the age of fifteen, he was sent away from home.'

Talking slowly, conserving his strength, Ralph said. 'I was a thief. I stole money and I even learned to break open gas meters to steal the coins inside.' He looked around the group of faces and added ruefully, 'I don't expect sympathy for any of this. I wasn't much more than a child but I was a criminal and it took a disaster to change me. I broke open a gas meter and I treated it roughly and moments after I left the house, fire broke out and the place was burned to the ground. I was accused of arson so my father told me to leave. I never went home again. But after that I never took a thing that I hadn't earned legitimately.'

The weather was warm and the doors stood open. Jack walked in, hoping for work as the summer was approaching and Abigail had told him that Ruth and Henry were looking for temporary staff. Ralph had slid down on the couch and was invisible to Jack as he knocked on the door and asked to speak to Henry.

'Not now. We're busy,' Henry said firmly.

Jack took a few more steps into the room, 'I'm looking for work, just temporary I know that, but I'll be glad of anything. I'll call tomorrow, about five, all right?'

As he turned to leave, he saw Ralph and gasped with shock. His face lost its colour and he looked as though he was about to faint. 'Dad!' he said.

'I don't have a son,' Ralph said angrily. 'Get him out of here!'

'But, Dad!'

'Get him out!' Ralph began to breathe heavily and Henry jumped up and showed Jack to the door.

'I want my inheritance!' Jack shouted, as Henry closed the door.

They all looked expectantly at Ralph. 'He's my son, but I never want to see him again.'

It took a while for him to recover, as the others absorbed the fact that Jack was their cousin, then Ralph told them the rest. 'I had a good business. A general stores in a small village, selling everything that the local people needed. The community was warm and friendly and I was happy and utterly content. Then the police came and I was arrested. Jack, my son, had been cheating everyone. He'd forged my signature on purchases I couldn't afford to buy for him and signed my name on several dishonest deals. It was my name on everything and, besides, he was my son. So it was I who went to prison for fraud. While I was there, Jack's mother committed suicide. She couldn't cope with the shame of knowing what her son had done to us.

'Prison didn't suit me,' he said wryly. 'I came out seriously ill to find the shop was sold, to clear my, or rather Jack's, debts. Of Jack there was no sign.'

'How have you managed?' Ruth asked.

'Factory work was all I could find with a record for fraud. That didn't suit me either. I was ill but I managed.

They discussed all this for a while then Ralph spotted the picture he had drawn when he was a child. 'Good heavens, you've still got my treasure!' He pointed to the picture. 'My treasure! How amazing that it's survived.' Ruth handed it to him and he held it, smiling at memories of a childhood that had ended too soon.

Jack had come back in by another door and was listening from the hallway. On hearing the word treasure, he burst in and snatched the picture from his father. 'This is mine,' he said, grasping it tightly against him. 'I should have had a share of the house when it was sold. I'm family too and I want what's mine.'

Jack began to run for the door but Henry stopped him. Ralph hardly reacted.

'Open it,' he told Jack. 'My treasure is hidden inside, and it's yours if you want it. Gently now; Ruth and the boys might like to keep the picture.'

With hands that trembled, Jack eased the picture out of its frame. Underneath the drawing was a picture of a lovely young woman with flowers in her long hair, sitting in a garden. 'This is only a cheap worthless print!' Jack said in disgust.

'Look underneath,' Ralph said. An envelope was attached to the back of the print with passé-partout. Panting with anticipation Jack eased the sticky tape away and opened the envelope. Ralph was smiling. Impatiently Jack tore open the envelope. Out fell one large, white five pound note, three ten shilling notes and coins totalling twelve and sixpence. 'What's this?' Jack demanded. 'A joke? Where is it? You told me about some treasure and I've searched for the family for almost two years, so where is it? I demand my inheritance!'

'That *is* my treasure.' Ralph was laughing. 'I started to save when I was nine. I wanted a motor bike.' Ralph continued to laugh. Nervously, the others waited to see what Jack would do, preparing to protect Ralph if he were attacked.

Jack glared at his father for a moment then ran out. He went back to Abigail's rooms. She was still at work and he gathered together his belongings. As usual, he'd made a mess of everything. He had a woman who loved him no matter what he did, a daughter called Melanie and a newly found family and he had to walk away from it all.

* * *

The family decided that Ralph should go to a nursing home where he would be cared for. Somewhere close to the sea which he believed would help him get well. Not too far away, so the family could visit him regularly. They all hoped that Jack would stay away and avoid worrying Ralph again.

Jack was walking towards the railway station and Ruth saw him and watched him go. As he reached the approach to the station a police car drew up and after a brief conversation, Jack got in and was driven off. So they hadn't seen the end of him. They would be put through the agony of seeing a man who they now knew was their cousin facing charges. She knew they would cope. Henry would help them ride it out.

* * *

Tabs was told the news of Ralph's return and Jack being a cousin, whose existence no one had known. In great excitement she went up to see Ruth. 'Don't you see, this means that my baby, Melanie Ruth, is a relation of yours? A sort of cousin!'

'Not sort of, but real. Tabs, you're part of our family!'

Talk of the unexpected development went on for days and weeks, with Jack in police custody. Remarkably, Ralph's health began to slowly improve. Gradually the talk about his return and the arrest of Jack eased and made room for talk of the wedding. One day when Ruth and Henry were visiting him, Henry asked, 'Ralph, will you be my best man?'

Life was full and Ruth knew how easily she could have lost it by being afraid to let go and take a chance. Ty Gwyn was a happy memory but now was the time to contemplate the future.

THE END

ALSO BY GRACE THOMPSON

THE OWEN SISTERS FAMILY SAGAS
Book 1: GOODBYE TO DREAMS
Book 2: PAINT ON THE SMILES

STANDALONE NOVELS
THE END OF A JOURNEY
NOTHING IS FOREVER

Thank you for reading this book.

If you enjoyed it please leave feedback on Amazon or Goodreads, and if there is anything we missed or you have a question about, then please get in touch. We appreciate you choosing our book.

Founded in 2014 in Shoreditch, London, we at Joffe Books pride ourselves on our history of innovative publishing. We were thrilled to be shortlisted for Independent Publisher of the Year at the British Book Awards.

www.joffebooks.com

We're very grateful to eagle-eyed readers who take the time to contact us. Please send any errors you find to corrections@joffebooks.com. We'll get them fixed ASAP.

Printed by Libri Plureos GmbH in Hamburg, Germany